Tell Me How This Ends Well

Tell Me How This Ends Well

A NOVEL

David Samuel Levinson

corsair

CORSAIR

First published in the United States by Hogarth, an imprint of the Crown Publishing
Group, a division of Penguin Random House LLC, New York in 2017
First published in Great Britain in 2017 by Corsair

1 3 5 7 9 10 8 6 4 2

Copyright © 2017 by David Samuel Levinson

The moral right of the author has been asserted.

A CIP catalogue record for this book
is available from the British Library.

HB ISBN: 978-1-4721-5293-0
TPB ISBN: 978-1-4721-5294-7

Printed and bound in Great Britain by
Clays Ltd, St Ives plc

Papers used by Corsair are from well-managed forests
and other responsible sources.

FSC
www.fsc.org
MIX
Paper from
responsible sources
FSC® C104740

Corsair
An imprint of
Little, Brown Book Group
Carmelite House
50 Victoria Embankment
London EC4Y 0DZ

An Hachette UK Company
www.hachette.co.uk

www.littlebrown.co.uk

For my mother

Every family has its joys and its horrors, but however great they may be, it's hard for an outsider's eye to see them; they are a secret.

—Anton Chekhov, "Difficult People"

Do not be daunted by the enormity of the world's grief.
Do justly, now. Love mercy, now. Walk humbly, now.
You are not obligated to complete the work,
but neither are you free to abandon it.

—Rabbi Tarfon, the Talmud

Tell Me How This Ends Well

JACOB JACOBSON;

OR, THE WHITE PEACOCK

Thursday, April 14, 2022

L os Angeles welcomed them with a dark, moody sky that broke open halfway through breakfast. The drizzle fell gently at first, then more profoundly, in sheets that ricocheted off the sidewalk, spotting the windows of the overcrowded IHOP on Sepulveda. Even at that late-morning hour, closing in on eleven, every table, booth, and countertop was occupied. Someone, probably the reedy, pimple-ridden shift manager, had set his iMuse to play every awful electro-punk-funk artist in his arsenal, an eternal, cacophonic loop of sinister screeches, the latest craze perpetrated on the teenage masses by a currently dying (again) music industry. The songs, which were forced upon them from four floating speakers hovering in the corners of the room, blasted through the bacon-grease-filled air. Each one collided with the other and sounded exactly like, if not worse than, the next, each vying for a top spot in Jacob's memory as the most craptacular and inappropriate accompaniment to breakfast, in this case pecan praline pancakes and Belgian waffles, which he and Dietrich were trying to consume while also struggling to carry on a conversation.

Around them, all was din and dystopia, and for a moment Jacob looked up from his plate of congealing syrup and butter, wondering if they hadn't wandered into some sort of bizarre casting call—girls in pale purple tutus performed pirouettes in the aisles; boys in Wranglers, cowboy boots, and spurs played horseback with imaginary whips and a few misplaced whinnies; a couple of the dads wore big red clown noses and frizzy orange Afro wigs; and many of the moms fed their saurian offspring lines from scripts, as they themselves shoveled eggs Benedict into their mouths.

"I thought you told me in L.A. the sun is continuous," Dietrich said, his German accent far more pronounced when he was tired or irritated. Or both, which was currently the case, Jacob suspected.

"And I thought you told me it rarely snowed in Berlin," Jacob said. "I guess we both did some exaggerating."

"I realize the historical and momentous ramifications of rainfall in this part of America, but still I was hoping we would leave that damp far behind us in Germany," he said, his heavy, dark soul more crestfallen than usual, his jet-lagged disappointment already palpable and nearly unbearable to Jacob.

Too tired to rise to the bait, Jacob just smiled, blinking his burning brown eyes, wanting nothing more than to get to his brother's house in the San Fernando Valley, take a shower, then fall into a deep, uninterrupted coma of sleep. However, the famished and equally fatigued Dietrich had spotted the quaint facade of the International House of Pancakes—"I hop, you hop, we all hop for IHOP!" he sang, pointing at the Dutch-inspired house with its orange cantilevered roof and blue trim—and had asked Jacob to stop. More like commanded, but Jacob was used to it. He applied a new varnish of syrup to his stack of rubbery pancakes in the hopes of revitalizing his appetite, which had flagged the moment the waitress had set the plate in front of him. So there they were, still only a few blocks from LAX, one of the most dreaded points of reentry into the country for Jacob, who never imagined he'd find himself back here so soon. God only knew how long it would take to get to Calabasas with this traffic, he thought, where his mishpucha, the immediate ones, were gathering like a terrifying golem made from the clay of behavioral tics and personality disorders—a litany of ills and a penchant for hypochondriasis and full-blown neuroses, with bouts of accompanying sanctimony, blinding narcissism, and a plain, old-fashioned, wrath-of-God-style guilt, which bound it all together in one neat package.

Speaking of guilt, any second now Jacob expected a deluge of texts and calls from the golem wondering where they were, he and Guess Who's Coming to Dieter—one of his dad's more amusing puns, although Jacob need not have reminded him that he was named Dietrich, not Dieter—and braced himself for the inevitable telephonic Jacobson onslaught by shoveling another forkful of cold, spongy pancake into his mouth. It was only after he was choking on the oversaturated hunk of surprisingly dry, inedible flapjack that he realized that none of them had a way of getting in touch with him—he still had his German cell, rendered useless here in the States—and relaxed, the muscles in his neck also relaxing, which allowed him to swallow, his throat having all but closed up when he pictured the grueling, emotionally withering days ahead.

He coughed in earnest and glanced up at Dietrich, whose face was blank save for that tiny moue of his, a wry smile Jacob still had trouble reading, although by then they'd been together for three years—the first two remarkably good, this one remarkably bumpy, with another two months left to go. For now, however, Jacob considered Dietrich the love of his thirty-eight-year-long life, loving him all the more when Dietrich slid his glass of watery orange juice toward him and ordered him to drink it. Was it too much to say Jacob's wants had changed already and that instead of a shower and bed, what he actually wanted was to fast-forward through the next four days, to look down upon L.A. from the height of thirty thousand feet out the tiny window of his tinier coach seat? How,

5

he wondered again, had he let his siblings talk him into this trip? It was one thing to subject himself to the unpredictable heart of Julian Jacobson, patriarch pro tem, yet a different thing altogether to wish his dad upon the unsuspecting Dietrich.

The coughing subsided. And with it so did the last of Jacob's appetite. It fled out the door into the rainy street, where one of those British-inspired double-decker tour buses, clearly lost and in search of more affluent pastures, like Beverly Hills, ran it over in cold blood. No matter, as Jacob had been talking to Dietrich just that morning about shedding the weight he'd put on in Berlin, due in large part to the addictively heavy German food and miraculously delicious, buttery pastry. (For a country of such historical darkness, they'd certainly managed to create the lightest, tastiest breads in all of Europe, surpassing, in Jacob's estimation, even the French.) Just another reason to push the plate of soggy pancakes toward the slim, marathon-running Dietrich, who, at twenty-six, never gained a single ounce and remained as lithe and striated with muscle as he was in the photos Jacob had seen of him at sixteen. The fucker. Dietrich, who finally finished his waffles, started on Jacob's plate, releasing a satisfied smile and a coo of pleasure after every bite.

"Knock yourself off," Jacob said, grinning at his own use of this idiomatic faux pas Dietrich had made on what was destined to be their second date, although neither of them knew to call it that back then. They'd gone for ice cream in the East Village and Jacob, having devoured his within minutes, took his spoon and dipped it into Dietrich's. "Knock yourself off," the German had said, as serious as ever. Jacob laughed, correcting him. If he had to guess, he'd have told anyone who cared that that was the moment he'd fallen in love.

"*Tu dir keinen Zwang an!*" Dietrich replied humorlessly, and Jacob understood he might have stretched the joke too thin, at least this morning when their nerves were, respectively, fried and fraying.

Dietrich proceeded to knock himself off, slicing the pancakes into precise wedges with his knife and fork, while Jacob flagged down the waitress, who dove at the table as if it were an end zone and she a wide receiver. "I am not your cashier. Pay up front," she said, then was gone, leaving a scintilla of powdered sugar and sweat in her wake.

Jacob left Dietrich to spoon up the syrupy butter and headed for the cash register near the door. Standing in line to pay for what had to be one of the most awful excuses for a breakfast he hadn't had the desire to eat in some time, he pulled out a Deutsche Bank ATM card and set it on the counter.

"We don't take that," said the cashier, a pregnant teen with braces. She pointed to a small laminated sign taped to the glass that read IN SCHWARZENEGGER WE TRUSTED, ALL OTHERS PAY CASH. Returning the card to his pocket, Jacob, bleary-eyed, pulled out a wad of bills and handed the girl a twenty. "Look, mister, do you want me to call the manager? American . . . *dinero*," she said, enunciating the words slowly as though he were a dumb foreign schmuck. She wasn't half wrong, as Jacob had been living abroad for well over two years and was acting just like, well, a dumb foreign schmuck.

He apologized and repocketed the twenty-euro bill just as Dietrich approached, peeling the proper currency from his fancy silver money clip, which was in the shape of an undulating German flag blowing in a strong breeze. Jacob glanced at the money clip, which shimmered faintly under the garish Suntopia solar-flare tubes, the opening lines to "The Love Song of J. Alfred Prufrock" gathering in a poetical storm inside him. When he and Dietrich emerged from the main carnival tent that was the IHOP into the cold, soaking rain that was L.A., the lines came up and out of him with an irrepressible urgency and, what's more, in a startlingly clear, effortless Deutsch (it must have been the fatigue, for he'd never been so nimble with Dietrich's native tongue), lingering on the last two lines, his favorite:

"*Oh frag' nicht, 'Was ist es?'*
Laß uns gehen und unseren Besuch machen."

" 'Oh, do not ask, "What is it?" Let us go and make our visit,' " Dietrich said.

As they hurried through the sloshy parking lot arm in arm, Jacob considered the heroic couplet and the voice of the boy who'd just translated and recited it. He loved Dietrich all the more for his willingness to go and make their visit, for his good-naturedness in the face of what was bound to be a fiasco of phenomenal proportions.

"Your inaugural meal in L.A. I wanted to pay," Jacob said once they were safely ensconced in the rental car. (Another rhyming couplet, this one left him drained of amusement, however.) He was acutely aware of not wanting to seem cheap in Dietrich's eyes. It was a fine balance. The harder he tried to master it, the more often it left him feeling like a skinflint or an utter mooch. He wanted to provide, to split everything fairly and evenly down the middle, from the rent they shared to the food they ate. But 1-2-3-Speak!, where he taught basic English to recent Russian and Israeli immigrants and business English, whatever that was, to German yuppies looking to emigrate to the financial districts of London and Manhattan, only paid a measly twelve euros per hour, which was, even by Berlin standards, insulting. As generous as Dietrich was with his money, Jacob knew there'd soon come a reckoning when he, Jacob's own personal Shylock, would demand Jacob pay up, lest Dietrich exact his pound of flesh another way. He didn't want to think about any of it, what with the heavy rains, the sudden merge onto the treacherous 405, which was nothing but red, beady-eyed taillights as far as he could see, and in a car that was not his, but he quickly did another tally of how much he thought he owed Dietrich—close to five thousand euros. This sum just happened to be the same amount that he'd withdrawn from his checking account in Berlin and that now lined the bulging front pockets of his stretchy, baggy jeans, stretchy and baggy because of the twenty extra pounds he'd put on in the past year alone.

"If it makes you feel any better," Dietrich said, pulling out the page of directions, which he'd printed before they left Berlin, "I will let you buy me dinner but not tonight. Didn't I tell you? I am to dine with Lucius Freund. He will prepare a delicious meal."

"Meal? Lucius Freund? What are you talking about? You told me you didn't know anyone in L.A.," Jacob said, his voice pinched with jealousy. "So who is he, huh? Who?" He thought he was joshing Dietrich, but if this were the case, why then did he feel the explosive aftermath in his capillaries and his circulation speed up, the razzmatazz of blood in his face? "He's German, this guy? How'd you meet him?"

"Jay, keep your eyes on that road, please," Diet said. Even after spending years of his life in Baltimore, at Johns Hopkins, then in Manhattan, at New York University, Diet still sometimes had trouble differentiating between *the, this,* and *that.* "Yes, Lucius Freund, he is a hunk of a man. I have been planning this rendezvous with him for weeks and months. So now is as good a time as any, I think, to tell you that I am leaving you for him. Please pull over and let me out. I cannot do this anymore."

Incoherent with exhaustion, Jacob nearly did as Diet ordered, though pulling over would have involved crossing four lanes of highway. Besides, who the hell broke up with someone doing sixty-five miles per hour in traffic like this on the fucking 405? This was a fucking joke. Wait. Was Diet actually joking? Jacob's jet-lagged brain could barely think straight. "Pull over? Are you kidding me?" he asked. Up ahead he saw red and slammed on the car's brakes just before his front end nearly married the back end of a black Mercedes SUV, which had stopped short. As he did, Diet was thrown forward out of his seat—rarely a passenger, he'd forgotten to buckle his seat belt—and banged his head against the windshield.

"Oh, oh my God," Jacob said, as Diet crumpled in his seat and went still. The Mercedes SUV, that wicked black carriage of evil, thought Jacob, found an opening in the congestion and sprang away, spraying the car with dirty, oily drops. Jacob tried the wipers, albeit to no avail—the cleaning solution proved useless, the wipers even more so, streaking the glass and further straining his already limited visibility. The rain came down harder and faster, intensifying Jacob's feeling of bewilderment and failure. He glanced at the unmoving man beside him, at the purplish welt forming in the center of his forehead, a mean-looking bull's-eye, and felt more love for him than he had ever felt for anyone in his entire life. Hadn't he raised his arm and flung it out in protection, an involuntary response to danger, right before he slammed on the brakes? "Why weren't you wearing your seat belt?" he asked. He wondered if Diet had suffered a concussion, if the impact would have long-term ill effects, and if he shouldn't get off the highway and hightail it to a hospital. But he had no earthly idea if there was even a hospital nearby. He looked around frantically for the page of directions but couldn't find it.

Jacob switched on the hazards and limped into the far-right lane, doing the best he could with the information he had, his copilot out cold beside him. He imagined what it would be like to live without Diet, and the very idea of it was unendurable. *What if his brain's bleeding? What if he's dying right this second?* Jacob thought, massaging the back of Diet's neck, which was still warm if lightly sweaty, a good sign. "You can leave me for Lucius Freak or Lucien Freud or Lucius Fiend or whatever his name is, but you have to wake up first. Wake up, wake up, wake up," he said, shouting into the claustrophobic confines of the car until his throat hurt.

As if roused by Jacob's magical words and by the even more magical sound of the deep, exponential concern in his voice, Diet awoke and blinked his eyes. "Baby, you are back!" Jacob said.

"I am back?" Diet asked. "Did I go someplace?"

"Don't make jokes," Jacob said, taking the next available exit. "I need to get you to a hospital. I don't even know if we're near a hospital, but I'm going to find out."

"*Schatz,* please," Diet said. "I am German, you are forgetting. Our crania are made of superhuman strength, like our wills," and he smiled, though it was a wan, used-up smile and hurt Jacob to see it. "I am fine. Really. Let us go and make our visit."

Jacob crawled off the 405 and out of the rain, taking shelter at one of the thousands of gas stations that sat on all four corners of every intersection, giving this world an even more transitory appearance. He couldn't believe he'd spent four years in Westwood, at UCLA, graduating on a Friday only to beat it out of there the same night, on a red-eye to New York, which was his home until he and Diet moved to Berlin. His collegiate days well behind him, he barely remembered them. What he did remember was the car, getting into it, getting out of it, filling it up, checking the tires, the oil, having the tires rotated, hauling his ass to Long Beach, where his brother lived at the time. His brother, the registered dietician and semifamous actor who was now married to Pandora, the proud parents of five sons: a set of triplets, twelve years old, and a pair of identical twins, five years old.

He remembered L.A. by night, the four-leaf clovers of interconnected roadways, everything set down and arranged like a vast, eerie circulatory system whose heart bled gasoline and whose lungs exhaled exhaust. *We're all leaving behind not just carbon footprints but a smogasbord of toxic delicacies for future generations,* he thought, picturing his nephews and trying to remember their names, which he couldn't. What he did remember were the semis, the tractor-trailers, the Pacific Ocean off to their left somewhere, and the romantic, russet-edged California sunsets, which, for as long as they lasted, made him feel nostalgic for his childhood in Texas. Even today, he still had never set eyes on anything as spellbinding as a Texas sunset. New York City came a close second. And Berlin—Berlin didn't even make the cut, though he often lied and told Diet otherwise. That was what coupledom had done to him—he perjured himself constantly under the oath of love he'd taken.

"I'm going to call an ambulance," he said to Diet, whose head remained tilted at what looked like an odd, uncomfortable angle. Jacob took a gentle hold of his chin and lightly turned his head to fit more squarely in the seat, so that the headrest supported his neck. "Does your neck hurt? Do you feel dizzy? Are you seeing stars? Do you feel light-headed?"

"My head hurts a little, but that is nothing," Diet said, stoical. "When I was a boy, I fell into a well in my friend Andre's backyard and bumped my head much worse than that. Twenty minutes later I was eating *Kaiserschmarrn* like nothing happened. I do not need a hospital, *mein Schatz*. If I start to feel weird, I will tell you."

"Look at me," Jacob insisted, as Diet turned to face him. "Tell me how tall the Fernsehturm is and when it was built." Diet let out a recalcitrant huff and answered: 365 meters high, Berlin's TV tower was erected from 1965 to 1969. "Now spell your name backward." Diet spelled his name backward. "What's the longest German word in the dictionary?"

Diet thought about this for a second, then took a deep breath and exhaled. "*Rindfleischetikettierungsüberwachungsauf-gabenübertragungsgesetz*. But I am not certain about it," he said. "I believe it was retired. Maybe it is the second longest?"

"Doesn't matter. What matters is that nothing got scrambled. But—and this is a huge *but*—the second you feel unwell, you have to tell me, and we're going to the emergency room," Jacob said, stroking the back of Diet's neck again and wondering if Diet knew just how much he loved that head of his and everything inside of it. "I think once we get to the Valley, it'd be a good idea if you were checked out by a doc-in-the-box."

"Jacob, please, enough," Diet said. "I am not a little child. If I die because of a slight bump on the head, then this is what is supposed to happen."

He hated when Diet spoke like this, full of a ghoulish fatality and cynicism that continued to take Jacob by surprise. Though he didn't share Diet's morbid determinism when it came to death and dying, there was something singularly freeing in it, he supposed. It lived inside every German he met and spoke to, a quality and view of life so un-American that for his first couple of months in Berlin he had a hard time taking any of it seriously, as if each German was born with his or her DNA already encoded with instructions on how to die. Death not as a horrifying, unfathomable, and unexpected end, the bogeyman of time, but as the ultimate categorical imperative, a duty to die to leave behind an impression on the world, an imprint of having lived, of having been there. Sometimes, though, Jacob wished Diet would just lighten the fuck up.

"Wait here. I'll be right back. And don't fall asleep," Jacob commanded, hopping out of the car and hurrying through the swash to the lonesome pay phone—perhaps the last pay phone in all of America—sitting beside bound stacks of firewood on sale for $29.99 and the large metallic bin of bagged ice, each going for a whopping $8. When had frozen water become a luxury item? Was it designer ice? In his absence, had Starbucks expanded into the niche ice market as well? If he didn't distract himself with such bagatelles, he knew he would fall apart completely.

Once he was standing at the pay phone, though, Jacob found himself at a loss. He observed the quaint plastic and metal relic with fascination, the coin slot, the tarnished keypad, the numbers and letters smudged off from constant use and abuse. Berlin still had its share of pay phones, but who used a pay phone in L.A. anymore? Drug dealers, he guessed, and anyone having some kind of dastardly business to do, that's who.

He took a deep, panicked breath, recalling the last call he'd had with his siblings a few months ago, a harrowing conversation in which they discussed their mom's failing health and the management of her care—or rather the mismanagement of it, they all agreed with alarm, even Edith—if it were left up to their dad.

"Ma should just move to Cali," Mo had said. "From where I'm sitting, that's an easy slam-dunk. So are we done here? Because the twins and I are almost at the studio." In the background, one of the twins had been melting down, shrieking as if he were being either held against his will or waterboarded by the other twin, Jacob hadn't been able to tell which.

"You better untie him and release him back into the wild, Mo," Jacob had said.

"That's a terrible thing to say," Edith had said, finally piping up.

13

She'd been so quiet that Jacob had all but forgotten her. "Hey, Bax, it's your auntie Thistle," thickly slathering the Southern accent in her voice and sounding, to Jacob, like Roy Rogers, if Roy Rogers had been a female with a BA from Harvard, an MA from Princeton, and a PhD from Georgetown. So more like Dale Evans, he'd mused, or Mr. Ed's other half. Mrs. Edith? "Bax, can you do Auntie Thistle a favor and—"

"Baxter Judah Orenstein-Jacobson, I need you to zip it right this instance or else you will never see your beloved Wii again," Mo had said.

It's instant, not instance, Jacob had thought dourly, rolling his eyes.

"Really, Mo. Threats?" Edith had asked.

"Hey, Thistle, when you're raising five boys—hell, even one boy; hell, even a houseplant—you can say whatever you want," Mo had said. "Until then, do me a favor and uckfay offay, okay?"

"It's a good plan, Mo, but you know Dad's not going anywhere," Jacob had put in, trying to redirect the derailing conversation.

For a moment, he had wanted to carry this outside—this call that had been shaping up to be yet another unpleasant round of hide-and-heat-seeking-missile with his brother and sister—and had gone to the sliding-glass door, finally deciding against it when he'd realized he'd have to bundle up in his parka and put on his snow boots because the balcony, which jutted out from the building and looked like a man with a protruding lower jaw, had been packed under a mound of fresh snow and months-old ice. Berlin in winter.

The sight of the balcony that night had had a profoundly negative effect on Jacob, recalling a remark he'd made to Diet, when they'd first taken possession of the flat, about how the balcony reminded him of his dad's obscenely pronounced underbite, which went hand in hand with the rest of his handsome albeit cavemanlike face, thick, bushy eyebrows, broody, overhanging brow. All he needed was a club, Jacob had told Diet, and his dad could have been part of one of those dioramas at the American Museum of Natural History. Also, he liked to grunt a lot and bang his fists.

"I heard that desert climates are better on the lungs for people with her condition. I read that someplace. I'll find it and email it to you," Edith had said. "She's seventy-two years old, though. Maybe it's just too late to do anything?"

"We shouldn't even give them a choice. We should just demand it," Mo had said.

"Um, again, good plan, Mo, but not exactly feasible," Jacob had said. "I mean, you have met Julian Jacobson, haven't you?"

"The old man just needs to relocate his habits out here. He can still garden, go fishing, and hit the gym—it's not like we live in eff-ing Georgia. No offense, Edith."

"None taken," she'd said, although clearly offended. "Look, I'm going to be brutally honest, because someone has to be: Ma's dying. She's never going to get better, only worse. And what, Mo, you and Pandora are going to look after her if, God forbid, something happens to Daddy? What about you, Jacob? You're going to move back from Berlin? And before either one of you says it, I may be a child-less spinster, but I'm not about to give up my cushy-ass job, which I love by the way and thank you very much, to be her caregiver. I love her to death, but it's just not something I see myself doing. What's the current state of her health anyway? Do either of you know? Ac-cording to Daddy, she could hang on for another year or more, but maybe that's just wishful thinking? At some point we're going to need to talk about some kind of managed care." Edith had gone on in her usual self-absorbed way. "But then again it seems Daddy's in tip-top shape and all of that. But you know how quickly that could change. It just takes one fall and . . . By the way, I've done some reading on those places and from what I've read they aren't as odi-ous as they once were. I'll send you both links to the articles."

Jacob had heard her tap-tap-tapping away on her keyboard to locate the links and shoot them off in an email. *Here is my sister,* he'd thought, *our Thistle of the Congregation of the Path of Least Resistance.*

"From what you've read? Edith, are you insane?" Mo had said. "Those places are La Brea tar pits of death and despair, and I'm not sticking our mother in one of them. She says he's taking good care of her."

"It's the least he could do after she's catered to that man's every single agonizing need for her entire adult life," Jacob had said.

"Remember what happened to Grandpa Ernie? He went in and never came out," Mo had continued, ignoring him.

"He was ninety-six years old," Jacob had said. "He wasn't going to come out even if they'd put him up at the Plaza."

"Look, I get that she deserves some happiness after all the shit Daddy put her through. Yes, okay, I admit it—he's never been easy to live with. But Ma chose him, stayed with him, and clearly still adores him," Edith had said.

"Here's to loving difficult men," Jacob had said, thinking about Diet, who was difficult in his own way, and Mo, who was difficult in his, and even himself, who, until quite recently, had thought he'd come to terms with and healed from the worst of his dad's treachery, all those years of unwarranted hostility, by finding Diet and moving to Berlin. Unfortunately, he'd begun to realize that he'd unwittingly managed to smuggle the tyranny of his dad in through customs with him. Pieces of him, at least, and the worst pieces at that.

"Okay, so we're here," Mo had said, "and I really have to go."

"Bye-bye, Baxter, bye-bye, Dexter," sang Edith. "See you at Pesach!"

"You're right, Thistle. She does deserve some happiness. And if Dad weren't around, we wouldn't even need to be having this conversation," Mo had said, almost as an afterthought. "It would be totally mute."

Moot, Jacob had thought, *not mute,* but he'd also let this go because Mo had started getting one of his brilliant ideas, which was

that Jacob and Diet should come to L.A. for Passover and that between Edith and him, they could come up with the money to pay for
the airfare. Though generous, the invitation had reeked of collusion,
and Jacob had called his siblings out on it.

"This isn't coming directly from the old man?" he'd asked, because it would have been just like him to persuade his two older
children to gang up on and guilt-trip his youngest.

"Not at all," Edith had said, though Jacob hadn't believed her.

"Mo, tell me the truth," Jacob had said because he knew Mo
wouldn't lie, at least not in front of his sons.

"It's the truth," Mo had said, put off by the insinuation, it seemed.
"I do get brilliant ideas sometimes, Jacob, you uckingfay utzpay."

"You mean like that thing you just said—'if Dad weren't
around,'" Jacob had said. "Care to elaborate?"

"Yeah, well, just thinking out loud. But seriously, have you guys
thought about what happens if she really does go before he does?"
Mo had asked.

Jacob had always assumed his mom would outlive his dad. He'd
spent his entire life dreaming of it, praying for it. Yet Julian Jacobson
was in fine fettle, as his sister had so kindly pointed out, as sound of
mind and body as he'd ever been, even at his advanced age. This had
been a sudden, horrifying revelation to Jacob, who'd tried to shake
it off but couldn't. It had made him shudder. It had nauseated him.
And if he'd let himself go there, he might even have said it brought
out a murderous rage and that he'd do and say anything to see his
mom happy again. "It just doesn't seem fair, does it?"

The three sat with this without speaking for a couple of minutes.
"What aren't you telling us, Mo?" Jacob had asked, full of suspicion.

"It's just . . . Give me a second," Mo had said. "Boys, Daddy
needs you to be good and quiet for a minute, so let's plug in your
ear bugs—that's what they call them; aren't they adorable?—for a
minute, okay?"

"So spill it, Mo," Jacob had said, and Mo had taken a deep

breath and given them their mother's most recent prognosis: bad. Superfucking bad. "How did you find out? Why didn't Ma tell Thistle and me?"

"Pandora just happened to call her on her cell right after she'd been to the doctor," Mo had said. "Four months. That's what Pandora said the doctors gave her." An absolute silence had fallen upon each of the Jacobson siblings, a silence that none of them had experienced since they had been children and taken their seats around the dinner table, their hands freshly washed and their mouths freshly zipped shut, sitting there like that until Julian took his own seat and their mother broke the silence by asking him how his day in the lab had been. "Apparently we're not supposed to know, so we never had this conversation, okay?"

"I just can't believe it," Jacob had said. "You're sure she said four months?"

"She should get a second opinion," Edith had said. "I hope that wife of yours was cognizant enough to tell her that, Mo. Did she? What does Daddy say about it?"

"Dad doesn't know. No one is supposed to know," Mo had said. "That's the way Ma wants it. Honor her wishes, Thistle, and don't open your mouth."

"Don't you take that tone of voice with me, Moses Jacobson," she'd said. "This is our mother we're talking about, and I'll do whatever I think is best for her, not what's best for—"

"Will you two just shut up for a second?" Jacob had interjected, pressing his fingertips against his closed eyes and massaging his eyeballs, which had ached from the backup of tears that he would not allow himself to cry, not yet, but after, later, in bed with Diet, who would hold him close and wipe the tears away with a finger. "You're right, Mo. It just doesn't seem fair. So what exactly are you suggesting?" he'd asked.

"I think another conversation might be in order," Mo had said. "That's what I'm suggesting. For Mom's sake, is all."

"For Mom's sake," one of the twins had repeated, unplugging

and wanting to join the adult conversation, one that, if he'd known any better, Jacob had thought, he would have understood that none of the adults wanted to be having, for it had seemed to him that it was far too soon to be having this conversation. Wasn't it only just yesterday that he and his mother had been wandering around Dillard's department store looking for school clothes for him, a secret trip that no one—not his brother or his sister or his father—knew about? *It's too fucking soon,* he'd thought.

"That's right, Dex. Good boy," Mo had said. "So, Jacob, let us know about Passover, because we'd love to have you. And about that other thing—just give it some thought. Well, this is Mo Orenstein-Jacobson signing off for now!"

"I don't see how it matters if Ma dies before Daddy," Edith had said. "He'd just go on as before and stay in that house until he couldn't cope anymore."

"Oh, cut the crap, Edith. If Mom goes before he does, then we'll never get rid of him. He'll lord his money, which is actually her money, over us and he'll force himself on you and Mo. Without her, he'll just get worse and worse, saying every horrible thing that pops into that reptilian brain of his. The only reason I even talk to him is because I know how much it'd hurt Mom if I don't. I love you, Edith, I do, but you need to wake the fuck up," Jacob had said. "So tell me again why I'd subject Dietrich to him, much less myself?" Yet as soon as he'd said it, he understood the reason why exactly. *For Mom's sake,* he had thought, reflecting Mo's sentiment.

"The five of us together again," she'd said. "Just think about it."

Now, in a sodden gas station parking lot, lifting the phone's receiver to his ear, Jacob thought about his sister, who was still floating on a tranquil (if not tranquilized) sea of denial when it came to their dad, how she'd never been as anti-Julian as he and Mo had been, because, as she claimed, she'd never had cause to be. Never had cause to be? Jacob could only laugh, recounting all the times their dad used to call her fat to her face and make fun of the boys she brought home. Though too young to remember all of it, Jacob was still definitely able to recall important moments and events, like when she had spoken up and asked to be called Thistle, invoking the name for the first time in the car ride home from her bat-mitzvah reception, Turtle Bay Country Club. A distant relation, a second cousin once removed whom no one recalled inviting, had kept referring to her as Thistle, like the leggy, fourteen-year-old model from Kiev with flowing, curly red tresses who had just graced the cover of *Vogue*.

"You want us to call you what?" their dad had snorted. "Sure thing, *Thistle*."

Their mom had tried to rectify the moment by changing the subject, as was her wont, everyone but Edith seeing the comparison between them as laughable and ludicrous, everyone including Jacob, who, at ten years old, had already taken considerable stock of his surroundings and deemed them toxic, sensing that he had a dad who was a monster and a big sister who was already exhibiting signs of a shockingly unhealthy sense of self, which was only going to lead her to further rejection and a life of abject misery, full of all kinds of sexual dysfunctions and intimacy issues—American Thistle resembled nothing of her supposed doppelgänger, except, of course, for the red hair, which she had inherited from their dad, who'd been a ginger himself up until he hit puberty when his hair went dark and straight. Poor Edith hadn't gotten the same break, however, her hair still just as fiery red and still reacting just as badly to any trace of humidity, puffing up like a dandelion gone to seed. It wasn't unusual for their father to tease her that Bozo the Clown had called, wanting his wig back.

After initiating a collect call to Mo, Jacob imagined the three of them—Mo, Edith, and himself—huddled together around a different pay phone somewhere in the sprawling San Fernando Valley, and deciding, probably through a hurried game of rochambeau, which of them would speak. He had a sneaking, awful suspicion, though, that because he was the youngest and thus usually dared and bullied

20

into mischief by his older brother and sister, it would fall on him to interview the hit men, whomever Mo had found to do it, probably former, disbanded Mossad operatives—the USA was rife with them now. "You aren't still a pussy, are you, Gay-Jay?" they would chide, treating him like a baby, even though they were more or less of the same age, all with receding hairlines, graying hair, skin tags, and gravity-compromised asses, all suffering from the same bad backs, shoddy knees, and chronic acid reflux. The life of a Jacobson in middle age. Mo didn't pick up, which foretold either good news or bad, Jacob thought, hanging up, only to initiate another collect call, this time to an old college friend and former lover at Eternal Hollywood, which had once been the Hollywood Gardens Cemetery until it fell into disrepair and financial ruin and was finally rescued from oblivion by the scion of the Kansas City Chalmers' fortune and the leading innovator in the death industry—Clarence Lee Chalmers, who had inherited the money and business from his family. Surprisingly, Clarence accepted the call, though he did not seem overly thrilled to hear from Jacob or remember exactly who he was. Was he being coy or playing another one of his passive-aggressive games with him, a holdover from their college days? Jacob wondered. Or was it that Clarence truly didn't remember him? In any event, the whole thing rankled Jacob, but then there was so much about Clarence that rankled him.

"You say I gave you my direct line?" Clarence asked, his slightly wispy baritone rolling out of him like a thick exhalation of smoke.

"Years ago," Jacob explained, reluctantly playing along. "We went to UCLA. We dated, did lots of drugs. You introduced me to ketamine and crystal meth and Thad Schneider, who killed himself. Any bells?"

"Thad Schneider," Clarence said. "Now, there's a name. But seriously, I did do an awful lot of drugs in college, so you can't take it personally if . . ." His baritone faltered, then trailed off and didn't return for a few beats during which Jacob swore he heard him meowing. Then he was back, continuing: "I do have a vague recollection of sleeping with a chubby Jewish boy who came from somewhere in Texas. Did you used to have a brown felt cowboy hat?"

Jacob wanted to lie—oh, how he wanted to lie—and tell him that he had never owned such a hat. He also wanted to hang up the receiver and forget the call had ever happened. But he needed Clarence, if any of this were going to work.

"You made me put it on a couple of times while we had sex, yes," Jacob said, humiliated. *I've never forgotten, nor have I ever forgiven you for it, either,* he thought.

"Big, fat circumcised cock?" Clarence asked.

"Yes, Clarence, you had quite a good time with my dick," he said, shaking his head in thorough shame, relieved that Diet was either unconscious or resting peacefully and not privy to any of this. Though he had to hand it to Clarence for remembering that part of him, at least, which shouldn't have been flattering, Jacob understood, but somehow managed to be. He took the compliment and squirreled it away.

"If this is a booty call, you're about fourteen years too late and thousands of miles too far east, aren't you?" Clarence asked. "Last I heard, you're still living in New York City? Is that where you're calling? The number is blocked."

"A booty call knows neither time nor space," Jacob said, continuing the ruse. But why was Clarence ending everything he said with a question mark? It was maddening. Pure, unadulterated madness, like Clarence himself, like making this call to him. Again, the urge to hang up almost overcame Jacob, but he resisted, for his mom's sake. "Look, the reason I'm calling is to say hello—so, hello!—but also because I'm actually in L.A., just flew in this morning from Berlin, and I thought it'd be great to catch up while I'm here."

"I'm free for lunch today," Clarence said.

"Today, as in today? No, I can't. I'm on my way to the Valley," Jacob said, glancing at the car and at Diet, who, from where he was, looked as if his head had come unscrewed from the rest of him and was about to roll off. Jacob nearly dropped the phone and flew to the car, but then Diet jerked awake, gazing out at the world with disoriented eyes. He cupped a hand to his mouth and breathed out, testing his breath, just as he did most mornings. "Dead bird! Dead bird!" he liked to warn Jacob, who didn't care and never failed to go in for a kiss anyway, but not before Diet leaped from bed and rushed into the bathroom, forestalling the moment and forcing Jacob to preserve his erection. He'd shut his eyes until Diet returned, bird-free, to lay a chalky, cinnamon-flavored kiss on him and wish his big, fat circumcised cock a *guten Morgen.*

"Hmmm. I suppose I could reschedule Pilates with Patty and meet for a Jameson on the rocks with Jacob instead," Clarence said. "Call me on my cell in a couple of hours to confirm exact time and place," and he rattled off an L.A. number, which Jacob easily memorized, as he'd memorized Clarence's direct line all those years ago when they'd bumped into each other at a men's gym in Chelsea, which Jacob did not mention now, because, for one thing, he'd spurned Clarence's advances, and for another, he had been headed to the locker room to change back into his clothes, as he found the place far too depressing and the men far too desperate and aggressive. "If you're ever in L.A . . . ," Clarence had said and written his number down on a card, which Jacob, the second he popped out into sunlight, ripped up and tossed away. But it'd only taken one glance at the card to etch Clarence's digits into his memory. In another life, Jacob might have been a world-renowned mathematician, as he'd always been good with numbers. In college, he'd declared a major in mathematics for a while, before switching to creative writing, upsetting his dad, who nearly disowned him. Looking back on it all, Jacob understood that that's what should have happened instead of what did; ever the mediator and people-pleaser, his mom had smoothed things out between them, although Jacob had done nothing wrong. Nothing but upset the old man's choke hold on him and the imagined future he'd had for his youngest progeny.

In the convenience store attached to the gas station, Jacob bought a map of greater L.A., a Diet Coke for himself, and a Coke for Diet. He also purchased a tube of K-Y jelly, a bag of assorted gourmet jelly beans, an L.A. Lakers cap, a large Igloo cooler, one of the fancy bags of ice, and two Nestlé Drumsticks. Getting it right this time, he put it all on his Visa, then left the store and grabbed the ice, happy in the knowledge that he was supporting all ice makers the world over or, if not the world over, then certainly in L.A., where water was at a premium and rarely, if ever, fell from the sky.

Despite his having thought that, it was still pouring down rain when Jacob returned to the car and slid into the backseat. "I'm back, Diet," he said, dumping the ice into the Styrofoam cooler, then nestling the Drumsticks and cans of soda inside and securing the lid. Through all of this, Diet remained asleep, which alarmed Jacob, who roused him, checking his pulse gently and pressing the back of his hand to his cheek. Diet's heartbeat was steady and normal, his skin room temperature, even warm to the touch. He'd heard about people knocking themselves out—knocking themselves off, he thought gravely—and staying knocked out for several hours.

Diet's eyes fluttered open. "Are we there yet?" he asked.

"*Schatz,* you've got to stay awake," Jacob said, climbing into the driver's seat, where he inspected the welt, which still looked angry and purple-red but hadn't expanded any and was still just the size of a quarter, which made it look as if Jacob had beaned him in the head with a baseball, which in turn made Jacob think about his dad, the last thing he wanted to think about at that moment.

"Jacob, please stop fussing on me," Diet said. "It's just a bump. I am not going to succumb."

Jacob didn't think he could feel even more terrible than he did, yet at the sound of this, he let himself imagine what might have happened—the two cars colliding and the accordion of metal and steel, the blood-soaked shards of glass as Diet was thrown through the windshield, another tragedy on the 405, this one of Jacob's own making, simply because he hadn't been paying more attention to the man beside him. To this end, he reached around Diet and grabbed the seat belt, buckling it in place.

"Let me sleep now," Diet said, his voice stern, nearly punishing.

Although Diet didn't blame him, Jacob understood that it didn't matter, for he'd continue to blame himself for the both of them. "Fine, but be prepared to be fussed over and monitored," Jacob said, kissing him.

With his copilot resting beside him, Jacob turned his attention to the map of L.A., the printed page of directions still lost somewhere under the passenger seat, though if he'd looked he would have found it easily enough, along with traces of the rental car's former occupants—a cinnamon-flavored toothpick, a peach pit, a rhinestone earring missing its back, a stale kernel of nacho-cheese-flavored popcorn, and a mother-of-pearl button.

Pulling out of the gas station and heading for the access road, Jacob cursed himself for not upgrading to a premium car with a built-in navigation system. He bumbled with the blinkers, indicating right when he meant left, and was finally allowed to merge his way back onto the ungodly congested, thoroughly frustrating 405, wondering as he did why anyone, much less his historically impatient, vengeful-to-a-fault-against-any-driver-who-got-in-his-way, road hog of a brother chose to live in such a carnivorously sickening city of cuckoo car culture.

Though Jacob had only been driving for thirty minutes, he was already more than ready to give the car back and hoof it. Perhaps he would have felt differently if he knew he wasn't going to be spending the next four days basically doing nothing but chauffeuring Diet around and shuttling back and forth to Calabasas, which he honestly didn't mind as much as having to deal with the car itself, the getting into and out of it, the short distances made long and excruciating because every single person in L.A. had the same exact desire at the same exact moment—whether it was to head to the grocery store or the beach, it didn't matter. Maybe cars, like people, were lonely pack animals, too, he thought, realizing that at the pace they were going they wouldn't make it to Mo's before nightfall.

"I can't believe you didn't put on your belt. What in the fuck were you thinking?" Jacob sulked softly, unable to let it go. He turned to Diet, whose thin lips were slightly ajar, and held a palm up to make sure he was still breathing. He was. It amazed him again how Diet could sleep anywhere and through anything, how he'd slept off and on during the arduous plane ride, while Jacob had just stared out the window, willing the plane not to crash. "You're lucky you're still breathing, you know that. What if I'd been doing seventy and bashed into the end of that stupid SUV?" The thought of it terrified him so much that he immediately refused it purchase and switched on the radio to distract himself.

The car filled with Willow Smith, whom he secretly liked, especially the iMHere she made about wrapping Christmas presents and delivering them via hologram to fans with so much less than she had. If he had that much money, he wondered what he would do with it all. "What do you think, Diet? Do you believe I'd be the kind of millionaire to give it away or to hoard it?" he whispered.

Jacob liked to think of himself as the kind of person who would give a lot of it away, though having lived in penury for so much of his adult life, he wasn't sure he would. This made him sad, both that he'd been living as he had—like a grad student, his dad liked to joke, though the joke often felt more like a dig, which it probably was—and that he couldn't even imagine having any kind of money at all, certainly none that he'd earned from writing his sad little plays.

"But all of that could change today," he said softly to Diet, who remained asleep, "because I'm taking a meeting with Clarence Lee Chalmers. Okay, not really taking a meeting, but I am going to meet him for drinks later, *Schatz,* if that's all right with you. Maybe you can tag along if you're a good boy." He rested a hand on his lover's denim thigh, palpating it. "Have I not mentioned Clarence before? Well, let's see—first off, I am not having an affair with him, not like you and this Lucius person."

Jacob honked his horn at a motorcyclist who was using the shoulder to zip ahead, disobeying the law and the natural order of things. "Look at this guy, Diet. Think I should follow him, huh? Think I should?" he asked. But he remained in his lane, crawling at a ridiculous ten miles an hour. "So you're really not going to tell me who Lucius is? Well, maybe it's better this way," he said, thinking for the first time since they'd arrived in L.A. that he was not looking forward to introducing Diet to his entire family, that he was more than dreading it, in fact. Not because they would treat him badly or boo and hiss when they learned that Diet came from Augsburg, in Bavaria, the original breadbasket of anti-Semitism, but because Jacob wondered if in some odd way he wasn't using Diet to test the limits of his family's acceptance of and love for him. It was one thing to date a German in theory, but something quite different to sit beside said German at the Passover table and break matzo with him. He knew this, just as they knew it, yet he'd given them all, including Diet, plenty of opportunity to back out.

Jacob didn't want to cause a scene, not with so much at stake, not with their mom in such fragile health and their dad being what he was, which was scary on any normal day but even scarier when he was out of his element. He predicted thrashing. He predicted the gnashing of teeth and the stampede of the four horsemen of the apocalypse right through his brother's villa on the hill. And he predicted blood—bloodshed, bloodcurdling screams, perhaps even a bloodbath or two.

"So let me tell you a little bit about Clarence," he said. "We met at UCLA way back in 2002. He's the son of Shreve and Wanda Chalmers of Kansas City, Missouri, and he's pretty much the most whacked-out, fascinating, self-destructive person I have ever met." And he told Diet the story about meeting Clarence at a Come Out & Dance Party—a monthly dance that the Gay & Lesbian Alliance, as it was known back then—put on in the Rotunda and that attracted hordes of men and a few women from all over Los Angeles and Orange County. "Lots of too tan chicken hawks coming to score a college boy, and there I was, in my tight Wrangler jeans, Justin roper boots, and big-ass belt buckle, looking to all the world like a misplaced rodeo reject, and there was Clarence, also in boots, snakeskin, towering over me at six foot two, though he looked a lot taller because he was long and lean. Not like me." He glared at himself in the rearview mirror and made a face. "Gay-Jay," he hissed and sucked in his cheeks, but no matter how hard he tried, he couldn't reproduce Clarence's cheekbones and finally gave up, focusing again on the traffic.

Up ahead, Jacob finally saw what the holdup was—a two-car collision, flares lit and sparkling even in the rain, and a cop directing them all onto the shoulder. As Jacob inched along and took a quick peek at the wreckage—and it was bad, with a dozen cops stationed at the scene, two helicopters in the air above them, and three fire trucks and two ambulances and several paramedics and what looked like the Jaws of Life to cut a trapped young man out of the passenger seat of one of the unrecognizable, charred, accordion-shaped cars—he felt the presence of death all around him and suspected that this was no ordinary accident, that it was quite possibly another suicide bombing and that the guy was dead. Rubbernecking people craned their heads out of windows to gawp and stare, but Jacob turned away from the wreckage, the sight of the accident, kept his eyes steady on the road, on the paroxysm of traffic that lurched and feinted, started and stopped. He didn't mention the accident or the dead youth to Diet when he continued. "Anyway, long story short, Clarence and I courted each other for a couple of weeks and then we fell into bed. The sex? Pretty awful. I guess if he'd been more my type . . . He's hairless and awkward in his body and the worst kisser ever, kind of like—" And Jacob paused suddenly, because the next words out of his mouth were going to be "kind of like you."

He gazed at Diet, whose eyes seemed to be darting back and forth under his paper-thin lids, and he thought about his desire for Diet, which had nothing to do with lust or predation. It existed outside the body and outside time, and though their sex moved him more than any sex he'd ever had, it wasn't all that good or all that fulfilling. It left him wanting. It left him missing Diet.

"So anyway, I'm hoping that I can talk him into producing my next play, whenever I write it, which is one of two reasons I agreed to this Jacobson family reunion. And the other reason—well, that one's a little more complicated," he said, finding an opening in the traffic and stomping on the gas and then they were flying at breakneck speed. The road opened up as the traffic thinned out. He glanced at the map in his lap, finding exactly where they were, and relaxed his fingers on the steering wheel just a tad, because they were soaring now, he and Diet, who did not know how to drive, had never learned. "I'm only telling you this because you can't hear me, which means you can't be an accessory, should anything go wrong," he said, "but the other reason is that my brother, sister, and I—we— are planning on murdering our dad." Having said it, something inside Jacob trembled to life, just like the car, which trembled to life under his grip as he approached seventy miles per hour.

Up ahead, a sign indicated that if he wanted to get to Calabasas, he should take exit 63B to merge onto the 101. He took the curve and merged again, slowing down considerably to join another stagnant pool of traffic, a wall of brake lights and fenders. He drove with a deep sense of regret and reservation, for a part of him wanted to forget about it all, forget everything he and his siblings had discussed, forget that his mom was dying and that his dad was going to die, even if he deserved it and she did not. He wanted to forget that he'd ever suggested this trip to Diet, forget about the Seder and Clarence Lee Chalmers. There was still time, he thought, to present an extraordinary excuse to his family about why he and Diet weren't coming after all. It would be so easy to lie, to tell them their originating flight in Berlin had been canceled on account of snow, which would not have been far from the truth—theirs had been the last flight out of Berlin Brandenburg before they'd shut down the airport and discontinued all other flights.

He'd even suggested to Diet they wait until travel conditions improved before chancing it, as a late-winter storm, an anomaly for that time of year, was gathering strength in the Atlantic and threatening to dump three feet of snow across New York City. And if they closed the airports in New York and New Jersey, God only knew in what city and on what runway they would end up. "It's a matter of timing and connections," he told Diet, who understood what was happening and took hold of Jacob's hand—Jacob who detested flying almost as much as he detested the prospect of having to spend four days with his family. "I will hold your hand the entire way," Diet said, kissing him. "I will not let anything happen to you, Jay." And he did hold Jacob's hand just as he said he would, and they'd landed on time and without any pother at a snowy JFK and made their connection to Hartsfield-Jackson in Atlanta, where he called Edith, who was flying out the next day, and where they again had to change planes. Diet never once let go of Jacob's hand, not in the entire twenty hours of travel they began in the late morning on April 13 and didn't complete until midmorning on April 14. In some way, he wished they were still on the plane, for he missed Diet's fingers twined in his own, the grip tight and reassuring, a pressure unlike any other and one that he'd remember until his dying day.

Now, according to Jacob's calculations, it was nearing 1:30 P.M. here in L.A. and 9:30 P.M. back in Berlin, which, he understood, accounted for the tremendous torpor he was experiencing in nearly every part of his body. He felt the drag thoroughly and throughout, an exorbitant physical and spiritual heaviness, as if every one of his cells and corpuscles were alchemizing, turning to lead. Or pleather, he thought, feeling suddenly at one with his seat, with every seat he'd sat in during the last twenty-four hours, from the taxi ride to the airport in Berlin to the cramped excuses for seats on every plane they'd flown on.

Jet lag was odd, and Jacob experienced it oddly, as both a shrunken and expansive form of himself, in touch with who he was and also out of touch with the rest of the world, which went sluicing by in a single wet blur. He knew full well that he was strapped into the rental car and speeding toward his brother's, yet at the same time was convinced he'd never left Berlin and was about to join Diet in bed. Afternoon and night, here and not-here, split in half only to be repurposed whole again elsewhere—these moments of concurrent temporality coexisted within him and produced the profound, eerie sensation of being and having been in several places at once. Though he was far from religious, he wondered if this weren't the closest thing to what life after death might be like—not the haunting of several different places at once but participating in several different manifestations of your own consciousness equally and at the same exact moment.

Ghosts in our own machines, Jacob thought, hitting the scan button on the radio and trying to find NPR, which he did, though it wasn't the show *All Things Considered* as he had hoped but another rousing rendition of *Little Brother,* a program in which ordinary citizens were witnesses to extraordinary events, catching every second of it on their smartphones. Today's guest was a native Los Angeleno who'd recorded a gang of teenage skinheads ambushing a young pregnant woman and bludgeoning her to death in the parking lot of Temple Beth Am, on La Cienega.

"It was late and at first I didn't understand what they were up to," the man recounted, "but then I saw them swinging these, well, they looked like homemade maces, tube socks stuffed with bars of soap that were hammered through with nails—even from where I was, I smelled the Ivory soap; I still can't wash my hands with the stuff without retching—and that's when I pulled out my phone because what kind of person would it make me if I hadn't done something?"

But you didn't do anything! Jacob thought, disgusted, unable to bear another second of such cold, calculated indifference, for the man, instead of dialing 911, decided to use his phone for other means, as a way of becoming a guest on what had become one of the most popular shows in the history of radio. Jacob hit the scan button again but not before the recording began to play and the young woman was shrieking for help as the gang closed in around her, their taunting faint but still recognizable: "Oven magnet," "Jew will die," and "Hitler was right." As an antidote and to combat the horror of the image of that poor young woman, who could just as easily have been a close friend or even his sister as anyone, Jacob settled on KJEW, a station his sister-in-law, Pandora, raved about, mainly because it plugged her business, Pandora's Box, for free. Today Jacob happened to land on the station right in the middle of an opera, the title of which was finally revealed to him during a station break—not a plug for Pandora and her ubiquitous Box, but one that reminded everyone that local Jewish baker and matzo maker Goldie Goldfarb was still taking special orders for Pesach, which lay just around the corner.

"Don't forget to clean out those cupboards of your chametz, ladies and gents, and donate all your yeasty, leavened goodies to charity, preferably to us here at KJEW," and the announcer rattled off an address somewhere in downtown L.A. "So harrumph and rise to the occasion, folks, and a mitzvah on all your houses!" He tapped a gong three times in succession, then added, "A big Jew-cy welcome to all those of you just now joining us. Congratulations again on spinning the dial and landing on us here at KJEW, because you do not want to miss another second of this remarkable production of *The Death of Klinghoffer,* brought to you by none other than the Metropolitan Opera of Jew York. No matter where you are or what you're doing, stop right this second and feast your ears on this," and up came the music, as if from the bowels of the car itself, mesmerizing Jacob, who normally disliked opera.

"Isn't that right, my sleeping *Schatz*? Opera and I don't mix, do we?" Jacob asked, creeping his way along Ventura Freeway until the traffic stopped again. "But hear this: If you don't wake up soon, we're going directly to the emergency room," and he removed his hands from the wheel to clap loudly at Diet, who opened his eyes and squinted against the somber afternoon light.

"Baby, you are back again," Jacob said in relief, while the music took a dramatic turn, darkening considerably and signaling the eventual murder of the invalid Klinghoffer by one of the terrorists in the Palestinian Liberation Organization. An absolute philistine when it came to opera, Jacob had never heard of this Klinghoffer person, much less how he'd managed to get an opera named after him and have a production of it staged at Lincoln Center.

"Oh, I think this is the part where they shoot Klinghoffer. It happens offstage," said Diet, who was as much an opera aficionado as Jacob was not. Jacob observed him carefully as he yawned and stretched, exhibiting only the telltale signs of having been asleep, nothing to indicate he'd fallen into a dangerous unconsciousness. Diet pulled down the visor and peered at the welt in the small, glowing mirror, wincing. "I am such the idiot. We will tell everyone who asks that I slipped in the shower. In *das kleinste Bad in der Welt*," and he grinned at the evocation of the nickname he'd given to their bathroom back in Berlin, which in fact was the smallest bathroom in the world at about four feet by three feet. Before the traffic started to move again, Jacob reached around into the backseat, producing a Drumstick and the can of Coke. He offered both to Diet, who grinned again and said, "*Schatz,* you make me the happiest German boy in the whole state of California."

"There's ice, too," Jacob said, "in case you want to use it on your noggin."

Diet reached over and caressed the back of Jacob's neck, his fingers frigid, which gave Jacob a jolt and made him whimper, which in turn made Diet say, "You like that, don't you?" Jacob said that he did. "We will save the ice for later," and he purred mischievously, bringing the cold, perspiring can of Coke up to his forehead, where he gently held it.

"You scared me, but you're feeling okay, right? You're not seeing double or dizzy or anything?" Jacob asked, while Diet removed the can and studied the map in his lap. "How many fingers am I holding up?"

"None, because I must navigate for you," Diet said, giving him a sideways smile. "I was knocked up for a long time?"

Though Jacob had warned him not to fall asleep, he couldn't bring himself to scold him, although he suspected that's exactly what Diet would have done if the situation had been reversed. A part of him wished Diet was still asleep, for now they would have to discuss the lingering, nagging question of this Lucius Freund character and who the hell he was and how Diet had met him and fallen in love with him—and he struggled with the insurmountable uncertainty of the future with Diet, which up until a couple of hours ago had appeared to him to be inscrutable. Sure, they had their issues, some more ongoing than others, but here was their chance to make a clean break with those other two men, the ones they'd left behind in Berlin, and concentrate on these men, this Jacob, who was driving and trying not to think about Diet's prior declaration—that Jacob pull the car over—and this Diet, who was busy studying the map of L.A. and directing Jacob to take exit 27B, then turn onto Mulholland Drive. *Let those other two men do battle,* Jacob thought. *Let those other two continue to assume the worst about each other, while this Diet and this me recommit to this relationship.*

"That rain makes me think we never left Berlin," Diet said, lifting his eyes from the map to stare out the windshield. "So far, L.A. has not proven impressive to me. It is an ugly place, I think."

"Oh? You can already tell that based on your extensive experience of it?" Jacob asked, knowing the moment he said it that it came out all wrong, for Diet withered in his seat and returned the can of Coke to his forehead.

"My head pounds," he said, more to himself than to Jacob, who understood that he'd accidentally wounded Diet again.

"L.A. is actually quite beautiful. You'll see, *Schatz.* I mean, it's no Berlin," Jacob said, backpedaling, softening his voice, his stab at trying to erase any trace of impatience and ire.

As focused as he was on smoothing things out with Diet, he nearly forgot about the exit, which he was going to miss if he didn't get over immediately. He shot into the far-right lane, cutting off a young Latino man with a big, fat teardrop tattoo who was driving a low-riding, restored Cadillac Seville. He had no other choice but to let Jacob muscle his way in, albeit hatefully and with horns and middle fingers blaring, all of which elicited a terrible, curdling cry from Diet that they were going to die. He shut his eyes and braced himself for an eventual impact that luckily never came. "What the hell? He was in my blind spot. Have a little faith in me, huh," Jacob said, breathing more calmly now that he'd left the 101, which would go on torturing other drivers for hours and days and years to come. (Though Jacob knew nothing about it, *US News & World Report* had just published a new issue that ranked driving in L.A. as the number one cause of stress, well above perennial favorites, moving and death, in just about everyone of any age.)

"That cowboy antic is sure to kill us," Diet said, giving him one of his all-too-familiar, all-too-punishing looks. "The roads here are always like this?"

Sitting up as high as they were, Jacob had a full one-hundred-and-eighty-degree view of the swirling, tortoise-green skies that hung over the San Fernando Valley and the close-knit terra-cotta-roofed homes that hugged the sides of the undulating hills and looked as if they might come away at any moment. He couldn't imagine how his brother and sister-in-law dealt with it all—the potential threats of sinkholes, earthquakes, and wildfires and the more real, more immediate threats of drought and suicide car bombers. All of these disasters just waiting to happen, and for what, to say that you lived in a mild climate where the sun shines three hundred and fifty days out of the year? *And wouldn't you know that we'd fly in on one of its off days,* Jacob thought, which was odd, because he had no real stake in L.A. either way. Yet the more Diet pointed out its flaws, the more Jacob felt personally assailed and needed to defend the city against him.

Heading north on Topanga Canyon Boulevard, they passed a Denny's, yet another iconic American breakfast spot, Jacob told Diet, who, it turned out, already knew about the chain from his stint in Baltimore, and who summarily dismissed it as "some of the worst American poison I ever put into my mouth." Which made Jacob wonder if Diet weren't holding on to some residual resentment, payback for Jacob's own role in their harrowing, horrendous first few weeks in Berlin when Jacob came down on Berlin hard, insulting the bland weather and the blander German food and accusing Diet of not seeing what he did each time they left the flat: Nazis in various guises everywhere. It didn't help that they were living directly across from a sports bar, which was an alleged gathering spot for neo-Nazi skinheads, or that Jacob spent many hours on the Internet, secretly viewing YouTube footage of Kristallnacht and portions of Leni Riefenstahl's *Triumph of the Will*. Diet called this dark period in Jacob's acclimation "The Month of Nazis Everywhere" and had even downloaded and printed out a translation of *Das Grundgesetz für die Bundesrepublik Deutschland* (*The Basic Law for the Federal Republic of Germany*) and read it to a terrified Jacob, who appreciated that his lover had gone to such lengths to soothe his fears, although it had little impact. For Jacob continued to see swastikas and hear "*der Jude*" in the air no matter what Diet did or said.

"Look, we're only here for a few days, so let's just give it a chance before condemning it," he said. "Or I can always just let you off on the side of the road and you can call Lucius Freund to come get you," and though he was smiling as he said it, his voice was pinched with jealousy again. "I just want to know if you were really serious or—"

"Jay, I made it all up," Diet said, keeping his face turned toward the window. Jacob couldn't help but register the sorrow in his lover's voice and beyond this the crisp, cold, vexing snap of exasperation. "It was a bad joke. We're taking your parents for dinner this night at Luscious Friend. Your brother recommended the restaurant to me when he called a few days ago. I reserved a table for us."

"I see," Jacob said, thinking he should just let it go, because Diet, like most Germans, had such a poor sense of timing and an even worse sense of delivery.

"I upset you. It was not intended," he said, his voice both detached and full of hurt, which moved Jacob. Out of all the men he'd ever loved, and the number was small and dwindling, he trusted Dietrich Krause the most, for Jacob could find next to nothing disingenuous about him—and he'd tried—which was why he'd believed his story about Lucius in the first place.

"Luscious Friend/Lucius Freund: pretty clever," Jacob said, though now that the initial shock had worn off, he experienced another, more menacing one and began to wonder if Diet hadn't used the ruse to test him, to gauge Jacob's reaction and thus his commitment. It wouldn't have been the first time.

"You must turn left onto Mulholland Highway, then again left onto Edelweiss Drive," Diet said, tracing a finger along the map to where Jacob had drawn a star in red ink to mark the approximate location of his brother's house. "Then it looks like a right onto Von Trapp Lane and this will wrap around into a caul-de-sac." Jacob had already ranted at length about the bizarre choice in subdivision names—Edelweiss Estates—and the equally bizarre choice in streets, ranging from his brother's to others like Pomerania Way and Graz Road.

"Cul-de-sac," Jacob said, correcting him, and pulled up to the guardhouse, which sat at the entrance to Edelweiss Estates, both men oblivious to the end of the rain and the clearer skies, the sun burning off what was left of the dark, mealy clouds. All of a sudden, the day was drying off, warming up, inundating them with sunshine.

"You with the reality show?" asked the guard, a puffy, middle-aged matron in her late fifties, the ridge of her oily forehead riddled with a constellation of pimply-looking sores, her chin with coarse gray hairs. As though she were merely an extension of the seat and made out of the same foam and plastic, she rose without getting up and leaned over to peer into the car, squinting at Jacob, then past him to Diet, who was fiddling with his seat belt, which seemed to be jammed, and muttering indecipherable German.

"But the show's been over for months. Didn't it get canceled?" Jacob asked as the guard shrugged, this motion of hers coinciding exactly with the raising of the mechanical arm under which the car slowly rolled.

"You have a nice day," she said, or might have said, if Jacob had been listening more closely. He wanted her to have said it, yet in the back of his mind he was convinced that what she actually said was "You are so gay." He would have asked Diet if he'd heard her, except Diet was still preoccupied with loosening his restraint and hadn't been paying attention.

"You're going to give yourself an aneurysm. Stop struggling," Jacob said, pressing a hand into the center of Diet's bony, concave chest and pushing him back into the seat. It was what he should have done earlier, of course, and the moment he realized it, he felt a quickening of his pulse and a tightening up in his throat. "Just . . . will you just . . . relax?" He massaged Diet's chest, the heat of him bursting right through the thin T-shirt and across Jacob's palm, a heat like no other, full of pain and regret and lust and apathy and love. Yes, there was love, and it traveled through Jacob's fingers and straight up his arm, radiating through the rest of him, warming his ears and his face, and finally coming to rest just behind his breastplate, where it remained, lodged like a fever, a memory of childhood—the minty Vicks VapoRub his mom used to swab on his chest whenever he caught the flu.

"Now, just slide out from under it," he said, gently drawing the slackening belt away from Diet's chest as Diet maneuvered himself past Jacob's hand.

"Baby, you are a genius," he said, kissing Jacob's knuckles. "You are my hero."

"Aw, t'weren't nothin'," Jacob said, the sun colliding with the dewy lawns up and down the block and throwing an emerald tint upon the land. "I do believe we have arrived at our destination," and he drove to the end of the cul-de-sac and up to his brother's house, which was not as garish or ugly as he had remembered.

An entire day after stepping onto a plane in Berlin, they were finally taking in the pink stucco facade of the two-story, Swiss chalet–style villa: the terra-cotta-tiled roof; the three-car garage; the freestanding basketball hoop; the overturned dirt bikes lying in the tall, drying, sun-drenched grass; the flourishing eucalyptus, palm, lemon, and orange trees; the boxwood hedges; and the climbing vines of wild roses, wisteria, and bougainvillea that spread out in purples, marigold-yellows, and reds, everything splashed in Technicolor and shimmering in HD. It amazed him that anything was alive, but then he understood that everything—grass, trees, flowers—had been genetically redesigned to survive on as little water as possible. He turned to Diet and said, "I'm apologizing in advance for anything rude and tasteless that any of them says or does." Then he leaned in and kissed Diet hard and square on the lips.

As he did, he heard what sounded like shouting coming from somewhere nearby and pulled away just in time to see his brother, Mo, round the corner of the house, throw his hands up in the air, and stomp off and then a shadow, which lengthened and grew the longer Jacob stared at it, the shadow that eventually became Julian Jacobson, his dad, who was pushing a lawn mower.

"Welcome to the next four days of your life," Jacob said, putting the car into drive and pulling up behind his parents' minivan, spotting the personalized Texas license plate, which read CROAKR, and laughing to himself at first, then aloud, until Diet asked him what was so funny. He explained what a croaker was—a kind of fish that makes a drumming sound by vibrating its swim bladder—and that it was his dad's all-time favorite fish to catch and eat, or catch and release, omitting the truly humorous bit, the ironic double entendre, which was ghoulish, Jacob had to admit, and gave him the shivers.

"I still do not get this," Diet said. "Explain it to me again."

"I will, *Schatz,* I promise. But now let's introduce you to the Old Man and the C." The *C* stood for colitis, but Jacob didn't feel the need to explain this right now, either. He'd also save it for later, or tomorrow, or next week when they were safely back in Berlin and ensconced in their lives, all of this already fading, much like his desire to see his dad, who yanked on the cord to start the mower, which emitted a puff of smoke before spluttering to life, and who began to mow Mo's unkempt, untamed front yard in earnest.

And though to the world it looked as if his dad were doing a nice turn for his elder son, Jacob knew that he was in fact doing it for other reasons altogether, which had little to do with helping Mo and more to do with his own embarrassment at the way Mo maintained his yard, which of course reflected negatively on all of them, the entire Jacobson syndicate and all dead and buried antecedents as well.

Jacob wasn't about to explain any of this to Diet and would save it all up for later, or perhaps, after meeting his dad, Diet, who was fantastically bright, would finally be able formulate his own opinion about the Jacobson patriarch, saving Jacob from having to explain why he and his siblings *had* to get rid of him. Although if you pressed Jacob, he probably would have said that plotting Julian's death with his siblings was just a lot of talk and that none of them was actually serious about offing Dear Old Dada. *I mean, it's not like Mo and I are the Menendez brothers or that Thistle is Lizzie Borden,* he thought, taking a deep, fortifying breath before stepping out of the car just as his dad turned away—on purpose? Jacob wondered, because he had to have seen them—and disappeared around the other side of the house.

Now was Jacob's chance and he took it, grabbing Diet's hand and leading him quickly up the sidewalk, which was still splotchy in places from the evaporating rain. Jacob rang the doorbell while Diet let out a howl of excitement at the prospect of a gecko clinging for dear life to the front door, only to have a smiling Jacob point out that it wasn't real.

"Ceramic. Imported from Israel," he said, flicking it with a finger. Three of the little inanimate reptiles adorned the salsa-red door, each with a different set of words painted across its avocado-green spine that, when read collectively, added up to Welcome to Our Humble Jewish Home. He looked for the expensive handblown-glass mezuzah, a gift from his parents on Mo's family's move into this, their second home, but found only two small screw holes and the outline of where it once had been attached to the glossy white doorjamb.

Let's leave, Jacob wanted to say, reaching for Diet. *There's danger here.* But it was too late to say anything, for the door creaked open, though no one was there to greet them.

"Hello?" Jacob called out, stepping into the house just as one of the twins, the not-so-invisible-after-all greeter, appeared from behind the door, a huge frown plastered across his face. He was clutching a remote control in his small hand and aiming it at the vaulted ceiling. On his shirt was an embroidered letter *D*.

"You must be Dexter," Jacob said, kneeling before him.

"No, stupid, I'm Baxter," he replied. "That's Dexter," and he pointed the remote at his brother, who stood at the top of the staircase in the same shirt, though his naturally had a giant letter *B* embroidered on it. "You be quiet," Baxter shouted, chasing a ghost or an invisible playmate or pet up the stairs, where he finally came to rest beside his twin.

"Charming," Jacob said, rising, and pivoted toward Diet, who had been hovering on the threshold behind him just moments before, yet who was now standing with Mo under the lemon tree.

As Jacob watched, Mo reached up and plucked off a small fruit and handed it to Diet, who brought it up to his nose and inhaled, his face lighting up with excitement again and chasing away the rest of the hooded darkness and doubt from his eyes. It was a marvel to see and for one brief second Jacob believed that all would go well, that bringing Diet with him to meet his family wasn't as selfish perhaps as he'd previously imagined, and that his family might embrace Diet as he did and congratulate Jacob on a job well done.

For there had been others, a litany of failures, though Jacob had known enough to never introduce any of them around, as he suspected it wouldn't have mattered anyway, because none of them had stayed long enough to take any real hold or have any real effect on his life. Besides, no one in his family besides Edith took any true interest in Jacob's romantic life, which caused a whole lot of friction and made him feel invisible, especially whenever they all used to gather to celebrate this or that Jewish holiday, though these gatherings had become rarer as they'd drifted further and further apart.

Jacob remained in the doorway, continuing to observe his brother and his lover, who returned the lemon to Mo, the air filling again with the roar of the lawn mower, his dad's re-approach, while Mo kneaded the lemon in his fingers, then absently tossed it into the air with one hand and caught it in the other, as if it were a baseball, which reminded Jacob of all the times he used to watch Mo and his dad playing catch, how he'd longed to join them but knew enough to remain on the wooden swing in the cool, canopied shade of the towering Chinese tallow trees, and how transfixing it was to watch the agile, confident Mo in the grass, his naturalness with the bat and respect for the game, the power in his young body, his windups as beautiful to Jacob as the pitches he let go. How jealous he was of Mo, until of course Mo shifted to his right or left and missed the ball completely and his dad erupted into heaves of taunting laughter, which altered Mo's countenance almost imperceptibly, an incremental darkness that crept across his face as he collected the baseball and sent it back to his dad, who hollered, "At least one of my sons doesn't throw like a damn pussy," and shifted his gaze from Mo to Jacob, who smiled blandly and took the insult, because what other choice did he have?

His dad maneuvered the mower, which choked once and died and had to be restarted, to the edge of the yard and followed the curb, and as he did, Mo shifted his body, tracking him, his face full of a familiar childhood mischief. Jacob sucked in his breath and took a step toward him, alarmed by what Mo was about to do but even more concerned for his dad, which surprised him. It had been so long since he'd felt anything for the old man and didn't even understand what he was feeling, until Mo gripped the lemon tighter in his fist, wound up his arm, and took aim at the senior Jacobson.

Before Jacob knew what he was doing, he was shouting "No," which he feared would be drowned out by the roar of the mower, yet

Mo lifted his eyes and registered it, letting his arm drop. He opened his fingers and the lemon fell into the grass, which swallowed it. If they were going to go through with it, and Jacob continued to have serious doubts that they actually would, he saw no point in purposefully antagonizing, even wounding, the old man, then having to deal with the fallout. Not that Mo would have even hit him, but why give the old coot further ammunition? Why merely bruise him when they could exsanguinate him instead?

" 'Fame is short-lived and you're the last to know when you're no longer hot,' " Mo said loudly and dramatically in an impressive and impromptu accent, channeling his favorite actor, the Australian-born George Lazenby, whose only claim to fame, as far as Jacob knew, was his portrayal of James Bond in 1969 in the rather forgettable *On Her Majesty's Secret Service,* after which he was canned from the franchise.

Jacob went down the walk to meet Mo, all ready to scold him for his passive-aggressive high jinks with the lemon, but instead veered off to help Diet, who was struggling with the suitcases, trying to lift them out of the trunk.

"Let me get those," Mo said, hurrying to the car to help. "That impression. It was pretty good, right? Tell me it was good."

"Yes, Mo, it was the best impression of Lazenby I've ever heard," Jacob said, rolling his eyes at Diet, while Mo lowered both extraordinarily heavy suitcases to the ground, which impressed Jacob, for Mo was nothing if not the caretaker and archetype of good old-fashioned chivalry and in his house the guest was king. "So I see the old man didn't waste any time," he added, referring to the yard. "How's Mom? Where is she?"

"She's with Pandora running some errands, then picking up the trips from school," Mo said, gazing with slit-eyed frustration yet also with a sense of wonder, it seemed, at the wide swaths his dad was making in the yard.

"Dad made it sound like she couldn't even walk to the bathroom," Jacob said.

"She can walk, she just walks superslow," he said, and something in his voice caught. "I can't believe she didn't get diagnosed earlier, Jay. What was she thinking? What was he? He didn't notice that his own wife couldn't breathe?"

Jacob had never seen the adult Mo cry and didn't care to see it now or ever, but luckily Mo got ahold of himself, the moment passing away without tears. "I don't mow the yard so much these days because the city told us not to, but do you think he cares?"

As Jacob and Diet made their exhausted way along the walk, rolling-dragging their suitcases behind them, Mo rushed on ahead of them into the house. "Baxter! Dexter! Come put your toys away! Your uncle Jay and his friend are sleeping in here," he said, his deep voice echoing through the rooms and carrying out the front door to Jacob, who paused and turned to wave at his dad, imagining the alternative scene and what would have happened if Mo had fired the lemon through the air. ("I don't grow just any lemons. I grow lemons specifically engineered to thrive in desert climates," his dad explained later, comparing his son's meager-sized fruit to the enormousness of his own back in Texas. "No common sense at all. I told Farmer Moans that I'd start him a tree and drive the sucker out here, but I guess he just likes those effete Meyer lemons better.")

He pictured his dad knocked unconscious and lying on his back in the grass, out cold for the remainder of the trip. The vision was so welcome and pleasant, so vivid, that Jacob didn't hear Diet calling to him until he was in the house and taking his place beside him at the wall of glass, which gave them a clear view into the backyard.

"Baby, you did not mention that pool," Diet said, pie-eyed and more delighted than Jacob ever remembered seeing him. "But it is . . . empty. Why? This is California, land of the blue swimming pools and one-point-three actors in every home!"

"The Great Drought: The Sequel," said Mo to Jacob, as if he'd been the one asking. "It was either drain it or pay a monthly luxury water tax so steep it'd make your nose bleed. Too bad you weren't here during the show. The network always kept it topped off, heated, and sparkling. But them days are over, or nearly over . . . Look, I should warn you guys about something before you settle into your room and unpack."

Just as the two leaned in to hear what Mo had to say—for some reason unbeknownst to Jacob, Mo was whispering—the letter *D*, which meant Baxter, appeared at the top of the stairs with what else but a nosebleed. "Dexter, what did you do to your brother?" Mo asked, hollering up the stairs.

"Nothing," Dexter boomed, his reply just as loud and grating as Mo's and making Diet cringe. "He's a liar if he said I did anything," and he appeared again beside his brother, wrapping an arm around the other's shoulders, each boy grinning from ear to ear. And in that moment Jacob was finally able to tell them apart, because Dexter with the *B* was missing two front teeth, while Baxter with the *D*, who was bleeding profusely from the nose, was missing two bottom teeth.

"Okay, well, you're dripping on the hardwood, which is going to upset Mommy, so get your butt in the bathroom lickety-split. I'll be right up," Mo said and turned to Jacob. "Don't tell the old man. Every time they come out here, Bax gets a gusher. He thinks the kid has leukemia, which he doesn't—it's just the dry air—but I don't feel like dealing with another round of Let's Make a Prognosis, starring Dr. Julian Jacobson." Jacob held one hand up to his own mouth, the other to Diet's, and mimed zipping lips. "Okay. Now, while I take care of Old Faithful, you guys make yourselves at home. If you're hungry, have a snack, but don't eat too much because I'm grilling tonight."

"Hey, what'd you want to tell us?" Jacob asked, but Mo was already halfway up the stairs and didn't respond. After he was gone, Jacob took hold of Diet's hand. "Are you as overstimulated and overtired as I am right now? It makes for a truly surreal experience, huh."

"It makes for a truly surreal something. I think I would like to stay at a hotel," Diet said. "It is already way too chaotic and loud, and I fear I will not be able to get any work done. We will also not have any privacy to carry out our, um, business."

"Baby, we discussed this," Jacob said. "It's important to every-one that I be here. Besides, this is what you signed up for. Don't back out on me now." After he said it, he realized how it made him sound, as if Diet owed him, which of course he did, thought Jacob, recalling the trip they'd taken to Munich to visit Diet's family, an eye-opening, nerve-racking weekend to say the least. "What's fair is fair."

"*Ja, ja. Sehr gut,*" Diet said, pressing a hand to the glass, as if he wanted to reach through and touch the imaginary lapping waters in the empty dreidel-shaped pool. "I must nap now, or I will never make it," his voice soft but stern.

They made their way upstairs to the guest room, where Jacob shut the door as Diet headed directly for the two large windows that faced the street. He drew the curtains, darkening the room, while Jacob fiddled with the pullout sofa.

"If you need anything, like towels and sheets, they're in the linen closet in the hall," Mo said through the door. "I'll be downstairs reading a script."

"How's your head?" Jacob asked as they made the bed, Jacob smoothing out the sheets and the blanket and arranging the pillows just so. He had recognized early on just how much Diet appreciated tight corners.

"It hurts a little, but I think I will be fine," he said.

"Mo suffered a concussion when we were kids," Jacob said, waiting for Diet's final assessment. He gave the bed the once-over, offering a tacit approval with his eyes, a telegraphed yes that Jacob had also come to recognize. Then and only then did he take a seat at the foot of the bed, where he was joined by Diet, who kneeled down on the pile carpet, a sudden supplicant.

"He got beaned in the head with a baseball. And you know what our dear old dad said that night at dinner? He pulled out a five-dollar bill, slid it across the table to Mo, and said, 'Buy the team another ball because I'm sure it got the worst of it.' Then he started to laugh."

"Is that not funny?" Diet asked, unlacing Jacob's shoes and slipping them gently off his feet. He set the shoes and socks aside. "To me, it sounds funny. Didn't Mo laugh?"

"Yes, he did, but that's not the point, is it," Jacob said, lying back on the bed and giving Diet full access to his jeans, which Diet proceeded to unbutton, then tug off as gently as he had the shoes and socks. "Anyone can say anything, but it's all in the tone and delivery. My dad has always had a peculiar way of communicating. Everything's a veiled threat, and I mean everything. Everything's tinged with guilt and obligation—and the trouble is, there's just not an ounce of love behind any of it. The meaning isn't in his message per se. The meaning is in the way I receive and interpret it." Jacob felt as if he were bumbling the intention of his explanation, making it more about the way he and Diet interfaced rather than a critical analysis of his dad. "I suppose I should feel sorry for him, but he makes even that impossible."

"Quiet now," Diet said, sliding up beside Jacob. "No more talk of meaning or of fathers."

He repositioned himself and dragged the blanket up and over his face, and after a moment his breathing deepened and his body relaxed, giving over to sleep. Jacob shut his eyes and tried not to think about his dad or about the rest of his family, whom he was going to have to face eventually. He tried not to think about his mom or the guilt he felt about having moved across an ocean—mainly to get away from all of them, the depressive, awful Jacobson clan, who had made growing up a nightmare of such extravagant proportions that he was sure that even if he did happen to write one play a year, he'd never be able to capture it all, to put it all down as it had happened, because no one would believe any of it.

There was just too much heartache and sorrow and bad blood to account for, all of it leading back to his dad. His dad who was mowing the yard, the sound of which traveled up the walls of the house and through the windows to find Jacob lying wide awake, unable to let himself go under, although he'd been up for twenty-four hours straight. His attempts to reposition himself on the bed, which was lumpy and offered little in the way of back support—leave it to Mo to buy the cheapest, least comfortable sofa bed imaginable—were met with further and further frustration, until he sat up, absolutely stymied by his own inability to sleep.

He climbed silently out of bed and went to the window, peering out to catch his dad standing in the middle of the front yard, staring up at the sky. He'd removed his shirt, which now dangled from his back pocket, and the sight of his hairy back with all of its moles and slippage of skin both saddened and disgusted Jacob. Oh, how he wanted to reverse time, to unwind it so that he'd never agreed to this trip. Yet here they were, here he was, and that said more about Jacob than it did about any of his siblings or his mom and dad, who had not been expecting him to show up, because for years now Jacob had been unreachable, too busy "being on vacation and writing in coffee shops," according to his dad, to make anything but the minimally acceptable amount of time for any of them.

Mainly because, Jacob reflected, putting his jeans back on, then his socks and shoes and padding to the door, he had never quite understood why, when he did relent and visit Dallas every couple of years, neither one of his parents seemed all that interested in him once he'd arrived. It was as if chasing him down produced far more excitement in them than his actually being there, for once he was in their house, he might as well have been a piece of furniture they'd ordered and had delivered—they moved him around the rooms but mostly just ignored him, his dad toiling out in the yard and his mom lying in bed with her tablet, scrolling through the news. And he always wanted to ask them, together and separately, what exactly they got out of these short, hurried, "required" visits.

He'd come to suspect that it was merely to affirm their roles as parents, to be able to brag to their friends about their youngest, the budding Broadway playwright, and oh, what a lovely time they had

had with him, which might not have been far off the mark for them but was wildly off the mark for him, for every second he spent with them was pure, unadulterated torture—from his having to behave in a certain way around his dad for fear of reprisal to pretending that when his mom leaned in to kiss him good night he didn't feel the slightest spasm of fear. Yes, he loved her, but she herself would have been the first to say that she hadn't always been the best parent, while in the same breath continuing to maintain that no one was perfect and that she and Julian had only done their best with the tools they'd been given.

So what was going to happen once she was gone?

How could he possibly be in that house without her to come between him and his dad?

He glanced back at Diet, wondering again if he'd be able to see what Jacob saw, what his siblings had finally come to see on their own, although it had taken them a ghastly thirty years to come to the same conclusion Jacob had made when he was just a few years old— that they all would have been better off without Julian Jacobson.

Downstairs, all was quiet and subdued. A sleeping Mo was sprawled out on the white leather modular sofa, the script lying open on his flat stomach, his thick, muscular legs crossed at the ankles— there he was, his semifamous older brother, this out-of-work actor, frustrated inventor, and author of the self-help book *Buff Bods,* in which Mo outlined for out-of-shape dads and their out-of-shape kids everywhere his six-point plan for getting and staying trim and in shape.

"You and you alone are the architect of your children's well-being," he wrote. "Overweight kids become overweight adults and overweight adults become a heavy liability—pun intended—on our country's health-care system."

Jacob only remembered the line because he'd edited the manuscript before Mo had sent it off to agents. He'd added the "pun intended."

The twins were not in the house but playing somewhere outside,

49

their voices carrying softly like the volume on a TV turned way down. Jacob went into the kitchen and grabbed the phone, then looked for and finally found a way into the backyard through the pneumatic door set into the wall of glass. The door breathed closed behind him as a slobbering, shaggy canine beset him, shoving its nose directly into his crotch.

"And you must be the new rescue, Nieves," Jacob said, rubbing the Scottish terrier's filthy white snout.

The dog glanced up at him with milky blue eyes and snorted hello, then pushed her head into the ground and yelped, clearly wanting to play. Jacob wound up his arm and threw a pretend ball into the air. The dog gave chase, skittering around the lip of the pool and losing her footing. For a moment, Jacob thought he'd sent the dog to her waterless death, but she righted herself and continued her high-speed pursuit of the "ball" to the far reaches of the yard, tumbling against the fence in a happy outburst of barks. While she sniffed and rooted around in the grass, Jacob made his call to Clarence Lee Chalmers, who eventually picked up on the fourth ring, his voice gravelly and phlegmatic.

"Hello, Jacob," Clarence said before Jacob could speak. But how did he know? "The wonders of modern technology. You're in the Valley at your brother Moses's, I assume, because you're calling from an 818 number and his name popped up on my caller ID. Mystery solved. Now, what can I do you for? Funeral arrangements? You aren't with the UCLA alumni association, are you? Because I swear those people can just suck it. I must get a call from them every week asking me to donate to—"

"Um, you told me to call you about getting drinks. So I'm calling you about getting drinks," Jacob said, flummoxed. Had Clarence forgotten his call from the apocalyptic gas station pay phone only a few hours previously?

"How demented of me," the other said. "I must have been astral-projecting again because I haven't touched a drop of alcohol in ages, not since I woke up one morning on the beach in Santa Monica stark naked with peanut butter in my hair."

Nieves retrieved the invisible ball and dropped it at Jacob's feet, then barked her piercing bark until he pretend-picked it up and pretend-tossed it into the air again.

"Anyway, if you believe anything I just said, you're still the same innocent you've always been, which is a remarkable coup," Clarence continued, and the hyena in him emerged and cackled wildly. "Why don't you meet me at Japón? Five o'clock sound about right?"

"Clarence, I have an important issue to discuss with you."

"As do I, doll. As do I," he said, serious all of a sudden, which gave Jacob pause. "Oh, Jay, it's going to be just like old times, except we're a decade and a half older and I'm a decade and a half richer. Now I have to go. The business of death waits for no man," and with that, he clicked off.

Somehow, Jacob found himself at the very edge of the pool without any recollection of how he'd gotten there. Clearly, though, he'd picked up his feet and put them down again, these feet that did not seem to belong to him, just as none of this—the house, the afternoon, the certain death of his mom—seemed to belong to him. As he stood there, his eyes blurry and burning, he braced himself for the inevitable approach of his dad, who came around the bend a moment later, utterly unaware of Jacob, who felt the same age-old tingling in his bones, the voice in his head that cautioned, *Run. Take cover.*

Long ago and far away, in a distant galaxy known as Jacob's childhood, he had kept a journal, many journals, that spanned more than a decade. From the time he started writing, at age five, to the last second of his tenure in his dad's house, at age seventeen, he'd recounted in them every mean and nasty word and deed that anyone had ever said or done to him. He'd hid the one he was working on in a secret slot in one of his pillows, a carved-out recess he'd made with a paring knife. When he was finished filling one journal, he'd add it to the collection of others, which he'd stored in a garbage bag under the toolshed in the backyard.

Sometimes, as luck would have it, there would be a day that he did not have to record a single episode and thus got to leave a page blank, though usually each day held more than one entry, sometimes several. When he read back over the journals later, after his parents had sold the dingy, cramped ranch house that Jacob and his siblings had grown up in and built their new dream home, a spacious, bright, seven-room, cookie-cutter monstrosity in a gated community, he made a startling discovery—the blank pages corresponded directly to his dad's being out of town, when he was either down at the coast on a fishing expedition or at some medical conference. This revelation ought not to have surprised him, yet it did, and he shared it, however reluctantly, with his siblings, who were aghast at first at the very notion of the journals, which he dubbed My Manifest of Meanness, then even more aghast at what Jacob was insinuating.

"Wait, are you saying what I think you're saying?" Mo had asked Jacob, who had joined his siblings at Canter's Deli on North Fairfax after taking the last final exam of his college career.

"He's saying Daddy was a monster," Edith said, taking a bite of her blueberry-filled blintz and smiling wildly, incongruously, as if she couldn't get a good blintz anywhere in D.C., which was where she was in grad school at the time and only in L.A. for a quick breather of a weekend. "He's saying that, episodically, Daddy accounts for most of the entries."

"No, I'm . . . Is that . . . ? Yes, I guess that's what I'm saying," Jacob said, attacked and on the defensive. "Are you guys going to sit there and tell me that you can't see it?"

"Oh, pray tell, supreme and worldly undergraduate brother of ours," Edith said condescendingly, "what exactly are we supposed to see?"

"That he's a sociopath. That he took great delight in being mean to me," Jacob said, which made his siblings smirk. "That he hit you in the head with a baseball, Mo, and that he never had his precious fig tree removed, Edith, although you were deathly allergic to it. Can't you see what all this means?"

"The baseball was an accident," Mo said.

"I ate the figs all on my own. No one forced them down my throat," she said. "You can't blame Daddy for what happened."

"Jesus, you really just don't get it, do you?" Jacob said, finally laying his cards on the table: "He wanted us gone, so that he could have Mom to himself again, because then it was checkmate. Because then he could take control of her entirely."

"Gone, as in . . . dead?" Mo asked, chortling again and dribbling his coffee all over himself.

"Jacob, I love that you have such a vivid imagination," Edith said, "but I think I speak for Mo as well when I say that while you present a compelling theory of Daddy's past—or is it his present?—indiscretions, need I remind you that a few scattered, empty holes in those . . . journals are hardly sufficient evidence to accuse him of what you're accusing him of? I mean, for fuck's sake, Jacob, you're talking about our dad. You need to let it go. It's not healthy to hold on to this negativity."

"Fine, just fine," Jacob said, getting up in a huff and stomping away.

Jacob, who loved his siblings, didn't speak to either of them again for well over a year and even then it was with some reluctance and trepidation that he took Mo's call. By then he was living in a tiny studio apartment in New York City and working at the legendary Chelsea Gym, which was more of a bathhouse than a real gym, although he didn't tell Mo this. He was twenty-two years old, a fresh, pretty face in a predominantly gay neighborhood, and while neither the job of being towel boy nor the hours he had to work was ideal, the men who came and went from the gym made it all worthwhile. Some of them were close to his dad's age and showered the most compliments on him. Though the men who dished them out made him fiercely uncomfortable to the point of feeling nauseated, Jacob took the compliments and ran with them anyway, for he had never in his life had so much positive attention heaped on him. Having grown up with a dad who never said I love you, never flattered or offered anything even remotely like a compliment, Jacob was unused to hearing how handsome, bright, and funny he was.

"I know it's too late to say I'm sorry, but, well, I'm sorry," Mo said. Then he told Jacob how he'd just suffered from what was apparently his first panic attack. "At least that's what the doctors called it. I thought I was going to die, Jay. That's how bad it felt. Came out of the fucking blue, too. Uncontrollable sweating, racing heart. Woke me up in the middle of the night."

"Mom used to get them," Jacob said. "Bet you didn't know that."

"You mean they're, like, inherited?" he asked, dubious.

"Everything's inherited," Jacob said. "It's in our blood, unfortunately."

"You ever have them?" he asked.

Did Jacob tell his brother that his anxiety manifested in a completely different way, that to combat it he found himself having random sex with strangers in the steam room of the gym, even once or twice on the roof deck after closing? Of course, back then he didn't think about anxiety at all or link it to his wanton sexual appetite. Back then, he just thought of himself as a randy budding writer who was racking up experiences the way others racked up debt.

"I mean I couldn't get out of bed for two days, Jay. I had to skip an important audition because I couldn't even leave my apartment."

"So you called to apologize and tell me you had a debilitating panic attack. While I sympathize, Mo, I can't say I'm surprised," Jacob told him without sympathy.

"Sometimes you sound just like him, you know that?" Mo snapped.

"And sometimes you should listen to me because I'm right, I've always been right about him. It's not my fault you and Thistle never saw what I did. What I still do. You mark my words: One day, we're going to be burying Ma because of him."

And look, here we are, Jacob thought, hating that he'd clocked it all those years ago during that fateful phone call with Mo. He turned to go back into the house before his dad spotted him, but it was too late; he let the mower die and joined Jacob at the pool. His face glistened with sweat, and he had grass shavings stuck both in his abundant albino-white chest hair and in the tousled crown of thick near-white hair of which he was quite proud; he'd only lost a small amount on top. The tonsure gave him the appearance of a monk, though he was about as holy as a desecrated, defiled temple, Jacob thought.

"The prodigal son doth returneth," his dad said, the moniker he inevitably threw around whenever he saw Jacob. (Technically, this wasn't Jacob's home, so he couldn't have been a prodigal, but he let it go. What good would it do to correct a man who was always right?) Swiping at his sweaty face with the back of his hand, he shook it off, some of the drops splattering Jacob. "Glad you could join us." This seemingly harmless welcome dripped with his usual acid. "Pandora and your mother are back from shopping at the Commons. I should go check on her and make sure she didn't do too much damage on my credit card. Be useful and finish up the yard."

"Yeah, sure, whatever," Jacob said, feeling unsafe and taking a step back, not out of fear of standing too close to the edge but of being just too close to the old man himself, who turned and strode away.

As if she sensed the passing of danger or just a rotten smell, Nieves returned, tearing graceless circles around Jacob, yapping and snarling in good fun, her ears standing at attention one moment, only to droop the next. *You hear things I never will,* thought Jacob, *just as I'll hear things this weekend you can't,* and he kneeled in the grass and stroked the dog's belly, picturing the turbulent days ahead and wondering which of them—if any—would make it out alive.

Jacob had wondered the same thing during that ghastly vacation to Disneyland when he was a boy, what proved to be the last Jacobson road trip, when his parents had climbed back into the car after a pit stop at Point Dume, his dad saying that once they got back to Dallas he was moving out.

"Your mom and I are getting a divorce," he had said. While Edith and Mo had reacted with surprise and shock, the normal response to such an announcement, Jacob had gone rigid and sat as still as he could, for he had been afraid of moving even a single eyelash and breaking the spell that he himself thought he'd cast. Hadn't he been wishing for this forever, for at least as long as he could remember, having only just turned seven? Hadn't he prayed each day for a miracle to take his dad away? Not his death per se, just to remove him from their lives and, oh, what lives they would live now that he was going, now that his mom had finally awoken to what Jacob had always known—that the man in the front seat could not have cared less about any of them. But then, when they had gotten home and his dad had packed his bags, he had just never left. Their mother could, in fact, withstand another straw and another without breaking, not because his dad had promised he'd change and stop being as mean, but because his mother had a heart and she loved the man and that was that—she recanted and he stayed. And in recanting, in overturning the decree of divorce, she had betrayed them all, although the saddest thing of all, thought Jacob, was that she had only ended up betraying herself.

"Oh, I forgot to mention that it's almost out of gas," his dad said, turning to him at the door. "The can's empty, so you'll have to run it up to the Exxon. And for the love of God, Jacob, remember: unleaded fuel only. You don't want to ruin another engine." He was referring, of course, to the ruined engine of the car he'd crashed when he was sixteen, or perhaps going back even further to the fire engine—a childhood Chanukah present—he'd set on one of the electric burners of the stove and melted, dared by his older brother and sister, who, when the time came, claimed complete innocence. It had been the first time in his young life that he'd realized he might not be able to trust his own brother and sister, an upsetting revelation that he entered into his Manifest, furious at them but more furious at himself for taking the bait.

Jacob tamped down his dad's dig long enough to throw up his hand in a wave. *Go with God, my soon-to-be-dearly-departed papa,* he thought.

Trembling and furious, Jacob yanked at the mower's cord, and when it coughed to life, he gave it a push, imagining his dad supine in the tall, spring grass, his arms and legs bound with rope and tied to stakes. He imagined his brother and sister standing over him, Mo leaning in to remove the gag in his mouth.

"Has he confessed yet?" Jacob asked on each pass he made, the acreage of yard dwindling. "Because I'm running out of grass."

"Not yet," said Mo.

"Daddy, you need to confess," said Edith, "or else he'll do it. He'll really do it, Daddy."

"Oh, shut up, Thistle," Jacob said. "He knows I'm going to do it. But I'm wondering what he's going to miss most—the balls that gave us life or that poor excuse of a dick."

Still, his dad remained as stoic and inexorable as ever, contending as usual that he'd never done anything wrong to any of them. "I'm your father. Untie me and we'll forget this ever happened," he said. "Your mother won't like it, that's for sure. She can't survive without me."

Jacob followed the path in the grass his dad had already made. The going was slow and tedious and required a lot of patience—a virtue Jacob had in spades. He'd been patient with his dad throughout his childhood when Jacob scored exceedingly high on an IQ test only to have his dad say it wasn't as high as his, patient throughout his teenage years when he came home from school having been bullied and his dad said that he probably deserved it, patient into his early adulthood when his dad refused to acknowledge or even deign to discuss his romantic life, the heartaches and joys—and this patience had served Jacob well and had helped him survive in the arid, ungenerous world of his dad's making. Yet all of that was going to change, because he was done being patient, done making excuses. Just done.

As the mower finally ran out of gas, choked, rattled, then went quiet, he took up the fantasy again and ran the mower over his dad, slicing off his dick, then backing it up to see what he'd done, his dad screaming, though no one could hear him because Mo had replaced the gag. His siblings turned away from the sight, the blood spurting out, the mower shredding and tearing and mutilating his hairy flesh until there was little left to flay. Then Jacob and Edith and Mo passed around the gasoline, sprinkling it over their father, who was still able to writhe and protest, and then the match and then the ashes.

Abandoning the mower as well as the fantasy, Jacob strode into the garage, where, instead of the plastic red container he'd come looking for, he found Mo sitting behind the wheel of the giant Expedition, just sitting there, gazing straight ahead, listening to what Jacob thought were wind chimes but were, in actuality, triangles. He tapped on the glass, startling Mo, who turned down the volume on the radio, then hit a button, lowering the automatic window.

"The mower's out of gas. His nibs ordered me to get more," Jacob said.

"Fuck the gas, fuck the mower, fuck the yard, and fuck him." Mo drew his eyes down and away. "She's dying and he still talks to her like she's some kind of wild, stupid animal," he said. "I can't take it, Jacob. I just . . . I don't want him here. And I don't want him anywhere near my kids."

The soft, anodyne pinging of the triangles punctuated the afternoon, a sad, wistful melody that echoed through the garage.

"Good, this is good," Jacob said. "When the time comes, I want you to remember this moment, this feeling, Mo. We're doing this for her, not for us."

He wanted to add that killing their dad would naturally affect them all, that it was as selfish an act as ever there was one. But he didn't say any of this because he knew his brother, knew that it might only take one misplaced word to unravel his resolve. And Mo wasn't even his real concern anyway—it was Edith who was going to take a lot more convincing, at least that's how it sounded the last time the three had spoken. Now he would have to wait until she arrived the following day to make sure she was still on board, that she wasn't having second thoughts.

"What happened to the German's head anyway?" Mo asked after Jacob had located the empty container and climbed in beside him.

"Really, Mo? 'The German'?" Jacob said, setting the container in back. "He bumped it."

"Good to know. I thought you might have thrown a lemon at him when he wasn't looking," he said, pulling out of the garage. "You don't have to come with me. It's probably better you don't." Jacob understood that his brother wanted, needed, some time alone. "I'm going to the store. Have fun with your nephews."

"By the way, what did you want to tell us?" Jacob asked before getting out.

"Oh, that," Mo said. "Well, I'm going to need you and the German—I mean, Dietrich—to sign confidentiality agreements and release forms if you want to be a part of the special."

"What special?" Jacob asked.

"Seems that some of our devoted fans petitioned the network. No one wanted us to get canceled and everyone was pissed when it happened. We got a ton of fan mail, Pandora, the boys, me. Anyway, the execs at the network thought it'd be a great idea to catch up with us a year later. We've agreed to let them film the family during the Seder. Passover with *The JacobSONS*! Isn't that awesome? You and Dietrich will be compensated for it in case you're wondering."

"Do Mom and Dad know about this?" Jacob asked.

"They've already signed on again," he said. "They've been on a few times before. There was that birthday special when the trips turned ten, don't forget. You're the only one who hasn't been on the show."

"That's because I hate reality TV and never wanted to be a part of it," Jacob said. "No offense."

"None taken," he said, though of course Jacob had offended him. He could tell by the way Mo curled and uncurled his fingers into fists. "But think about it like this: It's immediate exposure. Being on TV is like being ten feet tall. You'll never not get noticed again, even if it is because you're a sellout and your career's totally tanked and your wife is the breadwinner and is keeping your family afloat."

"It'll all be okay," Jacob said, though he wasn't sure he believed it himself.

"Up yours, man," Mo said, irascible. "Shit's falling apart all over the place and where have you been, in the land of sausage-eating Jew-haters? And after it's all over, then what? You go back to Berlin with Mr. Hitler Youth, 2022? How do you live with yourself?"

"Mo, you're being an idiot and incredibly unfair," Jacob said.

"Whatever you say," he said. "Now just get out, because I don't want to lose it on you."

Jacob descended from the Expedition. The second he did, Mo cranked up the radio's volume, then backed up and, not seeing one of the dirt bikes, which their dad had removed from the grass and left in the driveway, ran right over it, the bike snapping as if it were made entirely of plastic. *So this is how it's going to go,* thought Jacob, watching his brother drive away, the tolling of the triangles lingering in the warm, dry air.

Back in the house, Jacob tried to slip upstairs without being noticed, wanting to check on Diet before saying hello to his mom. He was making good progress and was more than halfway up the stairs when his sister-in-law, Pandora, appeared, crossing the landing. She glanced up from her iPhone, to which she was constantly, even pathologically, attached, just long enough to register him with a long, slow blink of her blue eyes and an even longer, slower curl of her collagen-injected lips, before returning her attention to her phone to finish up a text.

"You're here," she said, remaining with her face in her phone. "The trips are dying to see you. They're in there," and with an elbow she indicated the other wing of the house. "They call it the Resettlement. They're still very into the history of the Israeli-Palestinian conflict and what the hell happened over there. Sometimes, the UN gets involved and manages to save Israel, but most of the time they just play all that gory footage and hold mock trials for the war criminals and collaborators—needless to say, the first person on trial is often our dearly beloved president. Your brother and I aren't too happy about it, but maybe their worldly uncle can talk some sense into them. We sure as hell can't."

Pandora kept sending and receiving texts, as if this were her one true calling. "Your mom's resting in the guest room downstairs. Your dad's cleaning the grill. And Mo's . . . somewhere. I guess he went to the grocery store?" She paused, tapped out a text message, and sent it to him. They waited, unspeaking, until her phone dinged.

"Yep, that's what he's doing. So . . . I met your boyfriend a few minutes ago. Nice work. He seems lovely, even for a German. Just kidding." She glanced up from her phone again. "We're all glad you're here, Jacob," and with that, she sent another text, moving past him down the stairs and out of sight.

Jacob found Diet in the throes of unpacking one of the suitcases. The contusion on his forehead had gone down some and looked less angry and red, although this did not reflect his mood, which had soured. "I met your sister-in-law," he said, hanging up his shirts and pants in the closet. "She spoke to me like I was hard to hear."

"Hard of hearing," Jacob said, standing on the threshold of the closet, barring Diet, who tried to get around him. "I'm not sure Pandora's ever met a real-life German before. She grew up in Thousand Oaks and never left. Moving to Calabasas, which is just down the

61

road, was traumatic for her. You have to think about her as someone who grew up in the tiniest village in Germany, married, had kids, and just stayed. That's who Pandora is."

"As superficial as I sensed she was, I got the exact opposite sensation about your mother. I ran into her in the kitchen when I was getting a glass of *Wasser*," Diet said. "She was very nice to speak with. She kept wondering where you were. I told her I thought you were outside with your brother and this made her smile. We spoke only for a little while, but I felt as if I'd known her my whole life."

Jacob waited for Diet to say the same about meeting him, how he'd felt he'd known Jacob his whole life, too, but he said nothing, and Jacob got out of his way. "Remember that thing my brother wanted to warn us about?" he said. "You're not going to like it."

He told Diet about the reality-show special and how important it was to Mo that both he and Diet participate. "So this was the other reason Mo wanted you to visit," he said. "Well, I hope you told him this is out of the question."

"I didn't tell him yes or no," Jacob said. "Think about it like this: It'd be great exposure for me, *Schatz*. An instant connection to the fans I do have and perhaps a way to make new ones. You think I want to teach English to Israeli refugees for the rest of my life, or keep watching as friends land big movie and TV deals?" He sat down on the bed, falling silent.

"So what? I'm to be the token German at that table?" Diet asked. "Good for ratings, I suppose. The Jews who watch will love it."

"Yeah, well, maybe then you'll finally understand what it felt like for me during Christmas Eve with your family," Jacob said, then immediately wishing he hadn't. "Look, all I'm saying is . . ." He trailed off, his brain snagging on a previous branch of the conversation. "Wait a second. What did you mean when you said this was the other reason they wanted me to visit? What's 'the other reason'? I mean, the first reason."

"Did I say this? It is not what I meant," Diet said. "You are misinterpreting."

"It is what you meant," he said, knowing Diet was nothing if not concise and meant everything he said.

"I think I am turned upside down," he said, taking a seat beside Jacob. "I have terrible jet lag and on top of that probably mild brain damage, thanks to you."

"Aw, well, we can go to bed early tonight," Jacob said, leaning over and gently kissing him on the forehead.

Someone knocked on the door. Before Jacob could ask who it was, the door opened and in poured the trips: Brendan, Brandon, and Bronson, a perfect blend of Mo and Pandora, with a little of Edith and himself thrown in for good measure—they had the prominent Jacobson nose and thin, banded lips, but their faces were linear rather than oval and their ears were pinned back rather than sticking out from their heads. *You handsome devils,* Jacob thought. *Lady- or lad-killers-in-waiting.* It'd been several years since he'd seen them, and now at twelve they stood shoulder to shoulder before him, each with his hand behind his back. "What have you guys got there, huh?" he asked, getting up, the triplets pivoting in order to keep whatever they had hidden.

"Maw-Maw told us to bring this stuff up to you," said Brandon, Brendan, or Bronson.

"She did? Well, lay it on us then," Jacob said, as one of the trips stepped out of line.

"I'm Bran," said Brandon, who held out his hand and presented Jacob with two purple satin sleep masks, then stepped back into line.

"I'm Bren," said Brendan, who held out his hand and presented Jacob with two sets of earplugs, then also stepped back into line.

"And I'm Bron," said Bronson, who held out his hand and presented Jacob with a thermos and two plastic cups, though he did not get back into line. Instead, he took a step toward Diet. "It's a pleasure to meet you," he said, extending his hand.

Diet rose, took the little hand in his own, and shook it genially. For whatever reason, possibly because he was sleep-deprived, jet-lagged, and nervous, this moment moved Jacob to tears, and he turned to set the masks, earplugs, thermos, and cups on the bed, composing himself before facing the trips again.

"We brought presents for you all the way from Berlin," he said and looked at Diet. "Which suitcase are they in, *mein Liebling*?"

"I think not in that one," Diet said, glancing hesitantly at the other suitcase, which was still locked and zipped tight.

"Great. Well, I guess you'll have to wait until a little later. Oh, and boys, thank you for delivering this stuff. Now, do me a huge favor and tell Maw-Maw I'll see her in a few minutes?"

After they dashed out of the room, Jacob said, "How fucking sweet was that?"

"They seem like very well-mannered children, yes," Diet said, unscrewing the lid of the thermos and pouring the aromatic amber liquid into the two cups. "Your mother made this for us?"

"She made it for you," he said. "I told her how much you like tea. I also told her you don't drink alcohol. That smells like fresh mint from my dad's garden back in Texas. The tea's sun-brewed. Growing up, we used to have it all the time in the summer. The fridge was always stocked with pitchers of it."

"Your father brought the mint. This was nice of him," Diet said. "How bad a man can he be if he tends a garden?"

"I don't think they're mutually exclusive," Jacob said, a little put off. "I'm sure my mom picked the mint. It never would have crossed my dad's mind."

"It is delicious," Diet said. "And these other small tokens are so useful. I can see now why you always spoke so highly of your mother." His face darkened, as if he were overcome by a terrible thought. When Jacob asked if something was wrong, he added, "Nothing. I am just exhausted." He sipped the tea and smiled, which Jacob thought seemed false.

"After I see my mom, I'm going to meet Clarence," he said. "He's the guy I told you about on the plane. You don't mind hanging out by yourself for a couple of hours, do you?"

"Not at all. I will do some work. The Austrians are difficult clients, so I should get this translation to them earlier rather than later. If it gets too noisy," Diet said, reaching for the earplugs, "I will just invert these."

"Do you have any idea how happy I am you're here with me?" he asked, Diet's mistake only further endearing him to Jacob.

"Show me tonight, yes?" he said, glancing significantly at the other suitcase.

"Deal," he said and kissed him good-bye.

Downstairs, Jacob knocked on the guest room door.

"Mom, it's me, Jacob," he said, but when the door opened, his dad stepped out into the hall.

"Your mother's resting," he said. "You can see her later."

"I'd like to see her now," Jacob said. "I'm going to meet a friend for a drink and wanted to thank her for the iced tea and presents before I went."

"You finish up the yard?" his dad asked, continuing to stand in his way.

"I didn't fly halfway around the world to mow Mo's lawn," Jacob said. "You were right, though. It did indeed run out of gas."

"I distinctly remember telling you that you'd have to fill up the gas can," he said.

"I have an idea," Jacob said. "How about you go fill it up while I go say hello to my mother? You like to drive. Go make yourself useful."

"Listen, you little punk—"

"Jacob, is that you?" his mom called. "Honey, is that Jacob?"

"It is, Roz," his dad called back, though still refused to step out of the way. "He's just on his way out to meet a friend for drinks. He'll see you later."

"Oh, don't be silly, honey," she responded. "I've done all the napping I can do for one day. Jacob, come in here."

Jacob grinned a triumphal grin at his dad and opened the door, although he understood that this was nothing more than a pyrrhic

victory, for the entire weekend was destined to be full of such skir-
mishes. He was happy to shut the door behind him, for once he had,
his furiously galloping heart, which leaped and bucked at his rib
cage, quieted down.

"Here you are," his mom said once he was seated beside her. She
was sitting up, a paperback resting in her lap. "I know you can't stay
long, but tell me—did Dietrich like the iced tea?"

"He's drinking himself silly as we speak," he said. "Thank you
for making it and for our other gifts."

"In this house, earplugs are essential. In fact, I think they should
just hand them out at the door," she said, breathing heavily. "I don't
know if either of you use a mask to sleep, but I find that the sun's just
so strong and comes up so quickly here."

"We'll give them a whirl," he said, though he suspected they'd
go unused.

"Were you and your father—I thought I heard . . . Well, he's gotten so protective of me," she said. "He's actually been wonderful. I
joke with him about it because he's just not the same man I married.
I'm constantly asking him what he's done with the real Julian Jacobson," and she laughed, which filled Jacob with incredible sorrow.

"I'd take it as a blessing that he's finally acting like someone
else," he said.

"Oh, posh," she said. "I know you two don't always get along,
but please put the past aside, for my sake. Just try, that's all I'm asking. You can do that for four days, can't you? I just . . . I don't have
the strength to referee anymore. You understand, don't you?"

"Yes, of course," he said, thinking about this conversation,
which was already receding, and wondering if she realized they'd
been having similar versions of it for the last twenty years. "I'm on
my way to meet Clarence Chalmers. You remember him? He was my
roommate senior year."

"Didn't he model underwear?" she asked. "For Calvin Klein,
wasn't it?"

"Not underwear, just clothes. For J. Crew, actually."

"Oh, that's right. Your sister was spellbound when she met him. Utterly spellbound," she said. "She was beside herself when she found out he was gay. Is he still gay?"

"Of course he's still gay." He laughed. "Probably even gayer."

"Such a pity. I'd love your sister to meet a nice man for a change."

Then Clarence wouldn't do for her anyway, because he isn't nice, he wanted to say. Interesting, charming, even fascinating—but not nice.

"Oh, before I forget, Diet and I are taking you and Dad to dinner tonight at Luscious Friend. Apparently, Zagat rated it one of the best restaurants in L.A. Diet got us a table for seven-thirty, so we probably should have left yesterday for a reservation today."

"That's very sweet of you both, but your brother's grilling and, to be frank, I just don't think I have the energy to get back in the car. You know how your dad is. He got me up at the crack of dawn this morning because he wanted to beat the traffic."

"And did you beat it?" he asked, rising.

"What do you think?" She rolled her eyes. "It's L.A., I told him. If you didn't want to deal with the traffic, we should have flown. But then we'd have to rent a car, and it takes him a lot longer these days to figure out how things work, like the lights and the navigation system, which frustrates him. He also doesn't like to deal with LAX and I don't blame him. Everything's so difficult now, Jacob. When I used to take you kids to visit your grandpa Ernie, we sometimes had the entire airplane to ourselves. Do you remember that?" Jacob did remember it. He also remembered how relieved he was when his dad dropped them off at the curb and said good-bye. His mom yawned and shut her eyes. "Maybe I'll try to take another little nap before dinner."

He kissed her on the cheek, then left the room, only to run into his dad hovering in the hall. He stepped out of the shadows, startling Jacob, who tried his best to honor his mom's wishes by reaching down into the murky, gloppy pain to get at just one decent memory of his dad and him—and though he came up short, he willed himself not to give in to the bilious hatred he still felt for the man.

"How's your financial situation?" his dad asked.

A safe question, it had become as commonplace from him as asking about the weather. "Fine. It's fine. I'm teaching English. I love it." Jacob was not going to give him the least bit of satisfaction in knowing just how much he actually didn't love it, how much he wished that his last play hadn't closed after only a three-night run or that he was next to broke. And broken.

"That's good to hear." His dad reached into his pocket and produced a money clip made of sterling silver like Diet's, though this one had belonged to Grandpa Ernie.

It still amazed Jacob that Grandpa Ernie had left anything to his dad and he suspected his dad had pilfered it, as he'd pilfered his wife's inheritance—her tens of thousands of shares of tech, eco-tech, and med-tech stocks, the millions of dollars in other assets—having it signed over to him, then hoarding it, putting her on an allowance, and justifying it all by reminding her that she was stupid when it came to money, which might or might not have been the truth. What Jacob did know about his mom's relationship with money was that when it came to her children she was often generous with it, whereas his dad was uncommonly parsimonious, keeping a firm grasp on the purse strings and doling it out only when one of them was absolutely desperate and came begging for it.

"Take this," he said and pushed a fifty-dollar bill into Jacob's hand. "Treat your friend."

Before he could protest—he wasn't dumb enough to refuse money, not even from his dad—the man slid past him and into the guest room. Jacob knew this was nothing more than a payoff, not only for finishing up the yard, which Jacob now felt oddly compelled to do, but also for maintaining some sort of cordiality between them. It was a hollow gesture and had the same effect on Jacob it usually did—it lessened the hurt, reacting upon him like a topical anesthetic, delightful and numbing until it wore off, of course.

On the way to the rental car, Jacob removed the crushed dirt bike from the driveway and set it in the garage, busted frame, mangled spokes, and all. He wondered which of the trips it belonged to, which of them Mo would have to apologize to for destroying it.

It was nearly 4:00 P.M. and the torpor in his body had leached its way through him, giving over to an exhaustion of the spirit as well. Every movement he made and every thought he had felt twice as cumbersome, twice the weight as it normally ought to have, and for a moment Jacob wanted to turn around and go back to Mo's, collect Diet, abandon the luggage and this weekend, drive to LAX, drop off the car, get on a plane, and return to Berlin. He wanted to forget the agreement he'd made with his siblings, forget the conversations they'd had about murdering their dad, forget their mom was dying. Mostly, though, he longed to let go of the guilt he'd been carrying around with him ever since he'd left home at seventeen. The packing and unpacking of it, like his cutlery, like his clothes, into and out of boxes and the dark, seedy spaces into which he so often disappeared and that made him doubt his own ability to love anyone, especially himself.

Merging south onto the 101, retracing the route he'd made earlier with Diet, Jacob held his hands steady on the wheel and on the idea that he and his siblings were right and righteous, protecting a woman who could not protect herself. Yet in the back of his sleep-deprived, jet-lag-addled mind, he also sensed that killing his dad, if that's what was going to happen, meant something different for him than it did for Mo and Edith. He couldn't put his finger on exactly what it was or what it might eventually mean, though it niggled at him, like an itch in the middle of his back that he couldn't get to or scratch. There was a message in this madness, he realized, that kept appearing to him in flashes, like sunlight on bubbles, and just as evanescent and flimsy; every time he tried to catch it in his fingers, it popped.

He left the Valley and headed for the city of Los Angeles, in which for four years he'd labored under the belief and assumption that after graduating from UCLA he'd come away a full-fledged playwright. L.A.: the land of palms and palmists, charismatic charlatans and charlatanic charmers, a concoction of dreams and dreamers, and above all else a never-ending carnival of the flesh, which was nothing more than an attempt to hide the rot of the soul. Not that L.A. itself was soulless, but Jacob had to wonder if his own hadn't rotted through while he passed his time going from one man and one bed to the next, never once thinking he had anything in common with them beyond a penis and a penchant for being treated poorly—and then he'd met Clarence and all that changed. But he'd lost Clarence, the circumstances of which had had such an impact on him, had been a defeat so profound, that he gave up L.A. and swore never to return.

Yet here he was, back at the scene of the crime, his own, his body lying prone on the floor of the past, only to disintegrate once he touched it, leaving behind a chalky white residue. Who had garroted him from behind? Who had drowned him in the bath? He might have said it was Clarence, whom he had loved without limit, though by now he knew differently.

The drive to Hollywood took him well over an hour, then he was taking a right onto Santa Monica Boulevard, barely recognizing any of it, although he suspected it had never lost its sinister, down-at-heel disposition of twenty years ago. Everything and nothing about it resonated with him anymore, just as everything and nothing about it was new or different. Which made sense, he guessed, considering whom he was meeting and why.

After graduation, Jacob had rushed to the opposite coast—if California were the gold standard of coastlines, then this made the Eastern Seaboard what? The kosher-salt standard?—and straight into the heart of New York City, which indeed lived up to its reputation for never sleeping, or at least never sleeping without an Ambien or three, as he unfortunately came to learn, for though he'd fled the perpetual luster and glare of sunshiny L.A., he'd also managed to bring the dreary skies of memory with him. And though Jacob understood that Clarence Lee Chalmers was not directly to blame for running him out of town, he was indirectly responsible for ruining the last few weeks of his senior year and for what happened to Thad Schneider. He and Jacob both, though as far as he knew Clarence still refused to come to terms with the part he'd played in the tragedy—Clarence, a loud and proud gay man, had convinced the shy, closeted, besotted Thad to come out to his devout Christian parents because Clarence believed it would help Thad let go of his "gay shame." Clarence was supposed to have been there with him for moral support but flaked, missing the promised brunch with the Schneiders, too hungover after an epic night out with Jacob at Japón. In the days after, Thad seemed changed, though not for the better. He moved sluggishly around campus, his eyes darker and stormier than usual. Jacob asked several times if anything was wrong, but Thad just moved right past him without a word. A few days later, he hanged himself, leaving a note that started "Dear Clarence . . ." and ended "My love for you is eternal . . ."

Clarence had suggested Japón, and Jacob, speeding past it as if it were an optical illusion, a product of the sun, perhaps, or a mirage he hoped might vanish, registered the chill of that suggestion again, wondering why he hadn't spoken up and offered to meet him someplace else. Yet hadn't they spent many a splendiferous evening at Japón surrounded by every conceivable Hollywood type, from the likes of Willie Levine, the son of the head of Paramount, to Bernadine Bixby, the queen of movie gossip with the bifurcated tongue and every actor's, director's, and producer's friendly nemesis, as well as everyone in between? Clarence knew them all, for they all wanted to know him, this erudite, rich, blond-headed boy, a standout among even the most beautiful of them. And Jacob, his sidekick, nowhere near as striking, yet handsome in his own right, so blisteringly funny, so goddamn genuine, with his aspirations tucked away in his pocket and that big, fat Texan smile plastered on his face.

Yes, they'd often spent their evenings there, and sometimes Thad had even joined them, but not that final evening, when Jacob and Clarence drank the night away, partying well into dawn. A rowdy, drunken, and strange evening, Jacob recalled, that only got stranger later, as the two fell into bed together just as the sun came up and then slept the day away, spooning and fucking again and again, Jacob thinking Clarence had been returned to him only to realize with horror later that while they'd been in bed, Thad and his parents had been waiting for Clarence.

So Jacob drove right on past Japón, kept driving until he spotted the giant gold menorah glimmering in the distance and hung a right into Menorah Carwash Emporium, a more than pleasant sight. In college, he used to drive here all the way from Westwood to have his car cleaned and detailed, chiefly because he liked the owners, the Nathans, Persian Jewish refugees who'd faced persecution in their native Iran and come to L.A. in the early 1970s to escape the demonic shah. Elijah and Aviva Nathan, Ellie and Viva familiarly, were never without warm, generous hellos, always asking Jacob about his studies—"Keep your grades up and keep writing, my friend. I see an Oscar in your future," Ellie liked to say, and Jacob loving him so much that he didn't have the heart to tell him the truth, that he feared he'd never even get a play produced, much less win an award. They'd had a child, a son, who died young, though neither Ellie nor Viva ever talked about him, only to say once in passing that he was buried in Qom. Jacob kept in touch with them for a few years after his move to New York, then called their house one day to find the line inexplicably disconnected. He wrote and sent them a letter, which was returned unopened.

The mystery of what had happened to the Nathans plagued him for years and out of it grew the inspiration for his first three-act play, *Tell Me How This Ends Well*, which eventually found an Off-Broadway home at Rattlesnake Theater in the West Village—the story of a Persian Jewish couple who flee the shah and open up a car wash in Los Angeles and the surrogate gay son they adopt after their own drowns. The play won no awards, though the critics received it well, citing Jacob as "a young, talented hopeful with many more productions in him."

After he parked, Jacob went into the small, tidy waiting area, which looked exactly the way he remembered it—photographs of famous and not-so-famous actors and their cars lining one wall, nightscapes of familiar Los Angeles landmarks lining the other. When he asked the young black attendant where the Nathans were, he told Jacob that he'd never heard of them.

"Ellie and Viva Nathan," Jacob repeated. "I . . . I used to know them. They're the owners."

"Might have been, might have been," the attendant said. "Now it belongs to some Russian guy, Yuri something. So you want a car wash? We're running a special today—$89.99. That includes a rabbi saying a blessing over your car."

This was the same gimmick the Nathans had used and for a moment Jacob, beside himself with anger and remorse, wanted to reach across the counter, grab the guy around the collar, and say, "Tell your Russian cockroach of a boss that I'm the Nathans' son and an attorney and that he can't disrespect my parents by making money on their idea. Tell him to cease and desist, or else."

Instead, he wandered back out into the harsh California sunshine, got into the car, and sped out of the lot, glancing in the rearview mirror at the twinkling brass tines of the menorah and catching briefly, as if rising out of the dust of his grief, the ghostly figures of Ellie and Viva Nathan, waving. Were the Nathans still somewhere nearby, or had they succumbed at last to the horrors of the times, the "Jews in the News" segments on the nightly news that he secretly followed on YouTube—another torched synagogue, another murdered youth, another suicide bomber on the 405 or the 101, the anti-Semitism that swept across L.A. with the tenacity of a wildfire? Had they been frightened enough to give up at last, pull up stakes, and move away, becoming other people with other names? It was not unlikely. Nothing, he thought, was unlikely anymore. He felt unsettled by this train of thought, even after he pulled up to Japón, shut off the engine, and went inside to look for Clarence.

Jacob spotted him seated in a booth by the window. He did not approach Clarence immediately but remained at the door, drinking in the place as it were. Low-lit, still reeking of stale smoke, and still just as glamorously decrepit with its cracking red vinyl booths and black japan-topped tables, Asiatic flairs everywhere, from the Japanese calligraphy above the bar to the lanterns dangling from the ceiling.

"Death in the Afternoon," Clarence sang as Jacob approached, holding up his coupe glass, which contained the last couple of sips of a neon green–yellow liquid. "Hemingway thought he invented it— absinthe and champagne—but whatever. I'm pretty sure the drink's been in my family for generations, though." He laughed. "He did off himself, so how reliable can he be?"

"'Kills Like White Elephants,'" Jacob returned, sitting down across from him.

"Splendid. Just splendid. You must be a playwright."

"Only on Thursdays and only when I wear my Edward Albee underwear," Jacob said, the waiter appearing and setting a drink down on the table before him.

"I hope you don't mind, but I took the liberty of ordering for you. It's your usual—a Burnt Fuselage. You still like them, don't you?"

"Diet—Dietrich—doesn't drink, so I haven't had one in a while."

"A German?" Clarence asked, more surprised than his voice belied. "I can't imagine Pa Jacobson's too happy about that. But good for you! Revenge is sweetest when served with sauerkraut."

"My mom's dying, Clarence," Jacob confided, taking in his longtime, long-lost friend, the new shock of gray hair, the same pale green eyes, the sun-damaged skin. He looked exactly like himself and not at all like himself, if that were possible, a more deeply developed Clarence and also, at the same time, a more washed-out version, but even so Jacob could still see the boy he had once known, the boy he would have done and said anything for. He'd had a lifetime to memorialize him, to set him up only to knock him down, wish him ill, wish him well, and to sleep around trying to forget him.

"Oh, I'm sorry to hear that. I always liked Roz."

"It's a nasty, progressive pulmonary disease that's slowly suffocating her," Jacob said, though Clarence hadn't asked and Jacob wasn't sure why he'd said it, perhaps merely to underscore the severity of it and to make sure Clarence understood. "She's taking medication to slow it down, but her lungs aren't responding as readily as the doctors had hoped. I was thinking she'd go the nontraditional route—Chinese holistic medicine, some radical herbal remedies— but I've been voted off the island, of course, by Pa Jacobson." Saying all of this out loud, to someone who wasn't his brother or sister, merely confirmed what he had already suspected—that he wasn't quite ready for the pitying glances and sympathetic ears of others, not even Clarence, who dealt with death every day of his life.

"And so you'd like to discuss options with me? Get my advice on arrangements for her afterlife?"

"Not at all," Jacob put in, taking a sip of the drink, which, on an empty stomach, he could practically feel shooting through him. "She only has a few months left, actually. But maybe it could be extended, depending on the quality of her care." Jacob suspected that he was thinking magically, thinking wishfully.

"What about the quality of her life?"

Terrible, eerie questions to hear and to process and for a moment Jacob found himself in the clutches of an awful déjà vu, for hadn't they been sitting in exactly the same spot, drinking exactly the same drinks when Clarence had posed the exact same questions about Thad, before Clarence talked him into coming out, insisting that Thad's quality of life would improve greatly after he told his parents his big secret? "I don't know. She doesn't really like to talk about any of it. It all comes to me filtered through my brother and sister these days."

"And the illustrious Julian Jacobson? How's he coping with it all?

If I know your dad, not very well," Clarence commented, raising his fingers and flagging down the waiter. "Something told me that this wasn't going to be a run-of-the-mill, catch-up-with-cocktails kind of reunion. He's the reason you're here. Am I warm?" The waiter arrived promptly and set down a bowl of cold sesame noodles. "On second thought, we need this to go. Could you wrap it up, please?"

"Very warm. Some might even say hot. Hellishly, third-degree-burn hot," Jacob said. "Oh, my mom says he's being incredibly wonderful and attentive and all that, and this might even be the case, but you and I both know it's come a little too late."

"Yes, I suppose we do," he stated. Both of them laid fifty-dollar bills on the table at the same time. Clarence slid Jacob's back to him. "I've got this one. Think of it as a promise kept."

"No, I couldn't." Jacob slid Clarence's bill back to him. "It's my treat. A down payment on my mom's future."

As Clarence pocketed his bill, Jacob got up and went outside. Clarence followed a moment later, carrying the boxed-up sesame noodles. "I am truly sorry to hear about your mom, Jacob. She . . . when all of that happened with Thad . . . I've never forgotten her kindness. My own mother couldn't have been bothered. Did I ever tell you how she reacted when I told her? She went out shopping for French antiques and just never came back. My mother. Pillar of the community, head of the Junior League of Kansas City, and heartless cunt behind closed doors. Well, I always said you were the lucky one. I might have had a terrific relationship with my father, but of course it's my mother I always longed for. Funny how that happens." Jacob nodded. "You know I was only pretending not to remember you when you called. It was the shock, I guess. Part of me was hoping . . . well, a part of us always hopes, doesn't it?" Clarence said.

"Hope is a four-letter word," Jacob muttered, heading for his car.

Pulling out of the lot, he turned once again onto Santa Monica Boulevard, bracing himself against the night ahead by thinking of Diet and what was inside the other suitcase. This time of evening, the traffic was backed up for miles in each direction, the cars lurching to a stop and lunging forward like unsure toddlers on stubby, unsteady legs. It took Jacob half an hour to go a single mile, but then he was finally angling the car through the unadorned entrance of Eternal Hollywood, the ugly strip malls and uglier traffic dropping out of sight behind him. In Brooklyn, he and Diet had taken long afternoon strolls through the famed Green-Wood Cemetery, a vast system of hillside paths and roads that wound their way past ancient marble headstones, statuaries, crypts, and mausoleums, the graves crowded together to mirror, or mock, depending on how one saw it, the living arrangements of New York City itself—neighbor on top of neighbor, crammed into boxes, and lying side by side, a maze of underground tenants complaining unto eternity about the inflated prices of New York real estate.

From what Jacob had read and seen online, Clarence's cemetery sat on a hundred flat acres of land, the lawns superbly maintained and emerald green in the early evening sun. In the distance, Jacob made out the massive, white-marbled mausoleum and behind it, rising up in picturesque perfection, the equally white letters of the Hollywood sign. Jacob felt oddly compelled to go on a walk, for hundreds of famous actors, directors, and performers lay buried in Eternal Hollywood, though he figured he ought to wait for Clarence, who pulled up a few minutes later in his ancient sky-blue Scout, which, impossibly, he'd been driving since college. The two headed into the administration building, a beautifully restored Queen Anne with clinging ivy running up the sides.

They took a back staircase, bypassing a hive of staffers. "Death is the only industry in America that continues to outgrow itself," Clarence said proudly, leading Jacob to a door at the top of the stairs, which opened onto a vast empty space—a former chapel, at the far end of which sat Clarence's office. "I meditate in here on most mornings. You should try it with me sometime. Superb way to start the day."

"I don't doubt it," Jacob replied, examining the room tricked out in Far East Asian decor replete with burning incense, pots of living bamboo, and several different statues of Buddha, ranging from the miniature to the enormous, some in carved wood, others in bronze.

Four electrified Zen water fountains sat one to a corner, adding to the already soothing calm of the room. Jacob breathed in the jasmine-scented air and had to admit that Clarence might be onto something. "Mind taking off your shoes?" Clarence asked, removing his own, then bowing before one of the statues of Buddha. "I've been to Tibet several times in the last few years." Jacob remembered his attachment to *The Tibetan Book of the Dead,* which he carried around with him in college, though picturing him in Tibet, chanting with the monks, only made him laugh. "You're remembering the way I used to be, not the way I am. I don't hold it against you, though. Western philosophy teaches us that the past informs the present and that we must look at it from every angle if we're going to achieve spiritual enlightenment. Eastern philosophy tells us that it's our desire to change the past that leads us to unhappiness. That's why I meditate—to release the past and all the painful associations I've made. My only job while I'm meditating is to let these thoughts and feelings float by and pass away, like clouds."

"I saw an accident on the 101 today," Jacob announced. "Not while I was coming to meet you, but before that, when we were heading to the Valley. A burning car. A young guy trapped in the passenger seat. I can't get him out of my head."

"Come out here with me," he said, beckoning Jacob through a side door that led to a small, terrazzo-tiled balcony.

Jacob stepped out onto the balcony and took in the view, the dark shades of green spreading out below him. Though it might have been the final resting place for thousands of souls, to him it was nothing more than the shape of things to come—beautiful and tranquil, yes, yet also distressingly unreal. Clarence had transformed the grounds, rebuilt the mausoleums and crypts, and installed freestanding "memorial kiosks," which offered visitors virtual biographies of loved ones, all at the touch of a button and a swipe to the right or the left.

He'd dragged the cemetery into the twenty-first century by offering movie nights in which he projected Hollywood classics and popular cult favorites onto a large screen set up on one of the lawns. He invited famous singers to perform in the Rotunda of Reverences and created Shakespeare in the Tombs—a couple of years ago, Mo had been Macbeth to a packed house in the most-frequented summer event.

And standing there with him, as if Clarence were king and this his kingdom, Jacob realized that his old friend had remade the business of dying into yet another form of entertainment, a vastly lucrative sideshow. It had not surprised him to learn that the cemetery shared a wall with an empty backlot, a permeable membrane, his dad would have said, in which Clarence offered those on the other side of the wall further immortality on this side, his side, of it: death as spectacle, as the continuance of life. It's not what Jacob wanted, and it certainly wasn't what he and his siblings had planned for their dad. Moreover, he didn't understand the morbid appeal of any of it, the ritualized process of embalming, dressing the dead, the viewing, the wake. Jews were planted in the earth in a cedar or pine box and left to rot. Many Jews did not believe in an afterlife. And if there was one, he hoped by the time they met again his dad would have been through decades of postlife analysis.

"He was so young," Jacob continued, picking up the thread of the hellish freeway accident, which of course wasn't an accident at all but another suicide bombing. All that fire and smoke belching up from the wreckage and the young guy trapped inside it, this guy whom Jacob would never be able to get out of his head. "It reminded me of when I flipped my mom's station wagon when I was sixteen." *Except I was lucky enough to walk away from it,* he wanted to add. *I was lucky enough to live another day.* He'd been speeding through Hidden Glen, a subdivision in north Dallas, hit a patch of water, and hydroplaned, the car skidding out of control, the back end fishtailing, rolling over and over again, he and the car skittering to a stop and ending up in the middle of someone's front lawn upside down. "You can only imagine what my dad had to say when he saw what I'd done to 'his beloved vehicle.'"

"Do you have any good memories of him at all?" Clarence asked.

"Would you believe me if I told you I don't?" he replied.

"That's a shame, and not only for you," he said, taking a step closer to Jacob, the air shifting slightly and filling his nose with Clarence's scent, a mixture of deodorant and gasoline and beyond that the ripe and heady smell of his sweat. "You can't see it from here, but the crematorium is behind the mausoleum," he said. "I had it refurbished in 2017, everything state-of-the-art. You'll have to give me a day's notice, at least, but I don't foresee any problems."

Jacob reached into his jeans and extracted the euros. "I didn't have time to exchange them," he said, handing the wad to Clarence. "It's around seven thousand dollars, give or take."

This was Jacob's part in the plan—to make contact with Clarence again—and though he'd known this day had been coming, when he'd have to hand over every dime he had in the world, he felt as if he were losing so much more than merely money.

"Are you sure this is how you want it to go?" Clarence asked, pocketing the cash. Jacob said that it was how he, Jacob, wanted it to go, but that of course he needed to speak to his siblings. "Then you're going to need to choose an urn."

"I was thinking a used bedpan, or maybe a plastic cup like they make you pee in at the doctor's," he said, the sun sinking behind the hills and darkening the cemetery.

Suddenly, a clarion cry rose up from the grounds below, matched by several answering cries that echoed the pitch and sorrow of the first; when Jacob saw the source of the cries at last—a flock of pure white peacocks calling out to one another—he let out a hiccup of wonder. *Is it my imagination or are they actually levitating across the grass?* he wanted to ask. "They're exquisite," he breathed.

"Every day around sunset, they call out to the dead to let them know it's time to rise," Clarence said. "I love those birds. They're the pride of the cemetery."

"And do they? Rise, I mean," Jacob said, turning to leave, for it was time to make his way back to the Valley.

"I only bury the dead," he said. "I tend not to have too much to do with them after that."

Yet as they embraced and Jacob asked him for one final request, he got the distinct impression that Clarence was lying, that he might not have communed with the likes of Rudolph Valentino, Tyrone Power, or Bugsy Siegel, all of whom were interred in his cemetery, but that he might at least commune with the spirit of their lost, unfortunate friend, whose death ought not to have happened but had.

Pulling the car onto the road, Jacob pictured that regrettable evening all over again, finding Thad strung up with one of Clarence's club ties, and so preoccupied was he by the memory that he was completely unaware of the large white shape hovering directly in front of him until it was too late. He tried to swerve out of the way but to no avail, the tires riding up and over the peacock, crushing it. He braked, rolled down his window, and peered back at the snowy heap, which had exploded like a pimple, the feathers stained with blood and spread out against the asphalt, the once-unblemished body branded with a wide, black stripe from the tread of the tires. It fluttered a shattered wing, the eyes rotating ghoulishly, then it gave one last shudder and went still. Jacob wasn't sure what to do and sat there, feeling flattened himself, the blood draining from his fingers, which tingled with this horrible thing he'd done, as if he'd wrung the life out of the bird with his own hands. While part of him wanted to put the car into drive and speed away, deny what had happened in the last minute, and cut it out of his memory, the other part of him, the kinder, gentler, better part of him that Diet had fallen in love with, refused to leave things as they were—untidy, bloody, smashed to smithereens. He determined a quick and impulsive course of action: When he was sure no one was watching, he popped the trunk,

---

raced over to the bird, lifted it into his arms—it weighed far more than he could have imagined, as if made of sculpted marble—then laid it down gently in the trunk, shut the lid, and returned to the car, all of this in a matter of seconds.

He sped back onto Santa Monica, taking a right when he should have gone left, but he didn't care, because he simply had to drive—yet no amount of distance he put between himself and the cemetery could stifle the shrieking peacocks, which saturated the air around him. He fiddled with the radio, trying to find a new station—maddeningly, KJEW was still playing *The Death of Klinghoffer*—and inadvertently ran a red light, proving to himself once again that whenever and wherever his family was involved, Jacob was sure to go wrong.

Moments later, a police car drew up behind him, the officer flashing his headlights, turning on his siren, and getting on his bullhorn to order Jacob to pull over. *Overkill, thy name is the LAPD,* he thought. (If he and Diet had been back in Berlin, he might have joked that he was DWJ, Driving While Jewish, which Diet would have taken umbrage at, although the *Polizei* were infamous profilers, rumored to be able to spot a Jew simply by the shape and protuberance of his nose. "I bet they take classes on the assorted varieties of the *proboscis Judaicus,*" he liked to say. Understandably, Diet found this in utterly poor taste, though it never stopped him from making his own tasteless Jewish jokes.)

The officer took a hellishly sweet time approaching, which only ratcheted up Jacob's panic and fear. He had gone through life with an irrational terror of the police, though this time his terror was not unfounded, for he had been involved in a hit-and-run and had fled the scene, albeit with the body stowed in the trunk. An absurd idea popped into his head that someone, perhaps Clarence himself, had reported him to the cops. Were white peacocks on the list of rare and endangered species?

The officer demanded Jacob's license and registration in a voice that was steady and cold, uninflected, devoid of friendliness, and reminded Jacob of the cops who'd pulled him over in college, all the sweating he'd done while the cop wrote him up for speeding, for rolling through a stop sign, for a busted taillight. His mom had paid each fine, which totaled in the thousands of dollars, telling Jacob never to tell his dad, not that he needed reminding, because he knew exactly how his dad would have reacted if he ever found out—with shocking fury—but thanks to his mom he never did. At least that's what Jacob had thought, until, on Clarence's advice, he came out to the entire family during winter break of his senior year. And it was as if his dad had just discovered the storehouse of secrets and used them all against him in one fell swoop, a spectacular shit show of righteous indignation and moral superiority.

"I suppose you knew about this, too, huh, Roz? Is this another one of the secrets you two have been keeping from me?" his dad had asked, roaring at his mom, who shrank away, then glanced at Jacob, her face wounded and bruised as if Jacob had hit her. "So you really are a . . . faggot?" his dad had grunted, turning to Jacob. "Well, I can't say I'm surprised. But you sure as hell didn't get it from me." He'd made it sound as if it were something to catch, like a cold, and turned to his wife, shaking his head at her, his disgust made manifest in the wretched grimace on his face. "Don't blame me for making you a queer. You can thank your mother and her weak genes for that."

"Daddy, that's an awful thing to say," exclaimed Edith, who'd been the kindest and most understanding of them, followed by his mom, who'd cried silently in her seat beside a dumbfounded, disbelieving Mo.

"But he doesn't act or talk like a homo," Mo had said, addressing his dad, who'd kept glaring at Jacob.

"So it's really true? Well, let me tell you something—you're just lucky your mom and sister are here because if they weren't I'd jam a broom up your ass and watch it come out the other end."

"Honey, enough," Roz had said, her watery voice raised, but it hadn't been enough, for his dad had hardly finished with him and went on to tell Jacob that he was sick in the head and that he'd brought incredible shame on the family, acting, Jacob thought, as parochial and unsophisticated as ever, as if it were 1955 and not 2005.

"So I like men," Jacob had said. "So what? You like torturing mice to death, but you don't hear me calling you a murderer."

"Watch that mouth of yours," his dad had said, "or I'll make sure you never suck another dick again."

That was some day, Jacob recalled, when he'd torn out of the house and roamed around the neighborhood, returning well after midnight, after he thought everyone would be in bed, asleep. He'd been wrong, because his charming, compassionate dad had been waiting up for him. He'd been sitting on the sofa in the dark, Jacob's suitcase resting beside him on the carpet. And rising from the sofa, he'd shoved the suitcase at his younger son, saying, "Sodomy laws might have been abolished in Texas, but not on my property," and with that, he'd wandered into the back of the house and shut the bedroom door. Jacob had called a taxi and headed to DFW airport, where, after doing some finagling to change his ticket, he'd spent an uncomfortable, restless night sleeping on the floor. The next morning he'd flown back to L.A., where Clarence had picked him up and treated him to breakfast at IHOP.

When the officer returned, he handed Jacob his license, then peered into the front seat. "Is that blood on your hands and shirt, sir?" he asked. At this, Jacob began explaining that he'd been visiting an old college friend, the owner of Eternal Hollywood, and that there'd been this beautiful gaggle or swarm or murder—not a murder, but like a murder of crows, he said, not sure what to call a group of peacocks, if it even had a denotation. Then, from somewhere across the void of time and space the word came to him. "Ostentation," he whispered to himself, knowing how proud Clarence would have been with him for remembering, then realizing how upset Clarence was going to be when he found out that Jacob had just killed a valued member of this ostentation. He continued blathering that on his way out of the cemetery he'd been thinking about this boy he'd known when he'd been an undergrad at UCLA and hadn't been paying attention to the road and that he'd run over one of the birds. He went on, telling the officer he lived in Berlin and had flown into L.A. to spend Passover with his family, because his mom was dying of this rare pulmonary disease, and as he kept going, he felt himself spinning more and more out of control, unable to stop, worrying that at any second he was going to spill everything about his real motivation for coming to L.A. "I just paid off a friend to use his crematorium because nothing says 'I love you' like incineration," he heard himself say, though by then the cop had walked around to the trunk.

"Sir, could you step around here, please?" he called. Jacob did as he was told and approached the cop. "Open the trunk, please," he said, and Jacob, his entire body quaking with fear, depressed the button on the key fob, springing the lock on the trunk and releasing dozens of white feathers into the air, which startled the officer, who took a giant step back. "What is that, sir?"

Jacob stared down into the shadowy depths of the trunk, which held the peacock, although the longer he stared at it, the more it began to morph, becoming the body of his dad, the sight filling him with an incomparable relief and joy, for he understood that accidents happened every single minute of every single day and that perhaps instead of hiring an assassin, the idea of which they had bandied about, they should just handle it themselves without involving yet another party.

"Evidence of my guilt?" he simpered, noticing a small tattoo, a yellow Star of David, on the inside of the officer's left wrist. His name tag read "Lemke." Jacob smiled. "You're Jewish?"

"It's not unheard of," the officer replied unsmilingly. He was a short, compact man with a sturdy armature of muscle, buzzed blond hair, and a large, lopsided mouth, which sat just off center beneath his big, fleshy nose. Taken all together, his face, minus the eyes, which Jacob couldn't make out behind the mirrored lenses, was a pleasing arrangement of features.

"I'm Jewish, too. Ever heard of Mo Orenstein-Jacobson? Maybe you saw that reality show *The JacobSONS,* which aired on Bravo-REAL? It was only on for three seasons before they pulled the plug. Between you and me, I've never been able to sit through an entire episode."

"That's your family?" Officer Lemke stared up from his pad, then removed his sunglasses, revealing a pair of wide-set, summer-green eyes and long, dark lashes, which would have made even the most beautiful woman envious. Jacob figured he couldn't have been much older than thirty. His hairy arms sported a deep Mediterranean tan, indicating perhaps a Sephardic rather than Ashkenazic ancestry. "My cousin was a cameraman on that show. I can't say I was a fan of it, or your family, for that matter. I mean, I'm glad it went off the air, because I found a lot of it offensive."

Jacob had guessed that the mere mention of the wildly popular show might get him off the hook for whatever law he'd broken, but he was wrong in assuming such a thing and that the officer wouldn't have an opinion about the show either way. This was L.A., after all, and everyone was connected to Hollywood, even peripherally.

"I mean, if anything, it's just given people license—no pun intended—to think even worse thoughts about us."

"Do they think so badly of us now?" Jacob wondered, but of course they did. And he thought again of the Nathans and something inside of him rolled over and died.

"Are you trying to tell me you didn't watch the show?"

"They're my family, but I know my limits and couldn't subject myself to that kind of torture," Jacob admitted, though he didn't see that this was any of Lemke's business or why he felt the sudden need to justify anything to this stranger. Of course, when Mo asked if he'd been keeping up with the episodes, Jacob naturally lied and told him that he hadn't missed a single one.

"Well, bravo to you. No self-respecting Jew I know watched it other than to see just how hateful and dysfunctional your family could get. It was an utter embarrassment to the community here. They were pretty instrumental in getting it canceled, actually."

"It was just a stupid reality TV show," Jacob challenged, wondering if Officer Lemke didn't have some other reason for hating it, if it hadn't hit too close to home.

"We're all products of some kind of damage, purposeful or not," and with that, he handed Jacob a citation. "I'm giving you a summons for running a red light in the 9000 block of Santa Monica Boulevard. Feel free to contest it in court. Also, you can't be driving around with a dead animal in your trunk. Call the city and have them come out to dispose of it properly."

"Officer Lemke, on behalf of my horrible family, I apologize," Jacob said, feeling stung in so many different places that he wasn't sure where to begin to apply the balm.

"It's not your fault. They're your family and you love them. I get it. I'm not judging you. Well, maybe I am a little. I do count myself lucky not to have a father like yours, though."

"He's not that bad," Jacob blurted out, which would have made him laugh if he hadn't been so distraught.

"Maybe not, but I did see a couple of episodes when they all went to visit your parents in . . . New Mexico? Texas? Even on camera, he refused to play nice. The man's got an incredible sense of entitlement. And the way he talked to your mother?"

"I'm going to go now, if that's okay," Jacob said, bruised.

"Yeah, okay," Officer Lemke said. "Oh, by the way, you have a bench warrant out for your arrest—a few outstanding parking tickets from the early aughts. I'd take care of those fast because I can guarantee the next cop who pulls you over is not going to be as nice. Happy Pesach," he said and walked back to his squad car, leaving Jacob alone with the bloody corpse of the peacock and thoughts of his dad swirling through his muzzy head. After shutting the trunk, Jacob climbed back behind the wheel and rejoined the traffic, all of it pouring onto the 101 just as he was.

By the time Jacob returned to Calabasas it was approaching nine o'clock. He was happy to be back at Mo's, happier still to put some distance between him and the cemetery. Though he'd had an incredibly trying day, he couldn't deny just how awake he was, the adrenaline still pumping through him. If pressed, he might have said he'd never felt so alive, the world around him pulsing with a radiant, holy light, everything glowing in earnest and warm to the touch. Life. Even out here in the desert, where his brother had made a home.

Before going into the house, Jacob grabbed the cooler from the backseat and popped the trunk, thinking he would spread the remaining ice over the bird to preserve it overnight. But realizing that that would make more of a mess, he dumped the ice out on the ground. What was he going to do with the bird? Did he take Clarence's pet back to him, fully contrite and accepting of retribution? Did he toss it into some ravine in Topanga Canyon and pretend it never happened? *What is the etiquette here for getting rid of a body?* Jacob wondered, closing the trunk and heading into the house.

In one of the downstairs bathrooms, he rinsed off his hands and face, the water running pink with blood, which was also caked on his neck and right earlobe, though he had no recollection of how it had gotten there. He wondered what to do about his ruined shirt, for he had no desire left in him to explain the misadventure—he could just hear his dad erupting with laughter at what an awful driver he still was.

In some way, Jacob did have to wonder if the cop had spared him merely because he knew that what was awaiting him back in the Valley was far worse than any jail cell. It was a mitigating kindness that stayed with him as he left the bathroom and roved through the house, expecting his nephews to leap out at him at any second, rattling light sabers and whatever new gadgets and gizmos Maw-Maw and Paw-Paw had bought them. Yet the downstairs, lit up as it was, remained quiet, absent of the usual fracas Jacob associated with the boys.

On his way to the kitchen, he paused at the guest room and

pressed an ear against the door, though he knew he shouldn't, wanting to say a good night to his mom but not face the old man who would have to let Jacob know how disappointed he was in him for missing dinner. So he went to rummage in the fridge, his stomach grumbling. No sooner had he lifted out a platter of uncooked steaks than Mo, Pandora, Diet, and one of the twins entered the house through the side door off the garage. They headed for the kitchen, all of them chattering at once, Mo's voice rising above the others, his face, when Jacob finally saw it, clearly ravaged with anger and worry. They all moved into the kitchen, Mo reaching around Jacob to grab a bottle of beer.

"Baby, you are back from these wilds of Los Angeles," Diet said, drawing up beside him.

"What happened to you?" Mo asked, pointing the bottle at Jacob's shirt.

"Oh, this? Nothing. What's important is, what happened to *you*?" he asked Dexter, whose right hand was encased in a plaster cast that ran halfway up his arm.

"Paw-Paw slammed the lid of the barbecue down on my fingers," Dexter said matter-of-factly, without a hint of resentment.

"Paw-Paw did what?" Jacob asked, dumbfounded.

"It was an accident," Pandora soothed, glancing up from her phone long enough to register Jacob, who was kneeling down before Dexter.

"Are you okay?" he asked the boy, looking directly into his huge blue eyes.

"Yeah, I'm okay, Uncle Jacob," he said, "but it hurt like a bitch."

"Hey, language," Mo remonstrated, leaning across the counter and tapping the boy gently on the head. "Paw-Paw's already promised to take him up to the Commons tomorrow to pick out a toy. Isn't that right, Dexatrim?"

"Dad, don't call me that!" the boy said angrily, but through a big, toothy smile. "Mommy, is it okay if I go upstairs? I need to discuss an important matter with Baxter."

"No more summits today, though. Promise me you won't let your brothers talk you into playing Resettlement and that all of you will continue to honor the armistice," she instructed, running a hand through her highlighted blond hair and slumping down on one of the stools scattered around the island.

"I think I will escort you upstairs. It's been a long day," Diet said, taking hold of Dexter's other hand. "*Gute Nacht.*" He kissed Jacob, turned, and walked out of the kitchen, the boy asking Diet if he'd read him a bedtime story.

"I like him," Pandora said. "Congrats, brother-in-law. You did well."

"You mean you like him despite his German heritage," Mo insisted.

"No, I mean I like him because he's likable. That's what I mean," she retorted, glaring at Mo, who sucked on his beer. "Roz likes him, too. I'm not sure about Julian. It's so hard to tell with him."

That's because he's an asshole wrapped in a curmudgeon inside a misanthrope, Jacob thought, but said, "The inscrutable heart of Julian Jacobson."

"I'll drink to that," Mo said, chugging down the beer, then helping himself to another.

"Better go slow there, Easy Rider. You have a full day of activities tomorrow," Pandora chided. "Do either of you know my twister-in-law's ETA? I need to prepare myself psychologically for her arrival."

"Pandora, c'mon, that's not nice," Mo protested.

"I think she said around nine," Jacob said. "Oh, and before I forget. Clarence sends his best."

"Oh, yeah? What does the Prince of Death have to say for himself?" Mo asked. "Is he going to produce our one-man show?"

"What one-man show?" Pandora asked, swiping a glance at Jacob. "Did you write something for Mo? We should have a reading of it after the Seder!"

"It's still a work-in-progress," Jacob said, glaring sideways at Mo.

"Well, when it's ready, I'd love to read it," she said, her face once again at her phone. "So I have like fifty emails to answer. I'll be in my office if you boys need me," and with that, she left the kitchen.

After she was gone, Mo went to the swinging doors, which connected the kitchen to the rest of the house, and pushed them open, moving his head back and forth, while Jacob took a seat on one of the stools, staring longingly at the steaks. "I need to eat something," he said. "Then I need to pass out."

"Yeah, sure, okay," Mo said, returning. He got out a frying pan, added some olive oil, set two of the thicker steaks in the pan, then lit the gas burner. "I didn't want to say anything in front of the wife, because she'd lose her mind, but I'm not exactly sure what happened at the barbecue with Dad and Dexter. I think . . . I don't know what to think."

"What do you mean? Do you think he—Jesus, Mo, you think he did it on purpose? Even he couldn't be that—" But then Jacob stopped himself, for of course their dad could be that hateful, and he prickled at the image of the lid coming down on the boy's fingers.

"I don't know." Mo sighed. "It's just . . . it's what he said to me in passing after it happened."

"What? What'd he say?"

"He can't suspect anything, can he?"

"Tell me what he said," Jacob insisted.

"Well, he just . . . I thought I heard him mumble something about getting away with it. You don't think he knows, do you?" he asked.

"I can't see how he'd suspect anything unless you or Thistle opened your big mouths."

"Not me," Mo countered. "You think Thistle might have blabbed?" Out of the three of them, Edith had been the hardest to convince. Finally, though, over the course of several phone calls, Jacob, family archivist and keeper of Julian Jacobson's crimes against humanity, thought he'd been able to persuade her. "I hope she didn't screw us."

"Why would she do that? You don't have enough faith in her. Besides, you're starting to sound as paranoid as Dad," Jacob reckoned.

"He might have gotten more cantankerous, a touch slower, and harder of hearing, but he's still no slouch. It's just unfortunate that old age hasn't caught up to him yet and only seems to have improved his higher brain functions. How is it even possible that he shows no signs of senility?"

"Evil is clearheaded and never dies," Mo joked, which at any other time would have made them laugh, though tonight it merely extended the silence between them, the only sound coming from the steaks sizzling on the stove.

"I accidentally ran over one of Clarence's white peacocks, then five minutes later got a ticket for running a red light. All in all, it's been a spectacularly farcical day," Jacob offered after a while. "This hot Jewish cop pulled me over, though. Not a big fan of yours or the show. He pretty much thought you all single-handedly set the Jews back a hundred years."

"Yeah, that's great. Thanks for sharing, Jacob. I always love to hear that kind of crap, especially from a fellow Yid," Mo snapped. "What didn't he like about us? No, wait, don't tell me—he thinks our parenting style was 'too lax,' or that our taking the trips out of public school and putting them in Ilan Ramon Day School was 'too extreme.'"

"No, better than that, actually. He said it made him cringe whenever Dad was on camera. He also said that the Jewish community banded together to get it canceled."

"That's a lie," Mo contended. "BravoREAL came to us and offered us another two years. You know who pulled the plug? We did. Pandora and me. Not a bunch of torch-carrying, jealous Hebrews. We were getting death threats and we decided not to renew."

"Literal death threats?" Jacob asked.

"It was just the occasional call at first. 'Hitler had the right idea.' Click. 'There's no good Jew like a dead Jew.' Click. 'Gas the women and children first.' Click. Then the emails started coming to my account the last few months of the third season," Mo said. "They scared the crap out of Pandora. We got the FBI involved—

BravoREAL thought it'd be a good idea to run an entire episode about it—but they couldn't find the coward responsible. But then he began to target the trips. Somehow he got their email addresses and sent them these repulsive pictures of Nazis executing Jewish boys their age by shooting them in the head, except this twisted fuck photoshopped our sons' faces into the photos. Seriously psycho shit, Jacob. We gave them all new email addresses, but the same thing kept happening. You know the missing mezuzah by the front door? I told Mom and Dad it came off during an earthquake and broke, but the truth is, I came out one morning and someone had drawn a swastika on it with red nail polish. Can you believe there are actual people—real people with families and jobs and pets and friends—in the world who hate us so much that they'd terrorize my boys and come onto my property and do something like that?"

"They live and breathe and walk among us," Jacob said, thinking of his dad.

Mo forked the steaks, sliced through one of them, and asked Jacob how rare he liked it. "That looks about perfect," he replied, grabbing two plates from the cupboard.

Mo devoured his meat in a matter of seconds, washing it down with the rest of his beer, then belched loudly. "We'll discuss you-know-what when Thistle gets here," he said, rinsing off the plate and stashing it in the dishwasher. "I'm heading to bed. I have a ton of shit to take care of tomorrow," and he squeezed Jacob's shoulder on his way out of the kitchen.

"Night," Jacob said, taking a bite, then setting his fork and knife down, his appetite gone, for every time he looked at the steak swimming in its own coagulating pink juices, his mind kept veering to the image of the bloody stain the peacock had left behind on the asphalt. One minute the bird had been there, the next it was lying in a white heap on the pavement. One minute it had been crying out to the dead, the next it was joining them. *Long or short, precious or unappreciated, life makes dust out of everyone and everything eventually, incontrovertibly,* Jacob thought, cutting the steak up into bite-size chunks to feed to Nieves.

In the dark, vacant backyard, the air was cold and ripe with brine, although the sea was miles and miles away. A thick fog had settled across the yard. "Nieves, here, girl," Jacob called softly, approaching the redwood doghouse with the remains of his dinner.

The terrier poked her head out, snuffling the air, then shot out the door, barking and chasing one of her invisible nemeses. Jacob set the plate down, calling again to the barking, snarling dog, which tripped the motion sensors of the paranoid lights attached to the house. They blinked on, throwing the entire backyard into relief—and that's when Jacob saw the opossum, which the dog had cornered. It was big and white, the same size as the terrier, and it was curled up into a ball, playing dead, its rodent head and tail tucked up and away. Nieves kept drawing near to it and then retreating, baring her fangs, her fur bristled, the bell on her collar jangling like a door that kept opening and closing.

"Nieves, enough," he said, quickly grabbing her around the collar and picking her up, whispering into her ear that it was okay, that she needed to calm down. He held her close, even while she fought against him, poking her head through his arms to keep a constant and steady watch on her quarry. Then the lights went out. Jacob hoped the opossum would shove off now that the danger had passed. He couldn't see it in the dark, but still he sensed movement nearby and the next thing he knew, he saw a quick burst of white that stirred and parted the fog. "I'm going to let you go, but you better be a good girl," he whispered to the dog, which had stopped barking at last. "Go eat your meat." Once he set her down in the grass, she tore away, yipping and yapping again, this time at ghosts.

Upstairs, Diet was sound asleep, the novel he'd been reading lying facedown on the floor where it had fallen from his hands. *Die Leiden des jungen Werthers—The Sorrows of Young Werther,* Goethe's classic tale of a young man seduced and ultimately overcome by unrequited love. He picked up the book and set it on the nightstand, then went into the bathroom to shower, thinking about *das kleinste Bad in der Welt* back in Berlin and how yesterday—it was hard to believe it had only been yesterday—he had slipped into the shower with Diet, the first time they'd ever fucked in that tiny space. Mainly, they saved themselves for other places, darker, danker places, each carrying out the other's fantasy of power and aggression.

It all started two years ago, during their first Christmas together in Berlin, when they got on their bikes and pedaled out to Diet's sister's house in Lichtenberg, an area rife with gangs of neo-Nazi skinheads and their sympathizers. Jacob had read about the neighborhood beforehand, for it was often cited as being a hotbed of anti-Semitic activity by the ADL, whose website Jacob often found himself obsessing over. It wasn't snowing when they set out from their flat in Mitte on that cold Christmas Eve afternoon, but by the time they made it to the former Stasi prison that had been converted into middle-class housing—pristine white townhouses that sat in neat, tidy rows with tiny driveways that held tiny cars—the first of the flurries had begun to fall. They fell past the windows in gentle arcs as Jacob met Diet's family for the first time—his twin sister, Dagmar, her husband, Tomas, and their parents, Leopold and Griselda, both retired attorneys. Leopold was long and lean like Diet, Griselda somewhat shrunken with her son's same blue eyes.

Jacob removed his shoes, as was customary, it seemed, all over Germany, and then he followed Diet into the large, spacious kitchen, the heart of chez Krause, where the dinner table had already been set and Griselda was checking on the Christmas Eve goose.

"It's a tradition in our family," Diet said, leaning in and whispering to Jacob. "My mother makes her goose and we all tell her how delicious and juicy it is, though usually it's dry and inedible. You'll tell her you like it, yes?"

"Yes," Jacob said, heeding the warning in Diet's voice, a warning that he'd come to listen to ever since they'd moved to Germany, for Diet, who had hardly seemed German to Jacob while they'd been living in New York City, had renewed his marriage vows with his native country, embracing it with a scary nationalistic fervor.

Christmas Eve was more important than Christmas Day for most Germans, Tomas explained to him, after they'd all taken their seats at the table. His English wasn't terrific, but it was far better than Leopold and Griselda's, for he'd apparently lived in Brazil for a spell during college, where he'd learned both Portuguese and American English. "Not that bloody Queen's English," he said, chortling.

"He is loud and brash and stupid," Diet had said of his brother-in-law. "We don't particularly like him or the way he treats my sister. He's such a boor, and an insufferable, dismissive one at that. But you'll see what I mean."

Yet so far Tomas had been the friendliest of the lot—with a smile on his face, he offered Jacob "an authentic German beer and not that swill you have over in America."

The family chatted idly in German, and as they did, Diet kept turning to Jacob and translating what it was everyone was saying, which Jacob found sweet and kind, though wholly unnecessary, for it sounded very much like the kind of small talk his own family made. Jacob sipped his beer and looked out the sliding-glass door that led to a small backyard, where the snow continued to tumble through the dark, thinking how at one time this entire place had held prisoners of the state, of the DDR, and wondered when it had been decommissioned and turned into condos. He was about to ask Dagmar about it when she turned to him and asked in her broken English why he hadn't gone home for Christmas.

"Because I'm Jewish," he said, surprised by the question but even more surprised at Diet, who clearly hadn't told them he was dating a Jew.

"But . . . yes, okay . . . but . . . still . . . you celebrate Christmas, yes?" Dagmar asked.

"Um, no," Jacob said, feeling his heart galloping.

"Jews celebrate Chanukah," Tomas said proudly. "They hate Christ."

"We do not hate Christ," Jacob said, glancing at Diet, who sat there in pleasant silence.

"And . . . you are like Berlin?" Dagmar asked, clearly confused by who and what Jacob was. *Can it really be that she's never met a Jewish person before?* Jacob wondered. It seemed absolutely impossible, yet then he looked around at where he was and his stomach sank below his knees.

"I'm liking it a lot," Jacob lied, for Diet's sake.

"It's very strange for you," Dagmar said, though he couldn't decide if she meant it to be a question or a statement.

Jacob chose to nod in agreement and smile, though that didn't seem to satisfy Tomas, who pressed him to explain. "It's just . . . I'm having a bit of a culture shock," he said, already suspecting that this was the wrong thing to say, for Diet shifted in his seat and glared at him as if to say, *Now is not the time, Jacob.* "It's been a hard adjustment going from one of the most culturally diverse cities on the planet to a city that's predominantly . . . well, white and Christian." Though he wanted to stop himself and eat every single word he'd just spoken, he realized that it was too late and sat back in his seat, taking a long gulp of beer and hoping what he'd said had gone over everyone's head.

No such luck, for Tomas, who sat up in his seat and leaned his elbows on the table, had something to say about it. "But Berlin is different than the rest of Germany. There are all sorts of brown people here. There are Turks and those Israelis keep flooding in, but they all live among themselves. Oh, it's a big problem, don't get me wrong, but they want it that way. You are right, though. Germany is not as diverse as it could be, but we, Dagmar and I, are doing our part. We are making our country theirs, since they've lost their own. We hired an Israeli maid. Her name is Hannah. Isn't that right, Dagmar?"

"You have an Israeli maid," Jacob reiterated, feeling himself being drawn into this conversation against his will. "That's pretty diverse of you, sure. We had a German maid when I was a boy. We treated her well. She never had to take her shoes off in the house, though."

In the meantime, Diet chattered in German with Dagmar, his mother, and his father, who banged a fist on the table and shouted something at his son. Griselda jumped in and the three battled it out, which Jacob figured was nothing too unusual for them, considering how impassioned and litigious they seemed to be with one another. At least now it sounded as if they were finally talking about important matters, which made him feel even more left out, for as far as he could remember this kind of thing had never happened at the Jacobson table. At a certain point, Griselda got up to check on the bird.

"My wife is winking at me. This means the goose is ready," announced a jovial Leopold, who rose to help her.

"Did you hear any of that with Tomas?" Jacob whispered to Diet, who apparently had because he sat fulminating beside him, his face screwed up into one of those punishing looks that could only spell doom for Jacob later.

"Don't," Diet said, and that was all.

But it wasn't until after dinner, which was incredibly delicious (Jacob had repeated this many times to Griselda), when they went upstairs to sit around the tree and exchange presents, that Jacob felt the full effect of where he was and what Tomas had said and wanted to get out of there as fast as he could. He sat glum and silent, the full weight of his foreignness pressing down upon him. Worse than this, he had a terrible sense that he'd stepped into a house of xenophobes and anti-Semites who didn't understand they were xenophobes and anti-Semites, all of this further complicated by his love for and adoration of Diet, who happened to be a member of this family.

In typical German fashion, Jacob learned, they all opened presents with a quiet, subdued civility, one present per person, nothing outlandish or ridiculously expensive, just useful gifts like books for Diet, opera tickets for his parents, a new sweater for Dagmar, and a subscription to *Men's Health* for Tomas—and nothing for a sulky

Jacob, who hated himself for sulking, until Griselda reached down between her feet and handed him a small basket with what looked like roses in it but which turned out to be several pairs of socks she'd folded up and arranged to look like roses. He peered down at the beautiful woolen socks, all snug in the basket, then at the family, including his own Diet, who was sitting on the small sofa between his parents, all of their faces glowing in the soft candlelight of the *Weihnachtspyramide*—the Christmas nativity pyramid— and the white lights of *der Tannenbaum* and he wondered how he had ended up there, in Germany, with a German boyfriend who claimed he wasn't anti-Semitic but who didn't see anything wrong with what Tomas had said at the table and had not risen to the oc- casion, this man he loved who had brought him into this house and then refused to defend him, for this was a defining moment between them and Diet had let it go, had let Jacob down. It was all he could do not to pick up one of the pairs of socks and touch it to one of the candles that kept the Christmas pyramid spinning. But Jacob re- strained himself, though by the time they left on their bikes an hour later, he was more than ready to call it quits, to beat a hasty retreat back to the flat, pack a bag, and get the fuck out of Germany. Five months after their arrival and Jacob would fly back to New York City, absent Diet and into the full and glaring light of his family's We Told You So.

The snow. So much of it had fallen in just three hours that rid- ing their bikes was impossible, so they walked them in silence to the nearest S-Bahn station at Rummelsburg, got on the train, and rode it all the way back to Mitte in silence as well. It was, in Jacob's rec- ollection, the longest and most severe silence he'd ever endured and brought along with it terrible feelings of regret and remorse, for he understood that he'd upset the evening for Diet and that Diet would forever associate it with Jacob, the Jew who ruined Christmas Eve. He wanted to apologize, but more than that he wanted to ask Diet why he hadn't spoken up at dinner, why he'd let Tomas say what he had without so much as a word.

In the flat they removed their freezing, soaked shoes, then changed into dry clothes. Diet put the kettle on for tea and Jacob sat down at their rickety IKEA table, a hand-me-down from Dagmar. "That went well," Jacob jested, trying for levity. "I really liked Dagmar. And Tomas—that guy's a real hootenanny."

"My parents came all the way from Munich to meet you," Diet stated, remaining with his back to Jacob, his shoulders hunched and his spine rigid. Jacob could just make out each individual vertebra beneath the thin cotton of his shirt and wanted nothing more than to get up and wrap his arms around him, but he remained right where he was, for though he understood that he could not hold Diet responsible for what that idiot Tomas had said, he could hold Diet responsible for sitting there and letting him say it.

"Did you hear what he said to me?"

"They have an Israeli maid, Jacob. I don't get the major deal."

"The problem isn't that they have an Israeli maid. The problem is that your boyfriend happens to be Jewish—"

"Jewish, not Israeli."

"Don't split hairs. You know exactly what I mean," Jacob snapped, thinking about why it had all bothered him so much. "It was his tone of voice. It made me feel . . . like a dirty Jew. Like that's all Israelis or any Jew for that matter is good for. To clean up after you. I mean, them."

"This is not what he meant," Diet commented, turning around once the kettle had boiled and pouring the hot water into two mugs. "You aren't a dirty Jew."

"What if I am? What if that's how your family sees me?"

"I will not lie to you," Diet said, coming up behind Jacob and wrapping his arms around him. "There are plenty of Germans, French, and Poles who will still take one look at you and hate you on sight," he cautioned. "But do you really believe we are any worse than you Americans? Look at what's happening in the United States with those suicide bombers. You're safer in big bad Germany these days than in your own country."

"My country doesn't have the history yours does," Jacob pointed out. "My country didn't exterminate millions of people based on a single idea from a megalomaniac. But yours did. Your grandparents were party members. Are you trying to tell me that you don't have a single anti-Semitic cell in your body?"

"Why are you so terrified of being hated?"

"I'm not terrified of being hated. I'm terrified that you don't dislike the right people."

"Yes, okay. I understand. But I do not dislike you. I do not dislike anyone. What I dislike is that you hate yourself," Diet declared, taking a seat across from him. "You hate yourself for being Jewish, and you see that hatred everywhere and in everyone."

"I do not hate myself for being Jewish." Then Jacob thought about what he had just said and began to wonder if he didn't hate himself just a little, yet he wasn't sure it was because he was Jewish or a Jacobson, or for something as simple as merely being alive. "Well, okay, maybe I do. But I come from a long history of self-hating Jews. Another Jacobson curse I'm not proud of."

"How can we correct this? How can we make this better for you?" Diet asked, and his sincerity nearly broke Jacob's heart.

It began some days later in the dark of their bedroom, an idea fashioned out of Jacob's wish to shed any and all vestiges of this particular Jacobson curse and Diet's wish to exonerate himself from the atrocious guilt he'd inherited—that entire generations of Germans had inherited—from his grandparents, all of whom had been Nazis. It might be a way of wiping two slates clean at once, Jacob had said to Diet, who'd protested and fought against the idea but had, in the months since, come to see it as life-changing.

And it did change us, of course it did, Jacob thought, grabbing a towel and drying off. Not visibly at first, but over time Jacob was able to pass the dreaded sports bar without hearing *"der Jude"* in the air and to glance at the sides of buildings without looking for swastikas, although he did find them, but even then he understood that it was just a symbol, a sign of a single rotten soul and not one of another Jewish apocalypse. And Diet changed incrementally as well, shedding some of his renewed nationalism and owning up to his own latent anti-Semitism, which surprised Jacob, not that Diet confessed to it but that he was clearly working it out through Jacob, by loving the thing that scared him.

It had been many months since they'd begun their experiment, but in recent weeks he'd started to worry that the routine of it all had grown somewhat stale, that in fact their entire sex life had become old hat, and it was his hope they might be able to rekindle it there, in his brother's home, where it was even more forbidden to do what they were doing. The thought gave him an instant erection, and he beat off before leaving the bathroom.

No, Jacob wasn't proud of himself, but it still excited him to think about the other suitcase and what it contained, how imaginative they were going to have to be now that they were surrounded by his family. He'd never be able to explain to anyone just what went on between Diet and him, the reenacting of a moment in time bracketed by the world's sympathy on the one hand and now the world's renewed hatred and scorn on the other. The Jews of America had it bad, and it was only getting worse, which was another reason Jacob was not so happy to be back in California. He could not tell his family that he felt unsafe, especially not his dad or brother, who would have dismissed him for being paranoid and silly, reminding him yet again and at every turn how thankful he should be for getting out of that barbaric country, if only for a few days.

Jacob slid into bed beside a mummified Diet, who slept with the sheets drawn tightly around him. He wore the eye mask and had inverted—inserted—the earplugs, muttering softly in his native tongue as usual, a nocturnal habit Jacob found both charming and frustrating, for he was never able to make out anything Diet said. Jacob, who liked to sleep unfettered, forwent the mask and earplugs, falling asleep the second he shut his eyes.

His sleep did not last for long, however, because only a couple of hours later Jacob was awakened by a familiar, alarming noise—

familiar because it was one of the more frequent soundtracks to his childhood and he would have known it anywhere and alarming because it was close to midnight and his brother lived on a quiet, residential block. After throwing on some clothes, Jacob hurried downstairs and opened the front door to find the source of the noise: his dad, barefoot and dressed in his pajamas, mowing the rest of the yard. This sort of thing had happened a multitude of times during Jacob's youth, usually whenever his dad was experiencing a period of "heightened agitation and stress," brought on, naturally, by his "unsupportive, ungrateful wife and children."

His dad disappeared around the side of the house. Jacob gave chase, shutting the front door and heading to the wall of glass and through the pneumatic door to meet him. He stood on the patio, watching his dad push the mower in a single straight line, his glazed eyes fastened to a point in the distance. It always amazed him that, out of everything his dad could have chosen to do while he was sleepwalking, he chose to do yard work.

Jacob approached him tentatively, for he'd discovered that waking his dad when he was like this meant one of two things—he could snap out of it without consequence, disoriented though malleable, as someone hypnotized, or he could turn violent, throwing punches and screaming, as someone possessed. It was a constant toss-up, Jacob had learned, first from Mo, then from Edith after Mo left to pursue his acting in Hollywood, Jacob inheriting the burden from her not long after she left for Harvard. And his mom? She slept through it every time, though somewhere in the back of Jacob's mind he suspected this might have been her meager attempt at revenge, a passive-aggressive way of being rid of him, of not being responsible for anything that might befall him while sleepwalking. He knew his mother loved his father—she'd let him stay, for fuck's sake—but that same love had never touched Jacob, who now saw how easy it might be to end their troubles altogether, and an idea bloomed as he moved slowly toward his dad, who let the mower go.

It died in place, right there where the grass met the curved, pebbled apron of the pool, and as it died, so did the idea, for his dad began turning away from the pool and toward the house, as if being called back to bed. Jacob turned with him, hoping, praying, that a gust of wind might redirect him, might angle the dinghy that was his dad and steer him to his watery end. *Well, technically, waterless,* thought Jacob, when suddenly his dad was changing course on his own, as if he'd heard Jacob's thoughts, and he shuffled zombielike toward the pool, raising his arms above his head as if he were already swimming. And for one beautiful second Jacob saw it happen, saw him walk to the edge of the empty pool, put one foot in front of the other, pitch forward, head over heels, and fall flat on his face, breaking bones and cracking his neck. It would have been so easy to hurry the process along with a gentle nudge, even to push him, so that his body was propelled harder and faster into the concrete basin, ensuring his death.

But Jacob couldn't do it, wouldn't do it, because this wasn't part of the plan, because then there might be a chance he survived. Lord only knew how insanely lucky the man was—he'd beaten skin cancer and lived through two heart attacks and a raging bout of sepsis. Though it made Jacob sick to his stomach, he took his dad by the arm without waking him and led him back into the house, whispering in his ear, "I could have let you die, but that wouldn't have been any fun. We have something far more painful in store for you. What? What was that? Oh, you're sorry for all the times you called me a cocksucker, and you're sorry for all the times you made my mother cry, and you're sorry for missing Mo's first starring role on Broadway because you just had to go fishing, and you're sorry for breaking up Thistle's marriage. Well, guess what? Fuck you and fuck your apology." Jacob opened the door to the guest room, where his mom was asleep, the oxygen mask secured tightly to her face, and helped his dad into bed and drew the covers under his chin.

He stood above him, thinking back to a moment that he only knew from a photograph—as a two-year-old, he was sitting on his dad's knee as they watched what was destined to be the final launch of the Challenger space shuttle, which exploded into a fireball seventy-three seconds later. In the photo, he was smiling and tilting his head up to gaze at his dad, who was pointing at the Zenith's fuzzy green screen and smiling for a different reason altogether.

There was hope in the picture, so much hope and so much love, that it seemed impossible to Jacob that he'd grown up into the kind of man who would plot his own dad's death. *But there it is,* he thought, retreating quietly from the room. So much hope had become so much unendurable, needless pain, years and years of it, that even if Jacob wrote it all down, as he'd tried to do over and over again, he knew that no one would believe him and that his dad had counted on this all along, just as he'd counted on going to his grave as lucky as the day he was born.

Upstairs, Jacob slid back into bed. His mind whirled and raced with ideas, each of these breaking apart into thousands of thoughts and these thoughts multiplying and dividing exponentially into millions of possibilities with a gazillion different outcomes—everything hinging on the waffling Edith, for he and Mo could not move forward with their plan without her. She would take further convincing, though Jacob was at a loss as to how to move her. She was his older sister, yet in many ways she'd never quite grown up—their dad had seen to that by infantilizing her. Jacob knew he wasn't supposed to know about all the money Julian had sent her over the years, paying off her sizable student debt, buying her a car when her own finally broke down for good. Jacob didn't begrudge her any of this blood money. That's all it was, he understood, though he wasn't sure she did. Blood money for all the psychic bloodletting, the battery of subtle and not-so-subtle abuses that rendered her too weak and too timid to step out of their dad's shadow, where she might have seen him for the monster he was. He felt sorriest for her; if any of them had gotten the rawest deal, it was certainly his trusting-to-a-fault, utterly docile sister, her daddy's favorite plaything.

Even to this day, she continued to believe herself to be the daughter of a man who had loved her unconditionally. The truth, Jacob supposed, was just too intolerable to face. The irony, of course, was that she did face it in each of her disastrous romantic interludes—from her obsession with Sheik Cohen to her implosive marriage to Elias Plunkett to this new affair with a Displaced Israeli Male. Leave it to Edith to get involved with one of them during what was turning out to be a terrible time for the Jews in general. Violence against these DIMs was on the rise in Atlanta, which had taken in fifty thousand refugees at last count.

As if that wasn't bad enough, because of her skewed judgment when it came to all things romantic she was now facing the dissolution of her academic career—this scandal with one of her former students at Emory. The idea that she'd gone that far was alarming enough in itself, but that she wouldn't take any responsibility for it was plainly pathological and, quite frankly, a sure sign that something inside of her had broken irrevocably. He wanted to help her, yet he'd never been as close to her as he was to Mo, for she had always been her daddy's eyes and ears, tattling on Jacob for infractions big and small—accusing him of taking a stick of her chewing gum, stealing a quarter from her Golda Meir porcelain bank, or using her curling iron to curl his bangs—things he most certainly did but that she never should have been reporting on, Jacob believing as he did that the bond between siblings was a bond most holy. He never tattled on Edith, and he never quite understood how she could betray him time and again. He hated her blind faith and loyalty, yet couldn't hold it against her. Her daddy was all she'd ever had. What then could Jacob say, he pondered, to blunt that blind faith, to break that loyal oath she'd kept solemnly since they were little? How was he going to bring her around and convince her that what they were doing was more than justified, it was necessary? Think about Mom and her final few months, he might remind her, think about that, Thistle. And just as Jacob himself was thinking about it, Nieves let out a loud crescendo of barks, then fell silent, only to start up again a couple of minutes later. He reached for the earplugs, but not before he heard what sounded like crying, its origin unclear, and sat up in bed, startled. For a moment, he thought it might be coming from just outside the door.

When he was a boy, he'd awoken many times to find his poor, unhappy mom in her sheer nightgown sobbing just outside his bedroom and he wondered now if it might not be her again, wanting to slide into bed beside him, sobbing, apologizing for waking him up. "Your father kicked me again in his sleep," she'd often said, though this explanation never quite accounted for her tears or these visits, during which she'd unleash upon him all of her marital sorrow. She'd hugged him to her and kissed his neck, her warm, full, dangling breasts pressed against him, as if she'd been trying to comfort him and not the other way around. As if he'd been sick and had called out for her in his fevered sleep, except that he hadn't.

Jacob got up and tiptoed to the door, opening it and stepping out onto the empty landing. Everything was still and tranquil; the appliances hummed a domestic tune that resonated in the air and filled the house with reason. Returning to the room, he heard the crying again, fainter now, though just as clear, and it seemed to be close, emanating from a point just beyond the windows. If he'd been dreaming, he would have been able to pass like moonlight through the glass. He would have been able to transport himself into the trunk to comfort the peacock, as he'd comforted his mom.

"I hate to see you in so much pain," he would have said, just as he'd said to his mom on the nights she came to him. "What can I do to make it better?" He would have been able to hush the bird, as he'd hushed his mom, stroking her hair until she fell asleep in his arms, Jacob never feeling himself as powerful or as strong as he had on those nights she'd visited.

He wasn't dreaming, however, he was very much awake, though dead on his feet. He went to the window and parted the curtains, peering down at the car parked in the driveway, already imagining the morning, when he showed up at Clarence's with the peacock. Yes, that was the only way to deal with the situation. The bird belonged to Clarence, who would give it a proper burial, although he didn't relish the thought of having to return to the cemetery so soon or of seeing Clarence's fallen face when he delivered the dead bird back to him. *Better perhaps to call the city of Calabasas and have them deal with it,* he thought. Until then, Jacob, in his mental exhaustion and emotional fatigue, listened to the bird's sad, plaintive call, made all that much sadder because this call anticipated a response that would never come.

Abandoning the window, he returned to bed and inserted the spongy, orange earplugs, though every time he shifted his head, one or the other fell out. He lay like this for hours, suspended between worlds, between wakefulness on the one hand and sleep on the other, understanding that directly beneath him, his mom struggled to breathe and his dad, safely tucked back into bed, slept an unencumbered sleep, refusing the call of the peacock. Jacob found himself praying that Julian might die a natural death that very night and spare them all the trouble of having to kill him.

He also prayed that coyotes didn't come sniffing around the trunk, because that's all he needed—a pack of them howling, snarling, and scaring the neighbors, with whom Mo and Pandora were already having serious tsuris, according to Pandora, who'd asked them nicely and repeatedly to remove a certain prickly pear cactus from their front yard before one of the boys gouged himself.

An older couple, the neighbors dismissed Pandora and Mo's requests and continued to hold the boys' soccer balls and basketballs hostage, going so far as to spear them on the cactus and leave them out like decapitated heads, a warning to all children everywhere in the closed and gated community of Edelweiss Estates. If there was anyone brave enough to broker a deal between them, Jacob knew, it was his sister, Edith, consummate mediator and ethicist extraordinaire, who was set to arrive in the morning. Then the real fun could begin.

EDITH JACOBSON PLUNKETT;
OR, CAUCASIAN, JEW, OR OTHER

Friday, April 15, 2022

Edith emerged from the crowded, shadowy terminal onto the equally crowded, shadowy breezeway, dragging her broken suitcase behind her and taking her place in line for the airport shuttle. As usual, she'd overpacked, the Samsonite about to explode from the extra dress and heels she'd tossed in at the last minute. Thank heavens for Ephraim, her Israeli neighbor, who'd stayed over again last night and had helped her zip it up, or else she never would have made her flight. She'd also enlisted him to drive her to Hartsfield-Jackson airport, and as Ephraim was out of work and none too keen on looking for more, he didn't seem to mind doing her the favor. Besides, he said, the drive would give them an extra half hour of canoodling. Did it matter that he was sixteen years her junior and a pothead who was into hip-hop and wore his baggy jeans well below his waist? No, not to Dr. Edith Jacobson Plunkett, who, over the course of the last couple of years, had come to appreciate this newly minted species of DIMs as they were commonly referred to in impolite society. She saw their proliferation throughout the

111

southern United States as an unexpected silver lining to the thunder-cloud that had been the final annihilation of Israel—a population of swarthy, desperate-to-assimilate Jewish men who, along with the women and children of the former Jewish state (though she had less use for them), had been "transitioned" abroad after Syria, Iran, and Lebanon had invaded, conquered, and carved up Israel. They'd put up a good fight, the Israelis, but they couldn't make a go of it alone—the four million Israeli refugees America had accepted, the price the country had paid for its shocking and inexcusable neutrality née isolationism.

The shuttle finally arrived and they all piled in, the driver welcoming each one of them to Los Angeles, pronouncing it the way the Spanish settlers had intended, with all of the poetry packed within it, making Edith think of angels, which in turn made her think of Elias Plunkett, her ex-husband of several years. She wasn't ready to think about him, not yet, and turned her attention to the other passengers, some of their faces familiar because they had been on her flight. She wondered if those she recognized were heading to Pomona College for the conference and if she'd see any of them there, wanting to ask but chastened by her own shyness and fear of strangers. Even a simple ride like this put a fair amount of strain on the hypervigilant forty-year-old divorcée, who shuddered in her seat. Sometimes, it was all just too much. Sometimes, the people's eyes she met were filled with such accusation that she had no other choice but to turn away from them, which she did now, although she was wearing her big, black designer sunglasses that eclipsed half her face.

"And what a beautiful face it is," Ephraim had said last night while lying on top of her and thrusting himself deep inside her pussy. "And what a beautiful pussy it is, too," he'd said once he was finished and had helped Edith to finish as well. They'd kissed and cuddled, satisfaction glazing them like summer sweat, although the carriage house was cool, with every window thrown open, a light spring rain tapping out sonnets against the tin roof. She was not in love with him and, most likely, he was not in love with her, yet it had

112

been so long since she'd enjoyed a man's lips and tongue and cock—his anything—that she wasn't about to dismiss him merely out of some outmoded idea of moral relativism she had about herself. *Fuck love,* she thought, when Elias Plunkett plunked himself down in her head, brandishing his big light-saber prick at her like the nebbishy, Jedi-obsessed freak he was.

Just like old times, she mused without rancor, for enough time had passed for her to think of him fondly. Elias had shown her who he was fairly early in their relationship, small things that should have tipped her off that it would all end badly. She thought back to that tiff they'd had over *Star Wars,* which just kept escalating out of control: It started with episodes I, II, III, Elias claiming they outshone episodes IV, V, and VI, whereas she maintained the originals not only outclassed the prequels but put the sequels to shame as well, calling George Lucas a hack and a sellout. This was too much for the sensitive future professor of film to handle, and he stormed out of the apartment, got into his horrid lime-green Karmann Ghia, and drove away, returning a few days later to take his clothes back to his efficiency apartment, which was closer to American University, where he was getting a PhD in film theory. They remained separated for a few months, before one day he magically reappeared, showing up to her office at Georgetown with a canister of See's kosher toffees. And that was that, or almost that, for he'd also boxed up all of his *Star Wars* collectibles, not to sell them, never that, but to keep them out of her sight, although she'd never asked him to do anything of the kind. It made her feel inordinately sad and guilty—that he'd assumed she picked a fight with him over a bunch of stupid movie prequels and sequels, when the truth of the matter was, she knew now, that it had had to do with her subliminal discomfort at Elias's friendship with her dad, which had bloomed even as they'd first started dating in D.C. Julian had claimed that he didn't mind Elias being a Presbyterian so long as he didn't start genuflecting in front of him, though he was undeniably delighted when D.C. Elias (as he called him, Edith knew, not for his city of residence but because the

D stood for Decaf and the *C* for Christian, an abbreviation her dad used for anyone of the Presbyterian faith) proposed and decided to give up Christ "for her," although she hadn't asked him to do that, either.

The shuttle lurched and then stopped abruptly, the force of which unsettled her and shoved her into the elderly gentleman sitting beside her, who muttered, "Stupid kike bitch," under his breath, that is, if she heard him correctly.

Shocked and humiliated, she let out a gasp, reaching absently for the serpentine gold chain on which dangled a pendant in the shape of a chai, a present to herself that she bought with some of her bat-mitzvah money, a pendulum of precious stones—the het of pavé amethysts, the yud of pavé emeralds. It swung just above her ample décolletage, and she caught it in her fist in midswing, clutching it tightly as if it were a talisman to ward off any further attacks and muttering an apology under her own breath, then instantly hating herself for it. On the verge of tears, she got up and hurried to a seat in the back, her heart racing, hating herself even more for giving the old geezer the satisfaction of making her move, when, if the world were actually working properly, he would have been put off by the side of the road and made to walk to his destination, which, she hoped, was someplace in the lower intestines of hell. The horrible de rigueur etiquette of civilized society kept Edith from causing a fuss, though that's exactly what she wanted to do—she wanted to stand up to him, to become someone else, someone less afraid of what people thought of her, and to shed this thin skin of hers and grow another, a beautiful, waterproof hide, resilient when the rains of spring or the rains of shit came down upon her.

Instead, she sat silently in her seat, recalling the first time someone—one of her classmates in the sixth grade, a fat little bitch named Libby Ann McKenzie had called her a dirty Jew, back before it was a thing again. She wanted to ask the man in the front why he hated her when he knew nothing about her, other than that she'd bumped into him and that she was obviously Jewish and even more obviously a female. Where did the hate come from? She approached the question both as someone who'd experienced a wide range of prejudice—currently, she was in the throes of an unending sexual harassment suit in which she had been falsely accused—and as a professor of ethics. If she had to guess, she thought she probably approached all of her problems like this, first as an ethicist, then as a woman, which made sense because she specialized in the gender of ethics. How someone dealt with the issue of right or wrong was built into the genetic code, she believed. Either we were born with it or we weren't. She loved puzzling out the tougher questions, where gender and ethics met and the lines between them blurred. This was her arena and in it she flourished. Yet it was impossible to hand someone like the walking cadaver in the bow tie a list of her accomplishments and expect him to recant and apologize, awaken to his inhumanity, when he so clearly hated her a priori.

The shuttle lumbered up to the squat, putty-colored rental car building and she and her suitcase dismounted, the driver wishing her a pleasant stay in sunny (droughty, Jew-hating) Los Angeles. A few people, having just returned rentals, flowed around her, climbing into the shuttle and taking their seats.

Yet Edith wasn't aware of them, or of anything else for that matter, so fascinated and horrified was she by the elderly gentleman in the bow tie with whom she was having a staring contest. She wanted to remember him, for there he was, the face of the new anti-Semitism, an innocent-looking, well-groomed older man dressed handsomely in a business suit, who no doubt was on his way to pick up a luxury car, a convertible Mercedes coupe, to drive it to his rented beach house in Malibu, the top down the whole way. Was it terrible of her to wish a melanoma on his house? As they continued to stare at each other, she watched in absolute horror as he gave her the thumbs-up, then extended his index finger, fashioning himself a gun, bringing his thumb down and pretending to shoot her dead. No one else on the shuttle seemed to register this exchange, and the man grinned in self-satisfaction. Edith removed her sunglasses, propping them up in her untamed auburn curls, then lifted her own hands and shot him the bird, which to Edith was as far as she could go without coming apart completely.

When the shuttle finally drove off, carrying the hateful old codger with it, Edith watched it, quaking with anger, hurt, humiliation, and a tiny, wilting joy for having stuck up for herself, even if it were only the most minor and fleeting of victories and left her hollowed out and chagrined. Hadn't she taught her students better? Hadn't she carped about detachment and disengagement, about when to turn one's back on the evils that men did and when to acknowledge them?

"The high road must be a reward in and of itself," she told them year in and year out, until it lost all meaning and even she began to tire of hearing herself say it. "Act with Kantian goodwill, and you can never go wrong"—except that Kant was a rabid anti-Semite, as some of her Jewish students pointed out, so why should they trust him? Which of course led them down the rabbit hole into the murky, claustrophobic catacombs of man versus his ethics, man versus his philosophy.

Edith left her suitcase by the door and hesitantly approached the counter, where a buxom young woman with frizzy red hair and a glinting gold Star of David dangling from her neck said, "Hi, I'm Edith. How can I help you today?"

"Edith Plunkett reporting for duty," she replied, marveling that the girl seemed like a clone of her own younger self, while she tapped on her keyboard, keeping her eyes locked on the screen, clearly uncomfortable with Edith's staring.

"I can't seem to locate you in our system," the girl said. "Are you sure you have a reservation with us today?"

"Positive," Edith said, though she wasn't positive at all. "It went through Jocelyn, our department admin."

"Do you have a confirmation email handy by any chance?" the girl asked, just as sweet as Edith had not been at that age.

Edith rummaged through her purse and retrieved her iPhone,

which was still set to airplane mode. The moment she flipped the little digital button to off, the phone began to vibrate and light up like a disco as one text message, email, and voicemail after another was magically downloaded from the ether. She had to admit that Jacob had been right when he'd suggested she switch to the superfast, supersleek iPhone, which she looked upon with reverence as she did all things electronic and technical and well beyond her ken. Every time she used her phone it was like Chanukah all over again. After a second or two of scrounging and scrolling through her Emory email account, she finally came upon the errant message, which Jocelyn had forwarded to her and was dated last month.

"Oh, I see what happened. It looks like you did have a reservation with us, but it was for yesterday, which is why I couldn't find you. The system wipes itself clean every twenty-four hours," explained the girl to a horrified, perturbed Edith. "And of course our entire fleet is out," she added, "or else I could fix this problem for you immediately and get you into a car."

"I know this has nothing to do with you," Edith said, trying her best to stay composed, although with every passing second she was growing more and more unsure of herself, the ice-cold hands of panic and doubt pressing down upon her chest, "but I don't think Jocelyn made an accidental mistake with the dates, because Jocelyn never makes accidental mistakes with anything. I think she made a purposeful mistake, and I say this only because she and I have never gotten along, not after the incident with the boxes." And though Edith knew she was rambling, she couldn't help herself, not even when the people in line behind her began to grow irritable. "I'm on my way to the Valley to visit my parents. My mother's dying," she said, knowing how it sounded but saying it anyway. "So is there anything, anything at all you can do for me? Please?"

"I'm so sorry to hear about your mother," the girl said. "If you'd like to wait, I think I'll have a return in about half an hour," and she gestured to the next person in line, who, impatient and with nostrils flared, stepped up beside Edith. "I'm going to have to ask you to have a seat now, ma'am," she added, suddenly shuttered, cold and efficient with the power of her office.

Edith walked away and slumped down on one of the lumpy vinyl sofas, scrutinizing the girl from behind her dark lenses. It wasn't her tone so much as her refusal to recognize herself in the obvious features they shared that Edith took umbrage at. How often did you have a chance to meet yourself? For a moment, Edith's childlessness weighed heavily upon her, until she remembered that Mo was always cranky and tired and that her sister-in-law had had to get a tummy tuck and had once confided to Edith that she'd just as soon never have sex again than experience the wonderful world of morning sickness and preeclampsia. Besides, Edith had learned long ago not to miss what she would never have. She'd been down that road with Elias, and it had only led to the miserable dead end of divorce. The resemblance was just too striking to disregard, yet disregard it she did, for the Jewish girl who rented cars had no use for the Jewish woman who desperately needed one. At least this was the way it seemed to Edith, for every time she tried to get the girl's attention she dropped her eyes to the computer, ignoring her.

Fine. You just be that way, Edith thought, her phone pinging or ponging, dinging or donging, whatever the proper word was for the sound it just made, Edith doing her best to describe it approximately and finally settling on gonging, a single gong that raised absolutely no eyebrows, because everyone in the place had his or her face in his or her phone. The gong turned out to be a nudge from the Scrabble app, which she'd downloaded just that morning. The other player, TBS1946, wanted her to take her turn. She'd accepted the game while waiting at her gate in the Atlanta airport and had completely forgotten about it. She looked cursorily at her tiles, then at the open board. She was just about to play EMU, for sixteen points, when she glanced up to see the girl motioning to her.

"Okay, Mrs. Plunkett, you're all set," she said. "I've been authorized by my home office to upgrade you at no extra cost. I have you in a Chevrolet Express, returning Monday morning. Is that right?

I'm going to have one of my associates rinse the van off and bring it around to you."

"I'm sorry. Did you just say *van*?" Edith asked.

"It's either that or you'll have to wait another six hours," the girl replied. "You can always check in with us tomorrow to see if the fleet's been replenished." Upon hearing the word *fleet* again, Edith imagined an empty, expansive hangar that once contained hundreds of fighter jets, not compact cars, economies, or SUVs, the renters of them not drivers but pilots, all of them conscripted and headed off to war.

"Bombs away," Edith said, turning away from her would-be daughter, who called out to the next customer.

Outside, Edith texted Mo that she was on her way, ignoring his reply, "Pandora says to stay off the 405." As if she didn't know that already. Then she opened up the Scrabble app and played EMU, which connected with the S in TBS1946's previous word, SORRY. She loved the idea of connecting with someone in Phnom Penh or Shanghai or Paris, places she'd never been and still dreamed of going to. Mainly, though, she dreamed of traveling through the next few days with as little turbulence as possible, of talking Jacob and Mo out of making an irreversible, irreconcilable, and unconscionable mistake. She couldn't deny them their hatred of their dad any more than they could deny her the love she felt for him, and a part of her also understood that they'd gotten the worst of it, these handsome, devoted brothers of hers. They hadn't deserved any of it, not his cruelty or his threats, his taunting or his mean-spiritedness. He was sick and that was how his sickness had manifested itself, she'd explained to them. If anyone was to blame, it was their mom, Edith thought, their docile, people-pleasing mom, who never stood up for herself or her children. Even now, she imagined the way things were going to go once she arrived at Mo's, how Edith would take over for her mom, smoothing out the fights that were sure to erupt among the three Jacobson men. The roles had been played out so often that she, in some strange way, almost looked forward to stepping back into her own part. It'd been so long since they'd all been together in one place, since anyone besides her students and her fly-by-night, unmemorable lovers needed anything more than a mere sliver of her, that she luxuriated in the idea of falling back into the familial breast, however battered and bloody it was. And it *was* battered and bloody and it came now with the menace of death, which hung over her just as the utterly absurd notion of Elias again hung over her. She had heard that he'd left Atlanta for a position at USC, although they hadn't had any communication in ages. Elias, whose favorite Jewish holiday was Pesach, Elias, who'd given up the Father, the Son, and the Holy Ghost to marry her, then became the worst kind of convert, a rampant, rampaging Orthodox Jew. Of course, as these things went, the more avidly observant he became, the less she took him or any of it too seriously. Which was her mistake, not his, she realized, as a huge white van the size of a short bus pulled up and stopped, the associate hopping out and handing a mortified Edith a clipboard on which was attached the contract, which she reluctantly signed.

Then she was standing at the door, peering up at the dashboard and steering column and wondering how she was going to climb in and out, when he reappeared with a small yellow footstool, which he set down in front of her.

"You go up," he said, acting out a demonstration for her.

"Yes, I go up," she said, thanking him. Even after he disappeared around the corner, though, she continued to waver, doubt turning to insecurity and insecurity into paralysis. She'd never driven a cargo van, which was basically what it was, the enormity of the thing terrifying her. It wasn't just a gas-guzzling behemoth, it was also the kind of van kidnappers and murderers drove around in, searching for their next victim. "Up, Edith, go up," she said, putting one foot on the footstool, then the other, then one foot inside the van, hefting herself onto the seat while the associate set her suitcase in the cargo hold and slid the door shut. Edith thanked him, gave him a few wrinkled dollar bills, then strapped the seat belt around her five-foot-eight, one-hundred-sixty-pound frame, said a little prayer, put the van in drive, and off she went.

Instead of leaving the parking lot, she circled for a while, getting used to handling 5,500 pounds of steel and glass. It weighed more than three times what her tiny Smart car did and driving it felt like a giant betrayal, a blemish upon her own ethical standards. She was having a hard time reconciling her choice in rentals with what was happening in the world—a gallon of gas cost six dollars, water a scarcity, not just in California but in many areas across the United States, temperatures in Atlanta hovering around 104 degrees in the summer, carbon emissions continuing to slow, but nowhere near enough. Oh, the shame and hypocrisy of it all, even as she had lectured her students, future robber barons, capitalists, and financiers, on the advantages of living a civic-minded, conscientious life. The world was damaged and in extreme pain and here was Edith in a gas-guzzling van, part of the problem rather than the solution.

She drove with care, observing speed limits and stopping at yellow lights, pissing off the drivers behind her who leaned on their horns or pulled around her, flipping her off. Having lived in Atlanta for years, she'd gotten used to the slower paces, even liked and appreciated them, and didn't mind poking along behind a Sunday driver doing ten miles under the limit. The traffic in Atlanta proper could also be gruesome, but since Edith lived ITP, Inside the Perimeter, rather than OTP, Outside the Perimeter, the perimeter being that most-hated of roads, Interstate 285, she rarely was bothered by it. Until their divorce, she and Elias had lived in North Druid Hills, only a couple of miles from the Emory campus, and could walk to work, but really they had bought the house for Elias, who wanted to be near Congregation Beth Jacob and around the other Frum. Edith did not take to the enclave, which, she told her brothers, was dreary and drab, though she told her mom and dad it was peaceful and charming, the house a real gem. The three-bedroom split-level was not a real gem, but a real money pit. Yet Edith, who was still devoted to Elias back then, let him sink as much of their savings as he wanted into refurbishing it. She said nothing until one afternoon, six months after they'd moved into it, when she came home to find a bulldozer ripping up the patio and the well-tended flowering backyard, her one true solace in a world of frumpy women in wigs and podgy men in black frocks with long, untended beards.

When Elias himself got home that night, she met him at the door with a glass of wine. She served him his favorite meal—beef brisket with roasted fingerling potatoes, an iceberg salad running with Italian dressing—then cleared the table, made a pot of coffee, and set his favorite dessert—a platter of homemade lemon bars, her mom's recipe—in front of him. Beside herself with fury, everything around her gave off an intense, white-hot radiance, including Elias, who reached for the tin of powdered sugar, although she'd given the bars an ample dusting already. She let him dust his sizable portion even further before saying, "Were you ever planning on telling me about the addition?"

"Were you ever planning on telling me about Sheik?" he said, biting into the bar and chewing, his face instantly falling and losing its satisfied smile. She had absolutely no idea how he'd come to hear about Sheik, for she'd been more than careful about never mentioning him to any of her friends, much less anyone she and Elias had in common. Besides, she hadn't been in touch with Sheik in ages, and neither were there any paper or email trails, phone records, nor anything to have made her husband suspicious. "Are you sure you followed the recipe? This tastes . . . funny," he said, downing the first bar and taking another.

"To the letter," she said, eyeing the tin, which held a blend of powdered sugar and the finely ground-up stone that had once been her precious patio. "Maybe you just need more sugar."

Now, taking Pandora's advice to stay off the 405, Edith maneuvered the van onto Lincoln Boulevard, thinking about that night again, about ultimately conceding to Elias, who wore her down to a nub, interrogating her about Sheik, until she finally gave in, more out of exhaustion than resignation, and only after she made him promise never to bring up Sheik again. She let him build his addition, which, when completed, was supposed to house his vast movie collection. It was also supposed to serve as a screening room, replete with comfortable sofas and chairs, the movies projected onto a screen by an old-fashioned projector, which was to be mounted directly into the wall and operated by Elias himself, who, in a former life, had been a projectionist. *That, and a veritable huckster,* she thought, recalling how the plans for the addition never quite materialized. It turned out that Elias had other ideas for it, chiefly to turn the room into a new master bedroom, opening the original master up "to interpretation," he said.

"By interpretation, you mean a nursery."

"We are the only childless couple on the block. But don't worry, Edith. I know that children aren't in my future, not so long as you and I are married."

"What's that supposed to mean?" she asked, surprised, for they'd had this discussion so many times that Edith wondered if perhaps there might be something wrong with Elias's memory. "I like children, Elias, and if the world weren't so overpopulated, I might even think about having one, but I just . . . can't compromise myself like that ethically. I thought you understood."

"When you say stuff like that, you know what I hear? I hear good old-fashioned fear. That's what I hear. It's our biological imperative to repopulate the race."

"Jews aren't a race," she pointed out sternly. "It's that kind of thinking that ended in the murder of millions, don't forget."

"Why are you keeping such a stranglehold on your ovaries? Don't you love me? Don't I deserve a bundle of naches?"

Upon hearing her own husband invoke the same heavy, guilt-laden sentiment that her dad had used on her mom, who had not wanted a third child, Edith didn't break down into tears or throw one of her tantrums. Instead, she just smiled, surprising even herself, just as she had when she'd ground up the cement and added it to the powdered sugar. A big, fat, toothy smile, a Jacobson special, the

123

kind of smile she had been forced to put on when they had gone to sit for family portraits at Sears, a smile so full of false hope and good cheer that it nearly cracked her face in half to make it. She smiled at Elias, this man who, in increments so small and steady she hadn't even noticed, had turned into her dad, though of course it wasn't Elias who had turned into him but Edith who had turned into her mom, although she didn't recognize it at the time.

She recalled that day again, breaking out into a smile she'd only reserved for that most discomfiting family occasion, when her dad nitpicked them all to death—belittling her mom for her too red lipstick, Jacob for the irregular part in his hair, Mo for his poor choice in suits, and Edith for her weight, which he said ought to have embarrassed her the way it embarrassed him. Then taking it a step further, actually apologizing to the photographer for his daughter, "whom you might not be able to fit all of in the frame," he said, laughing. One moment out of a lifetime, yet how this moment informed the rest of her childhood, how she grew into the kind of girl who ate her feelings, then into the kind of woman who starved that little girl to death.

Elias, who was cleverer than her dad, however, rarely threatened her, which was why his threat that night was so disconcerting, as if her dad were speaking through him, reaching out through the vast distance that separated them. She could almost feel his fingers around her throat, his hot breath in her ear, scolding her again for not giving Elias a child.

No, Elias was nothing like her dad, for he never raised his voice or insulted her cooking or called her a stupid, dumb cunt. Instead, he simply took things from her—first the backyard, then the addition itself, which she ended up ceding to him rather than arguing over its purpose, then her car, because his just stopped running one day—until Edith sank into a definitive privation, both physically and spiritually. She walked the three miles to and from teaching her classes at Emory, telling herself it was good exercise, that he was doing her a favor, and she avoided the addition, which, instead of becoming the new master bedroom or even a screening room, he had turned into a shrine to and storehouse for his *Star Wars* collectibles and memorabilia. It was the brightest and cheeriest room in the house and he covered the multiple windows with heavy curtains to keep the sun from bleaching his posters and vandalized the beautiful cedar-paneled walls with oversize display cabinets for his figurines and accessories: the *Millennium Falcon,* TIE- and X-Wing Fighters, Darth Vader's Star Destroyer, and Jabba the Hutt's Sail Barge. From the ceiling, he hung a light in the shape of a Death Star and laid down a strange sort of spongy, rubbery flooring over the hardwood meant to imitate the mouth of the Exogorth into which the *Millennium Falcon* had flown. It was his room, and she let him do with it as he pleased, giving this to him because he was hers and she his—because, contrary to what her dad might think of her, she had enough love and compassion inside her for an entire household of his needy, imaginary grandchildren and for her one real, honest-to-goodness husband.

Lincoln Boulevard became the Pacific Coast Highway and Edith took it, following the coastline with its fantastical lines and curling motions, rolling out to her left, the water glistening like spun sugar under the sun. Another typically beautiful day in L.A. and her heart quickened a little at the thought of the talk she was to give later that afternoon at Pomona, then the reception to follow at which she would mingle with some of her field's leading luminaries, all of them gathering on this Good Friday to discuss the future of ethics and its role in the academy and the world. She drove from memory and took a right onto Topanga Canyon Boulevard, thinking about the last time she'd made this drive—just last year when she visited Mo and Pandora during her spring break.

By then, the reality show had already been canceled, which meant no more waivers to sign, no more worrying about how she looked every minute, and, most wonderful of all, no more irritating cameramen hovering around, waiting to catch her in an indecent act, saying or doing the wrong thing for all of America to see, judge, and comment upon. She had not liked having to involve herself in this whimsy of her brother's, his desperate attempt to resuscitate his unresponsive career, but to see her beloved nephews she'd had no other choice. She was happy when the show finally got canceled and told Mo as much, which pissed him off and produced a few days of pouting and bad blood. It wasn't that she begrudged him his desire to remain relevant as an actor, but she did begrudge him and Pandora their avaricious, pathological need to rub what they had in her face. And not just in her face but also in America's, in all the faces of all those people who were less fortunate, unhappily married, sadly childless, and wholly discontented with their lives. Family wasn't everything, as she had come to learn, and besides, she had to question her brother's motives even further, wondering how ethical it was to put his kids on display and open them up to heartbreaking criticism from other kids and what she had feared most, bone- and soul-crushing anti-Semitism—the vandalized mezuzah, the swastikas sprayed across the trips' lockers, the death threats.

It was back, this inevitable wave of intolerance for and hatred of the Jews. Yet this time it seemed all the more malevolent, for it came with a modern-day historical precedent, a cautionary tale, something to point to and to say, *Kill the Jews again, and this time the world dies with them.* No, this morning's episode was not her first time at the anti-Semitic rodeo, and she knew with sadness that it would not be her last. What she did know was that they were no longer safe anywhere, not even here in the United States, and this was yet another reason she was happy for the demise of *The Jacob-SONS.* Why give evil a map to your house, open the door, and invite it in for football and beer?

She admired and envied Jacob his tenacity and fortitude to remain off camera, a Jacobson glyph, the veritable Herculean strength it had taken him to say no to Mo and by extension to their dad, who spoke unflatteringly about Jacob on camera, dismissing him as "our wayward third-born." Their dad took it as a great, smiting slight,

Jacob's glaring absence reflecting poorly on the family and, worse, on him as a father. She hoped for Jacob's sake that he'd never seen any of those episodes.

Out of all of them, Edith respected her little brother the most, for he was his own person, the world and everyone in it be damned. She was thrilled he'd brought Dietrich and that she'd be able to meet him at last, though she had to wonder if Jacob wasn't in over his head just a little. It couldn't have been easy living in Berlin among the Germans these days, and if what he had told her about the Krause family were true, then she wasn't sure how long she'd be able to stay quiet. She understood his impulse to bring Dietrich along, yet she also worried that bringing him along might cause undue tension.

Edith's phone gonged again: another Scrabble notification from TBS1946, who had made his move, playing ABOUT for thirty-eight points. She was falling behind, which wouldn't have bothered her as much as it did were it not for the old, heretofore forgotten competitiveness that it stirred in her, the likes of which she hadn't experienced in ages. It was undeniable and crept up on her, just as her feelings for Sheik had crept up on her when they'd both been grad students, she at Georgetown, he at George Mason, where he was getting his MFA in creative writing. They lived only a few blocks apart—he and his wife in a brownstone on Swann Street, she with a roommate on 14th and T Streets in a moldy, dimly lit two-bedroom basement apartment—and had met because his wife had responded to the ad she'd placed in the *Washington City Paper:* Experienced dog walker for hire! Edith had a soft spot for dogs and anyone who owned and loved man's furry best friend. It was a perfect way for her to earn some extra cash while she put herself through school, she told Sheik's wife in the couple's backyard, where she and Edith sat under a blossoming cherry tree, while Tatiana and Sheik's toddler played in his little sandbox and Edith got acquainted with the three black pugs, Ernie, Trudy, and Frank, named for Hemingway, Stein, and Fitzgerald.

"I would have named them Wynken, Blynken, and Nod, but I didn't have the chance," Tatiana said, laughing. "It's okay. They're Sheik's dogs. They just inherited me."

"Oh, no, they're lovely names," Edith said, thinking of her grandparents while she scratched the dogs' ears, the pugs snorting with pleasure. "My grandparents had a little gray poodle named Tikkun. My aunt Shana named her," and for the first time in ages, she thought about this aunt of hers whom she'd never met, who'd died six days before Mo was born. "She was the apple of my grandparents' eyes."

"I'm sure she was," Tatiana replied, though Edith had been referring to Shana, dead at twenty-three, when she and her fiancé got into a head-on collision that threw her through the windshield. She hadn't died instantly, though, according to Edith's dad, who never spoke about her, but suffered an aneurysm ten days later. So for ten days the family swelled with hope, for Shana seemed to be making a full recovery, her broken clavicle aside. She had been walking around without knowing what was coming. "Sheik should be home from soccer soon. He coaches an inner-city league for boys in Southwest, near the Navy Yard."

This impressed Edith, for when she had accepted Georgetown's offer and begun looking for an apartment in earnest, one of her fellow colleagues had suggested that she stay out of D.C.'s other three quadrants—SW, SE, NE—and settle only in NW, or in Georgetown proper. She had taken his advice and settled in NW, though her neighborhood back then—the U Street Corridor—was just beginning to gentrify and was still pretty sketchy, a mash-up of immigrants and working class living beside the more affluent. She never once felt unsafe, though, for she had Dupont Circle within walking and biking distance and the Jewish Community Center, where she volunteered some of her time, just seven minutes away.

She liked D.C., catching the Capitol in the distance on rainy nights, the monuments rising into the night sky, the vast greenery of Rock Creek Park, the winding Potomac River, and how easy it was to get around on the space-age Metro, which went virtually every-where she needed or wanted to go, except, of course, to Georgetown, which didn't actually bother her because she was close enough to bike it. She had no need for a car and had sold hers the second she could, happy to liberate herself from her dependency on oil and do her tiny part for the environment. She loved her bike and went every-where on it, even in the rain and snow, and found herself on more than one occasion marveling at the centrifugal forces that caught her in one of the city's many looping traffic circles and spat her out, surprising her by redirecting her course. She was twenty-two, a year younger than her aunt had been when she'd died, and chock-full of curiosity, though even back then she had moments of extreme doubt and darkness, when bits of days fell away into nothing and she couldn't pull herself out of bed. These episodes were rare and didn't last long, not hard to shrug off when put into context—the pressures of her studies, to excel and achieve and forge a name for herself within the academy, and compounding all of this the added pressure of spinning the straw of acquaintanceship into the golden fibers of friendship, of finding an appropriate mate, of making her parents proud. And also—not to fall into old patterns of bad behav-ior, not to binge-eat, then starve herself, not to get into a cycle of privation and excess, but to toe a moderate line between the two. To live an ethical life on all levels, to become a new voice of reason and courage and to root out the older, wearier voices of irrationality and fear—this was her most solemn vow, and her most chief concern.

Edith and Tatiana finished up their business, Edith agreeing to walk the dogs three times a week, then Tatiana showed her to the front door, saying she'd be in touch to finalize the arrangements and to hand over the key to the house. Edith stepped out the door and was making her way down the stoop when a tall, darkly handsome man with long, tan limbs, dressed in soccer gear and clutching a soc-cer ball, appeared on the sidewalk. He had thick dreadlocks falling from his head and down his angular, square face. He was a few years older than she, and she knew without having to be told that this was

Sheik Cohen, husband of Tatiana and father of both the toddler and the pugs—but even so, she pretended surprise when he offered his hand and said, "I'm Sheik. You must be Edith," his thick, muscular arms wrapped around the ball, his head cocked at an angle, which made it look as if the dreadlocks, suddenly too heavy to bear, were dragging it down.

"Pleased to meet you," she said, blushing, turning away from him before he saw the lust in her eyes. "You have a lovely home."

"Thanks," he replied. "So what did you think of our three canine kids? Quite a handful, huh."

She spun around to respond just as he was moving past her up the stoop, and her elbow accidentally collided with his mouth, the ball falling out of his arms and bouncing away. Without looking, she sprang after it, paying no attention to traffic, which came to a screeching stop a few inches from where she was standing in the middle of the street. Swann Street, which was her favorite street in all of D.C., she told Sheik later, after she stopped shaking, returned the ball, and apologized again for bloodying his lip.

"Don't worry about it. I'll just tell Tatiana I dove for the ball and stopped the other team from scoring."

"I'd definitely appreciate that. I wouldn't want her to hate me," she said. "By the way, did you win?"

"We always win," he said, smiling, his straight, white teeth smeared pink with blood.

After they said good-bye, Edith crossed the street but did not leave right away. She lingered on the sidewalk, feeling dizzy and ensorcelled, aglow with the irradiation of a thousand different emotions, a flux of light and dark, warmth and cold, hatred and love, sorrow and joy, all of these allying and waging war within her simultaneously. She'd never experienced anything like it, as if the gentle hand of God and the spindly finger of death had touched her at once. And even as she finally roused herself and departed, leaving her place behind the tree and heading for home, she understood that all of this had more to do with Tatiana and less to do with

Sheik, whose dogs, she now understood, she would not be walking, although she could have definitely used the money.

Switching on the radio, Edith flipped through the stations and tried to locate KJEW, for she'd just remembered the satellite office they kept at Pomona, which was going to do an interview with her and eventually air it, and her talk, in tandem. She couldn't find KJEW, but she did end up pausing on NPR to listen to the last few minutes of *Fresh Air* with Terry Gross, who was still going strong as ever. As if it were just yesterday, she recalled when Sheik had been a guest on the show and how surprised she'd been to hear him all the way in Atlanta.

She and Elias had been driving to meet some friends for dinner and there he was, discussing his novel, which had just won some huge international literary prize, Edith going still with discomfort, the sound of him filling her with agony. She did not dare move or change the channel, for Elias loved *Fresh Air* and would not have taken her interrupting it lightly. When he'd brought up her acquaintanceship with Sheik—that's how she'd taken to thinking of him, merely as an acquaintance she'd briefly known in a past life—she'd wanted to ask him how he knew about it but didn't. But then it didn't seem to matter, for he'd mentioned Sheik just that one time, during the construction on the house in North Druid Hills, and hadn't ever broached the subject of him again. It was Edith's hope that that night Elias had forgotten all about him, that they'd listen to the interview without consequence and then she'd reach out and casually change the channel. Sitting beside Elias without moving or breathing, she'd listened to Sheik go on and on about how startled he'd been to learn he'd won the prize, that he had no idea it came with such a sizable cash award—two hundred thousand dollars to do with as he pleased. It was then that she'd let out her breath and scoffed, whispering without meaning to, "Like he even needs the money," then had fallen silent again, praying that Elias, who had been concentrating on the road, hadn't heard her, or that if he had, wouldn't question her about it.

And he hadn't, not then anyway. It would take another few months of talking around things, of fighting, of trying again, of giving up, of trying once more, before he finally asked her point-blank about the comment she'd made in the car. "Sheik Cohen," he said one night from the doorway of the addition, his playpen, as she'd come to refer to it, first merely to herself, then to her friends, then to him as well. "I finally finished that book of his. The one that won that big literary award." He was crying, at least that's what it looked like to Edith, who remained just outside the room, her back and hands pressed against the wall, her spine as rigid and straight as it had ever been, every muscle tensed, and her breath quick and shallow, as if she were about to pounce, to rip out his tongue before he said another word. "Now I understand why you were so coy when I brought him up and never wanted to talk about him. You were . . . involved with him, or whatever you want to call it, and then I came along? Is that it, Edith? I was the schmucky booby prize? Am I getting the timing of that right?" he faltered, accusing, wiping his eyes. "You're the dog walker from the book, aren't you? Is any of it true? Any of those things he wrote? Poisoning the dogs and writing his wife all those sick, threatening emails and notes? Did you stalk their child? Were you obsessed with him?"

She pressed herself harder against the wall, until she imagined she could feel the pulse of the house itself, a slow, dying pulse to match the slow, dying pulse of her marriage.

"It's fiction, Elias. A novel. He embellished. It's what he does," she said. "I couldn't stop him from writing what he wrote. He never liked me. It was his revenge."

"For what, though? What did you do to him?" he asked.

Edith pulled up to Mo's house still in a state of remembering, all of the good times, all of the bad, and all of the forgotten moments in between. There had been so much good and it had gone on for years, until that moment in Atlanta when she heard Sheik's voice on the radio, broadcasting his story for anyone to hear and discover, then it all fell to pieces. She never saw Sheik again, but hearing his voice, well, that had been enough. She couldn't stop herself from loving whom she loved any more than Elias could stop himself from falling out of love with her. Which is what happened, a glacially slow progression of withdrawals on his end that resulted in a bankruptcy on hers.

She parked the van in the curve of the cul-de-sac, understanding that once she stepped through that salsa-red front door and took her place among her family, she would have to keep a careful watch over what she said and how she said it. She would have to arm herself with smiles, her best and only defense against a Jacobson onslaught. And as she climbed out of the van, she had to remind herself again why she was there in L.A.—to give her talk, to check on her mom and dad, and to knock some sense into her brothers, whom she loved but who she was certain had lost their minds. They were not murderers, and she was not about to let them turn her into one, either. She was Dr. Edith Jacobson Plunkett, a professor of ethics, with a CV as long as Ephraim's dick, and if nothing else, they had to respect her position in the world, how hard she'd fought to get where she was—and how hard she was fighting to keep her life from unraveling any further.

Von Trapp Lane was still and silent, everyone off at work, Edith imagined, making her way up the walk and taking in the state of the lawn, which looked as if someone had started to cut it, then pooped out and gave up. Having lived in real cities like Boston and D.C. before moving south to Atlanta, which was not a real city at all, in her estimation, just a concatenation of villages and good old-fashioned sprawl, she had cared little about lawns or their magical, rigorous upkeep—until they'd moved into the house with its sumptuous, flowering backyard. Truth be told, Edith despised anyone with a lawn who farmed out the maintenance of it to others, namely to migrant workers in big pickup trucks. This practice was rampant in Atlanta, where, on any given spring, summer, or fall morning, the air was choked with the obnoxious, whiny cry of one or more leaf blowers, the bêtes noires of her existence, which inevitably woke her up and cast a pall over the rest of her day. She hated the damn contraptions, which accounted for far more noise pollution than any amount of Boston or D.C. traffic ever could and released the same harmful emissions into the air. When had the rake become a relic and her fellow citizens so lazy?

Though everyone, including the pundits and talking heads she admired, seemed to believe that an explosion in population was the leading factor in western civilization's decline, Edith herself opined that the advent of the leaf blower had heralded its downfall. The leaf blower, and the field of nanotechnology, which had made great strides in being able to cure a whole host of cancers as well as the virus that caused AIDS. People were simply living longer, into their hundreds, thanks in large part to continued governmental investiture in the multitrillion-dollar pharmaceutical industry—the same industry that still had not been able to find a cause or a cure for her mom's illness.

Edith also took note of the house, which she did every time she visited, because it was lavish and beautiful and put her own little carriage house to shame. Though she made a decent salary at Emory and could have afforded a grander place, she did not get the kind of monetary assistance from her parents that Mo did. Sure, her dad had helped her out from time to time when she was in a bind, but it was nothing compared to Mo's supposed need—seven mouths to feed, a mortgage, private-school tuitions. Still, it hurt her to know that her dad, who controlled the purse strings, viewed her life as less valuable than Mo's simply because she was unmarried and childless. Granted, it was Jacob who really got shafted, for she knew her dad barely even registered him as a living, sentient being, preferring to keep him at arm's length, seeing his homosexuality as a kind of affliction rather than a way of life. Jacob had told her he had neither asked for nor received a dime from her parents in years. Which was probably for the best, because it meant that he was not beholden to them at all.

She pushed on the door and it gave way, then she was in the vestibule, marveling again at the modern decor, the tasteful elegance of what her mom and dad had helped Mo and Pandora afford. A new, giant flat-screen TV graced the far wall, its shiny black surface reflecting her movements through the large, spacious room. She waited with both excitement and dread to be set upon by her family, who didn't appear, even after she called out again, louder this time.

"Where the hell is everyone?" she asked the indifferent air.

Perplexed, she'd gotten out her phone to text Mo when she heard a squeak behind her and turned to see her mom wheeling herself out of the guest room. The sight of her in the chair, the green tank of oxygen resting in her lap, nearly brought Edith to her knees. She hadn't seen her in over a year and in that time her mom had grown frailer and more faded, as if she were becoming a ghost right before Edith's eyes.

"My little girl." Her mom smiled, throwing her hands out in front of her, upsetting the tank, which slipped out of her lap. It landed with a crash on the hardwood floor, then rolled away and yanked the tubes out of her nose, pitching her forward out of the chair. Edith was at her side in a shot, lifting her back into the chair, then grabbing the heavy tank and settling it in her arms, like a newborn infant. "Pandora's at boot camp, Mo's at an audition, and Jacob and his German friend went to Fleischmann's Market just up the road. They should all be home soon," her mom said after she was breathing more normally again.

"And Daddy?" she asked, alarmed at how they'd all gone off and left her alone.

"He's been fiddling around with the lawn mower all morning," her mom said. "You know your father. Can't sit still for a second."

"How are you feeling, Ma?" Edith asked, still somewhat in shock at seeing her in the wheelchair.

"Don't worry, dear," she soothed. "I can still walk. It just takes so much out of me."

"So the meds aren't working?" Edith asked.

"Roz, you know what that idiot did? He didn't leave the gas can, which means I have to run up to Exxon myself." This was her dad, who suddenly appeared, oblivious to Edith's presence.

"Honey, Edith's here," her mom said, and that's when her dad finally registered her.

"Hi, Daddy," she exclaimed, going up to him and giving him a long hug.

"That your van I saw drive up, Eddie?" he asked as she let him go and stepped away. "I thought it might belong to the city of Calabasas."

"Why the city of Calabasas?" she asked.

"Because of that dimwit brother of yours," he snorted.

"Jacob ran over an ostrich," her mom explained, "and your father called the city this morning to have them come out and take it away."

"Not an ostrich, Roz. A peacock," her dad corrected her gently, without any hint of his usual aggression and self-righteousness, which alarmed Edith for reasons altogether different from her previous reasons for alarm.

"Even when I was a girl, I always got them confused." Her mom laughed.

"How did Jacob kill a peacock?" she asked.

"You'll have to ask the genius when he gets back with Marlene Dietrich."

"Honey, you're terrible," her mom said. "Don't you dare say that in front of Jacob."

"Why? You think it'll offend the German? I think not, my lovely Roz," he said sweetly, making her mom giggle like the fresh-faced Catholic schoolgirl she had been in a different life.

What the hell is going on around here? Edith wondered, feeling dizzy with relief and warm with suspicion, for even at his best, she had never seen him act this nice to his wife. She thought for a moment that she'd come to the wrong house, that body snatchers had stolen him away in the night and replaced her usually cantankerous, ill-tempered daddy with this replica, who looked and sounded like him but wasn't. An adult changeling. Had she stepped into Jacob's last play, in which this very thing had happened? For her mom's sake, she didn't want it to be an act, yet she knew her dad, perhaps better than any of them, and now she understood that on top of keeping a careful watch on herself, she would also have to keep a careful watch on him, realizing that if any of them were going to make it out of this weekend alive, it was going to be up to her.

Edith left her parents kibitzing and went out to the van to grab her suitcase. While she was wrestling it to the ground, her phone gonged again—another nudge from TBS1946. *My, but you are impatient,* she thought, leaning into the dark, empty cargo hold to shade her phone's screen from the sun so that she could get a look at the word he'd played, only to realize that the hold was not as empty as it appeared, for lying in one of the wheel wells was what looked like a used syringe. The sight of it made her skin crawl and raised goose bumps all over her arms. She straightened up and quickly slid the door shut, hurrying with the suitcase through the grass and into the house, trying to knock the image of the syringe out of her mind by picturing Ephraim, naked and asleep, in her bed. The ploy worked and soon enough Edith was able to concentrate her attention on her tiles, laying down the eight-letter word COLOSSAL, using the O in ABOUT and all of her letters, to make a bingo. Her phone went wild, lighting up with all kinds of digital pyrotechnics and emitting all kinds of delightful sounds.

She spotted her parents in the backyard, her dad pushing her mom in the chair. It looked to her as if he were angry, his face distorted under the morning sun, this face she had come to loathe and love—sometimes more the former than the latter, she had to admit. She approached the wall of glass and sure enough she could hear him blustering, pointing at the barbecue for some reason, screaming about Mo. The angrier he got, the faster he pushed the chair, until he was directly at the lip of the pool, her mom's feet dangling off the side. Edith stepped so close to the glass that her breath fogged it up. As her dad tilted the chair back and spun it around, she let out a gasp, for she'd caught the look on her mom's face, a look she wouldn't be able to soon forget—the sudden terror in her mom's eyes that gave way to a peaceful, resigned calm, as if she understood that it could not, would not, happen any other way than this.

It was over in a matter of seconds, then her dad was pushing her along the smooth flagstone path that ran through the backyard, his own face drawn, full of its own terror and resigned calm. She watched them for another few moments before abandoning the wall of glass and struggling to get her suitcase upstairs and into the guest room, which seemed to be already occupied. *Fuck me and the duck I rode in on,* she thought.

After slumping down on the bed, Edith got out her phone and tapped out a message to Ephraim, whom she'd promised herself she wasn't going to contact.

I arrived in L.A. safely, got called a kike bitch on the way to pick up my rental car, but the reservation had been made for yesterday (on purpose) and so I have to drive around in a cargo van, the last renter of which I'm sure was a murdering drug addict, who left a syringe behind. My dad's acting strangely and my poor mom looks haggard and has been confined to a wheelchair, though I don't know if she's in it against her will or not. The room I normally stay in when I visit has been given away to my gay younger brother and his German lover, who I'm sure after four days of being around us will leave an anti-Semite (if he isn't one already), thanks in large part to my older brother and dad, who hate Germany and all things German with a blinding passion. How's your day going? Do you miss me yet? EJPxo

Edith thought long and hard about sending this text to her neighbor, with whom she'd been sleeping for only three months. Thought long and hard about what she'd witnessed between her parents just moments ago in the backyard. What was she to believe she actually saw? Certainly not the incomprehensible horror that she was imagining at the moment, nothing like that from the man who'd given her life, whom she'd called her daddy for forty years. And yet there were her eyes, which had not betrayed her, and her intuition, which she usually trusted. But how was she to trust in this when it was simply too big and too gruesome?

Erasing everything except the last two lines of the message, she sent it to Ephraim, who responded a few seconds later with a smiley face in black sunglasses. She supposed he was trying to be cute, that the smiley, sunglasses-wearing emoji represented her, and though she appreciated the gesture, it still flabbergasted and disappointed her, then began to gnaw at her when she realized that this was going to be the extent of his reply. Seriously, he couldn't do better than that?

She got up and went to the window, looking out at the other houses on Von Trapp Lane, noting with dread the sudden arrival of a big pickup truck pulling a flatbed trailer, which was full of all kinds of power tools and landscaping apparatuses—two lawn mowers, an industrial-strength power saw, giant pruning shears, and a couple of leaf blowers. *The scourge of the modern world,* she thought, her heart sinking when three men jumped out of the truck and unloaded the trailer, first the mowers, then the saw, then the pièce de résistance, the infernal leaf blowers, which two of the cigarette-smoking men started up immediately, even before a single blade of grass had been cut.

Turning away from the window before she did something impulsive, like open it, lean out, and scream a nasty string of expletives at them, Edith's eyes fell on the nightstand and the pair of neon-orange earplugs perched atop it. They looked remarkably like candy corn and had the effect of whisking her back to a long-ago Halloween night, circa 1988, when she was just six years old and didn't want to put on the costume her mom had chosen for her—a witch's outfit replete with a warty nose and all, which Edith was convinced her mom had picked out only to spite her, because she was sure her mom thought it reflected her true nature. Reluctantly, Edith slipped the costume on, to her mother's great delight, which only made Edith cringe and withdraw, eventually locking herself in the bathroom and weeping hysterically until her dad intervened. He knocked on the door, and when Edith finally allowed him to enter, she told him that she hated the costume and didn't want to be seen in it and could she please stay home with him, please?

"Leave her with me," he said to her mom, who left the house shortly thereafter with Mo and Jacob to take them trick-or-treating.

Edith sulked in her room, where she took a pair of scissors to the costume and shredded it, stashing it in her closet so that her mom would naturally find it. She paced the carpet, fingers balled into fists, muttering under her breath what she would do to her mom if indeed Edith had been a real witch—turn her into a zombie; make her do her every bidding, from Edith's homework to her stupid chores; set her on fire and watch her skin melt away until she was nothing but bones, which Edith would grind up to use in all kinds of potions against her enemies, all the kids who taunted her for having red hair, for being Jewish—one potion to blind them, another to cleave their tongues and make them sprout horns, as they often accused her of having. A potion to help them see clearly that the Jews had nothing to do with killing Christ or with murdering babies to drain them of blood for making matzo. How dumb and gullible these enemies of hers were! She blamed it all on her mom, who'd volunteered to educate her class on Judaism, although she wasn't a true-blooded Jew, merely a convert, and not a particularly good one at that—she knew only a little Hebrew, enough to get by, at least enough to join in the recitation of the Kiddush, the Sabbath blessings over the wine, the bread, and the candles, though it was usually Edith who liked to do the prayers to impress her daddy. She was his Bride of the Sabbath, he said, which made her extraordinarily happy, happier still to know that she showed up her mom.

It was getting dark out when her dad knocked on her door and asked Edith if she wouldn't mind helping him with an important task. They went down to the den. "I don't know about you, but I like it when it's just you and me," he said, patting the seat beside him. "What a stupid costume your mom picked out for you. She can be an idiot sometimes, can't she?" Hearing this made her feel closer to him while at the same time it also made her feel crummy and want to hit him, because she didn't think it was a nice thing for him to say about his wife.

"It . . . it wasn't that bad, I guess," Edith said, sitting down beside him.

"What I mean is, if anyone's a witch, it's her, not you," he said. "I look at your mom sometimes and think she must have cast a spell on me, because I just don't think she deserves me. Does that make sense?" Edith said that it did, although it didn't, not at all. "You know what? It's good you didn't put that costume on because then you would've ended up just like her. Promise me you won't tell her I told you, but late at night when she thinks we're all asleep, she reaches into the back of her closet, past her dresses and shoes, where she keeps her own witch's outfit, and she puts it on, grabs her broomstick, and flies all over town, turning girls and boys into snakes and frogs."

"Daddy, it's not nice to lie," Edith said sternly, although she was giggling, which hid her discomfort and belied her fright, for what little girl wanted to hear about her mom being a bona fide witch?

"What makes you think I'm telling a lie?" he asked as he handed her the remote control, then lifted up the pillow to reveal a bowl of candy corn nestled in his lap. Edith grinned and reached into the bowl, grabbing a handful of candy corn, then aimed the remote at the TV, filling the screen with *It's the Great Pumpkin, Charlie Brown*. "Before we watch it, you have to promise me you'll never go snooping in your mom's closet. If she ever found out I told you who she truly is, she'd be incredibly angry at your daddy and banish me to some deserted island, where I'd have to live all alone and never see you again. You wouldn't want that, would you, Edith?" No, she wouldn't want anything like that. "Then be my good girl and keep Mommy's secret." She said that she would forever and ever, until death did them part. "Thank you, Eddie," her dad said, invoking his pet name for her, which he did sometimes when he was being supersweet.

Eddie. How long it had been since she'd thought twice about that night, thought twice about that absurd nickname. Eddie. As if she were a boy, as if she had ever needed another reason to hate herself and her place in the world—a boy's name, not a girl's, a complete disregard for who she was, his daughter, not his son, and how she'd once loved hearing him use it, though today, for whatever reason, it had sounded different to her, passing forcibly from his lips without the hint of warmth, as if he were passing a kidney stone instead. She recalled how she'd come home for the holidays after her first semester at Harvard and finally found the courage to ask her dad to stop masculinizing her and calling her Eddie, especially in front of a boyfriend she might bring home. He'd stared at her as if she'd just swatted him across the face. "You going to give me a lecture on that women's lib crap like your mom used to?" he asked. "I thought you were better and more evolved than that. I thought you and I had a deal." His response surprised her, for she'd had no idea the deal had come with strings. "Speaking of boyfriends, your mom and I were beginning to worry you might like carpet munching instead."

"Funny, because Mo and I were thinking the exact opposite of you," she said, leaving Jacob out of it, because he still lived at home.

"What's that supposed to mean?" he asked.

"Nothing, Daddy," she said. "It doesn't mean a thing. Forget I said anything."

On some level, she had to laugh at him, at the way he barreled and caromed and careened his way through the world, bouncing off its sharp edges, never admitting any wrongdoing or that he was bleeding from the gashes those sharp edges left in his sides. In this way, his only daughter felt extremely sorry for him, seeing him as just another old man terrified of losing his wife. She adored her mom, though she had awakened to this slowly, after she'd moved out of the house and began to open up to her friends about her home life. How her dad had spoken so hostilely to her mom and to her brothers, how he had always seemed to favor her, Edith, over them. "He doted on me," she'd once proudly announced to her freshman roommate. Yet the more she spoke about her childhood, relaying both good and bad memories, the more she began to wonder about the sincerity of her dad's adoration.

There were months during her freshman year, she remembered, when she found herself unexpectedly missing her mother. She would call home, cringing whenever her father answered, yet she spoke to him anyway, pleasantly if hurriedly, before asking him to pass the phone to her mom, whom now, from a distance, she'd begun to see as a warm and sympathetic ear. She felt robbed, she told Elias later on one of their first dates, resenting her dad for stealing her mom away from her, for feeding Edith's fears and corrupting what might have been an easy, natural friendship and love between mother and daughter. Edith couldn't blame him entirely, though, for had she not loved him nearly as much, she might not have been as easily persuaded to turn her mom into such a sinister presence.

Edith was not Mo or Jacob, both of whom had an indefatigable reservoir of love for their mother. Yet in the waning hours and days of her mom's life, Edith thought that her being there for Passover might act as a palliative for her mom, a way for Edith to make up for mishandling her girlhood. More than anything, though, being around her family again only brought to light what she'd feared for years—that she'd chosen the wrong parent to love and emulate.

That said, Edith still found it hard not to begrudge her mom some of the mistakes she'd made in her own life and was glad not to have inherited her mom's one seemingly tragic flaw—a dogged pleasantness that clouded her ability to see things clearly, for unlike Edith her mom found the good in everyone and in all situations, no matter how awful both were. She'd had one defining moment to turn that same doting pleasantness inward, to alter the terrain of the future, if not for herself, then for her brood, her boys specifically, yet on that ill-fated road trip, which ended at Point Dume, she climbed

143

right back into the car and Edith had known instinctively that noth-ing would come of any of it. She knew her mom loved her dad, but even more than that, she knew her mom could not possibly give up her creature comforts or the pride she took in being a doctor's wife. So her dad would stay, he would be forgiven, and the pleasant walls of her mom's pleasant life would go up again, protecting her from him. Her mom had done her best to build this wall around them, her children, as well, yet with far less success, Edith thought, though the thought wasn't bitter, just bittersweet.

She gently dragged her suitcase to the door of the guest room, this suitcase that matched the one sitting on top of the low-slung bureau in the corner, the same model of suitcase Mo also owned and had stashed in the attic—matching luggage, a present to them all from their parents on Chanukah a few years ago. And before she knew what she was doing, Edith switched the suitcases out, leaving hers and taking Jacob's, a practical joke she knew he'd find amusing. Besides, the room ought to have been hers. She still wasn't convinced Mo hadn't given Jacob preferential treatment, which shouldn't have bothered her but did, for it meant that she'd have to bunk with her parents, just like she had to do when they went on those regrettable car trips, Mo and Jacob getting to share a room while she'd been stuck on a cot or a sofa. *Look, Invisible Girl to the rescue again,* she thought, grabbing from her suitcase the dress and heels she was going to wear to Pomona, then zipping it back up.

She rolled Jacob's suitcase, which was far lighter than hers, across the floor and carried it down the stairs, almost crashing into a tall, thin, blond mustachioed hipster wearing cut-off jeans, a tight, sky-blue T-shirt that said APPLEBEE'S OR BUST across it, red suspenders, and lace-up black Doc Martens, looking very much as if he'd just stepped out of the Stonewall Inn in Greenwich Village, circa 1973 or 2013, she couldn't tell the difference anymore. He was eating a croissant while simultaneously reading a book, which he held up to his face and didn't see Edith, who had to sidestep out of his way. He seemed to be in a hurry to get upstairs and away from Jacob, who was in hot pursuit.

"So that's it? The great statesman, Dietrich Krause, has spoken and there's nothing else to be said?" he said, pausing momentarily to hug her before following his friend up the stairs and out of sight.

Edith rolled the suitcase into the guest room and left it—wouldn't you just know?—beside the rollaway, already set up, imagining the fun she'd have trying to get to sleep, with her mom in the bed suffocating to death and her dad alternating between farting and snoring. She wished for Ephraim, that she'd asked him to come with her, envying Jacob his friend, though not envying the friend's mustache, which she found laughable. That, and his suspenders, but perhaps those were fashionable in Berlin as well? And what was with his forehead and that reddish welt? A zit he tried to cover up?

She knew nothing about fashion except for what she saw of it in Atlanta, which wasn't all that impressive. In the beginning, Edith tried her best to find all that was beautiful and interesting about her home, yet somewhere around year four, she realized she wasn't quite cut out to live in the south and certainly not in Atlanta, which, she came to understand, was nothing more than a fraternity- and sorority-infested overgrown beach town without the beach. Sometimes, though, she wondered if her real issue stemmed not from the place but with how she had been welcomed at Emory; even now, as she stepped out of the room, which smelled oddly of camphor and smelly socks, she thought about Jocelyn and the boxes. Jocelyn with her curly white chin hairs and obsession with *The Lord of the Rings,* with the odd assortment of moles on her face, who was not a lesbian, as Edith had assumed, but married to an actual man, not an imaginary one, as Edith had also assumed, who had been born sitting at her desk and was the true heart and soul of the ethics and religion department. The same Jocelyn who congratulated her in an email when she'd gotten the position at Emory, then had no recollection of who Edith was, even after she wandered into Jocelyn's office and announced herself, having just driven all the way from D.C., freshly married and ready to rumble. Granted, it was the end of summer and three months had gone by between that welcome email and her arrival, but still Edith found herself having to explain who she was all over again, until Jocelyn finally put it all together, the naked bulb of her face lighting up momentarily with recognition before darkening again and burning out completely.

"Then those must belong to you," she said, pointing at the eight boxes, which were stacked in the middle of the small, cramped room. "I'll have them delivered to your office lickety-split."

"And by lickety-split, she meant two weeks later, which was fine because Elias and I went to visit my folks in Dallas," she had told Ephraim last night on the way home from an Emory function to which he had escorted her.

"She seemed nice," he'd said. "I was expecting—"

"The bride of Godzilla?" Edith had asked. "No, she's quite affable. Just not to me." She proceeded to tell him about that late-August afternoon, when, for the first time, she unlocked her office, which they'd painted in the meantime, about the sunlight spilling through the window onto the boxes, about how they'd been arranged in four stacks of two and how horrified she was to find that someone had covered one of the boxes with swastikas and graffiti—GO HOME JEW CUNT. GAS ALL KIKES. ADDRESS UNKNOWN: RETURN TO HITLER . . . "I reported it to the head of the department, who apologized profusely and contacted the president of the university, who contacted campus security. Nothing was ever resolved and no one was ever caught, of course. Don't ask me why, but I always suspected Jocelyn. She's the only one who had direct access to my boxes. And, yes, before you start defending her, I'm well aware that any number of people could have done it, from the UPS guy to the campus movers, but that just seems like a stretch. I know I shouldn't have said anything to anybody, but I was new and foolish and told a couple of people over drinks that I thought Jocelyn had done it.

Anyway, it was a stupid, rash thing to accuse her of, though I still think she did it."

She never told her parents, especially not her dad, about the incident, because she knew exactly what he would have said. He'd been quite vocal against her taking the job at Emory in the first place—her dad, whose one big dream, she knew, had been to become a dentist and who'd attended Emory University dental school but had flunked out his first semester, although he'd never not made a passing grade in his life. Julian blamed Emory's history of anti-Semitism—in the '60s, Emory had designated prospective dental-school applicants as Caucasian, Jew, or other and judged them accordingly—though Jacob preferred to believe that rather than flunking out for being a Jew, Julian had flunked out merely because he couldn't hack it. "They're just lucky I never liked sticking my fingers into other people's mouths," her dad had said, "or else I'd sue the hell out of the momzers. You can take that job, but don't come crying to me when something happens. Caveat emptor, Eddie. Caveat emptor."

It was with an incredibly heavy heart that Edith had found herself the victim of the same kind of anti-Semitic sentiment that had ousted her dad and led him to what he claimed was a far more suitable and fulfilling profession in respiratory physiology. The irony of this still left her brothers cold, that he'd spent his entire life studying the mechanics of breathing only to have a wife who couldn't. Her brothers also noted the coincidence of this and pondered the root of their mom's illness, which the doctors said was idiopathic, its origin both uncertain and unclear. Jacob took Edith down a terribly uncomfortable road, saying all sorts of damning things about their dad and what might have led to their mom's ruined state. "He may not be directly responsible, but you can't rule out his peripheral involvement," he said the last time they'd all spoken.

"What are you saying? That he's somehow the cause of it?" she asked. She was sitting in her office at school, the door closed, the lights off, the campus emptied by spring break, going over and over the conversation she'd had with the head of the department about a certain midwestern boy and former student of hers, who was still demanding Edith change his grade and had moved forward in his sexual harassment suit. "If you're saying what I think you're saying, I think I can't hear any more of it. I won't hear any more of it, actually." She nearly hung up before Mo cut in.

"Look, I wasn't going to mention this, but I guess, well, I guess it's time I did," he said. Then he told them a story so utterly outlandish it made even Jacob, the consummate cynic among them, guffaw in disbelief. "You can laugh all you want, but it's totally true. That's what the old man said to me. I have no reason to lie to either of you."

"You realize what you're doing, don't you?" Edith asked, perusing her email history with said former student, wincing at the boy's tetchy, disrespectful replies to her quite assured, quite reasonable explanations as to why she could not change his grade. "You're fishing. You're inventing reasons and filling them with false meaning as a way to justify killing him. So he was mean and nasty. So he treated Ma with disdain. That's always been her problem, not ours, as far as I see it. No, I'm sorry, but wishing him dead and making it happen are two totally different things. Unless, of course, your motives aren't as noble as you claim."

"What the hell is that supposed to mean, Thistle?" Jacob barked. From his tone, it was all too clear and frightening that she'd struck pay dirt.

"Have you even considered the fact that Ma's health won't suddenly and miraculously improve just because he's gone? Or that killing him might even kill her faster? You keep talking about her quality of life, but from where I'm sitting, she has everything she wants and needs."

"Except the most important thing," Jacob argued.

"You mean love," Mo added, his voice tiny, breakable.

"You think he's taking care of her because he loves her, Thistle? Even you can't be that naive or that blind," Jacob spat. "And if what Mo said is true, he's only taking care of her because he doesn't see any way out of it but through, and because he knows that if he doesn't take care of her, he'll lose his hold on her and her money."

"I was wondering when you were going to make this about that." Edith laughed.

"I didn't make it about money," Jacob protested. "Mo did."

"What are you so afraid of, Jacob? That if Ma goes first, he's going to cut you out of the will?" she asked. "Even if he did, Mo and I would still give you your fair share. Isn't that right, Mo?"

"Maybe, maybe not," Mo said.

"Fuck you, Mo," Jacob snapped.

"Boys, boys, boys, I just don't see the good in any of this," she pacified them. "I love you both, but I don't think you've asked yourselves the truly tough questions—like what happens if we get caught? Do you want to spend the rest of your lives in jail for killing a man you hate? Doesn't that seem unwise to you? Doesn't that sort of give him a kind of poetic justice?"

"How many times am I going to have to say this, Edith? We aren't doing it for us, we're doing it for Mom," Jacob said. "You may not love her as much as we do, but you can't sit there and deny that she'd be better off without him, just as we'd have been better off without him."

"She made her bed years ago," Edith said.

"Then we need to unmake it for her," Mo interjected, coming to life. "He's brainwashed her into believing all marriages are unequal and loveless, that all marriages are based on tit for tat, that all marriages work the way his does. Most marriages do not work that way. Mine sure doesn't. You think Pandora would stay around if I ever treated her the way that asshole treats Mom? Hell, no! She'd take my kids away from me, and I'd probably never see them or her again—and I don't like to admit it, but she'd be right."

Edith found herself reluctantly agreeing on this point. She had been married and had treated her husband badly one too many times, all of her lying and obfuscating, all of her withholding, her inability to show genuine affection, genuine remorse, genuine forgiveness. He'd been the one to leave, to file for divorce, not Edith, who would have stayed with him indefinitely. Elias might have taken things from her, but they were only things—a backyard, a room, a car. And if she were truly being honest with herself, she would have seen that he hadn't taken these things from her so much as she'd willingly relinquished them to him. On some level she had known that the parts of herself she couldn't give him freely, like compassion, like love, she had to give to him in other ways.

She came to understand all of this at that precise moment, while standing at the wall of glass in her brother's stunning, many-roomed home. It sickened her to see herself in such a sudden, harsh light, but even worse was that her marriage hadn't fallen apart because she let it but because she let Sheik back into her heart.

Edith hung the dress up and stashed her heels in the hall closet, then, with still a few hours to kill before she had to leave for Pomona, she went out into the backyard for a swim only to discover that the pool was empty. Which made what she'd witnessed earlier between her mom and dad that much more confusing and terrifying—but certainly her dad had only been fooling around, hadn't he?

The last time Edith had visited, she'd spent most of her time in the pool, out of harm's way—harm being Pandora, with whom Edith had never quite found comfortable footing. Having grown up in the Valley, in Thousand Oaks, Pandora Orenstein-Jacobson was everything Edith was not, an alien species of Jew crafted out of Botox and collagen injections, silicone implants, and some of the most luxuriously long blond hair that Edith had ever seen, the color and texture of which, Edith was certain, existed nowhere else but in L.A.

Nieves ran in circles around her, yapping her little head off, then parked herself at the edge of the pool, snarling and snorting, while behind Edith, her dad banged on the glass, motioning for her to come inside. Before she went in, though, she stepped to the edge of the pool and looked down, recoiling in disgust, for on the bottom lay a large white bird, its feathers bloody, its wings fluttering, though she couldn't be sure this wasn't the result of the wind surging over it. She screamed just once, thinking it might draw the attention of someone, her dad, say, who was still tapping on the wall of glass. But no one came. She kneeled beside Nieves and petted the frothing, agitated terrier, trying her best to calm her down, but to no avail. The dog simply wouldn't be consoled and kept running circles around the pool, certain that she was protecting the Jacobson family from an attack of feathers.

Edith went back into the house, passing her dad, and straight into the dining room, where the rest of her family, sans the trips and the twins, who were at school, were gathered at the table, feasting on bagels, lox, and cream cheese, compliments of Jacob and Dietrich, who apparently were not speaking to each other and sat at either end of the long, rectangular table.

"Unless I'm seeing things, the peacock climbed out of Jacob's trunk and is now sunbathing at the bottom of the pool," Edith said.

"Maybe it wanted to go swimming also." Dietrich directed this at Jacob, who ignored him. "Or maybe it just wanted to snatch a tan."

"Catch a tan," Jacob muttered without glancing at Dietrich. "It's 'to catch a tan.'"

"Someone was supposed to call the city this morning and have it removed," Mo said, also directing this at Jacob, who also ignored him, and reached for another piece of lox.

"And someone's children clearly can't be controlled." It was her dad. He stood in the doorway, his face painted with that all-too-familiar, shit-eating smirk of his—the smirk that sunk a thousand ships, as Edith's brothers like to say. The same smirk that Edith found herself wearing at times when she wasn't wearing her mom's vacant smile. "I have an idea. Let's place bets on which one of your little monsters threw it in the pool. My guess would be one of the triplets. What about you, Mo?"

"Julian, please," Pandora protested. "There's no need for you to use that tone."

"Excuse me?" he said. "Your unruly kids dump the decomposing body of a rabies-infested animal into your pool, but there's no need for me to use that tone? Boy, are you going to let your wife talk to me like that?"

"Honey, come sit down over here and have a bagel," her mom said, already reaching for the platter of lox and the tub of cream cheese.

"Not until I get an apology," her dad objected, crossing his arms.

It was time for Invisible Girl to remove her cloak and step out of the shadows before things got seriously ugly and out of hand, yet something inside of Edith refused, wanting to see where this would go and what would happen if she didn't. "Pandora didn't mean anything by it," her mom mollified him. "Did you, Panda?"

"Hey, Dad, maybe you just need to learn how to take a joke," Mo said, glancing over at Jacob and smiling.

This was, of course, the repetition of the same words their dad had used on the boys whenever he teased them and made them cry about getting a bad grade on a test, or not being able to fit into their suits. Jacob smiled back, though he did not lift his eyes from his plate.

"Just whom do you think you're talking to, boy? I'm not one of your faggot actor friends. No offense, Jacob," her dad said. "You see what I mean about him, Roz? The same spoiled ingrate as always."

"Apple, tree," Mo responded.

"Jacob, I will be in that room overhead," Dietrich said, rising. "Mrs. Jacobson, I feel quite sorry for you," and with that, he got up and left the table.

After Dietrich was gone, Edith turned to Jacob and said, "I'll take care of this. You go take care of him." Jacob kissed her on the cheek in thanks, then headed out of the dining room. "Now, Daddy, you and I need to have a little chat."

"It's going to have to wait, Eddie," her dad said, "because your mom and I aren't welcome here."

"Not if you're going to act like a four-year-old," Mo said, spearing a slice of tomato and laying it on top of a heap of salmon and red onion, then taking a large bite. "Ma's always welcome."

"Come on, Roz, let's go pack," her dad huffed.

"Will you people just put a tack in it for one effing second?" Edith said. "Jacob did not fly halfway around the world to be subjected to your bullshit, Daddy, and neither did I. If you can't be nice, maybe you should go. But you can go without Ma, because she's staying."

"Oh, Thistle, that's nice of you, but I couldn't possibly," her mom said.

"You know what? Fuck this and fuck all of you," her dad said, storming out of the room and out of the house, leaving the front door wide open.

Edith was certain her mom would follow him as she always did, but considering her weakened condition, she remained at the table, peering down at her plate. Edith also thought her mom might cry, for this was how she often responded to anything irregular and upsetting—a burst of tears, the effect of which was to produce in her children a terrible sense of inadequacy and guilt. "Let him go," her mom said with a sigh, after Edith got up to close the door and returned. "He didn't handle that very well. But honestly, Mo, he's hurt you didn't thank him for lugging that stupid barbecue with us all the way from Texas. I told him we should just buy you a new one when we got here."

"Um, Ma, I did thank him?" he protested. "What more does he want from me? That I get his name engraved on the damn thing? Besides, I'm pretty sure he slammed the lid on Dexter's hand on purpose. Isn't that right, Pandora?"

This was the first Edith had heard about Dexter's hand, and it alarmed her. "What happened to Dexter?" she asked.

"Her ball-and-chain broke two of his fingers," Mo said, pointing at her mom, who just sat there, stunned by the accusation that her husband, their dad, could have done anything of the kind.

"Oh, Mosey," her mom murmured. "If you believe that, I don't think we have any other choice but to leave."

"You aren't going anywhere," Edith commanded. "And he doesn't believe it, do you, Mo?"

"No, Ma, I suppose I don't," he said hesitantly. "But you better keep an eye on him. I wouldn't want him ending up like that peacock." Which made Edith wonder if that was how it was going to happen, if they'd just make it look like an ordinary accident—another old man slips and falls into a drained pool, breaking his neck. Hadn't this been one of the ghoulish scenarios her brothers had discussed on the phone?

A commotion erupted in the backyard and diverted Edith's attention away from the table. She looked out to find Nieves barking at her dad and her dad barking orders at what turned out to be the three Mexican day laborers from across the street. "Shut up, you dumbass dog," her dad said and gave her a swift kick, horrifying Edith. The dog rolled in the grass and lay still for a moment before getting up and slinking off, while the men gathered at the pool, staring down at the peacock, her dad trying his best to communicate with them.

"Andale, muchachos," and he held a fifty-dollar bill in the air. "First one to get rid of it," he said, waving the bill at them, then folding it up and returning it to his money clip.

The three men formed a loose-knit huddle, speaking rapidly in Spanish, when suddenly one of them, the shortest and chubbiest of the three, reached up with the flat of his hand and smashed the taller, broader leader in the nose. A fight broke out among the two, the shorter man wrestling the taller man to the ground, bashing his face into the earth, while the third man lowered himself into the pool, grabbed the peacock by the neck, then hurled the carcass up and over the side, where it landed with an unpleasant, mushy thud at her dad's feet, splattering some drops of blood onto his clothes and his glasses. Her dad reeled in disgust, pitching backward, twisting himself through the sunlight and air like a contortionist, her seventy-year-old, brittle-boned, acid-tongued dad, who suffered from terrible ulcerative colitis and the terror of losing his wife. And as he fell, Edith held her breath, her brain screaming no, while the rest of her trembled yes—the scene both horrified and titillated her, for how often were you able to bear witness to someone else's punishment, the unequivocal delivery of instantly gratifying karma? There he was, his body seconds from the ground, his head seconds from crashing against the corner of an uneven, jagged flagstone, and Edith, unable to watch, shut her eyes and listened for the second thud of the morning.

When she opened her eyes again a few moments later, her dad was leaning all of his weight against the taller man, who'd caught him. His head rested in the crook of the man's arms, his eyes closed, and for a second Edith wondered if he hadn't had a stroke. "Daddy," she said, pressing a hand to the warm, sun-drenched glass, and as if hearing her, he opened his eyes, lifted his head, and, using the man as leverage, righted himself.

"Looks like your hombres deserted you," her dad said and glanced around, neither mentioning the fall nor thanking him. He removed his bifocals, which were speckled with blood, and breathed on the lenses, wiping them off with a handkerchief. "You want the fifty dollars, amigo, you take that thing with you," and he pointed to the mangled body of the peacock lying in the lush green grass. The man looked down at the bird, then back up at her dad, sizing them both up before tossing his hands into the air and walking away without a word. "Well, fuck you very kindly," her dad said, giving the peacock a kick and releasing scores of tiny white feathers into the air.

Edith turned her face away just as her phone gonged, announcing a new text message. It was a short video of Ephraim in the shower, lathering up his lean, hairy chest and firm, basketball player's ass, some of the suds dangling off his thick, circumcised dick, which he touched, fondled, and masturbated, saying her name as he did. The sight of him and his erect cock made her skin prickle all over, but it was the sound of her name that truly made her wet. Never in her life had she had a lover who said her name the way he said it, who truly wanted her to know that his big, unshaven balls and perpetual erection were for her and her alone. No, she didn't love him, but who cared about love when this was on offer—a six-foot-two, green-eyed, black-haired former Israeli soldier, her own puppy dog, who lived mere seconds away and whom she could call for sex anytime she wanted. Again, she rued her decision not to invite him along, yet still maintained that it would have been torturous for him. She didn't want to subject any lover to her dad's grilling, and certainly not a potential boyfriend—although her relationship with Ephraim was never going to amount to more than what it was.

Still, something about the video was not quite kosher—beyond the content, of course, which Edith still found both exciting and unsettling—though she didn't have time to figure out what it was, because Pandora was upon her, saying, "Hey, there you are! We need to leave in a few if we're going to make our appointment at Rejuvenate."

"We're rejuvenating?" Edith asked.

"It's the new spa at the Hollywood Stardust Hotel. A day of beauty for you, me, and Roz," and she smiled that phony smile of hers, further exasperating Edith and making her want to punch Pandora right in her spongy, phony lips.

"I have to be back here by three-thirty to get to Claremont by five."

"It's only eleven-fifteen, Thistle," Pandora reassured her. "I think it's safe to say we won't be mud-bathing for four hours."

"Oh, they have mud baths!" She beamed, ignoring the second part of her sister-in-law's comment.

"It's a surprise for your mom from her two doting daughters. You can pay me back whenever," Pandora chirped. "She's been so blue lately, you know." Did Edith know this? She wasn't sure she did. "I just hope we can leave the boys alone without them killing one another."

The first true thing to come out of Pandora's mouth since Edith's arrival, and it made her laugh and warm to her sister-in-law. "Wouldn't it just be so nice if they did, though." Edith shuddered at the implication. "What I mean is, they're all so stubborn. Pure Jacobson cavemen."

"No need to explain. I know what you meant," Pandora said knowingly. She looped an arm through Edith's, leading her back into the dining room, which was now empty of Mo as well. "Roz, do think you're up for a drive into L.A. with Thistle and me? I need to pick up some things for tomorrow night: a couple of jars of gefilte fish from that little place on Wilshire and another box of chocolate-covered matzo, a request from my boys, whom I cannot deny a thing," and she smiled again, though this time she seemed to mean it.

"That sounds lovely, Panda," her mom said. "I could use a little diversion, I think."

"A diversion?" her dad asked. He was standing in the doorway, looking to Edith as if nothing had happened and apparently nothing had, except for the dark spots on his pants. "What was that about a diversion?"

"Oh, there you are, Julian," her mom said. For the first time that morning, Edith detected the faintest intimation of disappointment in her mom's voice. "Did you take care of the rooster?"

"Yes, Roz, I took care of the rooster," he said, although as far as Edith knew, the dead bird was still lying in the grass, baking in the hot California sun.

"Oh, good, I'm so glad to hear it," she said. Then, "Oh, I said rooster, didn't I? I meant peacock. These damn pills make me so loopy, Thistle."

"It's okay, Ma," Edith soothed. "You can be as out of it as you want. This isn't a loopy-free zone."

"Not pills, Roz. The medication," her dad nagged, less gently this time, an edginess to his words that might have startled Edith if she hadn't heard it a million times before.

"But is there an actual difference?" inquired Jacob, who had returned from upstairs. "I mean, I've just spent the better part of the last few seconds trying to figure out what the real difference is and I just can't. I think you're splitting hairs, Pop."

"Pills refer to medicine, a dosage, whereas medication refers to treatment," her dad said. "Look it up if you don't believe me, but it seems any wordsmith worth his salt would appreciate the distinction."

"Duly noted," Jacob badgered, this round of sparring, Edith hoped, at an end. "Dietrich and I are headed out. Thistle, tell me again what time you want us to be at Pomona."

"Oh, I think it's probably better if you don't come," she said, flustered, for she'd forgotten she'd invited her entire family to her talk. "I mean, I think you'll just be bored out of your minds. Besides, I'm sure Dietrich would rather see the sights than listen to me deliver a dry lecture on the state of ethics in America." She yawned for emphasis. "See, the topic's even putting me to sleep."

"You don't know my boyfriend too well, then," Jacob mused, "because this is right up his Teutonic alley."

Her dad went rigid when Jacob said *boyfriend,* his face darkening. Edith, worried that he'd malign him again, cut in immediately. "Okay, ladies, time to hit the road," and she gestured to Pandora, who helped her mom out of her seat, the two heading to the door that led to the garage.

"Wait one second," her dad said, following them. "I don't think you're in any shape for this, Roz. You heard what the doctors said. Plenty of rest."

"Oh, Julian, please stop fussing. I feel perfectly fine," she said, waving him off, but not before he'd come between the door and the two women. "If I get tired, I'll take a little snooze in the car."

"Who's going to carry your oxygen, huh?" he asked. "It's pretty heavy."

"I think we'll manage, Julian," Pandora said, as Edith went to retrieve the tank from the guest room and ran into Mo, who was just exiting the kitchen. "You and Jacob play nice with him," she whispered.

"Who, me?" He feigned innocence. "We'll be fine, unless he cracks wise again about Jacob's sexual orientation or says another disparaging word about Pandora or you. Then I'm going to snap his neck in two and dump his ass in the bottom of the pool."

"Sorry? *Another* disparaging word about me?" she asked softly. "Please tell me it's not the Emory thing again." Her dad still took umbrage at her accepting the assistant professorship and for making tenure in the interim, which meant she wasn't leaving Atlanta anytime soon. It was still a sore subject between them, but Edith refused to believe him so small and petty that he'd use it to demean her behind her back.

"Oh no, it's even better than that," Mo said. "Apparently, last month you missed the fifth anniversary of his retirement. 'She couldn't even bother to call and congratulate me. After all, that job put a roof over her head, fed her three square meals a day, and sent her to Harvard. She must have been too busy sexually harassing another student to pull herself away even for a moment.' That's what he told me, Thistle. I just happened to call them, and Ma reminded me to say something nice to him. Jacob was in Berlin, so he's off the hook. Besides, I'm not sure the old man would've cared one way or another if he'd called anyway."

"Oh, that's rich," she said, trying to modulate her whispering, though it was becoming increasingly hard to smother her anger. "I fly into Dallas to surprise him on his last birthday by taking him to Sea Island for dinner and giving him a two-hundred-and-fifty-dollar gift certificate to Orvis, and he has the gall to complain about me? Did he ever once extend himself when I was going through my divorce? What about when Jacob was in the hospital in Berlin? If it were my child who'd almost died, you better believe I would have dropped everything and gotten on the next flight."

"You and I didn't go, either," Mo said. "What does that say about us?"

"We aren't his parents," she said. "But neither one of them does anything all day—Ma, when she was feeling better, used to have lunch with her friends, and Daddy, since his retirement, doesn't stray far from that garden of his. Yeah, really important stuff they just couldn't possibly leave. Who cares that their child's in the hospital?"

She thought back to that terrifying moment when her mom called to deliver the news about Jacob, how he'd developed a blood clot during the long plane ride to Germany and how this blood clot had broken off and traveled to his lungs. Had she known then the extent and gravity of the situation, that he might have died, she would have dropped everything and gotten on the first flight to Berlin. Yet Jacob, when she spoke to him, told her not to come, that Dietrich was taking good care of him. Never one to be fussed over or comfortable being the center of attention, he downplayed it all, including what had been a superlative pain in his left calf—he thought he'd strained a muscle—and his subsequent collapse on the U-Bahn, which she only found out about later, after it was all over. Jacob spoke just once to her about those six long, excruciating days that he spent in Charité hospital, and that was only and again to commend Dietrich, who'd shown up each morning with flowers and a stack of DVDs (*Family Guy, The Simpsons, Seinfeld*), staying the whole day until the windows went dark and the nurse came into the room to remind him in a scolding, punitive tone that he'd overstayed his welcome and that he had to leave *augenblicklich*. After she'd gone, however, Dietrich dismissed the dismissal, climbing into the narrow bed and curling up beside Jacob, whispering German nothings into Jacob's ear, while the other three patients turned their faces away to give the lovers some much-needed privacy. "The guy is a miracle," Jacob had told Edith later.

"Speaking of not going, I don't think I can make your talk. You aren't mad, are you?" Mo asked.

"You can catch the next one," she said, relieved, thinking of the van, which made her picture the cargo hold and the syringe she'd found. "Let's say you found a syringe in the back of your car, what would you do with it?"

"You found a syringe in my car?" Mo asked, horrified.

"No, in the van," she said. "Pretty creepy, huh."

"You should get rid of it. Don't throw it in one of our garbage cans, though. The kids are curious little shits and who knows what's on the needle. If you want, I can take care of it," Mo offered.

"No, I'll do it," she said. "But thanks anyway."

"And as for my coming to one of your other talks, you can count on it."

Which was sweet of him to say, though she knew Mo would never attend one of her lectures, just as he knew she would never see one of his movies. She loved him, even respected him, yet the roles he chose were often mindless, the movies often full of exploding cars and buildings, nothing more than video games projected onto the screen. Entertaining schlock, perhaps, but ultimately empty and a complete waste of his gargantuan talents. Her dad maintained that water sought its own level, yet in her opinion, Mo was far better than the bumbling cops and archvillains he repeatedly played. She hoped one day to see him prove her correct.

In the room, Edith grabbed the green canister, which was resting in her mom's wheelchair, wondering if she shouldn't pack it in the car as well. But it seemed to her that it was better for her mom if she walked, however slowly, to retain some sliver of independence. She suspected that part of her mom's depression came from having to rely on the wheelchair to get around. This saddened Edith, for she understood that one day soon, maybe next week, maybe next month, her mom would be confined to the chair for the rest of her shortened days, erasing yet another bit of freedom.

She found the two women sitting in the Expedition, Pandora

behind the wheel, her mom in the passenger seat. To her surprise, when she climbed into the backseat, she also found her dad, who was buckling himself in. "Daddy, what are you doing?" she asked.

"What does it look like I'm doing, Eddie?" he said matter-of-factly.

"Well, it looks like you're coming with us to get manicures and pedicures," Edith said.

"Oh, is that what we're doing?" her mom asked. "I haven't had a mani-pedi in ages!"

"I don't see any reason why—"

"Julian, you need to get out of this car right now," Pandora said without looking up from her phone. "I don't mean to hurt your feelings, but you aren't invited. Girls only."

"Roz, tell her it's okay if I come along," he said.

"Honey, please, you're acting childish." Her mom laughed. "He hates being without me, don't you? You have a dozen projects to occupy you until we get back. You could finish mowing the yard. You could try to fix Brendan's bike. You could tag along with Jacob and Dietrich, who I'm sure wouldn't mind, but you're going to have to apologize for what you said, of course. You could help Mo cleanse the house of hidden Pop Tarts and whatever else the kids have hoarded."

"Don't leave me alone with them," he pleaded.

"Don't leave you alone with whom? Your sons?" her mom asked. "Why ever not?"

"Are you going to tell me you haven't noticed the peculiar way they've both been acting?" he barked. His voice held such genuine panic and fear in it that Edith couldn't bear to look at him and had to turn away. "They're up to something."

"Our boys?" her mom asked. "Up to what, Julian?"

"Well, if I knew that, Roz, I'd be even smarter than I already am, now wouldn't I?" he said snidely.

"Good-bye, Julian," Pandora said and clicked the automatic door lock.

Reluctantly, he unlatched his seat belt and opened the door. "If you come home and I'm dead, I want you to call the police and have them launch a full investigation," he said.

This made the two women in the front seat break into laughter, and though Edith finally joined in, her own laughter rang hollow and untrue, for she was thinking about the syringe she'd found in the van and wondering what it contained.

"Don't be so morbid," her mom scolded him. "You brought your fishing gear with you. Well, drive yourself to Malibu and fish off the pier. It's a glorious day to be outside, Julian. Go fly a kite. Go for a walk. Live a little."

As her dad shut the door and Pandora backed out of the garage, Edith had to force herself to speak, for her dad's eerie declaration had left her numb and mute.

"What do you think that was about, Ma?" she asked once they'd turned onto Mulholland Parkway and the house was out of sight.

"Your dad can be such a Paranoid Percy sometimes," her mom said. "Honestly, I don't know what to do with him. He follows me around like a shadow! I can't go anywhere these days without him popping up to check on me. It's getting bizarre even by his standards. I keep asking him what he did with the real Julian Jacobson, because this version of him is not the version of the husband I know. I'm not complaining, though. Well, you've seen it, Thistle. Look at what good care he takes of me. He drives me right up to the door and lets me out. He hasn't been down to the coast to go fishing in I don't know how long. Between us, though, I wish he'd find a hobby that gets him out of the house more, because he's driving me bonkers."

Yes, Edith had seen it, though she had also seen the real Julian Jacobson show himself as well. There was that, and now there was the added strain of her earlier conversation with Mo, which only complicated matters further. For the first time in ages, Edith had no idea what to make of her dad. Normally, he was so oblivious to the impact his behavior had on those around him that the best way to deal with him was not to deal with him at all, not to engage him when he was acting paranoid and crazy, and not to react to anything negative he said. She knew that he fed on these sorts of unfortunate interactions, especially those with his sons. It came as a great surprise, then, to hear that he sensed a disturbance in the force, to quote Elias, who would have gotten a kick out of learning that her dad suspected that there was a plot to kill him afoot, true though it may have been. She prayed her brothers didn't do anything foolish or rash while she was off getting her pimples squeezed and the calluses on her feet sanded.

"He won't let me out of his sight," her mom went on. "Sometimes, when I take a nap, I open my eyes and there he is, sitting in the chair across from me, staring."

"That's creepy, Ma," Edith said.

"Your father's not creepy, Thistle, and I resent you saying that he is," she said. "What's creepy is what I keep hearing on the news about those suicide bombers right here in L.A. There was another one just yesterday on the 405. Isn't that right, Pandora?"

"Another Jewish family," Pandora said. "Jacob told me the police diverted traffic onto the shoulder, but that he drove right past the car. They closed the entire freeway a little later, after it was definitively ruled a terrorist attack."

"I swear, when you and your brothers were kids, the worst thing I ever had to worry about was that you'd get into a car with a stranger and that I'd never see you again. Now, though, Islamic extremists killing innocent people by driving right up beside them with a bomb? I wish you and Mo would take the kids and get out of L.A., Pandora."

"And go where, Roz? This happens all over now," she said.

"The answer used to be Israel," her mom said, taking a deep breath. "But you can thank Washington for that. Refusing to come to Israel's aid? America first? Has the world lost its mind?" She was breathing heavily and fell silent, then took another big gulp of air and continued. "Where was the UN? Where was the EU? Heads in the oil, that's where. Oh, it nearly killed your father the day the Arabs invaded. I never thought I'd see it—a Jewish holy land where nothing Jewish remains." She panted at this last part and shut her eyes to catch her breath.

"It's a bad time to be a Jew," Edith declared, thinking suddenly about Justin Cohn, that poor Jewish colleague of hers who'd been out for a predawn jog in an empty and deserted Piedmont Park one Sunday morning when he tripped—was tripped with an invisible wire, said the article in the *Atlanta Journal-Constitution*—and as he lay on the ground, a gang of vicious youths in Hitler masks descended upon him from out of nowhere, brandishing bats and beating him until they'd broken nearly every bone in his body and left him to bleed to death. "They knew who I was," he said later to Edith, who'd gone to visit him after she'd heard that he'd awoken from his three-week coma. "They have a list and our names are on it. All of our names, Edith." The memory made her think about her upsetting morning on the shuttle, about her young, vulnerable, brave doppelgänger at the rental car agency, who too was still brave enough to wear her flashy gold Star of David, even in these darker times, or to spite them, Edith hoped. And what was her part in all of this mess, what was Edith doing to stem the tide of hatred and intolerance?

Well, for one thing, she was about to deliver a much-anticipated talk called "Death to the Rumors: The Unethical Portrayal of Jews in Film and Theater," and she was trying to talk her brothers out of murdering their dad, and she was sleeping with a displaced Israeli, who'd been ousted from his homeland, though she wasn't sure the last one counted, even if it made her feel better and gave her an inner sense of peace she hadn't experienced in years. "Peace always starts with the self," she liked to tell her students, who shifted in their seats like restless statuary, eyes vacant and limbs heavy. She tried to reach them on so many different levels and in so many different ways until she felt herself bleeding emotionally from the effort. "Change only happens when critical mass meets critical thinking," she also told them. "Be the thinker, not the thought." Oh, these minor spiritual pep rallies she threw for them, her voice rebounding through the lecture hall and the silence that boomeranged back at her, deafening in its totality. Were they all such lost causes? Edith wondered, thinking again of her dad, when her phone gonged—TBS1946, who'd played another word, or rather exchanged five tiles and passed his turn to Edith, who had taken a considerable lead.

She glanced at her tiles, shuffling them around, while her mom and Pandora discussed the Passover meal, the Passover guests, the Passover wine, and the Passover TV special. "I'm sorry, but did you just say 'TV special'?" Edith asked, exchanging three of her own tiles and skipping her turn as well.

"Didn't Mo tell you?" Pandora asked.

"No, apparently it slipped his mind," Edith said.

"Norman Glick, the executive vice president of development and talent for BravoREAL, thought it'd raise awareness of anti-Semitism here in America and with any luck globally. A percentage of the revenue is going to the L.A. chapter of the Israeli Relief Fund. It's amazing how many Israelis we've accepted just in the past six months."

"Yes," Edith said, thinking of Ephraim, whose aunt, uncle, and cousins had relocated to L.A. last year. "I'm surprised Daddy agreed to appear on camera again, though."

"Well, he knows it's for a good cause," Pandora said. "Besides, Passover just wouldn't be the same without him," and she winked, glancing into the rearview mirror at Edith, who winked back. *What the hell is going on here? Did we suddenly call a truce that I don't know about?* Edith thought, panicking a little when she realized she might not dislike Pandora as much as she still desperately wanted to.

"Do you think—I was thinking of inviting someone to the Seder," Edith said.

"Have you been holding out on us, Auntie Thistle?" Pandora asked. "Nu, so who is he?"

"No one. Just an old friend from college," she said.

As far as Edith knew, she had no friends from college in the L.A. area, though, and absolutely no idea whom she'd invite anyway, but she wanted to leave the option open, just in case, for she didn't think she could endure the Seder alone, without the comfort and support of her own foil. Mo had Pandora and the kids, Jacob had Dietrich, her parents had each other, and whom did Edith have? No one but the gorgeous, inappropriate Ephraim, who was far too young and who sent her videos of himself masturbating in the shower. Though not in his shower, she finally realized. She muted her phone and played the video again, her surprise turning to shock and her shock to disillusionment when she recognized the pink tiles of her own bathroom and the bottle of shampoo he was using to jack off. Yes, it was titillating, and yes, it turned her on, and, yes, it made her want him that much more, yet it also disgusted and frightened her, for she had no idea how he'd gotten into her house, much less why he thought it was a good idea to send her an illicit video of his crime. Clearly, he believed she wouldn't mind, and worse, that he hadn't done anything wrong. *The utter chutzpah,* she thought, her anger stoked. Perhaps the Israeli Army had trained him in the art of breaking and entering, but what about in the art of stalking, for what else was this but that?

Edith remained surprisingly calm, focusing on nothing but the hillside scenery that flew past the tinted windows. Because the traffic was light, they cruised along at a comfortable speed, Pandora remarking that she'd never seen the freeway as clear as it was that day.

"Well, it is Easter weekend, dear," her mom said. "Maybe all the Gentiles decided to leave en masse."

"Let's not jinx it, Roz," Pandora said, heading through a relatively clear Laurel Canyon, and then they were winding and wending and being spit out onto Hollywood Boulevard, her mom oohing at the distant Hollywood sign, which Pandora pointed out to her.

"The last time I was on this street was with Mo, oh, thirty years ago," her mom said, her chest heaving, as if the memory were too strong for her to carry. "We stayed at what your dad would call a fleabag motel somewhere around here. Mo had an audition with an agent not far from the motel. I left you at home with Dad, Thistle. Jacob was at sleepaway camp. Do you remember that?"

"I do, Ma," Edith said, recalling those two days she'd spent with her dad.

Ten years old and just beginning to show signs of the woman she would one day become, the buds on her chest, the soft red hair sprouting between her thighs, the shifts in temperament and height and weight, her figure altering and lengthening and losing its boyish, flat lines to become fuller and rounder, girlishly shaped, beneath the loose-fitting clothes she wore out of embarrassment and hatred of her body. All sorts of changes happening on a molecular level, including one that nobody could see and that went undetected until one fateful night: Her daddy loved figs and ate them in every conceivable variation—jars of fig preserves, fig butter, and fig compote lined the shelves in the pantry, boxes of homemade fig bars were wrapped delicately and stored in the freezer. Edith disliked the smell and texture of them, everything associated with them, but that didn't stop her from going out into the backyard and picking some fresh figs from the fig tree to surprise her daddy with that night after supper, which her mom had cooked the day before and left for them.

Her daddy came home from the lab more tired and grumpier than usual, yet Edith had a secret weapon to counter his bad mood—she'd diced the figs, added some lemon zest and sugar, then made homemade whipped cream, just as she'd seen her mom do a thousand times. She covered all of it and stored it in the very back of the fridge to hide it from her daddy, who sat down at the kitchen table without a word while Edith heated up the baked chicken and wild rice, then dressed the salad. She set the table and poured him a glass of water. The meal began in relative silence, her daddy lost in his own thoughts, either grunting at her questions or letting them pass unanswered: How was work today? Did you have any breakthroughs in your experiments on the mice? These questions only seemed to make him more sullen and withdrawn, yet Edith kept at it, for she knew him and knew that all he needed was to get some food into him, then he'd be his pleasant old self again. And that's more or less what happened—after a few bites, his mood shifted and he began to tell her about his day, going into great detail about it, mainly about how the grant he'd applied for had been accepted but that he was only getting a mere fraction of the money he needed to continue his research. He was going to have to fire his lab technician, for he could no longer afford her, which meant he'd have to do everything himself.

"Unless you want to help me," he said, smiling. "I could always use an assistant. Who knows? Maybe you'll become a scientist like your old man. It'd be nice if one of my children followed in my footsteps and did something useful." She knew he was referring to Mo. The whole family knew how he felt about Mo's dream of becoming an actor. "Well, if you can't be smart, you might as well be entertaining. Isn't that right, Eddie?"

"Mo has a right to follow his dreams, doesn't he?" she asked, clearing the table only after he was finished. There were rules to follow, and Edith made sure to follow them, for she'd seen how touchy he could be when these rules of his were broken—no getting up from the table during dinner, no speaking out of turn during dinner, no interrupting him during dinner (or at any time, for that matter), no elbows on the table, no plates left unfinished, no second helpings unless he had already taken his, and no clearing the table until he had set his knife and fork down. She rinsed the dishes and put them in the dishwasher, then got out one small bowl and a dessertspoon, placing them before him. "I hope you left room for dessert, Daddy," she said, grabbing the figs and whipped cream from the fridge.

She served him the figs, scooped some whipped cream on top of them, then sat down again, a little antsy to go to her room and practice the flute for an upcoming band recital. Still, Edith knew enough not to ask to be excused, for this was another rule of her daddy's that he didn't take lightly—he let them know when it was time to be dismissed. She sat there, listening to him talk about the chair of his department, who was stepping down, and how they wanted her daddy to replace him.

"I already turned them down," he said. "I'm right on the cusp of a breakthrough in my experiments, and if I take that crappy promotion—and it is crappy, Eddie, don't you believe otherwise— I'd be giving up two years of intense research. On the other hand, how many people can say they love what they do? I wake up every morning and can't wait to get to work. I stumbled on the perfect career, but it's only because I'm exceedingly lucky."

Edith was proud of her daddy, for he was the first Jacobson in the family to go to college and to get a PhD. By contrast, his younger brother, Edith's uncle Bernie, had never finished high school and had gone into the merchant marines. Now he owned a couple of pool halls in downtown Dallas, was superrich, lived in a huge house, and was on his third wife. He had fathered three kids—wild, pot-smoking, delinquent losers, according to her daddy—whom she liked but rarely saw. The difference between her daddy and her uncle was as startling as the difference between her and her own older brother, whom she loved but found silly and frivolous: Edith, who was book smart, took after her daddy, while Mo, who was street smart, took after their uncle Bernie, a consummate hustler and businessman with ties to the Jewish mafia. Mo even resembled Uncle Bernie, who had blue eyes, a square chin, and a lean boxer's physique, more than he did their own dad, which raised the eyebrows of the three siblings, though their speculation was later quashed when Mo finally confronted their mom, who denied the allegation outright, reminding him that she'd stopped attending breakfasts at their grandmother's because she couldn't stand to be around Uncle Bernie. "He's a class-less pig," she said. "Your dad might be many things, but at least he's not a serial divorcer. It doesn't surprise me he can't keep a wife. He may be physically attractive, but that's about where it ends." (At his untimely death at sixty-one, he left behind a mountain of debt and a burner phone, which his fifth wife discovered in a desk drawer, with the names and numbers of countless paramours.)

"Delicious. Just delicious," he said, spooning some of the figs into his mouth. "My compliments to the chef."

"Thank you, Daddy." Edith beamed.

"Don't tell your mother this, but your figs put hers to shame," he said. "I don't know what you did to them, Eddie, but they taste ambrosial."

It was a word she'd never heard her daddy say about her mom's cooking and she sat there, as proud as she could be, studying the figs, which didn't look nearly as gross or as distasteful to her as they once did. If her daddy liked them, well, she'd probably like them, too, despite her mom's repeated insistence that she didn't like them. She asked him if she could have a taste of his.

"By all means," he said, offering her his spoon. "Don't forget the whipped cream, Eddie." He slid the bowl toward her.

She added some whipped cream, then held the figs between her lips before shutting her eyes, quickly emptying the spoon, and swallowing it all down, smiling as she did.

"Well, wasn't I right?" he asked. "Ambrosial."

She took another small bite of the figs, then a sip of water to wash the taste from her mouth, because quite frankly she didn't like them. "Yes, Daddy, delicious," she lied, her eyes watering from the bitter aftertaste. "May I be excused now, please?"

She ran to her room, where her stomach began to hurt. And not just hurt, but also to swell. Her skin itched, her lips were sore, and her mouth felt as if someone had taken a mallet to it. She tried to lie down, but half an hour later, she was finding it difficult to breathe and to see, for her eyelids were swollen shut. Still, she did not call out for her daddy, who she knew was in his study and not to be disturbed.

Climbing out of bed, she stumbled into the hall, making her dizzy way toward her daddy's door, but found the floor tilting away from her. Her legs, unable to support her, buckled, and she collapsed outside the study. One of her hands must have hit the door, because a few moments later, she heard it open. She tried to speak and found she couldn't, but she did hear him, not his voice but the sound of his shoes on the carpet and the rush of air on her face as he stepped over her.

She lay like this for minutes, waiting for him to do something, then heard him again somewhere nearby, in the kitchen, she thought, because she heard the fridge open and close, bottles rattling. Again, she tried to call out to him and again her voice was lost, nothing more than a whisper, a breath. She tried to get up, but her body refused to respond, her stomach churning and her face on fire, every inch of her chilled. *Daddy, where are you?* she thought, cocooned in sweat and blind to the world.

She recognized that she was in the throes of an allergic reaction; she'd learned about them just the previous week in science class. Anaphylactic shock. That's what was happening, and she wanted to scream out to her daddy that she was sick and needed his help, and she tried with all of her might to speak and to open her eyes again, and while speaking was impossible, she did manage to crack one of her eyelids open long enough to catch the murky image of her daddy standing directly over her, a terrible, creepy smirk on his face. Then she must have blacked out, because the next thing she knew she was waking up in a hospital bed and a nurse was checking her blood pressure.

Yes, Edith remembered those two days and how nice her daddy was to her after that and for the next few weeks, until the episode faded and both of them forgot about it. But now, as they pulled up to the Hollywood Stardust Hotel, Edith fixated on the fact that her dad had tempted her into eating the figs.

"I never told you this, Ma," Edith now said, as Pandora's phone rang and she answered it, speaking to what sounded like an advertiser who wanted to buy ad space on Pandora's Box. She pulled up to

172

the valet stand, continuing her conversation about the price and size of ad space. "But Daddy let me try those figs."

"Oh, Thistle," her mom said. "You must be misremembering. Whatever put that idea in your head?"

She decided against telling her mom the truth, out of fear of ruining the lovely day and also out of a deep sense of commitment to herself to keep past grievances from impinging upon this visit.

"Well, it was all one big misunderstanding, wasn't it," her mom went on. "You always were a little too curious for your own good. Julian told me how you snuck the figs behind his back. I felt awful that I wasn't there for you, Thistle." After they climbed out of the car, she reached out and hugged her. "I love you so much. You're my only daughter, and I only ever wanted you to be happy. You know that, don't you?"

"Of course, Ma," she said, tightening her grip on this frail, unwell woman, who she suspected might be crying. They stood like that for a couple more minutes until Pandora said it was time to go inside and get muddy. "I'll meet you in there," Edith said, reaching for her phone because she'd gotten another text from Ephraim: Didn't like the video?

She wanted to respond, but now wasn't the time, for the text she wanted to send would most certainly ruffle him and perhaps lead him to call her. She didn't want to talk to him, not until after she'd relaxed and had a chance to contemplate her feelings. She silenced her phone and slid it into her purse, heading through the glass doors of Rejuvenate to join her mom and Pandora in the mud.

Ninety minutes later, the three women emerged from a refreshing regimen of warm mud baths and hot spring soaks, to take lunch in a "controlled environment" off the main lobby of the hotel. Edith, who was not used to being pampered, marveled at the surroundings—the careful attention to detail that made her believe, if she shut her eyes, that she was in an actual Amazonian rain forest—the chirrup of crickets, the warbling of birds, the comforting swish of wind that blew over them. Until all of a sudden, a downpour, artificial thunder-claps, but she was protected—they were all protected—underneath a giant umbrella. Rejuvenating Rain was also part of the experience, and though Edith felt rather guilty about the amount of water it must have taken to make this experience as authentic as possible, she was more than pleased to set aside her moralizing and just go with the capitalistic, bourgeois flow of it.

They ate kale salads and washed them down with cucumber water and seaweed smoothies, everything emerald green and smelling of the earth. The water, Edith learned, was desalinated seawater, delivered daily. She had no idea just how much her share in this day of beauty was going to cost her, but even this didn't matter to her. She took her last bite of salad and said, "So, Ma, how much are you enjoying yourself? Isn't this fantabulous?"

"Yes, oh my, yes," her mom said, her face ruddy with color, the ashen quality of her skin all but a memory. "This has been such a pleasant surprise, Thistle. I can't wait for my massage."

She looked healthier and more vivacious, her old self again. Even her breathing seemed to have improved, as if she'd left the disease along with her clothes in the locker room, though Edith knew this was just magical thinking. *If only it were that simple,* she thought, wishing her mom a speedy recovery, yet understanding that no recovery was forthcoming. She would never get well, never get better, only worse from here on out, and it suddenly felt to Edith that her chief directive now was to make sure her mom lived out the rest of her days on the planet like this—comfortable, cared for, and bundled up with love. All of the things that should have been given willingly, all of the things she'd had to fight tooth and nail for, from a new washing machine to a proper allowance to maintain her dad's house, to stock it with food, to keep it clean, to make sure none of them ever went without—Edith would make up for all of these now. It shamed her to realize how awful she'd once been, how she'd once looked upon her mom with pity and disgust, never seeing the sacrifices she'd made when Edith wasn't watching, that happened well within the inner keep of her marriage. She'd laughed at her mom both behind her back and right in her face, had feared her for her witching ways, secure and strong in the notion that her dad was right, although, of course, she never found any evidence of her mom's allegiance to the black arts, not in her closet, which she inspected regularly, or in the books and magazines she read, or in the conversations she had on the phone when she thought Edith wasn't around. Still, the young Edith had fretted about the supposed hex she'd put on her daddy to trap him, wondering if his outbursts, when he called her mom such nasty names, which would've gotten Edith spanked, were his way of combating the spell. On one level, she had always suspected it was just a silly game, yet on another had grown up quite attached to the belief, almost hoping it were true, for it would have explained so much about what had gone on in that tiny house on Persuasion Drive.

An attendant cleared the trays of woven hemp from the table and announced it was time for massages. Edith reached out to help her mom up, but her mom shooed her away and rose without trouble, walking as if she weren't debilitated at all. Edith smiled after her, saying, "If I hadn't seen it with my own eyes . . ."

"You know that we're the carriers of men's pain," Pandora said, "and that we keep it in our bodies." Edith had never heard this before, yet in some strange way it made perfect sense to her. "I love your brother, but when I agreed to marry him, I told him that if he ever hurt me the way your dad hurt your mom, I'd leave him in a heartbeat. I like him to think of it as a spiritual prenuptial agreement. And it goes twice for the kids. Abuse might run in your family, but it doesn't in mine." Though Edith didn't appreciate Pandora's self-righteous tone, she couldn't deny that Jewish Barbie did have a point. "Does it bother me that Mo would rather stay home with the kids instead of looking for a real job? Yes. Does it worry me that he's a forty-two-year-old, out-of-work actor? Yes. But you know what doesn't bother me? He doesn't let Julian bully him. He's had to work on it, for sure, but he stands up to him when he needs to, because that father of yours, whether you want to believe this or not, ought to fall down on his knees and give thanks for the family he has, especially for that wife of his who still puts up with his bullshit." *Let's hear it for my mother, Roz, patron saint of unappreciated wives,* Edith thought. "Look, I know this is hard for you, Thistle, but I wanted to get you alone to discuss Julian. After what happened with Dexter, I'm thinking seriously about asking him to leave."

"You want to throw my dad out of the house?" Edith asked, moving past the attendant, who handed her a towel and pointed to cabana 3 at the end of the hall. "Does Mo know?"

"Not yet," Pandora said, pausing outside of cabana 2. "I thought you might bring it up with him. It'd be better if it came from you, don't you think?"

"Pandora, they drove all the way to L.A.," Edith said. "Jacob and I flew in specially to celebrate Passover with them. Now you want me to speak to Mo about asking them to leave?"

"No, no, you misunderstand me," Pandora said. "Not Roz, just Julian. We love having Roz around. It's your dad, Thistle." She pulled her phone out of her robe, touched the screen, then handed it to Edith. "Press play."

It was a video, but Edith saw at once that this was a video of a completely different nature from Ephraim's. For the first few seconds, there was nothing but black, as one of the twins spoke to Mo on the phone, but then suddenly the picture started: The camera caught what had to be Dexter's face—he was missing two front teeth—then it panned across the front yard, settling on Jacob's rental car for a second before spinning around to settle on Edith's dad, who was fiddling with something in the back of the minivan. Dexter held the camera on his paw-paw, who had no idea he was being recorded, apparently, though it wouldn't have mattered because Dexter had no idea what he was witnessing. And to be honest neither did Edith, other than that her dad was doing what he normally did—futzing around reorganizing the back of the minivan, shifting his fishing gear, then grabbing a green canister, which he shifted as well, but not before fiddling with something on its side. The video went on for another moment before going black again.

"Okay, so Dexter's a budding director," she deadpanned. "What was I supposed to see?"

"Oh, Thistle, for such a smart, accomplished woman, you can be such a complete dumbass," she said. "Do I seriously have to spell it out for you?" Yet before Edith could tell her that yes, she had to spell it out, Pandora's masseur tapped her on the shoulder. "Just think. I'm sure you'll figure it out," she said impatiently, then disappeared into the cabana and shut the door.

Edith lingered in the hall, caught between two impulses: to storm into cabana 2 and demand to see the video again or to storm into cabana 2 and pop Pandora in the mouth for having the gall to insinuate what Edith believed she was insinuating—that Dexter had caught her dad tampering with her mom's spare oxygen tank. Absurd. Beyond absurd. *Delusional,* she thought, reaching absently for her phone. She considered calling Mo and telling him about the video, but if Pandora hadn't told him about it yet she might just be making matters worse. Whether or not Edith believed the implications of the video, her brothers would take one look at it and that would be that. There would be no talking them out of their plan to kill their father, even though the video was inconclusive.

She wanted to talk to someone, anyone, but had no one to call. She couldn't call Ephraim, who had sent her a dozen more texts, which she ignored without reading. She had several missed calls from him as well, which only further fueled her anger and discomfort. She thought about calling Jacob, but he didn't have a working cellphone. She scrolled through her list of contacts, past Sheik Cohen, whose number she'd kept, though she knew she shouldn't have, pausing only when she got to E Pluribus Unum, as she'd fondly once referred to Elias—out of many, one. For many years he had been that to her, until her feelings for Sheik had rekindled. If she could speak to anyone about her sister-in-law, it'd be Elias, who still knew her the best of anyone, although they hadn't spoken in ages.

She was about to call him when she got another notification from TBS1946, who'd finally played his turn: YOUR, for a whopping fifty-four points, which brought his score alarmingly closer to hers.

Her blond-haired, blue-eyed, muscle-bound masseur stepped out of the cabana, said hello, then instructed her to go inside and lie down on the table. Based on his accent, Edith put him from Eastern Europe.

"Where are you from?" she asked, slipping out of her robe and hanging it on a hook, while he potchkied around with the musical selection, his back to her.

"I am Tomasz, from Poland," he said with a thick accent. "From Kraków."

He finally settled on a relaxing avian motif—owls, starlings, doves, and songbirds—while Edith lay faceup on the table, her towel draped over her pussy and breasts, thinking of her unruly, dark red bush, in which Ephraim liked to bury his face, and so she'd kept it longer than usual. Now she rued not having trimmed it, though she couldn't have foreseen this, that she'd find herself naked on a massage table. "I hear Kraków is quite lovely," she said as Tomasz grabbed the oil, squirted some into his palms, and rubbed them together to warm them up.

"I give you deep Swedish massage," he told her. "You tell me if too much pain, then I be more gentle."

They kibitzed for a few minutes while he kneaded her freckled shoulders with his thick, meaty fingers. She shut her eyes and gave in to the pleasure of the pain, sighing through it, transporting out of herself, and floating away. She looked down upon this Edith, with her long, lumpy body and odd-sized breasts, her large, aquiline nose, a gift from her dad, her bulbous chin and thin-lipped mouth, gifts from her mom. She thought about her brothers, envying Mo his long black eyelashes and thick head of floppy black hair, and Jacob his full lips and small, Gentile nose, his shockingly blue eyes, like a malamute's, or as he liked to say when they were kids, like a Malamud's, meaning Bernard Malamud. She was plainer than both of them and for this reason she'd nurtured her intelligence, sensing that this would be her way through the world. Which was okay, considering that she actually did have quite a high IQ, definitely higher than her brothers', though this wasn't all that surprising, since women often had higher IQs than men anyway. It was her dad who rated them, while they all sat around the dinner table, discussing school and grades, and he'd inevitably turned to Edith and said, "You're lucky you take after me," gazing upon the rest of them—Jacob, Mo, and her mom—with contempt. She was the apple of his eye, and she'd used it to her advantage as often as she could, getting out of chores and being treated that much better because her daddy valued her intellect over the others'. Yet he never said she was pretty, never told her she was graceful in her prom dresses and high heels, never took photos of her the way he did her brothers. It left a hole inside of her that no amount of cock could fill, though she'd spent years trying.

An hour later, the massage was over, and she was putting her robe back on.

"Have you been in L.A. long?" she asked Tomasz as he shut off the music.

"I live here few months. I like. I used live in Berlin," he said. "But weather bad and too much Turks. I don't like. They lazy. They make mess wherever they go. Every time you hear problem, it's the Turks."

"My brother lives in Berlin," she said, his comment rankling her. "He says he's met some wonderful Turkish people," although Jacob had never said anything of the kind.

"I like lots sun and beach and girls," Tomasz said, wiping his hands on a towel. "If no trashy Hebrews, would be paradise."

And there it was, just like that, her second confrontation of the day. How many others had she not recognized, odd, uncomfortable, strained moments between her and a stranger, which remained unaccounted for, though they lingered like a bad taste in her mouth? A sideways glance, a date declined, a party invitation that "went missing in the mail." All of these everyday occurrences might not have been so everyday when added to all of the other offenses she'd experienced.

She glanced at Tomasz, wanting to tell him off, but figured instead she'd write a letter to the owner of the Stardust Hotel itself. *Fuck you and the tip you rode in on,* she thought, clearing out of the cabana quickly without saying good-bye. In the locker room, Edith changed back into her clothes, then texted Pandora that she'd meet them in the bar. It was close to two-thirty and though ordinarily she wouldn't have ordered a cocktail, she felt she owed it to herself. She downed her first lychee margarita in less than five minutes, then ordered another. While she waited for it, she pulled out her phone, still refusing to engage with Ephraim, who'd sent her a few more frantic texts. Instead, she opened up the Scrabble app and perused her tiles, finally using the Y in YOUR to spell TYRANNY, for sixty-eight points, and reclaiming a sizable lead. She was already quite buzzed from the tequila. She wanted to pace herself and dipped her hand into the bowl of caramelized almonds, then asked for a menu. A quick nosh before Pandora and her mom appeared and it was time to get back into the car and make the dreaded return trip to Calabasas, where anything might have happened among the three Jacobson men.

Halfway through her second round, her mom and Pandora showed up. "Ma! Pandora! I ordered some munchies. A fig pâté and some fried calamari and lots of bread! Take a load off. Here, try this," and she shoved her drink into her mom's face.

"I don't think she should," Pandora cautioned. "It might interfere with your medication, Roz."

"Oh, screw the medication," Edith said. "It's a lychee margarita, Ma. Ly-chee!"

"I don't think one little sip will kill me," her mom said, taking the glass and swallowing a much larger sip than Edith was expecting.

"Atta girl, Ma," she said. "Finish it if you want."

"We need to get going if you want to make Claremont on time," Pandora said, her face in her phone.

"Screw Pomona. Screw my talk. And screw ethics," Edith said. "I don't have any idea why I even bother half the time. I mean, you've seen the shit storm waiting for us out there," and she pointed to the windows and the world beyond. "Well, haven't you? I mean, we all grow up thinking the world's like this, but it's really like that, and then we're suddenly adults and the horrors that befall us—it's all just so undignified. We tell ourselves life is random, because that's the only way we can get through it. We say 'life's unfair,' but it's worse than that. Why didn't you ever tell me it was going to be worse, Ma? You could've at least warned me!"

"Thistle, did something happen, because you're sounding like—"

"Like what, Ma? Like Daddy? Is that who I sound like?" she asked, her voice shrill, her tongue sopped with tequila and her mind with panic, for she had absolutely no idea how she was going to make it another two days in L.A. She stared at her mom, who swam in and out of her vision, and nearly burst into tears for the way she'd treated her. It was all too much.

"No, I was going to say you're sounding like you're premenstrual," her mom said.

"Oh, that's just great. Reduce me to my uterus, Ma," she said. "It's nice to know that feminism rides again with Roz Jacobson." *I might not sound like Daddy,* she thought, *but sometimes you do, Ma. Sometimes you do.* "So do you have any wisdom to impart to your unhappily unmarried, unhappily moppetless, unhappily drunk daughter on this Friday afternoon in Los Angeles?" She pronounced Los Angeles the same way the shuttle driver had that morning, and it made her feel tremendously, deliriously joyous and superior to every other person in the chichi hotel, except for those who pronounced it correctly anyway because the whole region and all the land in it rightfully belonged to them. She wished she were the kind of person

who took stands and joined protests and attended marches and rallies, but instead she was the kind of person who stood up in front
of a classroom and enjoined her students to take action, to get involved, to care about this or that cause, then she went home, opened
a bottle of chardonnay, and watched Netflix until it was time to go
to bed. This had been her life for years until lately, until Ephraim,
although after the video she didn't see much point in him anymore.
"Shall I tell you about my life in Atlanta, Ma? Do you want to hear
how your daughter got herself involved with one of her students and
how that student didn't like his grade and how your daughter's now
being brought up on sexual misconduct charges?" she asked just as
the fig pâté and fried calamari arrived. "Daddy ought to get a big
kick out of the details. Vengeance is best served with dipping sauce,"
she said, stabbing one of the circular squids with a finger and dropping it into her mouth. "Damn, but these little critters are chewy,"
putting on a thick Southern twang.

"Thistle, why don't we get this to go?" her mom said, wrapping
an arm around Edith's waist and leading her into the lobby.

"Don't forget to have them box up the baguette chips," Edith
called to Pandora. "Oh, Ma, I'm sorry. I must be such a disappointment to you. Ever since . . ." But she stopped herself.

"Ever since what?" her mom asked, moving apace and keeping
up with Edith.

"Ever since your diagnosis," she said. "I know we haven't always
gotten along and that's mostly been my fault, I see that, and I'm not
blaming you for the choices I've made these past few months, but I
just can't bear the idea of losing you."

"Shh, Thistle," her mom said. "Your dad's taking good care
of me."

"You keep saying that, but is he? Is he taking good care of you?"
she asked. This was the tequila talking, yet she couldn't stop herself. She kept mentally replaying both the moment at the pool that
morning and the video of her dad at the minivan, and the more she

replayed them, the more sickeningly clear each one became, until she could no longer deny the truth. "What I mean is, wouldn't you be happier if you moved out here and were closer to your grandsons? I've also heard that a drier climate can do wonders for the lungs."

"Your father and I have discussed moving out here many times, but all of our friends are in Dallas. California's also prohibitively expensive," her mom said. "We pay enough for water as it is. I think your dad would fall over dead if he ever saw just how much Pandora and Mo spend on water every month." This was her dad talking, of course, her practical, pragmatic, defeatist dad. "It's a nice thought, though, Thistle." She climbed into the Expedition, which Pandora had just unlocked.

Handing Edith her boxed-up goodies, Pandora said, "I just got an SOS from Mo. Julian is apparently on the rampage. Do you know anything about a missing money clip?"

Edith knew nothing about a money clip, missing or otherwise, but she did know about rampaging men. The committee on sexual misconduct was made up mostly of men, her colleagues who'd known her for years and had awarded her tenure and were now coming after her. Emory University had a zero-tolerance policy on sexual harassment of any kind, and although what Edith had done had been misconstrued completely, she was shocked and appalled to learn that her peers still considered her behavior "morally suspect." All she'd done was befriend a troubled boy and console him in her office, with the door wide open. It'd been her mistake to hug him—that's where she'd gone utterly wrong. Hug him a second too long, but it'd felt so good to care about someone else for a change, to hold this pasty-faced, gawky sophomore in her arms and let him sob about his parents' imminent divorce. Some of her current and former students wrote letters of protest to the dean, calling the whole affair a witch hunt, causing Edith even more unease, as it brought up images of her own mom and the witch hunt she had conducted furtively throughout her childhood. She'd gotten so obsessed that she'd reached out to Arthur Miller, writing him a letter in which she beseeched him to come and help her. He never responded, which was just as well.

In the backseat of the hot SUV, Edith gazed at her mom and laughed at the girl who'd written that letter and who'd been full of such alarmed, virulent fear. How silly she'd been to be afraid of the sick, withered woman in the front seat. Edith had to hand it to her dad for dividing allegiances, for manipulating her into believing such a demented, twisted myth. To call it what it truly was—a lie— meant that she'd also have to call her dad what he truly was, and she wasn't ready for that just yet. She rummaged through the bag and brought up the calamari, passing it to the front seat after she herself had nibbled on it.

"Anyone for fig pâté?" she asked.

"But, darling, don't be silly. You can't eat figs," her mom said.

"People grow out of allergies, Ma," she said. "I just thought . . ." But whatever Edith thought was quickly dispatched by the look on her mom's face, a look that held a fleeting sadness in it and beyond this a tremble of worry.

"Yes, that might be true," her mom said, "but why take the chance, dear?"

"What am I missing here?" Pandora chimed in. "I don't care for figs. They make me bloat."

"I can't eat them because the last time I did, I ended up in the hospital . . . I nearly died."

"You nearly died?" Pandora asked, horrified, glancing at Edith in the rearview mirror. "Edith, don't take this the wrong way, but just how much have you had to drink because it's clearly messed with your judgment? I mean, I've heard of having a death wish and all that, but this is just ridiculous, even for you. Besides, we aren't about to let you weasel out of the Seder that easily." Pandora smiled at her, which only made Edith want to devour the pâté that much more, and not just the pâté but also every single fig within a ten-mile radius.

She wanted out of this, Edith suddenly realized, and if it meant harming herself to do it, then so be it, for there was only so much she could take and she had about reached her limit. Her mom was dying, her dad was awful, her brothers were plotting his murder, and she was sitting in the back of this SUV, wondering how she'd gotten there, how she'd let her life get so completely away from her.

"Darling, just give me the pâté. I have a bit of a sweet tooth. Anything to wash away that kale, which left a gritty taste in my mouth," her mom said.

Edith relented and handed the pâté to her, along with the baguette chips and a plastic knife. While Edith and Pandora shared the calamari, her mom monopolized the pâté, which was fine with Edith, who was just happy to see that she had an appetite, considering the medication often left her nauseated and without one. "Hey, Ma, pace yourself," she said, but her mom took no notice and shoveled more and more of the thick, creamy slab into her mouth. "Since when did you develop a taste for figs? You never used to go near them."

"That is just not true, Thistle," her mom said. Yet as far as Edith could remember, it was true, which only made her wonder why her mom was lying. "Maybe you're thinking of Mo. My word, but there was one fussy eater! He wouldn't go near a single fruit or vegetable. The fights we used to have!"

"Sounds like someone else I know," Pandora said. "Baxter won't touch them, either. It's pizza, bagels, hamburgers, or nothing."

"When we used to take the kids to McDonald's once upon a time, I'd have to scrape off all the onions, pickles, and ketchup on Mo's hamburger, or else he'd throw a total conniption fit," her mom said. "Remember that, Thistle?"

Edith did remember. She also remembered that when her daddy ended up coming along, he demanded that Mo eat his burger, onions, pickles, ketchup, and all. "Why do you think you deserve special treatment, huh, boy?" he used to ask a sullen Mo, who raged silently and refused to eat until he got his way. She'd admired this quality of his, his ability to stand up for himself, for later it became even handier when he had to stand up not just for himself but also for Jacob, whom her dad used to corner and shout at, saying, "Well, which are you—a little boy or a little girl?" Jacob, who got bullied at school only to come home to take more bullying from her dad. At the time, of course, Edith found it hysterically funny, though she slowly realized that she only laughed to hide her own mortal fear, for he could turn on any one of them at any moment, and often did. His bullying knew no bounds—he liked to keep the house at a steady 80 degrees Fahrenheit in summer, which they all found far too warm, and an even steadier 61 degrees Fahrenheit in winter, which they all found far too chilly. Sometimes, at night, her mom raised or lowered the thermostat by a few degrees, and it was up to one of the kids, usually Mo, to return it to where it had been before he noticed. This worked well for a while until he eventually caught on. The next day, he installed a plastic cover with a lock, the key to which he had on him at all times. His excuse for keeping the house either too hot or too cold, he said, had to do with their part in conserving electricity and saving the environment, although Jacob rightly understood that it just came down to dollars and cents. "Cheapie the Jew rides again," Jacob liked to say of him behind his back. Mo seconded this and gleefully joined in the roasting, while Edith abstained.

An hour later, Pandora pulled onto Von Trapp Lane just in time to pass a police car driving away in the opposite direction. "This doesn't bode well," her mom said, her voice fragile and throaty once again. Edith looked at her, the transformation she'd undergone at Rejuvenate reversing and quickly undoing itself the closer they got to the house.

Mo and Jacob were stationed in the yard with unhappy looks on their faces. Jacob raised a hand into the air and pretended to stab himself in the gut. Had Invisible Girl arrived on the scene just in time to step out of the shadows and put things right?

Pandora pulled into the driveway and the second she came to a stop, Edith leaped out and hurried over to her brothers. "You didn't . . . Did something happen to Daddy?" she asked, glancing at her brothers for signs of blood. Blood had not been a part of the plan.

"Perish the thought, dear sister," Jacob said, "for our father, King Julian of Crapmenistan, is resting peaceably in his chambers and expelling intestinal gas through his anus, no doubt."

"Oh, that's so funny, Jacob," Mo snorted, mock-laughing. "But thanks to this one's boyfriend, who opened his damn German mouth, we now have a serious problem, because the old man's threatening to leave."

"Dietrich said what to Daddy about what?" she asked, her head still muzzy from the tequila.

Worse, though, she was suddenly queasy, her stomach churning from the fried calamari, which was not sitting well. In fact, none of this was sitting well with her. She desperately wanted to put on her dress and her heels and hightail it to Pomona, where she'd be treated with the respect of her station as a leading luminary in the field of ethics. But did anyone in her family ever take an interest in her career? Did they ever see her as anyone but the unattractive middle child whose marriage had fallen apart, who continued to struggle with her weight, and who had sex with wildly inappropriate men? No, the moment she stepped back into the family fray, she was as invisible as ever, which was just another reason she wanted nothing to do with her brothers' asinine, murderous plot. She loved her mom, but her mom's life was her own and had nothing to do with Edith anymore, nothing to do with any of them anymore. What made her brothers think that killing their dad would somehow restore order to the universe? Wasn't it better just to cut their losses and walk away?

"I was cleaning out the trunk of the rental car when Diet came out of the house to tell me that Dad was 'on the war course.' And sure enough the old man appeared a second later and he's carrying on about his money clip and he knows for a fact that the Mexicans stole it. He's making a beeline directly for them, hollering about INS and immigration and how they had no business in this country, although he had no idea if they're illegal or not. But leave it up to him to assume the worst, right?"

Yes, leave it up to her dad to assume the worst about others and leave it up to Jacob to assume the worst about him. "So add this to his list of offenses," she said. "Bravo, Jacob."

"I haven't finished yet," he said. "So he's standing at the curb, shouting at them to return his money clip and that there better not be a single dollar missing, when Diet taps him on the shoulder," and Jacob demonstrated it on Mo. "'Dr. Jacobson, instead of shouting at them, maybe you have misplaced your money clip in the house,' he said. And of course this doesn't go over well with the old man, who actually mocks Diet. Yes, mocks him, accent and all. I'm about to say something when Diet crosses the street to speak to the three men, who are loading the equipment back onto the trailer. That's when our dear beloved dad goes into the house and calls the police. I should mention that Diet's pretty much the most morally upright person I've ever met in my life. He honestly believes in the goodness of others, even in that thing we call a father. Once I made a nasty remark about the Gypsies who hang out all over Berlin selling postcards and while you're browsing, the kids pickpocket you. It happened to Grandpa Ernie when Ma and I took that trip with them to Europe. Anyway, the Roma are actually not nice people. I made an off-the-cuff remark about them to Diet, like how they're parasites feeding off the kindness of Germany and should be rounded up and deported. This completely set him off and he said, 'This is the same line of reasoning the Nazis used on your grandparents,' which absolutely took me aback, because the Jews weren't preying on unsuspecting Germans or tourists, they were very much a part of the fabric of German life, so the comparison, I told him, was fallacious and—"

"Yeah, he's definitely the most morally upright anti-Semite who's ever stayed in my house," Mo said.

"—insulting. But upon later reflection, I saw he had a point," he continued. "And by the way, Mo, you can just suck it. Every German isn't anti-Semitic and every Jew doesn't hate the Germans. Case in point," and he pointed to himself.

"What about when you went to visit his parents in Munich and they took you to the symphony? You said his dad 'got a glint in his eye' when he pointed out Hitler's old residence, then went on to say how much 'he admired the man.' These were your words, Jacob."

"Boys, enough!" Edith said, stepping between them. "I can't listen to any of this right now. Besides . . ." But she lost track of the thought, for the heat, albeit dry, was going straight to her head, and her stomach was bloated and cramping, as if someone were drumming on it from the inside out. Contrary to the comment her mom had made earlier, Edith was not premenstrual and had just had her period, which meant one of two things—either the Stardust Hotel had served her rejuvenating squid or she was letting her nerves get the better of her.

Turning, Edith walked away from her brothers into the cool house, to lie down on the sofa, hoping that whatever this was would pass. She fell almost instantly into a deep sleep in which she dreamed her mom had turned her into a white peacock that Jacob then ran over. She awoke with a start to find her mom standing over her.

"It looks like we're leaving," she said. "Your father's loading up the minivan."

"Ma, you do realize that it's rush hour in Los Angeles," she said. "Maybe you guys should at least wait until tomorrow morning."

"You know your father, Thistle," her mom said. "He just wants to go, so we're going."

"What about you?" she asked. "What do you want?"

"I think you already know the answer to that," her mom said.

"Then let him go on his own and you can fly back," she said. "Your children came here to spend Passover with you and Daddy, but if he's going to be difficult, it's probably better that he leave before someone loses an eye."

"I can't let him drive back alone," her mom said. "He's terrible with directions, you know that. He'll end up in Mexico if I'm not there to direct."

"The minivan has a state-of-the-art navigation system, Ma," she said. "All he has to do is tap in your address and it will tell him exactly where to go."

"I know where I'd like him to go," her mom said. "This may be my last Passover with all of my children and grandchildren, and he's behaving like a real schmuck. Maybe if you asked him to stay, he'd change his mind? You know he's always had a soft spot for his Eddie. You are your father's daughter, after all."

At any other time, these words might have soothed, even inspired her, yet now they only managed to intensify her panic and distress. Part of her wanted her daddy to get as far away from there as possible, while the other part of her wanted to honor her mom's wishes. Circumstances being what they were, Edith knew her only chance at convincing her dad to change his mind was to convince herself that he would be safe, that all of this talk about killing him was just that—talk—fantastical, improbable, discreditable talk, a way for her brothers to cope with the eventual loss of a parent, and the far more likable and agreeable of the two.

Before going to speak to her dad, Edith grabbed her dress and heels from the closet and went into the bathroom to change. She applied lipstick, eyeliner, and mascara, thinking as she did about Ephraim and fretting over how she was going to handle him and his runaway messages. That he'd broken into her house was one thing, but that he'd defiled himself in her shower was something else altogether. Was she going to have to take out a restraining order against him the way Tatiana had taken one out on her? Granted, her crush on Sheik Cohen had carried her into some pretty harrowing, uncharted waters, the currents of which had kept drawing her farther out to sea on the rickety raft of her own romantic delusions. The ethical standards by which she'd gauged his interest in her had been faulty, she'd realized that long ago, faulty and full of extraordinary loopholes. It was unfortunate that it had all ended the way it had, yet if anyone came out the rosier for it, it was Sheik, who'd gotten a novel out of it, spinning the grisly events into book sales and media appearances. She still hoped, some thirteen years later, that his publisher had dropped him, that he'd spiraled into one of his drunken, psychotic depressions, and that Tatiana had left him. While Edith wasn't exactly thrilled with the woman she saw staring back at her in the mirror, she was even less thrilled about wishing harm on Sheik, his career, and his marriage. Not to care—wasn't this what years of therapy had taught her? Wasn't this what she ought to have been reaching for still?

Edith found her dad at the minivan rearranging the suitcases. His fishing rod, tackle box, and waders lay on the driveway, her mom's spare oxygen tank sitting on top of the cooler. Edith had been fishing with him many times and thought this might prove her only way in.

"Daddy, you're not really going, are you? I was hoping we could spend some time together in Malibu. You know, fishing off the pier," she said. "Mo says it's some of the best fishing in the area."

"He says that, does he? Well, I tell you what. I know when I'm not wanted," he said. "I only want to be around people who want to be around me."

"Don't I count, Daddy?" she asked, the sun bearing down on her, inducing a painful throb behind her left eye, which, if she weren't careful, might bloom into one of her legendary migraines.

"You're the only one of my children who does," he said.

"Then stay for me," she wheedled. "I'll protect you," and the moment she said it, she wished she hadn't.

"From your brothers? Those two broke-ass, ungrateful punks?" her dad snarled, his face pulled into a menacing sneer. "No need, Eddie, because your father's going to have the last laugh yet."

"If you stay, you have to promise to play nicely," she said. "If not for me, do it for Ma. Will you do that?"

"Roz wants to get the hell out of here as much as I do," he said.

And you probably truly believe that, Edith thought. "I've told Mo time and again that those boys are growing up into TV and computer junkies and that they need to sit still and read a book. Exercise the mind, not their fingers or their mouths. You can't wring intellect out of a stone, I suppose." Meaning that her dad believed that Mo was raising his kids to be just like him, raising them to be shallow, entertainment addicts. But Mo was an incredible father, far better than her dad had ever been.

"I've already talked to Ma about your staying and she's okay with it," Edith said as her dad removed the suitcases and she returned the fishing gear to the minivan. She went for the cooler, lifting up the green tank, and froze, for it was perceivably lighter than her mom's other tank. She checked the knob surreptitiously, but there was no sign of tampering. The seal on it hadn't been touched or broken, a fact that Edith found both strange and disconcerting.

She set the tank in the back, recalling her conversation with Pandora, still refusing to believe the worst about her dad, who was already wheeling the suitcases down the sidewalk. She half hoped he might pause to take notice of the way she was dressed, to tell her how pretty she looked, and to ask where she was going, yet he simply held up a hand in a wave, then disappeared into the house and shut the door.

Edith pondered what was a fairly normal exchange with her dad except for one thing—the earlier apprehension, which he'd expressed about his sons, had vanished. Something had changed his mind about leaving, and it certainly wasn't Edith.

"I can't protect you from them, Daddy," she said to herself, turning to the house to find Mo and Jacob heading for her.

"Nice work, Thistle," Jacob said.

"Yeah, you certainly earned your keep," Mo said.

"I didn't do it for you," she said. "I did it for Ma."

"Then even nicer work," Jacob said, helping her into the van. "You sure you don't want me to drive you?"

"No, it's fine," she said, reaching for her seat belt.

As she did, she quickly glanced back into the dim cargo hold for the syringe, but it was gone. Though beads of sweat rolled down her face and back, her skin was chilled, her pulse excitable, and the spot above her left eye twitching and throbbing. No, she couldn't protect her dad from them any more than they could protect her mom from him. Whatever was going to happen was going to happen whether she wanted it to or not. But all of this would have to wait until later, she conceded, bidding her brothers good-bye. Driving off, she caught them in the side mirror, their faces as blank and eerie as she'd ever seen them, inscrutable but for the smiles they wore, smiles that belied the uncontainable relief and bitter scheming they hoped to mask.

When Edith came to the stop sign at the end of the street, she paused longer than necessary, thinking, *No, I can't let them do it. I won't. What kind of ethicist would I be if I did?* But then she continued on, following her phone's instructions to merge onto the 101 going south, then onto the 210 going east. She felt good behind the wheel of the van and was able to look down into the other cars, everyone headed home or to someplace else this weekend, which marked both the Hebrews' flight out of Egypt and the resurrection of Jesus Christ. She thought about that Jewish family who'd died such a horrible death on the 405, suspecting it was only a matter of time before it happened on one of the quiet streets in Toco Hills, or on Interstate 85 in Atlanta, out north toward Sandy Springs, where many Jews lived. The world was an unsafe place for the Jews these days, her people, who wanted nothing more than to be left alone. They'd given Israel back, yet the world still came for them. How could anyone have guessed that a mere eighty years after the end of World War Two the Jews would be made to roam the world yet again? It was despicable what was happening, which only made what her brothers wanted to do that much more reprehensible. How could they ask her to be part of such a macabre plan, to take another Jewish life, when they knew every single Jewish life was precious, so easily and readily extinguished? If they'd thought it through, they would have understood the pitfalls, the traces they were bound to leave behind and that the police would surely investigate. She was not about to go to jail because her brothers wanted to do a nice turn for a woman who might not survive into next month.

Over an hour and a half later, Edith finally arrived in Claremont, which sat in the Pomona Valley, the San Gabriel Mountains rising to the north and the Chino Hills to the south, the college itself sitting in the middle of town. The first thing she noticed upon driving through the gates was the ravishing beauty of the campus, full of luscious green lawns and giant palm trees, the architecture done up in the Moorish style with Spanish-tile roofs, everything perfectly manicured and maintained. The second thing she noticed was just how much lighter she felt driving through this campus as opposed to Emory's, whose heavy white-marbled, neoclassical-designed buildings she found oppressive and ugly and very out of place, looking more like the Acropolis than a top-tier, research-one university. She was unhappy to see that while the rest of California was dying of drought, this institution of higher learning was awash in water— *pun intended,* she thought, passing an enormous fountain that might well have irrigated one or two hundred acres of farmland.

The third thing Edith noticed on her drive along N. College Avenue toward Pearsons Hall was the emptiness. Where was everyone? Had the students already left for Easter? The fourth thing she noticed—actually it went hand in hand with the third—was the police presence, both campus and municipal, which made her wonder if some dignitary or important politician weren't nearby. Was that fascist President Cox, Republican granddaughter of Richard and Pat Nixon, speaking on campus? (She still found it amusing that in comparison to the many other adjectives used to describe her, the least offensive of them all was "Republican.")

Edith parked in the Harrison Street lot as her contact, Magda Stern, had instructed her to do. She headed to Pearsons Hall, while all around her circulated stony-faced police officers, wearing riot gear and Bluetooth devices and carrying what looked like magic wands. Something was afoot; Edith heard in the distance the echo of loud, thunderous, indecipherable voices—a rally in progress. She recalled her undergraduate days in Cambridge, when she'd particitated in womanly causes like Take Back the Night and humane causes during Israeli Apartheid Week and Palestinian Awareness Month, when she actually manned a booth and handed out pamphlets. Today, she looked back in shame on her younger self, who'd been such a vehement anti-Zionist, someone who'd never made the connection between the way she felt about Israel and the way she felt about herself. For years, she kept her involvement in these hateful, ignorant demonstrations a total secret, never divulging the part she'd played to anyone—that is, until Sheik came along. Sheik Abdullah Cohen, with his Israeli mother's flirtatious mouth and his Lebanese father's fuck-me eyes; Sheik Cohen, with his rack-and-pinion mind and spark-plug heart. Edith had neither fallen for him the first afternoon they'd met on the stoop nor the next time, when they seemingly ran into each other at a bar in Adams Morgan. A poet back then, Sheik had just come from a grueling workshop in which his classmates had eviscerated his work, while she had just come from a meeting of BDI (Boycott and Divestiture of Israel), though she didn't tell him that. Instead, she told him she'd been out walking dogs in the neighborhood.

"Speaking of, Tatiana said she never heard back from you," he said.

"Back from me?" Edith asked, remembering she'd never responded to his wife's email, which she'd sent two months ago. "Oh, about the pugs."

"I was sure we'd found our dog walker," he said.

"It's nothing personal," she said, regretting it immediately because of course it was personal. "I've just been so overwhelmed with school and my other clients. Bad timing, I guess."

"We tried someone else," he went on as if he hadn't heard her, "but the pugs didn't take to her. They liked you, though," and he smiled that buttery, infectious smile of his that nearly broke her heart and resolve. "I'm definitely not one for the hard sell, but I know good people when I meet them. I need to feel comfortable handing my kids over to a total stranger, but seeing as you're not a stranger, I'm willing to give you the benefit of the doubt and trust you with them."

"The benefit of the doubt?" she asked. That's when he told her he'd seen her outside the brownstone on more than one occasion. "Probably so. Once I find a route I like, it just becomes habit," although as she said this, her pulse quickened and the blood roared in her ears. She was sure she was going to faint and dug her nails into her sweaty palms. She'd never felt anything quite like this before, the need to stay hidden yet also the need to be found out, and these two needs went on warring inside of her for the rest of the time it took her to finish her drink, make up an excuse to leave, and say good-bye. She was hurrying away from the bar when she heard him call her name and then he was beside her, leather backpack slung over one shoulder, her phone in his hand.

"You might need this," he said, though all Edith heard was "You might need me." After she thanked him, he held out his hand for her to shake and said, "See you, Edith," then he climbed onto his bike and pedaled away.

She watched him go and knew that he knew what she'd done. He knew who she was yet didn't seem to care. She'd been following him all over D.C., an exciting, thrilling game of hide-and-seek. She never got too close to Sheik, especially when Tatiana was around, for Edith didn't trust her to understand the fun they were having. As she had wandered through the explosive, Mardi Gras–like razzle-dazzle of Adams Morgan that Friday night, with people milling about on the sidewalks and the singles bars and hookah lounges packed full of eager young women dressed in scanty, skanky miniskirts and the predatory, equally young men who hungered after them, she'd understood then that Sheik loved her and that if it hadn't been for Ta- tiana, she might have had a chance—Tatiana who'd bewitched him into believing she wasn't the old, ugly hag she was, for Edith saw right through her, just as she'd seen right through her mom.

As she climbed out of the van, Edith thought about this, thought about the aftermath, about meeting Elias, marrying him, and leav- ing D.C. to settle in Atlanta. Having never done well with the police, she recoiled at the sight of so many of them gathered in one place and hurried into the building. No one was there to greet her, the hall itself quiet and still, as if someone had pulled the fire alarm and ev- eryone had evacuated the building never to return. She walked from one end to the other and back again, then got out her phone to text Magda only to find that she had a few missed calls from the woman, who'd also texted her. According to the first, the department was being forced to "postpone the conference due to unforeseen circum- stances." Her second text advised Edith not to come to the Pomona campus at all, because "things are escalating and it's not safe. The president has advised all Jewish employees to vacate the premises until further notice. I have left for the day. I'm sorry about this, Edith. I was looking forward to meeting you."

Well, that's just fucking great, Edith thought, not even bother- ing to reply, for her fingers were trembling too much to compose a text anyway. Even from where she was, she could still hear the grumbling of voices and beyond this another sound, which, when she stepped outside, turned out to be a helicopter. It was hovering over the campus and looked to be from one of the local area news stations. What the hell was happening? Edith wasn't sure she was all that interested in finding out, especially since the university pres- ident himself had issued the warning. She rushed to the van and had almost made it when her phone gonged. She was still in mo- tion and glanced down at the screen for one split second—TBS1946 had played another word—not looking where she was going until it was too late; she stepped off the curb, her left heel giving out from under her, and down she went, launching her phone into the air. She watched it land on the hood of a BMW, bounce off, then go skittering across the parking lot. When she stood up, she found that she'd split her dress right down the side, put a hole in her stocking, and broken two nails. She got up and walked in dazed circles, fighting back the excruciating pain in her hip, wanting to cry though finding herself unable to muster a single tear; she was as dry as California itself. At one time, she'd done nothing but cry, for her failed marriage, for her mom, but mostly for having lost Sheik, her one true love. She could already feel the giant bruise forming, a commemoration of this humiliating moment, just as she carried around another bruise, invisible yet just as agonizing, of her last encounter with Sheik at the police station.

After hobbling across the parking lot, Edith retrieved her phone, which was unharmed, then laughed a doleful, unhappy laugh when she saw the word TBS1946 had played—MOTHER. All around her, the police were mobilizing, the helicopter hovering, and the voices bellowing, yet Edith no longer cared about any of it. She cared only about the word on her screen, the word, which, the longer she stared at it, came to have far more weight and importance than she'd ever given it. She'd been telling herself she'd come to L.A. for the sole purpose of delivering her talk and being celebrated by her peers, and that Passover with her family was merely an auspicious coincidence, yet she saw now, as she limped over to the van and struggled to climb in, that perhaps she'd gotten it all wrong. Perhaps the true test of her mettle was not to be found in her perceived success as a renowned professor of ethics, but somewhere else, in the smaller, quieter, thankless acts of goodness—she was thinking about her Jewish next-door neighbor Abigail, a seventy-four-year-old widow who ran a bed-and-breakfast out of her house. She was thinking of all the times Abigail had asked her to drive her to the grocery store, or take her to the Chabad house, or go on a walk with her around the neighborhood, and how Edith inevitably declined each of her requests, not because she didn't like Abigail, because she did, but because she saw Abigail as someone to fear, Abigail who had reached the end of life and had little to show for it, and because of this, Edith kept her distance, stopping to chat when she had the time, though never going in for a cup of tea. Edith did other things for her—she put back her garbage bins, collected her mail, picked up litter in her yard, and sent potential guests to her B&B. She kept on the periphery of Abigail's life, actively participating in it without having to deal with the woman herself, without having to watch her struggle to walk to the mailbox, to hear about her arthritis, her angina, her constipation and failing bladder—all things Edith knew would happen to her eventually. But of course these were merely excuses. If she'd been honest with herself, she would have understood that she simply didn't want to have to see Abigail die or miss her when she was gone.

In the van, Edith gazed at her phone, giving herself a minute to shake off what had just happened. She shuffled the tiles, then sized up the board, all of the possible combinations and configurations of letters. As she did, she saw an odd, surprising pattern take shape. It couldn't possibly have been, yet there it was, a sentence developing out of the random assortment of words TBS1946 had played—IAMB, SORRY, ABOUT, YOUR, MOTHER. Edith studied the arrangement again, just to make sure she wasn't hallucinating, that the fall hadn't addled her brain. She blinked her eyes, then looked down again, noting the same series of words, which formed the same incontrovertible sentence.

TBS1946.

She'd just assumed this handle—hers was EdiTHICIST, the same one she used on Twitter—was her opponent's initials and date of birth, though now she realized that it stood for *The Big Sleep* and the year in which the movie had premiered, 1946. Elias's favorite film. Elias, whom she hadn't heard from or spoken to in ages. He'd left the film studies department at Emory a couple of years ago to take a position at USC, where, as far as she knew, he was still teaching. It had once seemed odd to her that she'd come all the way to L.A. and not see him, but having visited Mo several times and not called, she hadn't seen the point this time, either: They hadn't remained friends during or after the divorce. Still, only Elias could have been this clever, *or this manipulative,* she thought, to get in touch with her like this. The Scrabble app had its own built-in messenger service, which she enabled, tentatively tapping out "Elias, is that you?," then hitting send.

She waited a few minutes for a response, and when none came, she started up the van and put it in reverse. The pressure of her foot on the pedal produced a searing sting in her hip that radiated down her leg, making her wince and cry out in such pain that she inadvertently took her hands off the steering wheel. The van, already in motion, launched backward, running up and over the curb and crashing against a small fountain, the abrupt stop tossing Edith forward into the suddenly inflated airbag. The impact upset the glove compartment and the plastic door popped open, vomiting up all kinds of receipts and maps, a compass, a pen, a half-eaten chocolate doughnut, and among all of it a small electronic device Edith had never seen before.

By the time she opened the door and stepped out, she was set upon by three police officers, who swarmed around her, Bluetooth devices lit up and wands at the ready.

"Suspect is a white female, mid-fifties," one of them said. Edith glared at him, though she said nothing. "Negative, suspect does not appear armed or dangerous." He turned to Edith, who was swaying in place, dizzy and dazed, her hip in agony. She plunked herself right down in the grass and lay on her back, her dress coming apart, the breeze cool against her bare skin. She kicked off her heels and stared up into the trees, the call of the birds and the voices washing over her. "Ma'am, I'm going to need to see your license. Ma'am, can you hear me? Are you hurt?"

"Yes, all over," she said, referring more to her pride than to her literal person, though her person had taken quite a beating, too. Five minutes later, a medic was at her side to check her vitals, which turned out to be normal. "Did I damage the van?" she asked, still on her back, the grass tickling her neck and making her giggle. "I should call Edith," and she reached for her phone.

"Ma'am, your name's Edith," the officer said, kneeling down to hand her back her license, which must have fallen out of her purse and onto the floor of the van. "You aren't diabetic, are you?"

"Diabetic? Me? No, why?" she asked.

"We found this little gizmo. It checks blood glucose levels," he said, showing her the device.

Just as she was examining it—"Nope, not mine"—a massive chunk of the circular fountain, which had been supporting the weight of the three-ton van, broke off and fell to the ground, the water spilling down the sides in thick torrents and splashing her. The van lurched and rolled back, the bumper and undercarriage scraping against the masonry and releasing a terrific screech. "Oh, oh no. Somebody do something," she said, watching it all happen with pure horror on her stricken face. "We have to save the water!" She wasn't sure why she was being so hysterical about it. She turned away from the sight of the ruined fountain and the van's damaged back end and looked down at her phone, which was still clutched in her hand and which had gonged again—a reply from TBS1946.

"Yes, it's Elias. I wanted to surprise you and come to your talk, but it looks like it's been canceled. I'm still on campus. I can meet you at the west end of the quad directly behind Bridges Auditorium. Find me?"

"I'll be right back," she said to no one in particular, the police not seeming to care where, or even if, she went.

Bedraggled and bemoaning the state of her appearance and of her life, Edith limped away, breathing through the pain in her hip. She followed the echoing thunderclap of voices toward Marston Quad; she'd already determined this to be the place Elias and the rest of the campus were gathered, though for what purpose she had no idea.

What exactly could have been so important that they'd canceled her talk, so threatening that the president had issued such a dire warning? *This isn't Nazi Germany in 1938,* she thought, approaching the quad from the north. *This is California, USA, in 2022.*

Nearing the quad, Edith saw an even greater assemblage of police, the bulk of whom were also in riot gear. She tried to make out what was happening at the far end of the quad but got the distinct impression she'd be safer right where she was, stationed against a giant oak and scanning the passing faces for Elias. She didn't want him to see her like this, not for their first meeting in so many years, but she also figured it didn't much matter, for Elias had never bothered to notice her appearance one way or another. Now that she had discovered with whom she'd been playing electronic Scrabble, she'd felt both resentful and ashamed. Part of her had been hoping her opponent might be a handsome, single man in the Atlanta metro area. Not that she was in the market for a handsome, single man, but considering she was through with Ephraim, recognizing that she would never find the courage to answer his texts or return his calls, the thought of having a potential date upon returning home appealed to her. Granted, if she'd been following her own handle logic, then TBS1946 would have been far too old for her. Her intuition had failed her again, as it had failed her when it came to Ephraim and all those who'd come before him, including Elias, though of course it had all begun with Sheik.

She still wondered how she could have read him so incorrectly, how she'd gotten it all so spectacularly wrong, and how she'd allowed herself to become that person who'd gone to such obsessive lengths to keep him, especially when he'd never belonged to her. *Oh, the absolute horror of it,* she thought, spotting Elias, the slouchy back of him, which she would have recognized anywhere. She nearly called out his name but stopped herself, because she heard a voice coming from the opposite end of the quad. The speaker was speaking into a mic and though what he was saying was muffled, the voice itself gave her the shivers. Edith stepped out from behind the tree and headed toward it, as if it were a siren song luring her to her rocky, watery death. She paused to touch Elias's shoulder before winding her way through the crowd, many members of which were chanting anti-Semitic slurs and hoisting signs in the air. She came to a cordoned-off area, which stretched from one end of the quad to the other, a line of police officers guarding its perimeter from the surging, aggressive demonstrators. She felt someone pressing against her and when she turned to see who it was—Elias, naturally—she also saw a staggering sea of swastikas held aloft by what appeared to be every make and model of American, from white, black, and Hispanic to young, old, male, and female. Some of the men wore turbans, some of the women hijabs.

"What is this?" Edith asked Elias, dispensing with salutations and small talk. They could catch up later, if they made it out of Pomona alive.

"It started out as a memorial service for the son of the family who was murdered yesterday on the 405. But it's devolved into this," he said. "He was a senior, graduating in May. Maximilian Vogel. Head of the Jewish Federation of Students, wanted to be a doctor and a volunteer at one of the new medical centers the Israelis were building for the Palestinians in Gaza before the invasion." He turned to look behind him at the angry, hateful mob.

"And him? The one who's speaking? Who's he?" she asked.

"I think it's pretty obvious who he is," he said without rancor, for which she was grateful. "That's Zion Abdullah Cohen. He's a freshman here at Pomona." Edith waited for him to add, "As if you didn't already know that," but he didn't. She was thankful to him for not accusing her of knowing it, although she did know, had known for quite some time, ever since she'd agreed to give her talk. She'd gone to Pomona's homepage and there he was, all six feet two inches of him standing beside his dad, the prominent writer with the receding hairline and the graying dreadlocks, Sheik Abdullah Cohen. "Maximilian was his best friend," he said.

Over the shouts and hisses of the protesters, Zion addressed the mourners, who were sitting facing him, and spoke unsentimentally about Maximilian—Maxi, as he called him. It seemed impossible to Edith that she hadn't seen the boy since he was five and there he was, eighteen years old, the spitting image of Sheik, with traces of Tatiana thrown in for good measure—his outsized ears, for example, his pert little nose and high Russian cheekbones. He was beautiful and, for a moment, Edith imagined that he was hers and beamed with the kind of pride she would have reserved for her own courageous son or daughter. "I didn't know he'd be here. I'm sorry," she said, speaking to Elias, though he was deeply involved in listening to Zion and probably didn't hear her.

"The kid's articulate. I'll grant you that," he said, turning to her.

It was then that someone in the crowd lobbed an egg at Zion, which grazed the top of his head and careened off to smash in the grass. He wasn't as lucky with the next egg, which hit him right in the center of his forehead, the impact of which knocked him back, though only for a second, because he righted himself immediately, cleared the runny yellow yolk from his face and chin, and kept going, while Edith spun around and stood on her tiptoes, trying to find the culprit.

Around them, the sickening slogan of the afternoon, "The only good Jew is a dead Jew," erupted out of the mouths of the mob. Another egg was lobbed and missed, then another and another, and Edith kept wondering when the police were going to step in, but they didn't budge. The sixth egg broke against Zion's shoulder, the seventh against his chest, yet he kept going, louder, stronger, repeating Maxi's name, while the eggs kept coming, lobbed from nowhere and everywhere, and Edith left her place and elbowed her way through the crowd, knowing she was going to get into serious trouble for what she was about to do.

Elias trailed behind her, calling her name, but Edith refused to stop for one single second until she'd reached the van. It was sitting exactly where she'd left it, the police and medic having moved on to more pressing suspicious persons, and she climbed in, the pain in her hip spectacular and grim, but she would use it, she would not squander it, not like the wasted water in the empty fountain, the jets still firing into the air. Elias was suddenly at the van and he climbed in after her, saying, "You can't be serious," but she was. As serious and determined as she had been on her wedding day, as serious and determined as she had been in trying to take her own life after she and Sheik finally fucked on his bed while Tatiana was away and Zion was playing downstairs and Elias was taking his oral exams at American University. She'd left Sheik that afternoon prepared to lose Elias, to tell him the truth—"I'm in love with Sheik and he's in love with me"—and ran into Tatiana on the stoop and the two chatted briefly, airily, the small talk of would-be friends. Then a couple of days later, an officer at her door, a restraining order, and her call to Sheik, who would not call or text her back—all of this hidden from Elias, to whom she blamed the attempted suicide by pills on the torture of academia and exhaustion, imploring him to believe that she'd collapsed emotionally under the weight of an avalanche of stress.

Now, seated beside him, Edith remembered making a lewd joke about him and his orals as Sheik went down on her and he laughed right in her pussy and didn't stop, her body bucking on the bed, his tongue roughhousing her clit. "I'm sorry," she said now, repacking the airbag and stuffing it back into place, then putting the van in drive. It shuddered and groaned and squealed, then the tires finally found purchase and off they went.

"Sorry for what?" Elias asked. He was thicker and bulkier and seemingly sadder than the last time she'd seen him. He'd cut his hair short, the peyos gone. Out of his black frock and hat, he looked like himself again, Elias Plunkett, the boy in jeans and a plaid shirt whom she'd met while she'd been waiting for Sheik to come around.

"For everything," she said, "for this," and she maneuvered the van down N. College Avenue until she came to Marston Quad. "Get out," she said. "I don't think you're going to want to be Clyde to my Bonnie."

She revved the engine to emphasize her point. She was tired of being afraid, tired of being mistreated, tired of a world that had not learned from its mistakes, that still came after her people and wanted them gone, disappeared, erased, dead. She was tired of living as if all of this hatred were okay, as if it were somehow justified, as if people didn't have the freedom or the moral intelligence to choose between right and wrong. She was sick of the excuses, sick of being accused, sick of being sick of her fellow man. Mostly, though, she was sick of having to look over her shoulder, of speaking to roomfuls of people and having what she said fall on deaf ears.

"Don't tell me what to think," he said, strapping himself in.

"No, Elias. Maybe you didn't understand. I'm going to need you later," she said, which seemed to do the trick, because his face went from dark to light and he finally got out. Then she was pulling the van off the road and onto the quad, where she began a slow assault of honking, not wanting to hurt anyone. It couldn't be said that Edith didn't have a touch of murder in her heart, as she leaned on the horn and the crowd began to disperse and fall away, the signs coming down, either chucked at the van or abandoned altogether. She pressed on, leaving deep declivities in the earth, but she didn't care, what she was doing was more important—she was parting the Red Sea, heading for the line of police officers, who were suddenly on the van, swarming around it, as Edith came to a complete stop, never once taking her eyes from Zion, who was still orating, still gesticulating, holding up pictures of Maximilian and saying "We will never forget him," saying, "Life is short but he will live long in our memories." He had much of his father in him, she suspected, and even from where she was, she could sense the charm and charisma oozing out of him. She watched him for another minute, then opened the door and stepped down onto the lawn, where she was immediately arrested, handcuffed, and led to a squad car. Some of the protesters booed, hissed, and spat at her, while others merely ignored her. Throughout it all, though, her ride to the station and her subsequent booking, Edith remained firm in her conviction that she'd done the right thing.

Good for the Jews, bad for Edith Jacobson Plunkett, who then spent the next three hours in the Claremont Police Station hoosegow until Elias finally showed up and bailed her out, though not without letting her know he thought what she'd done was senseless, selfish, and stupid.

"You could have hurt someone," he admonished her once they were outside. "What then?"

"But I didn't," she replied, leaning against his car. Her hip was killing her. She massaged it gently, caressing what she knew she would find later, after she'd undressed, the ugly bloom of a bruise, her battle scar.

"It's not a battle, Edith," he said, climbing in and unlocking the passenger-side door. "The barbarians are already through the gates. The bonfires have already been lit."

"Don't you mean the storm troopers have already captured the *Millennium Falcon*?" she asked, trying for levity, though her tone made it sound mocking, and she regretted having said it.

"You'll be happy to know that my obsession with *Star Wars* happened in a galaxy far, far away," he said, going on to tell her how he'd sold his collection a couple of years ago. "I realized I was putting far too much energy into that world and not enough into this one."

"But you were so devoted," she said, picturing the room and all of his collectibles again. For whatever reason, hearing that he'd gotten rid of it all saddened her.

"Now I'm devoted to other pursuits," he said, pulling out of the lot. "Figurines of Princess Leia and Chewbacca? You had every right to leave me."

"Elias, I didn't leave you," she said. "You left me. Remember?"

"Maybe it's better if we don't talk about this," he said, heading for the 210. He gallantly insisted on driving her back to Calabasas, since the van had been impounded. "How's Roz, by the way?" he asked. "I was sorry to hear she's been ill."

"We spent the afternoon at a spa, which lifted her spirits for a while," she said. "Mud baths, hot springs, and fungal wraps. It was all very 1990s L.A." As she went on to tell him about her mom, and her job and life since then, she kept wondering how he'd come to know about her mom's illness and finally put the question to him.

"Julian told me," he said. "We've remained in touch. He never said? I suppose he thought you'd take it badly. Are you taking it badly?"

"Not at all," she said. "But you do realize he never liked you or had a kind word to say about you when you were his son-in-law and even before that."

"Yes, I discussed all of that with him," he said. "As his therapist, he actually approached me with it."

"His *what*?" she exclaimed, stupefied. "You're a therapist now? Since when?"

"Since I left the suffocating classrooms of academia and went back to get my degree in social work," he explained.

"Let me get this straight: My the-examined-life-is-not-worth-living dad has not only been in touch with you, my ex-husband, but you, my ex-husband, are also his long-distance therapist?"

"Well, technically I'm a licensed clinician," he said, correcting her. "But therapist is less of a mouthful."

It was odd for her to hear that her dad had discussed his obnoxious behavior with Elias, its target, for she'd never known him to discuss his onerous behavior with anyone, much less with his own family. She supposed it was easier for him to unburden himself with someone like Elias, who lived thousands of miles away and had little investment in him, who wouldn't judge him for his past and his maniacal indiscretions. Still, she didn't like it, and she got the sense that Elias was about to unburden himself as well and that whatever he had to say was going to reverse the alchemy of the moment, turning gold into lead and lead into foolscap, on which she would pen her magnum opus, beginning with the line *It didn't end well for any of them.*

"You do realize I can't take you or any of this seriously," she said, thinking of her day, its morning with Ephraim that had become her evening with Elias. *Will the wonders of this complex, internecine clusterfuck of a life never cease?* According to her phone, it was 9:30 P.M. She'd received no new messages, no missed calls, no notifications of any kind, which was more than okay with her, even if it was surprising, considering how many emails she got a day from various departments and various functionaries at Emory, the latter keeping her apprised of her case's status, cc'ing and bcc'ing one another ad infinitum right on down the line. "On Monday, I have to meet with another evidentiary committee. This committee is separate from the Committee on Honor Code Violations," she explained, "which is also separate from the Sexual Harassment and Misconduct Committee, which is also separate from the Faculty and Student Relations Committee, which first dealt with the complaint about four months ago. They're trying to get rid of me, Elias. But I'm sure my dad has kept you abreast of the situation. I'm sure he's thrilled to be proven right. He always hated that I took that position at Emory, even if it had nothing at all to do with him."

"Speaking of," Elias said. The traffic on the 210 was light in both directions, the blue-black sky stretching out above them like another road, this one traveled by dreams and dreamers. "You're not going to like what I'm about to tell you, but I don't think it's fair to you or to me that I should have to keep carrying it around. I don't think you'd want that. I know I don't." She knew without having to be told that what he was about to say had to do with Sheik, and she wondered what else Elias had learned in the interim between their divorce seven years ago and tonight. What other terrible things had come to light? "That fight we had about Sheik Cohen and the remark you made about him in the car. Remember?"

"How could I forget it?" Edith asked.

"You accused me the next morning of knowing far more than I

should have about him. I don't remember what I said in response, but whatever I did say was a lie." They were flying through the air, the night a gaping mouth devouring everything in its path, including her will to turn to Elias and tell him to be quiet, that she didn't want to hear any of this because it no longer mattered. "It was Julian, Edith. He told me about Sheik. He told me about what you did. He told me all of it," he said. Edith let what he'd just confessed hang between them, saying nothing, offering nothing. She'd always assumed her mom had mentioned Sheik in passing, which was her way, of course, her mom who never meant any harm but who had a way of causing it anyway. To hear it had been her dad all along, though, who'd come between Elias and her, didn't make much sense, until of course it slowly did. "I know for a fact he feels terrible about it," Elias concluded.

Still Edith said nothing, letting the navigation system punctuate the silence with directions—a left onto Mulholland Parkway, another left into Edelweiss Estates, then past the empty guardhouse and under the raised metal arm. *Not so secure, your gated kingdom,* thought Edith. They were on Von Trapp Lane, then curling around the cul-de-sac. Edith commanded him to keep driving, so he did, looping and looping around.

"You know for a fact he feels terrible about it," she said. "Were those his exact words, or are you paraphrasing? Or are you covering for him? My mom covers for him. That's how she's spent the last forty years of her life, catering and covering for a man who treated all of us like your worthless figurines, collecting us and moving us around the house for his own pleasure. Did you know that? Did I ever tell you about the time he—" But she stopped herself as Elias stopped the car. They were idling in the driveway, the lights of the house dark except for the upstairs guest room. "I have to go inside now, Elias," she said. "Thank you for the ride." She unbuckled herself, stepped out into the cool, starlit evening, the air tinged with eucalyptus. She took a step, then leaned back in and added, "If you don't have any plans for the Seder tomorrow, why don't you join us?

Or you can just watch the festivities on TV. I think the network's going to stream it live."

She didn't wait for him to respond but shut the door and made her way up the sidewalk, her hip and feet and ego aching. She kept waiting to hear the sound of Elias pulling out of the drive, but he didn't. Instead, he just sat there, thinking, she imagined, about the next word he was going to play. She half expected her phone to gong again before she'd even gotten to the door, yet her phone didn't gong or ping or pong. It remained as dark and lifeless as Elias himself looked from the deep interior of the car, where the dim light of the dash cast his face in eerie relief and made his eyes shimmer, like the eyes of the coyote that appeared in the yard. It had something in its mouth, something white and furry by the looks of it, and Edith shuddered, knowing it was the little rescued terrier, Nieves, and that come morning, she'd have to break the bad news to the family.

"Get out of here," she yelled at the coyote, which slunk away, across the street and out of sight, though she could very well have also been speaking to Elias. It didn't much matter if he heard her or not, for he was already pulling out of the drive as if he had, flashing his headlights once, then he, too, was gone, disappearing down the block. She watched him go, then went into the house, where she found Mo sitting on the sofa in the dark. He pointed the remote control at the giant TV, yet nothing happened, the screen remaining dark, just a flat black expanse on the wall. She hobbled over and took a seat beside him, switching on the small lamp, a Tiffany-glass knockoff, on the end table, which lit the ceiling in colorful, cheery diamonds. She reached over and grabbed the remote, just as she used to do when she was a girl and her stupid older brother didn't have the sense to realize the batteries were dead, or that Jacob had stolen them to power one of his toys. She removed the back and, sure enough, the batteries were missing. "And so ends the case of the inoperable remote," she said, setting it down on the coffee table.

"What the hell happened to you?" he asked, turning and staring at her.

"Emotional earthquake, 8.9 on the Richter scale," she said.

"Welcome to sunny California," he said. "How'd your talk go?"

"It didn't." She sighed and told him about the travesty that had been her evening. "I'm going to need someone to drive me back to Claremont to pick up the van," she said.

"Well, you win hands down," he said. "You definitely had a more exciting day than any of us."

"It wasn't exciting at all, Mo," she said, but when she thought about it, she had to admit it had left her feeling different about herself, bigger and less fearful of the world, if only a little. "Oh, well, okay. It actually was kind of thrilling. I mean, I've never been arrested for anything in my life. They actually led me away in handcuffs! Like I was some crazy, lawless fugitive."

"Speaking of that," he said, leaning in closer.

She knew what was coming and wanted to head him off at the pass. "Before we get into any of that, I need you to answer a question: What do you know about figs?" she asked. Mo gazed at her, not understanding the question or its importance. "What I mean is, what do you know about figs as they pertain to me? I mean, I know I'm allergic. But when exactly did we know? How'd we find out?"

She expected to hear the story about how she'd been hospitalized while her mom and Mo were away, but her brother gazed at her as if he had never seen her before, his eyes huge in his head. "You really don't remember?" he asked.

"Remember what?" Edith asked, alarmed.

"We were playing in the backyard and I turned my back on you for like a second and all of a sudden you were just lying facedown in the dirt under the fig tree. I can't believe you don't remember."

"But what am I supposed to remember?"

"You took a bite of one of the figs that'd fallen off the tree and went into shock. We had to rush you to the emergency room. I was probably like seven, so you would have been . . . five? We've known that you're deathly allergic to figs since you were five. Why are you asking me that, though?"

Then slowly, because she couldn't believe it, because she'd always suspected it, though until today, when she'd been so tempted to play Russian roulette with the fig pâté, hadn't truly been able to accept it, she told her brother about those two days when he and their mom were in L.A., how she'd eaten some of Daddy's figs, which Mo remembered, but what she really wanted him to know was what she'd learned that very afternoon from their mom—that their dad had encouraged her to eat the figs and then lied to Roz about how it had happened. "Why would he tell her I snuck them?" she asked. "Do you think he just forgot about my allergy, too, and didn't want to be scolded? Parents make mistakes all the time, Mo."

"Parents forget birthdays and anniversaries. Parents don't forget their children's food allergies. I know exactly what my kids can and can't eat," he said. She hadn't wanted to believe it, for in believing it she'd be forced to reexamine other episodes—his beaning Mo in the head with the baseball, covering the pool without first checking to make sure Jacob wasn't swimming along the bottom, as he was wont to do. These were accidents, according to her dad, yet nowhere in Edith's memory could she locate the one phrase that would have undone at least some of the harm—*I'm sorry*. He'd never said he was sorry for what had happened to Edith that night, and now, coupled with what she'd learned from Elias, she was beside herself with disappointment and sorrow, for she, too, had always defended her dad against the likes of Mo and Jacob. It was more than simple, ordinary sadness, though, for it set off in her a series of unsettling, uncomfortable reactions, touching a deep, dark, oily well that was ignited into flame, which licked at her organs, singed her nerves, and burned her down from the inside out. A silent combustion of historical proportions, never before seen or felt with such an intensity by her, who was slowly coming to know it all differently, everything she'd ever trusted and believed in falling away to reveal its essence, not of what it was but of what it wasn't, not a heart fashioned out of flesh and blood but a sooty heart of cold, hard coal that went on beating in the next room, oblivious.

"Do you think he's vindictive?" she asked, although she'd already come to this conclusion on her own. She thought about the harmless practical joke she'd played on Jacob by switching the suitcases and all at once felt even worse than before.

"He's a lot of things, but yeah, I'd say that's one of his more obvious, unlovable qualities," Mo said.

"Then I know exactly how we can do what you want to do," she said, just like that, just that easily. "Furthermore, I know how we can do it and not get caught." She told Mo her suspicions about the syringe, noting, though, the slight hiccup that it had disappeared. She prayed her little brother had done what he always did and appropriated something of hers that didn't belong to him. *Patterns,* she thought, and hoped this particular pattern held true, for this could be a little miracle of murder.

"I told Jacob about it, so, yeah, he probably pilfered it. You know he can be really motivated when he wants to be. Look, I've got to get to bed. We can discuss all of this tomorrow," he said. "The three of us," and he reached over and hugged her. She melted against him, this big brother of hers, finally accepting her place among them, finally understanding that they had no other choice.

"Before you go, I have a tiny confession to make," she said, then told him about switching the suitcases because she thought Mo had given Jacob preferential treatment. "That's always been my room, you know, but I . . . I thought it'd be funny."

"Yeah, about that," he said. "Luckily for you, the German figured it out before Jacob did and we switched them back. I don't know how he knew, but he did. His naturally keen sense of deceit really came in handy, I guess."

"I kept meaning to switch them back but just didn't have the chance," she said. She didn't think of herself as a vindictive person usually, *but then again I am my father's daughter,* she thought with a shudder, and she understood that she'd have no choice but to fully embrace and harness this quality, as they all would have to, if they were going to see this thing through.

"Look, don't beat yourself up," Mo said. "Jacob's none the wiser—the German promised he wouldn't tell him. Sorry, I had to give them your room."

She hugged Mo, who then drifted upstairs. She slid out of her heels and then slipped quietly into the downstairs guest room, where her parents lay sound asleep, her mom's breathing gravelly, her dad snoring lightly. Other than this, the house was quiet except for the sudden slamming of the front door, which made her wonder who was going out at this time of night and for what purpose. But she let this go—she refused to let herself worry and wonder about every little thing under Mo's roof—and approached the bed, where she stood over her dad and gazed down at him, this man who looked like every other man she'd ever seen asleep, except that he wasn't like every other man, he was Julian Jacobson, her daddy, her should-have-been protector. If anything, he had been the bogeyman who lived under her bed and the creature in the closet who wanted to eat her alive and the sad, pathetic ghost who did not know he was already dead.

The rollaway sat in the far corner of the room, nearest the window. Someone had opened it and made it up, probably her mom, she thought, climbing out of her dress and into the small, spongy bed, forgoing her nightly routine.

She slid under the covers and lay on her right side. As she spread her arm out under the pillow, which was how she always slept, something fell to the floor. Sitting up, she leaned over and shined her iPhone toward the spot where it had fallen and there it was, the syringe, just lying there. *Jacob,* she thought. Leaving her little presents under her pillow—a dead butterfly, a crushed frog, the decapitated body of her Barbie doll—just as he used to do when they were kids.

Edith reached down and picked up the syringe, then lay back, staring at the liquid inside it, which she understood was insulin—it hadn't taken much of a leap to realize that the last renter of the van had been a diabetic who had probably dropped the syringe by accident, that it had rolled under the seat and kept rolling, lodging itself in the wheel well where Edith had discovered it and from where Jacob had retrieved it. Insulin—fast-acting, fatal in large doses, and untraceable back to them. *Insulin—it does a body good*, she thought, imagining the three of them, she, Jacob, and Mo, holding him down, injecting the insulin between his toes, then waiting for it to work its magic and shut down his heart, this heart that beat only for itself, this damaged, destructive heart that she finally knew without a shadow of a doubt had to be silenced. Sitting up, she pointed the syringe at him as if it were a magic wand.

"Figs, Daddy? Really? You let me eat figs?" she whispered. "What did I ever do to you? What did any of us?" Yet even as she said it, she suspected she was asking the wrong questions and that a better one might have been: "Did you ever even want us, Daddy?"

Now that she was hopped up on adrenaline and too riled to sleep, Edith decided to check her phone. She read Ephraim's texts, all seventeen of them, each one more intense than the next, darker and more disturbed—and all because she hadn't replied to him immediately, all because she hadn't known what to say or how to handle it. The first few were pleasant enough. But then the tone and frequency of the messages changed, the time stamp indicating that he'd sent the next several messages within minutes of one another, and these were alarming for their prescience and their assumptions—that she was disgusted by him and what he'd done, that she didn't understand how much he loved her, because if she had she wouldn't be acting like this, all pouty and silent, wouldn't be ignoring him if she truly liked him. He called her a fat bitch and a spoiled cunt and a selfish twat, demanding that she answer him, that she call him immediately, then he reversed himself in the next text, apologizing profusely and blaming the frustrating job hunt and his ex-girlfriend for making it impossible for him to trust another woman. Edith felt terrible for him, but even more for herself, because, although he could not have ever made things right between them again, he certainly didn't have to make things worse by insisting he wasn't a bad person, that he was just having a bad day.

Pandora was right. We do carry men's pain around in our bodies. And she wondered if she'd been too permissive with Ephraim, too desperate, too earnest, or if he just happened to be one of those men who took great pleasure in scaring the woman he allegedly loved. She waffled between wanting to respond to him and understanding that engaging him would only further fuel his mania. Still, she hated the idea that he thought he'd intimidated her, that he thought he'd won.

From experience she understood that the best way to take away a man's power and render him useless was to pretend he didn't exist. With trembling fingers, she tapped out a single line of text—"Who is this?"—then sent it, already erasing him from her phone and her memory, already undoing that first meeting, that first kiss, the first time he was inside her. She had liked him and would miss him, but she was done granting passes and swallowing excuses. She was done trying to figure out how to navigate the waters of this man's, any man's, broken, embattled psyche. Mainly, though, she was done trying to understand the brutality and violent tendencies that lived within every one of them, including her adoring brothers and her less adoring daddy. *Yes, even them,* she thought, lying back on the bed, certain that her dad must die, yet still uncertain, even after everything she had learned and had said, if she wanted any part of it.

MOSES ORENSTEIN-JACOBSON;
OR, THERE'S A KRAUSE IN MY HOUSE!

Saturday, April 16, 2022

Moses ran. He ran as if he were being chased, like Babe Levy in *Marathon Man,* or as if he were training for the Olympics, like Harold Abrahams in *Chariots of Fire.* He might have been running in place and going nowhere, but even so he felt that he was putting some distance between himself and the past two days, between himself and the rest of his life. He ran to shut off his brain. He ran to keep running, because that's what his body wanted.

At forty-two, he was arguably in the best shape of his life, which took both diligence and sacrifice, alimentary and otherwise. What he'd given up to look the way he did! And how could he not, considering that his face and body were his prized possessions and an integral part of his livelihood and his identity? He did it for Pandora and the boys. At least, this was what he told himself when he rose at 3:30 each morning to be at the gym and on the treadmill by 3:45. He did it for other reasons, too, not least of which was to undo all that his parents, especially his dad, had done to "reward" his obedience—

filling him with banana splits, hamburgers, extra-cheese pizzas. The greatest of all ironies then being that his dad immediately turned on him, chastising Moses for being too fat to fit into his clothes and publicly shaming him in the huskies section of Dillard's, the trauma of which sometimes revisited him when he was out shopping with his own boys. Then he'd have to cower in one of the dressing rooms until the fear and panic passed, or he'd have to call Pandora, who would appear a few minutes later to round up the kids and let him slip away. It'd take a few hours of intense weight lifting and cardio to expunge these memories, but then Moses was as good as new, returning from the battlefield of the past having once again slain the fire-breathing dragon that was his dad.

"You give your dad way too much power," Pandora had told him once early on. "He's just a big, dumb bully."

"Yeah, but he's my big, dumb bully," Moses had replied.

"Change the conversation you have with him in your head and you can change the conversation you have with him in real life," she had advised him.

"He doesn't do conversation," he'd said. "He just stabs with his mouth."

"The first time I heard him call you an idiot, I was in the other room and thought I'd misheard. The second time, I was just too shocked to say anything. But you remember the third time, don't you?" Yes, he remembered it vividly, remembered how Pandora had turned to his father and asked him nicely not to use that word again when referring to the man she loved. This had been a first for Mo, a woman, who loved him, standing up to his father in defense of him.

"My mother liked to pick on my brothers," she'd told Mo later. "My father's more like Roz. He just stood by and watched her do it. I love my mother, but when she started picking on me, I had to put her in her place. You're going to have to stand up for yourself eventually, Mo, because I'm not about to spend my life with a pussy." Then she'd told him to fuck her because there was nothing like a good fuck to chase the idiots out of their heads.

He thought about that conversation as he glanced down at his wristwatch, where a red digital heart pulsed rapidly on the small glass display above the words "Target range achieved, begin your cooldown, Moses," which he did, or which the treadmill did for him automatically, the two devices paired and synched. His pace slowed until he was walking briskly, taking long, steady strides.

As his body cooled down, his mind heated up, imagining the next couple of days and all the planning he still had to do. He was happy his siblings had come, though a little less happy about that stupid mezuzah Jacob had bought for them in Munich. How could Jacob have possibly thought it would make a good gift? "You should have seen Pandora's face when he and the German presented it to us," he'd told his pal, Gibson, as they'd arrived at the gym. Gibson Gould—né Gary Goldstein—of the American James Bond franchise, a role Moses had been up for and which had gone to his best and oldest pal, or his best and oldest enemy, depending on the day. These days, he was more prone to see Gibson merely as a soulless hack, but he kept this opinion close to his bulging pectorals. He never wanted to stray too far from his friend's good graces, just in case, and he remained eternally grateful for Gibbs and his parents, Donald and Anita Goldstein, without whom he never would have survived Julian Jacobson's house of horrors. "They 'presented' it to you? What? Like an Oscar? Or a Golden Raspberry?" Gibbs asked. "'And now in the category of Tackiest Trinket That Should Have Remained Hidden in His Suitcase, the award goes to . . . Oh, it can't be! I can't believe it! The award goes to . . . Herr Schmuck Jacob Jacobson!'"

"That's funny, Gibbs," Moses said, not laughing. "They'd already screwed it into the doorjamb, so what were we going to do?"

"Kiss it and make up." Gibbs cracked up.

"Jew slay me," Moses said. "Jew really do." He decided not to tell him about what his son had found hanging in the guest room closet.

Moses stepped off the treadmill and headed for the empty locker room, where he took a quick shower, dressed, then proceeded to the juice bar to reconvene with Gibbs, who was talking on his phone. Moses ordered his usual smoothie, a concoction of plankton, molasses, and raw quail eggs, and drank it all down, gagging on it a little. Though he knew it was good for him, its congealed, gelatinous texture left behind a slimy coating and a dirty aftertaste that only a sugary treat, say, a Krispy Kreme doughnut or three, could take away. Luckily for him, the Krispy Kreme near his gym opened early and after saying good-bye to and fist-bumping Gibbs, who indicated he'd call him later, Moses jumped into his dad mobile, an Apple Car—a space-gray station wagon made of a durable, scratch-resistant, titanium-and-steel polymer—and zipped out of the lot.

Moses loved this time of morning most, when the streets were deserted. In just a few hours the traffic would be backed up for miles, despite the warning the new mayor had issued to those caught driving alone in L.A. proper during peak commute times. Steep fines, points on one's record, possible suspension of one's license, even some jail time for repeat offenders. (That Edith had made it to them in Calabasas without getting pulled over struck him as miraculous.)

Here, in the Valley, at 4:30 in the morning, Moses had no need to worry, especially since the traffic lights were on timers, remaining green, the speed limits having been lifted on certain roads like Ventura Boulevard during certain times, of which this was one. He was free to drive as fast as he wanted. Everything and anything to accommodate the automobilists in their automobiles, to get and keep people moving, to get them to their destinations as quickly as possible, reducing their carbon footprint and its accordant guilt.

After buying a dozen assorted doughnuts and piping-hot black coffee, Moses pulled back onto Ventura, his watch lighting up with Pandora's face, which spoke the text she'd just sent him: "Okay, I got Edith and Jacob up. I'm not happy about it and neither are they. In the future, please handle your morning plans the night before, Mo. Your inability to plan ahead is still an issue. Get your shit together.

Now the whole damn house is up. What is so important about a stupid sunrise anyway? Your sibs don't seem to give a shit about it, FYI." Pandora Orenstein-Jacobson, his beloved, angry wife and the mother of his sons, all of whom he worshipped, from the twins, feisty Baxter and maudlin Dexter, to the trips, budding lady-killers all, mealymouthed Brendan, sweetmouthed Bronson, and foul-mouthed Brandon. He was blessed—*my God, but am I blessed,* he thought—with this family of his, which was crumbling around him thanks in large part to his own inflexibilities, according to Pandora, who demanded, as she threw him out of the house two months ago, that he either stop going to bed at eight o'clock, attend some social functions with her, ones with her friends and not just industry people, and fuck her once in a while, or she was going to divorce him.

His watch instructed him to make a left onto Tujunga Avenue, then a right onto Dilling Street. "Your destination is on your right," announced George Lazenby, whose voice Moses had been able to lease, download, and install directly from iTunes. It was well worth the $29.99. Sometimes he liked to let himself get lost just to hear Lazenby, whom he considered his patron saint, give him directions.

"Thank you, George," he said, imitating Lazenby's accent, which he'd perfected over the years and brought out on occasion to amuse the twins, who screamed with delight, or during auditions in which he was called to play "a man of a certain age." It once amazed him that he'd be able to play men of a certain age one day, and now that he could play men of a certain age, he didn't want to and found the whole idea discouraging. He was happy that being a man of forty-two in Hollywood was nothing like, say, being a woman of forty-two, or even of thirty-two, but parts for a strong male lead under forty, which he continued to try out for, were becoming scarcer and scarcer, especially for men who refused to have work done, who preferred the dignity of a timely decline. Moses's smile was still his own and he was proud of that. *No scalpel or knives or needles have gone into the making of you,* he thought, glancing at himself in the rearview mirror, before stepping out of the car and heading across the street to 11217 Dilling—otherwise known as the *Brady Bunch* house.

Sometimes, instead of going to the gym, Moses came here just to eat his doughnuts and drink his coffee and watch the sunrise, recalling that fretful, disastrous trip he'd taken with his mom to L.A. when he was just a boy. Two days in a dingy, crappy hotel room in Hollywood, which sat right around the corner from Grauman's Chinese Theatre, as it was still called back then. Two days during which he'd met with several agents and managers, all of whom liked him and none of whom wanted him, the Jewish boy from Dallas, with his operatic singing voice and ability to recite from memory a monologue from his favorite Neil Simon play, *Brighton Beach Memoirs*. Two days of traipsing across L.A., his mom as enthusiastic as he was about the next agent and the next, until there were no more agents to see and she told him she had a surprise for him and the next thing he knew they were at the drive-thru of In-N-Out Burger on Sunset Boulevard.

"This is my surprise?" he'd asked, confused and deflated, although he did have to admit that his love for a plain old hamburger—the bun and the meat, that is—knew no bounds. He could eat them for breakfast, lunch, and dinner, eat them standing on his head, eat enough of them to turn into one himself, his mom liked to joke.

"Partly," she'd said. "I've heard they make the best hamburgers, even better than at McDonald's. I'll get you whatever you want, within reason."

Yet what he wanted she couldn't buy for him, not there, not at a stupid burger joint sitting next to his mom, who was trying to make him feel less lousy but only managing to make him feel lousier. These were their last moments in L.A. before they had to get on a plane back to Texas, back to the one place he dreaded more than any other—that ugly, awful cramped house on Persuasion Drive. Everything about it was just wrong, from the cracked foundation to the leaky roof; because his dad never saw the leak firsthand, it actually didn't exist. The leak didn't affect Julian directly, because it was in Moses's room and Moses was a paranoid, schizophrenic, obsessive-compulsive liar, according to his dad, who liked to accuse him of such both behind his back and to his face, and so he naturally had to be lying about the rain that soaked his bed and led to his dad also accusing him of wetting himself in his sleep, which Julian said was far more likely. His mom, too, hated the house and sometimes on Sunday mornings, while his dad was at Maw-Maw's for breakfast, she'd take Mo and his siblings on a drive through better neighborhoods, looking at houses with big, open, airy floor plans, lots of windows, a skylight in every room, like the houses in Bent Tree and Preston Hollow and Highland Park, like his best friend Gary Goldstein's house.

Moses had tried to order a bunch of different things, but in the end his mom had said his eyes were bigger than his stomach and only ordered him a cheeseburger, French fries, and a large chocolate milkshake, which she said she would share with him. His mom was big into sharing, and whenever they all went out to dinner, which was rare, she asked if anyone wanted to split a bite with her. For a long time, Moses had assumed they didn't have enough money for her to order her own meal, but really it was because she liked to watch her figure. Which made him laugh, because his mom was thin and gorgeous, though it also made him sad because he knew her unwillingness to order her own dinner had to do with his dad, who often made nasty cracks about how they were going to need an extra booth one of these days to accommodate her wide load. "Honey, don't be mean to me," she'd say, but that was all, saying it without force or resolve, so that it simply dissolved into nothing, a whisper.

No, what Moses hankered for was twofold—to move to Hollywood and act in bigger commercials (he'd starred in local commercials already), TV, and movies, and to make enough money to buy his mom the house of her dreams, a huge, sprawling, ten-room house on twenty acres of land or even an apartment in Manhattan; sometimes late at night he heard her in Jacob's room, sobbing about how much she missed New York City and how much she hated Dallas. Moses could have taken or left Dallas, where his dad had been born and his dad before him and so on down the line, all true-blooded Texans, Moses the sixth generation.

After they got the bag of food, his mom told him to close his eyes and keep them closed. He told her that was silly and stupid but did it anyway, opening them once by accident, because doing it proved much harder than expected, so then she covered his eyes for him with her free hand, which couldn't have been comfortable for her, but oh, well, it's what she wanted, so he went with it. Ten minutes later, his mom let her hand go and when he opened his eyes, he wasn't sure what he was supposed to be looking at: They were on an ordinary street that looked a lot like the street on which they lived back home. But then she was pointing and saying, "Look," and he followed her finger and that's when he saw the house.

"Whoa!" he exclaimed, already reaching for his Kodak disposable camera. "Cool!"

And it was cool, especially to the twelve-year-old Moses, who forgot all about the food in his lap. He climbed out of the car and stood at the curb, snapping one picture after another, thinking about Peter, Greg, and Bobby, about Cindy, Marcia, and Jan, those TV kids he saw almost every day in reruns and with whom he'd grown up, laughed, cried. Oh, he wasn't so stupid or naive as to think the house wasn't merely a set, or the show more than a sitcom; he knew none of it was real. He still marveled at the potential of it all, the love, make-believe or not, that lived within those rooms, so unlike the rooms of his dad's house, where love, if it existed, happened sporadically and only if certain conditions were met, like good grades, like following orders, like being seen and not heard. "Do you like your surprise, Mosey?" his mom asked, climbing out with the food and sitting on the hood of the car, where he joined her a moment later.

"Very much!" He did, and he loved her all the more for it. "I have a great idea. When I make enough money, I'm going to buy it and we'll all move in," though of course by "all" he meant Edith, Jacob, his mom, and himself. His dad, as far as he cared, could go live in a fishing village in Mexico, for that's how he liked to spend his time anyway, away from them, fishing, whenever he could.

They ate their meal and talked, as the afternoon turned to evening, until it was time to head back to the hotel to pack. On the plane, Moses imagined what might have happened if just one of the agents had said yes, how different his life—their lives—would have been. There was no way he wouldn't have shared his riches with his sister and mom and baby brother, because Moses, the firstborn, felt an extraordinary obligation to keep them safe and at the same time an even greater obligation to himself to see his dreams fulfilled, whatever it took.

His watch cuckooed for 5:00 A.M., a sound that drove Pandora insane and that made the boys fall over with laughter. He loved it when they laughed, for it chased away any doubts he had that they hated and resented him as he did his own dad. And what a terrible thing it had been to admit, yet admit it he had, first to Pandora— his beautiful, savvy wife, who knew a thing or two about difficult people from her mom and her granddad, a real estate developer who'd made his fortune in the San Fernando Valley and was the brains behind Edelweiss Estates, the first gated community built to attract the kind of resident who could both afford and want to live in a Swiss chalet–style villa—then to his siblings last month. They'd been discussing their mom's quality of life—Edith in Atlanta, Jacob in Berlin, Moses here in L.A.—and he'd mentioned in passing just how great it would be if their dad weren't around. "What are you suggesting?" Edith had said during that first call. Mo hadn't been sure that he'd been suggesting anything, not then, but during a more recent call, when Jacob told them he and Diet had indeed decided to spend Passover in L.A., Mo had again brought up how great it would be if their dad weren't around, this time adding, "If she only has four months, shouldn't we make them the most amazing four months of her life?"

"What are you suggesting?" Edith had asked again, to which Jacob had replied, "Oh, for fuck's sake, Thistle. Ethical cap off, unethical cap on. He's suggesting that we kill him, as in off with his head."

"As in off with his head," Moses had repeated. "As in, 'Shot through the heart, and you're to blame, darling.' As in 'Will it be poison put in my glass?' "

From the hood on which he reclined, his ankles crossed, Moses made out the approach of a car, the headlights cutting thick triangular wedges through the solidified dark. In the distance, a dog barked once, and the air held the pleasant aroma of coffee and doughnuts and beyond that the faint fragrance of citrus and exhaust. For a moment, he turned his eyes from the street to the sky, where three or four helicopters hovered somewhere above him. These days, he couldn't look up without seeing them, these whirlybirds, as his kids called them, that kept watch on and over them all, a police presence even up there in the L.A. skies. They were everywhere, at all times of the day and night, huge mechanical peace-keeping insects and the crews who flew them—the mayor trying to reassure her Jewish population, which numbered in the millions, the vast majority of them Israeli refugees, that they were being adequately protected. *It was nice to know they had at least one ally,* Moses thought, as the car crept past him, then parked, the night going completely still and black again. Then the ding of a door opening and the sound of footsteps on gravel, then another door, then another, which made him sit up and turn around and that's when he saw not two but three shadows moving toward him and that's when he said, "Fuck," under his breath, though his voice carried in the sudden silence, the helicopters having departed for more interesting and dangerous skies.

The three planted themselves before him, Edith between Jacob and Dietrich, each of whom had an arm wrapped around her waist to keep her from falling. "Your hip still hurts, huh?" Moses asked. He thought she said yes, though it was hard to tell because Dietrich was speaking in his horrible language to Jacob. "What was that, Herr Krause?"

"Mo, just knock it off," Edith snapped. "None of us wants to be here, wherever this is, so just get to the point."

"Please don't make me the enemy, Thistle," Moses said, climbing down. He reached into the car for the Krispy Kreme box, the cups and napkins, all of which he set on the hood. "I thought it was just going to be the three of us. No offense, but why'd you bring him?"

"I've been teaching him how to drive," Jacob explained. "And after we're finished here, we're going down to the beach to watch the sunrise. Then we're going to fuck in one of the coves. That's why he came along, Mo." For whatever reason, this made Moses laugh, both with and at his little brother. "What's so funny about that?" Jacob asked.

"Nothing. Everything," Moses said, taking a doughnut and pouring himself a cup of coffee. "I'm assuming that his being here means you opened your big mouth and told him about our little plan."

"Not even close," Jacob said, also taking a doughnut and pouring a cup of coffee, which he handed to Dietrich before going back for his own and for Edith, who reluctantly took a seat on the hood.

"Jacob did tell me about that plan of yours," Dietrich said, "but he did not mean to tell me."

"What'd you do? Torture it out of him?" Moses shot at Dietrich. "Or did you use some kind of German mind game?"

"Mo, what the fuck is your problem?" Jacob glared at him. "Leave the guy alone already."

"No, this is okay, *Schatz,*" Dietrich said. "Your brother is clearly uncomfortable with me being here."

"Or anywhere," Moses said. "Look, it's nothing personal, but I have to agree with our dad on this—and I try very hard never to agree with our dad on anything—and just say that I find it utterly baffling that out of all the guys in the world you could have ended up with, Jacob, you chose him. I guess I'm just trying to make sense of what you find so irresistible about him that you couldn't find in someone else, say, who wasn't German." As soon as he'd finished speaking, a light went on in the house across the street, drawing his attention away. "Do you know why I wanted you to meet me here, besides the obvious reason of discussing how to do away with you-know-who?"

"Mo, he knows who you-know-who is," Jacob said. Moses hated when Jacob spoke down to him. It was a quality that came from the Jacobson side of the family that Moses luckily hadn't inherited, and he found it extremely off-putting. Usually he just dismissed it, yet this morning, the superiority in Jacob's voice infuriated him and made him want to pinch his head right off his neck. "And not to overstate the ludicrous, but we still don't know where 'here' is," Jacob continued. "Maybe you'd like to fill us in."

Moses reached out, grabbed his brother's chin, and turned it forty-five degrees to the right, until they were all staring at the house.

"No fucking way," Jacob said, "4222 Clinton Way! How the hell did you do it?"

"Magic," Moses said, "and Mom."

"That house belongs to someone famous?" Dietrich asked. "Why did you just say '4222 Clinton Way'? I thought this was Dilling Street?"

"Edith, be a peach and pull up Wikipedia, please," Jacob said. Edith brought Wikipedia up on her iPhone. "Now type in 'the Brady Bunch house' and hand the phone to Dietrich."

"Yes, I know that show," Dietrich said, "but I never watched it. My parents did not allow it. They believed TV was the curse of the modern world and that what came out of Hollywood was evil."

"Not evil. Just tacky, hilarious, quintessential America," Jacob said. "The three of us grew up on the reruns," and without having to say another word, the siblings took a few steps closer to one another and to the iconic house, where they stood in awed silence, each knowing the details of it inside and out.

About as well as we knew our own childhood home, Moses

thought. And he recalled both with fondness and resentment how often he'd rearranged the living room and dining room furniture to match the layout of the Brady floor plan, knowing the hell he'd get for it later when his dad returned home from work. But it was all worth it, for there was nothing like leaving one world for that other one, however briefly, nothing like banishing himself from the dark-paneled prison of his dad's house to emerge reconfigured in the brightly lit, Technicolor rooms of Mr. and Mrs. Brady. He craved those rooms and the love that existed among them, especially after he grew up and discovered that some families interacted, if not exactly as they did in the Brady house, then as close to it as he could find. The Goldstein family did, of course, and he spent as much time as possible with them when he was a boy, loving Gary's parents and his sister, the laughter that rose from the dinner table, the kind words they spoke to and about one another—the exact opposite experience of dinner with Roz and Julian Jacobson. Oh, his mom tried, yet she was often told she was being too chatty and to shut up. And he'd sit there across from his dad, fuming, not only for his mom, who he wished would pick up her steak knife and stab it through his dad's windpipe, but also for his brother and sister, who didn't know what Moses knew—that life inside the four walls of the Jacobson house was fraught and terrifying, though it did not have to be, that life was full of all kinds of people who behaved nothing like their mean, viperous, and unpredictable dad. Because what was the point of being a family if four out of five members of it wanted you dead?

"So how should we do it?" Jacob asked matter-of-factly. "It doesn't make that much difference to me as long as he suffers. An old-fashioned stoning works, though. What about you guys? I mean, it's very wrath of God and sort of in keeping with the Passover theme."

"If we were keeping with the Passover theme, then we'd drop him off in the middle of the desert without food or water," Moses said. "He wouldn't last forty hours, much less forty days in that heat."

"But given his luck, it'd start raining and manna would start falling from the sky," Jacob quipped.

"You're both sick. You know that?" Edith said. "How can you discuss this here out in the open before God and the ghosts of the Brady family? It's indecent," and she pushed off the hood to take a seat inside the car.

Moses glanced at Jacob, who shrugged and turned to follow Edith. Behind him, he heard Jacob tell Dietrich to go and practice his driving. "Remember: The small pedal is the gas and the big pedal is the brake. And quit using both feet, Diet. Just your right one. Also, try to keep both hands on the wheel at twenty-two and fourteen hundred o'clock, like I taught you. Now come here and smooch me," and the two kissed deeply, which sickened Moses, not the kissing of another man, but the kissing of this man, who had such an unfortunate provenance and history.

"Maybe Dietrich should join us," Moses said once he'd grabbed the doughnuts and coffee and settled in the front seat. "I mean, it is in his blood to murder innocent Jews and all."

"That'd be true if Dad were innocent," Jacob said, refusing to take the bait. "Besides, he doesn't have a murderous bone in his body and thinks what we're doing is reprehensible. He doesn't want any part of it."

"I'd still like to know how Herr Krause found out about it, Jacob," Moses said, digging in the box for a doughnut and taking a large bite. It tasted of childhood, of Saturday-morning cartoons, and for a moment, Moses felt wistful when he remembered sitting beside his dad in the red convertible VW Beetle, speeding through the quiet streets of Dallas on their way to the Donut Hut on Saturday mornings. Perhaps this was the fondest memory he had of his dad and he held on to it briefly before releasing it, knowing that if he were going to go through with this, he had to keep such distracting, extraordinarily rare memories at bay. And they were distracting and they were rare and they could never make up for all of the others, which crowded around him and rekindled his bloodthirsty fury.

"You're going to laugh when I tell you," Jacob said, also reaching for a doughnut.

"He's not going to laugh," Edith told Jacob. "You're not going to laugh, Mo. I certainly didn't."

"That's because you don't have the keen sense of humor that Mo and I do," Jacob said. "You've always been too serious, Thistle. Better yet, let me quote from the book of Julian: 'You need to lighten up, Eddie.'"

"Please don't do that," she said. "Please don't ever use that phrase in my company again," and she took a quick sip of coffee as if to wash down that bitter memory. "And by the way, I do, too, have a sense of humor. Do you think I could actually sit here and talk about any of this if I didn't?"

"Touché," Jacob said, as the lights came on in some of the other houses up and down the block and Dietrich shot past them, all the windows down and the radio blasting opera, the windshield wipers going full tilt, though the sky was cloudless. "Teaching him how to drive has definitely been an experience. It's either going to bring us closer together or completely rip us apart," he said. "I don't envy you, Mo. Five boys. Five cars. Five times the worry."

"They're all going to take the bus," he said and part of him meant it. "Which reminds me. How about a fatal car accident? We can get him all liquored up and put him in a car at the top of Mulholland Drive. With all those hairpin twists and curves, I can guarantee you he'd never make it out alive."

"First of all, the man hasn't even touched a drop of Manischewitz in years and blesses a cup of grapefruit juice on Shabbat," Jacob said. "Second of all, whose car, Mo? Yours?"

"Nah, mine has that sensor on the steering wheel that locks the driver out if he's over the legal limit," he said. "I don't know. Why not their minivan?"

"He's not going to die in a drunk-driving accident," Edith said, raising her voice. "What if he ends up killing someone else in the process? I vote lethal injection."

"You don't even know what's in that syringe," Jacob said.

"I have a pretty good idea," she said.

"Yeah, what if it's just, like, water?" Moses asked.

"Water? Why would someone fill a syringe with water?" Jacob asked, irritated, and took another doughnut. "That's pretty lame."

"Just as lame as telling your boyfriend our plan, I'd say," he said.

"It wasn't on purpose," he whined, which made Moses want to sock him in the mouth. Yet he restrained himself and channeled his aggression, packing it into a pure white snowball of hate, which he lobbed with all of his imagination at the memory of his dad—a much younger Julian Jacobson and a much younger Moses out in the backyard. "I thought he was asleep and that I was just talking to myself—you know I like to hash things out like that—but he wasn't asleep, he was 'resting with his eyes shut'—by the way, he's a terrific faker—and he says he woke up right in the middle of my soliloquy and heard me say it. So you can yell at me all you want, but it wasn't my fault."

"No, but it's certainly proven my point," Moses said. "He can't be trusted, and neither can you. It's not like Pandora knows anything about it."

"Oh, don't give me that holier-than-thou shtick," Jacob said. "You know who you sound like, don't you? You sound just like—"

"Don't you say it," Moses said. "Don't you dare—"

"Just like Julian Jackoff Jacobson, that's who," Jacob said as Moses reached into the backseat and smashed his raspberry-jelly-filled doughnut in his brother's face. "You stupid motherfucker," Jacob hollered. "You got raspberry in my eye."

"Boys! I didn't come here to watch you two revert back into unruly apes or to point fingers or to harangue Jacob for his truly idiotic faux pas. I came here to discuss murder, so let's discuss it before I change my mind and stab one of *you* with the syringe I just happen to have in my purse. Now will one of you please hand me a fucking doughnut?"

So they discussed and they squabbled and they presented arguments for and against hanging him, for and against drowning him, for and against shooting him with his own gun, which he never went anywhere without and was locked up in the glove compartment in the minivan, a loaded Glock .45. Edith felt strongly that they should do it quickly and humanely, however they were going to do it, which of course led her right back to the insulin, and again the brothers rejected the idea wholesale. "Don't we *want* him to suffer?" Jacob asked. "Isn't this the point, that he knows why and who and for what?"

"It's too bad we can't just stick him in a cage and shoot him up with tumor cells, though I know it'd take way too long for him to die," Moses said, recalling all the times he'd gone to work with his dad at the lab, where he kept dozens of adorable albino mice and how many times he'd helped his dad with the chloroform pellets, dropping them through the holes as the mice ran around in circles, their bodies swollen and disfigured from the cancer cells that his dad, who specialized in rare forms of pulmonary disease and their mutability in and effects on the lungs, had injected into them. Which was noble, he understood, yet he couldn't ever forget the look of pure satisfied glee on his dad's face when he handed Moses the big yellow bucket and told him to clean up the cages after all the mice were dead. It didn't take more than twenty minutes for every last mouse to shudder and die, their tiny bodies still warm when he lifted them out by their tails and set them gently in the bucket, all the while reciting the Mourner's Kaddish, the prayer for the dead, over them. He'd hated this business of his dad's, who went about his own without so much as a blink of an eye, as if he hadn't just taken fifty lives, torturing them first, their bodies wracked and riddled and bloated, all in the name of science. Moses had hated all of it—the antiseptic, silent halls, the gamy, rotten stench of death that wafted through the lab, and the twitching pink eyes and noses set into the purest white faces Moses had ever seen—imploring him to release them, which he longed to do, though he knew the price he'd pay for it if he did.

"They're just filthy rodents," his dad had said on the way home.

"They carry pestilence and disease, Mo. They serve a purpose. You can't feel sorry for them." And yet Moses had. He'd felt sorry for them, but still sorrier for his dad, who clearly had no idea just how much his killing of the mice had killed off something inside Moses as well. He'd known enough not to expect his dad to philosophize or to impart any sort of wisdom about the meaning of life and death, yet his nonchalance and dispassion had continually astounded and infuriated Moses, who'd often wondered if this was what years of studying lung cancer in albino mice had done to the man, or if the penchant for such a thing had been present in him all along, from the start. It would take Moses years and years before he grasped the true horror of it all. And even then it was Jacob who had to make the connections for him, had to show him the inappropriateness of what his dad had done to him, of using Moses, his own son, to kill the mice. "But that's not the worst part," Jacob had said. "The worst part is that he didn't give you a choice."

Yes, that was definitely a part of it, Moses thought, as Dietrich zoomed past them again, flashing the headlights. Yet to the eldest Jacobson sibling, the worst part wasn't that his dad had never given him a choice, but that in killing, in having the capacity to kill, whether he'd liked it or not, he'd seen some latent quality in himself that had allowed him to believe he was more like his father than not. And even that worst part had another aspect to it as well, which Moses still had a hard time accepting, although Jacob had laid the evidence out for him on the phone last month. It was this that Moses clung to, because it made the idea of killing his dad that much less personal and that much more doable. This aspect that took on monstrous proportions as he replayed those moments in the lab when he dropped the pellets into the cages and sensed the pleasure his dad took in watching him do it. This pleasure, Moses realized, came not from seeing his son snuff the life out of the mice but from a different, imagined scene altogether that had to do with his dad's innermost feelings about his own family, relatives of these trapped, caged mice. On those chilling afternoons, his dad had turned Moses into someone he wasn't and never wanted to be, an accomplice, but more than that, a psychic stand-in, for he suspected, though could never prove, that murderous fantasies festered inside his dad.

It did not surprise Moses that, of the two, his mom had fallen ill and was finally succumbing to the metaphorical poison, which his dad had laid out for her. It did not surprise him, but it sure as hell pissed him off. "I've got it," he said, lifting the last doughnut out of the box and dividing it into three equal pieces. "It's going to take all three of us, though." Then he told them his plan. "Think you guys can find everything you need by tonight?"

"I still say we just burn him alive," Jacob said.

"Patience, Jacob, patience," Moses said. "You want to have a little fun with the man first, don't you?"

"I suppose," he said, sighing. "Though I wish you or Thistle had spoken to Clarence, too. He always liked you guys, and I got the distinct impression he still hates me for what happened in college. I don't even want to think about how much he's really going to hate me when he finds out I murdered one of his prized pet peacocks and didn't tell him."

"He only hates you because you broke his heart," Moses said. "And as far as the peacock goes, leave that to me."

"I didn't break his heart, because he doesn't have one," Jacob said, laughing. "And I know for a fact he doesn't, because I saw what he did to Thad Schneider, both alive and after he was dead. You can't imagine the extent of his depravity."

Moses didn't have to, because Jacob had told him, though he clearly didn't remember having done so. Clarence had taken it upon himself to contact Thad's parents, acting as the would-be funeral director he would eventually become, telling them he would be honored if they allowed him to arrange their son's burial because Clarence loved their son and wanted his afterlife to be peaceful, as opposed to the earthly hell it had been, referencing how shitty

239

Thad's parents had been to their son about the whole homosexuality thing and how if they only hadn't been so rigid and unfeeling none of this would have happened. Mr. Schneider broke in and said he had it all wrong, that they had actually accepted their son's homosexual lifestyle, informing Clarence that Thad had actually killed himself because he'd found out Clarence had been sleeping around on him. "It devastated him," Mr. Schneider said. "You can read his note. In fact, why don't you come to the house so I can stuff it down your throat?" Then he hung up, leaving a bewildered Clarence to phone Jacob, whose guilt in the whole tragedy had only been more grimly confirmed.

Yes, Jacob had told Moses all about Clarence and Thad and it had shocked and surprised him, but it was Jacob's heart that had surprised him all the more, for he sensed that Jacob, even after all these years, still harbored feelings for Clarence and wondered what it said about his little brother that he did.

"Depravity comes in many shades," Edith said, curled up against the door. She roused to life and began to tremble, rolling down the window and leaning her head out. "How can the air not have any air in it?" she asked, dry heaving.

"Depravity is as depravity does," Moses said, which elicited a slight grin from Jacob and dyspeptic groans from Edith, who finally threw up onto the grass.

"Morning sickness?" Jacob asked, unable to control himself.

"Oh, just let her be," Moses said. "Thistle, you okay?"

"Will you just look at us? Look at what we're doing," she said. "It's just . . . I know I said I'd go along with this, because you're my brothers and I love you, but I'm not sure I can stand the idea of torture." She wiped her mouth with the napkin Moses handed to her. "Have you even bothered to ask yourselves how you're going to live with it afterward?"

"And have you even bothered to ask yourself how he's lived with himself for all these years?" Jacob asked hotly. "He tried to kill you with figs, Thistle, and Mo with a baseball, and me, well, he didn't

240

try to kill me so much as try to drive me to do it myself. I'd be lying if I said I won't take great pleasure in seeing him dead, but it seems to me you've forgotten that we aren't doing this for us, we're doing this for Mom. Remember her? She's the woman in the wheelchair who needs fucking oxygen tanks to breathe because of him."

"I see your point," Edith agreed with resignation, though her voice was shaky. "But maybe . . . I don't know. I'm still not convinced that he had anything . . . Blame is a bad game to play, Jacob. That's all I'm saying."

"Thistle, please shut up. I can blame him all I want, especially for not paying more attention to her health," he said. "I can blame him for not seeing how much she was struggling."

"Kids, kids, kids!" Moses said. "I think we can all acknowledge that this goes well beyond blame. Thistle, if you want to back out, back out, but then you don't have the right to tell us how to kill him. Look, I'll make you a deal—you help us with the festivities this evening and we'll think about the insulin. Jacob, is this kosher with you?"

"I suppose it doesn't matter how he dies just as long as he does," Jacob said. "So, yeah, okay. I'll think about the insulin, although it's far too humane for him."

"Edith?" Moses asked. "What do you say? Do we have a deal?"

His sister glanced at him, then past him to the house, above which the sky lightened, going from the bruised black of night to the dark, chalky blue of dawn. Soon, the inviolate, relentless L.A. sun would be up, shining down upon them all, Pandora and his sons, his mom in her wheelchair, and even upon his dad on what was to be his last day on earth. "Yes, okay," she said at last, falling back into the seat and shutting her eyes.

"Jacob, get ahold of your German and go fuck on the beach, while I drive Thistle to Claremont to pick up her van," Moses said. "Let's rendezvous at Canter's around ten A.M. They're one of tonight's sponsors and made banners I need to pick up."

"Oh, right, today's the day. *A Very JacobSONS Passover*," Jacob said. "I'm kind of looking forward to getting to the plagues tonight, especially that old standard—the slaying of the firstborn. No offense, Mo."

"None taken," he said.

"Hey, exactly what time does the camera crew arrive?" Jacob asked.

"No camera crew this time," Moses said. "The network's sending out a technician to install webcams in most of the rooms. Cuts down on overhead and production costs. We're going live in T minus twelve hours or whenever sundown is, whichever comes first."

"You know, Mo, sometimes I wonder if Dad didn't get it right when he said you were a mountain of stupidity," Jacob said. "You do realize we won't have a split second of privacy all night, right? How the hell are we going to carry out our coup de grâce if every one of our movements is being tracked?"

"I guess we'll just have to improvise," he said. "Life's an improvisation, Jacob. But you already knew that."

"Oh, that's rich. I didn't sign on for this Passover reunion special when I agreed to come out here," Jacob said. "And I haven't said anything because I wanted to support you in your hour of gross and needy self-promotion. I know you've had it hard, what with all the shit going down in Hollywood, but guess what? I'm finally saying something."

"Are you backing out on me? Is that what you're doing?" Moses asked, feeling the first wave of heat in his face, which often accompanied one of his panic attacks. He started sweating uncontrollably, big, fat drops that poured down his back and sopped the constricting elastic waistband of his boxers. He wanted out—out of the car, out of his clothes, to jump into the nearest pool and sink to the bottom. He felt himself going from zero to sixty. How had he let it all come to this? How had he put such stock in a profession that was failing him as his brother was now failing him? Yes, the rise of anti-Semitism had begun to eat Hollywood from the inside out, and though no one said so, Moses had heard rumors that the Jews who still ran many of the studios were being pressured to cut back on their hiring of Jewish actors—which may have explained his career's recent nosedive. There was a part of him that found this excuse a little disingenuous and a little too convenient. *What if I'm not getting roles anymore because I just suck?* Moses thought, then reversed out of this opinion by reminding himself that he did, in fact, not suck, that good, solid roles in good, solid films were pretty rare, even for those with flourishing careers like Gibbs's. Still, the facts were the facts—Jews in Hollywood were being ousted, or leaving on their own, though nothing was ever said out loud and certainly nothing was on the books, not yet, but that day was coming, he suspected. And then major box-office draws, even the Gibson Goulds of the world, could kiss their successes good-bye.

Thinking about this did nothing to stanch the flow of adrenaline coursing through him. Moses glanced down at his watch, expecting to see the digital red heart pulsing dramatically, but the screen was black, which made everything seem a thousand times worse. He shook his wrist as if this might reactivate the watch, wondering if his wildly beating heart had overloaded it. The little black screen upset him, but not nearly as much as the idea of Jacob backing out. "If you want out, tell me right now, this second, so I can make other arrangements," he said. He had thought they'd been talking about the special, though all of a sudden he wasn't sure.

"What other arrangements?" Jacob asked, climbing out. He stepped into the middle of the street to flag down Dietrich, who came barreling toward him, and Moses averted his eyes; he was certain something deep inside the German would not be able to stop himself from running Jacob down. Yet there was nothing, no scroop of tires, no impact, no thud, which meant Jacob did not go flying through the air, broken and bloody. There was merely the morning wind in his ears. Then Jacob was back and leaning into the car, saying, "I was talking about the special, Mo, not the other business.

But good thing I brought it up or we wouldn't have known about your 'other arrangements.' A contingency plan, Mo? Really? When were you going to tell us that you were thinking of hiring an outside party?"

"Calm the fuck down, Jacob. It was just an idea," Mo said. "Don't tell me you haven't had a similar thought."

"Actually, I haven't," Jacob growled. "I didn't fly halfway around the world to—"

"You know 'outside parties'?" Edith cut in excitedly, sitting up.

"You'd rather farm this out to someone else, wouldn't you?" Jacob accused. "You'd rather let someone else have all the fun and take all the glory for something we planned. Unbelievable. You're a coward, Mo. A coward and a traitor."

"I'm not saying that," Moses said. "All I'm saying is that you may be right about tonight. Let's be honest—none of us wants to get caught or go to jail, not on account of him. I have a family to think about, besides."

"Oh, and what about us? What about Thistle and me? Because we haven't produced a litter of five, our lives don't matter? Throw us to the lions, but you and your offspring run free?"

"I'm not saying that, either," Moses said. "But better to get it all out in the open now rather than later. Isn't it better to know where we stand?"

"You know what? I have a sunrise to see and a blowjob to give and to get, so I'm going to say *auf Wiedersehen*," Jacob said, walking over to the idling Dietrich, who slid into the passenger seat, and off they went. Moses was convinced that as they pulled away he heard the German singing, " 'Go down, Moses, way down in Egypt's land. Tell old Pharaoh, let my people go.' "

"That didn't go so well," he said after Edith climbed up front and buckled herself in. "You don't think I'm a coward, do you? My kids are my life, Thistle. I just don't want anything to go wrong. If that makes me a coward, then so be it. We just have to be incredibly careful, which is why I was thinking about a gun for hire, because let me tell you—I'll be damned if I'm going to let my boys grow up without a dad the way we did."

"We didn't grow up without a dad," she said, "but I know what you mean."

"I still think about the day the old man announced he was moving out. It would have been better for all of us if Mom had divorced him, you know. So don't sit here and tell me you're having second thoughts, too. Don't tell me I'm going to have to do this by myself."

"You know where I stand," she said as he put the car in drive. "If we're going to do it, I want it to be quick and painless. Those are my stipulations. I don't want to look back on this with regret."

"How could you ever look back on it with regret? Don't you think Mom deserves some peace and happiness? I don't think I need to remind you that she's dying, do I?" he said.

"And I don't think I need to remind you that the man we want to kill is taking care of her, do I?" she asked. "She seems perfectly happy to me, Mo. Who are we to assume she isn't?"

"And who are we to assume she is? Has she said as much?" he asked. "We're her children and we know what he's like and how he could turn on her in a heartbeat. We lived in that house. We were there. We experienced life with Julian Jacobson. Fuck, Edith, you were there, too."

"All I'm saying is, you can't have it both ways," she said. "You can't speak to us about fearing for your children in one breath, then about torture and murder in the next. It doesn't work like that. You have to choose, just like you're making us choose." *Leave it to Thistle to lay it all out in black and white,* Moses thought. She was right, of course, and in being right, she was forcing him to examine not only certain precious beliefs he held about life and love but also the belief he held about himself, that when the time came he'd be able to carry out the deed. "I'm sorry. I didn't mean that. You're not forcing Jacob or me to do anything," she added.

Moses lived somewhere in between his siblings, not hating Julian as much as Jacob did or loving him as much as Edith did, and because of this, his decision was that much harder. "Let's not talk about it anymore," he said, feeling very much alone.

"I don't know," she said as if she hadn't heard him. "Maybe we should try to give him one more out."

"Like what? Ask him to divorce her?" he asked, laughing. "Like that's going to work."

"Not ask. Demand," she said. "Make him an offer he can't refuse."

As far as Moses was concerned, there was only one kind of offer his dad couldn't refuse, and there weren't enough shekels in the whole world to satisfy it. "You do understand he's been playing a long game," he said. The goal had always been his mom's fortune— all eight million dollars of it. His dad was nothing if not predictable that way, predictable and single-minded. And what better way to make his claim on her money stick than to pit his own children against him and thus demand his mom choose sides? *And we all know how that usually went,* he thought. In a way, he couldn't help but find his dad's play at concern brilliant, for it only bolstered his cause and pulled the wool further over his mom's already failing eyes.

Moses had had no idea about the money until he took that fateful trip with his dad down to the Texas coast, to Rockport, a small fishing village where Uncle Bernie owned a house. One night they'd gone out to dinner at Hamburger Haven, and eleven-year-old Moses had asked his dad to tell him the story of how he and his mom met.

"Was it love at first sight?" Moses asked. His dad, ever careful with his words, talked around his question, saying he'd been dating Roz's roommate. "So you thought she was pretty?" he said.

"I don't know, Mo," he said. "I guess I must have. I certainly didn't know what a talker she was, that's for sure. Some women hate spiders, your mom hates silence. It's like living with a radio twenty-four hours a day. Drives me bat shit, I tell you. When you find a woman of your own one day, just make sure she knows when to shut her mouth."

"But you love her, right?" Moses asked, surprised by his own nerve.

"Love," his dad said. "I have no idea what love is."

This might have been the end of the conversation, yet Moses, for whatever reason, kept pressing on, emboldened by his cheeseburger, as well as by what felt like a real, honest heart-to-heart with his dad, the first they'd ever had.

"If you don't love her, why did you marry her?" At the time, he still had quite a fondness for his dad and thought the feeling was mutual. But that night was the first time his dad revealed himself to be both completely disingenuous and a consummate swindler.

"Well, I'll tell you," his dad said, taking a gulp of beer, then setting it back down and putting on that sinister smirk of his, which should have clued Moses in on what was coming. "Your mom's many things—not particularly smart, or capable in the kitchen, or even all that beautiful, but she's completely devoted to me, which you should only be so lucky to find in a wife. Devotion and loyalty. That's what makes a man happiest." He took another pull on his beer. "It also doesn't hurt when your wife's parents are filthy, stinking rich. Do you understand what I'm saying?" Confused, Moses said that he didn't. Then his dad leaned across the table and said, almost in a whisper, "I'm an incredibly lucky man, Mo. Not because I married your mom but because I married an heiress. Money is only an issue when you don't have it. You'll see what I mean someday."

Moses had spent the next thirty-one years of his life keeping his dad's awful confession a secret, for he knew that if he ever told his mom it would break her spirit. He now finally understood that part of her inability to leave his dad was his fault, for he had never told her. Not that she would have believed him, and even if she had, he was sure his dad would have come up with some sort of plausibly deniable excuse—that Moses misinterpreted what he'd said, that the boy didn't like him and so of course invented this horrible lie—all the while knowing that Moses knew the truth.

"What if it isn't money but something else we can use to compel him to divorce her?" Edith asked, bringing up the video Pandora had shown her. "It should still be on her phone."

"What the fuck, Thistle? Why didn't you mention this earlier?" Moses said hotly, turning the car around and heading back toward Calabasas.

"She's your wife and it's on her phone, Mo," Edith said. "I didn't know she hadn't told you about it, so don't blame me."

"This is our ace in the hole," Moses said, ignoring her, for it didn't matter to him which of them had kept the video from him, because now he had it—the offer his dad simply couldn't refuse.

"Then we don't have to kill him?" she asked.

"On the condition that he agrees to disappear—and I mean vanish, up in smoke, never to be heard from or seen again," he said. "But it all depends on what's in that video and if it frightens him enough to leave."

Then it was as if a dam burst in her, for suddenly she was opening her mouth and spilling out another vital piece of intel, which she had also been keeping to herself. "You saw that? You saw him nearly tip Ma into the pool and you didn't think to tell us? What. The. Fuck?"

"Ma didn't seem the least bit scared," she said. "She was laughing. So what was I to believe? It's not like he didn't know I was there. I mean, he looked directly at me and smirked." She bit her lip. "Oh, God, that smirk. I see what you mean. It's more leverage for us, isn't it?" *Someone, please, tell me how this is going to end well,* Moses thought. "Maybe we'll have a happily-ever-after, after all," she said.

"Maybe," he said, turning into Edelweiss Estates, past the drab, useless guardhouse, empty again this morning, the mechanical arm hoisted high in the air, allowing unimpeded access to anyone who wanted to do his family harm. *Including me,* he thought, determined to see this whole macabre affair through to the end, no matter the consequences. Jacob was right—this was far bigger than they were. And it was gaining momentum, Moses felt it, gathering a force and life all its own, a penny dropped from the fifty-story building of his imagination. After pulling into the drive and parking behind the Expedition, Moses said, "If anyone asks, the sunrise was beautiful."

"*Alles klar, Herr Kommissar,*" she said, saluting.

"Do me a favor—use that ugly language only on the German and keep it far away from me and mine," he said, climbing out into the bright, warm sunshine.

"You can't tell me you actually have a problem with Dietrich, who happens to be one of the sweetest men in the world. I'm thrilled Jacob found someone like him, Mo," Edith said, "and you should be, too. You're being unfair and childish. We invited both of them to Passover, we helped pay their airfares, and now that they're here you're behaving as if you never invited him in the first place. What gives?"

"Why do I have to like everyone?" he asked. "Jacob doesn't particularly like Pandora, but I don't make a federal case out of it."

"This is different, and you know it," she said. "It's one thing to align yourself with Daddy—and we all know how he feels about Germany—but it's another thing to disrespect Jacob and his relationship. He's in love with a German, and so the fuck what? You need to get over it if you don't want to alienate Jacob any more than you already have."

"Maybe it has to do with the fact that he's a latent anti-Semite. Or maybe it has to do with the fact that one of the boys found a Nazi uniform in the upstairs guest room closet. It was hanging right beside a filthy schmatte that looked like a camp uniform. There's a yellow Star of David embroidered into the pocket of it. I can show you if you want."

"I'm sure there's a logical explanation for it," she said, though her voice was chilly and he could tell the news had had a sobering effect on her. "They're probably just costumes for one of Jacob's plays. It could be as simple as that. You can't always jump to the worst conclusion. You aren't Daddy."

"You've always been good at giving him the benefit of the doubt," he said. "And look where it's gotten you. Look where we are now."

"Don't be cruel," she said, massaging her hip.

"Pandora has drawers of Zyklon B—I mean, oxycodone—from her last tummy tuck," he said. "You should help yourself."

"No more speaking German for me, no more references to cyanide gas for you," she said. "Stop being morbid. It's a gorgeous day and we're all together and before I forget, Elias might be coming tonight," and she hurried on ahead of him into the house.

"Wait a second," he said, hurrying in after her. "You're in touch with Creepy the Jew? Since when?"

"You know I always hated when you called him that," Edith said from the stairs.

Moses gave chase, nearly overtaking her, but she ducked into the guest room away from him. He caught his breath on the landing, where he happened to glance down to see something both oddly repulsive yet uniquely beautiful, for he'd never before witnessed anything quite like it in his entire life. He recoiled at the sight—his parents, in the living room below, locked in a long, slow kiss—and turned toward Edith, who exited the guest room with a wry smile on her face. "If you're going to accuse Dietrich of concealing Nazi paraphernalia in your closet, you might want to make sure you have actual proof," she said. "Next time, don't try so hard to win me over to your side by lying. It just makes you look like a sore loser."

"He must have moved them or hidden them," he said. "They aren't there?"

"Nope," she said. "Check if you don't believe me."

"I believe you," he said. "What I can't believe is what just happened down there," and he pointed to the place where his parents had been and were no longer. "I might have to get a lobotomy to remove it, and when I tell you you're going to wish for the same. Ma and Dad were *kissing*."

"You saw our parents, Roz and Julian Jacobson, kissing, as in sucking face, as in smooching, as in osculating?" Edith asked, shocked.

"Yeah, all of those except the last one, whatever it means," he said.

"It's just a ten-cent word for kissing." This was their dad, who'd come up the back staircase. "And why shouldn't I kiss your mother and what business is it of yours?"

"Maybe because I've never ever seen you two kiss," Moses said. "Maybe because I always just assumed you had to like someone to kiss them?"

"What about you, Eddie? Do you also have an opinion like your brother, the genius, which you'd like to share?" their dad asked. "No? Well, I'm glad we had this little chat because I'd hate for there to be any confusion about my ongoing love and devotion to your mother." He was laying it on thick and speaking well above his normal range, because his mom was within earshot. Sure enough, Moses caught her out of the corner of his eye, wheeling herself out of the kitchen and back into the downstairs guest room.

"Oh, there's no confusion on my end," Moses said. "Yours, Thistle?"

"None on mine, either," she said.

"That's good. Now, if I were you, Mo, I'd let that wife of yours, who was up at the crack of dawn, sleep in and see about waking those kids up and fixing them a decent breakfast full of complex carbohydrates," he said. "You remember what I always used to tell you kids—breakfast is the most important part of the day. That, and kissing the woman you love," and with that, he turned to go back downstairs, humming what sounded to Moses like "Chad Gadya."

"That awful, smug son of a bitch," he snarled, recalling the day a couple of months ago when Pandora threw him out of the house. He'd called his parents sobbing and his dad had gotten on the phone and told him what a stupid piece of shit he was and that he didn't know the first thing about women or how to treat them, and Moses had just sat there, weeping and shaking, for in some way his dad was right, though it was impossible to take him seriously because if he'd

251

learned anything from his dad, it was how *not* to treat a woman. Pandora was nothing like his mom, though. When Moses raised his voice to her, she did not shrink back and try to appease him but rather reared up and came charging at him, this woman he'd married and whom he loved more than anyone in the world. He'd spoken terribly to her over the years, he knew he had, and he was trying to be better, trying to make it right, if not for his or Pandora's sake, then for the boys'. While he might not have been the perfect husband, no one could tell him he wasn't a good dad. He never shouted at his boys unless circumstances demanded it, and he never told them they were stupid or inadequate or insignificant or made them feel as if they weren't wanted. He tried to protect them from the world's phenomenological vengeance and curses both medieval and institutionalized: kike, Yid, Christ killer, Hebe, dirty Jew.

Moses crossed the catwalk that bridged the two wings of the house and entered the war zone of his sons' carpeted kingdom, a sprawling, cluttered land of Wiis, Xboxes, tablets, books, soccer balls, basketballs, baseballs and gloves, a pennant of the L.A. Dodgers, a poster of the Dallas Mavericks, and a couple of Israeli flags that served as window shades—the trips were still vehement Zionists and before the dissolution of Israel had often spoken of wanting to visit. The trips' media lounge (their former playroom) was still set up to look like a mock UN, with a table, three chairs, and three tiny flags of Israel. Last year, they had watched with disgust the real UN tribunals that had taken place in the days following the Three-Day War, which would not have gone the way it did had it not been for the absolute neutrality of the Europeans and Americans, having elected leaders who fervently embraced a new brand of isolationist nationalism. The rise of ISIS and the flood of Muslim refugees from war-torn Arab nations had convinced the west to leave the Middle East to itself, and they'd simply sat by and watched as enemy nations, with the help of Hamas, terrorized Israel's cities and invaded its borders. An unholy alliance between liberal anti-Zionists and right-wing protectionists had meant that for the first time in modern history, the United States of America refused to come to Israel's defense. Things were shifting all across the nation and coalitions that would have been utterly unthinkable a few years ago were suddenly welcomed, championed, and celebrated by those Americans who'd grown tired of the conflicts in the Middle East and wanted an end to it once and for all. The gut punch came when the United States joined the other nations of the UN in recognizing the dissolution of Israel, which was carved into thirds—one part each for the victors Syria, Lebanon, and Iran—the outraged, still nationless Palestinians absorbed in the process.

Unlike his children, Moses couldn't bring himself to watch it all unfold on TV or read about it online. He couldn't believe it was happening, and couldn't believe it hadn't happened sooner. All the while, every Jewish person he knew had gone into a kind of mourning, removing himself or herself from society just as he'd removed the mezuzahs from his doorways. The world had finally gotten its pound of flesh—not even a century after it was founded, Israel was no more—and life for America could go on as before. *Except that life did not go on as before, for even a single drop of rain there had significant consequences here,* Moses thought, waking the trips up and rustling them out of bed.

"Who wants pancakes as big as Texas?" he asked them.

"I do, Daddy!" said Bronson, the first of them to rise, for he loved the mornings best, just like Moses, whom he most took after. Moses roused Bronson's brothers, whispering, "Pancakes, pancakes," into their ears, then dashed across the hall to wake the twins, who were already up and getting themselves dressed. A minor miracle. One of those kinds of miracles that only happened when he wasn't looking, when he wasn't paying attention to the here and now but rather to the fluctuating possibilities of a future in which his wife no longer resented him, his acting career picked up steam, Jacob saw Dietrich for who he was, Edith rescinded her invitation to Elias, his mom grew stronger, and his dad, terrified of finally being unmasked for the psychopath he was, fled the house, the state, the country, the world, never to be heard from again.

The twins—Dexter with his broken fingers, Baxter helping him into his shirt, then into his shorts and shoes, which he tied for his brother, double-knotting them so the laces wouldn't come loose. Five years old and already so different from the way he and his own siblings treated one another. *But then look whom we had as role models,* he thought, hating himself for thinking badly of his mom, though there it was. She, too, had done her part in fomenting distrust among them all, so much so that for years the three had been divided, each to his or her own cell and to his or her own life. It wasn't until much later, after they'd all moved out, went to college, and had a chance to live on their own, that they'd even begun to be able to see one another without rancor. He didn't want that for his children.

The trips bumbled into the bathroom, pushing and shoving one another in good fun, whooping and hollering, until Moses went in and shushed them, telling them to be quiet, that their mom had gone back to bed. "If you wake her up, I'm going to have to take away all of your electronics," he threatened. "Just remember that, okay, guys? Don't make me the bad guy, not today. We have a long, long day ahead of us. Let's all try to get along."

He left them, these good-looking boys of his, to brush their hair and teeth, then set out again across the catwalk, treading more lightly the closer he came to the bedroom so as not to wake his wife. Before he entered, Moses removed his shoes and tiptoed through the dark, the heavy curtains drawn against the sun. He stood perfectly still to allow his eyes time to adjust, trying to make out the outline of his beloved—his beshert, his destiny—beneath the quilted comforter. They'd been together for fourteen years, many of them good, some of them not so good, yet Moses would not have traded in even one of the bad years, for to live without her, well, there was just no living without Pandora Orenstein-Jacobson, whose last name he'd taken as well, because that's who he was, because that's who she needed him to be. The idea that he hadn't slept in the same bed with her in over a month distressed him, for no one knew about this part of the separation but them—they'd kept it a secret from everyone, especially from his mom, the news of which would have killed her, as it was killing him.

Before everyone had arrived, he'd slept in the guest room across the hall, sneaking back into the bedroom before the boys woke up. Now that the house was filled to the rafters, however, Moses had to be more creative and discreet and had been sleeping at Gibbs's house on Calabasas Lake, which was even larger and grander than Moses's. *But of course it is,* he thought, as his eyes finally adjusted to the relative dark and Pandora's phone vibrated from somewhere deep in the folds of the bed: She often fell asleep with it in her hand. Her attachment to her phone irritated him beyond measure, yet he was trying to let it go, just as she was trying to let certain irritating idiosyncrasies of his go as well. They were trying.

Slipping under the covers, Moses found himself caring nothing about finding the phone or the video on it, nothing about anything except being right there, beside Pandora again. He curled up inside the cocoon of their marital bed, everything melting away, a shedding so profound that for a moment he could almost believe they were younger and still madly, deeply in love and they hadn't yet had children and were still living in their first apartment in Thousand Oaks and he was getting commercials right and left and the studio kept extending his role as psychiatry resident Floyd Foxx on the hit L.A.-based sitcom *Our Time's Up,* and his mom was breathing regularly and his dad was trying to find a cure for lung cancer and Jacob was in Brooklyn working on another play and Edith was in grad school falling in love with Elias and trying to get over her affair, exaggerated or not, with Sheik. He could almost believe it until he accidentally pressed himself against Pandora, who said, "Knock it off, Mo," breaking the spell that he had cast and vanishing everything with it. Then she rolled over, away from him, and as she did, her phone, which she'd been sleeping on, lit up with new notifications. As he reached for it and turned on his side, his back to her, he listened for the sound of her breathing, the lap of her tongue against the roof of her mouth, as if she were trying to remove peanut butter, then other sounds, which he'd come both to love and to loathe—the click-clack of her jaw, the burble of her stomach, the occasional, sighing fart—all signs she was once again asleep.

Moses slid out of bed and hurried with the phone into the twins' room, where Dexter was struggling half in, half out of his shirt. "Where's your brother?" he asked the boy, the lower half of his face hidden.

"Downstairs," he muttered as Moses went to help him. "I was trying to put on a different shirt, Daddy."

"I can see that, yeah," Moses said. He slipped one of his son's small arms through one sleeve. "Hey, Dexter, will you do Daddy a favor and say Mommy's passphrase into her phone?"

"Why do you have Mommy's phone? Is yours broken?" the boy asked pleasantly, without any hint of suspicion.

What a great age to be, Moses thought, missing his five-year-old self. "Yes," he said, "mine's broken," and oh, how he hated to lie, but it was just easier and more expedient and this explanation seemed enough to satisfy Dexter. He knew her passphrase, had heard her say it many times, but he couldn't match her modulation.

"Okay, but I want you to know I'm doing this under the dress," Dexter said. *Under duress,* which made Moses smile. He held the phone up to the boy's mouth and told him to say, "I love Moses," then waited for Dexter, who he gambled still sounded enough like his mom to fool the voice recognition software. "I love Moses," he said at last, yet the phone did not accept the string of words and remained tantalizingly locked.

Moses had only gone into her phone once before, many years ago, when she was in labor with the triplets. He'd forgotten his phone in the car, and Pandora, out of her mind with pain, had thrust the phone into his hand and had told him her numeric passcode—

how technology had changed—ordering him to call her dad. When he mentioned it later, she completely denied having given out her passcode, laughing at the very idea. But that was a different world, when she still loved and trusted him and kept him close to her heart by using a simple chain of numbers, their anniversary, to lock and unlock the secrets she kept. He gazed down at the phone, at the screenshot of Pandora and him holding hands, remembering the day of that photo shoot a few months ago. To his mind, it was the last good time they'd had together before Pandora cooled to him, the house becoming a place of battle rather than of respite. He stared hard at the phone, trying to imagine a new set of words, the right ones in the right combination, that would give him the access he needed, for something told him he'd find things on her phone that she'd rather not have him see—changing her passphrase was proof.

More than ever, Moses wanted to unlock the phone and threw out random phrases to Dexter to say—"I love my boys," "I love Nieves," "I love my life," "I love Calabasas"—but none of them worked.

"Can we go downstairs? I'm hungry," Dexter said, drifting toward the door.

"Sure thing," he said. "And thanks for helping me out, champ."

"I'll always help you out, Daddy," he said. "You can count on me."

My boy, Moses thought with such longing and love in his heart that for a moment he was utterly ashamed of himself for turning him into an accomplice. Luckily for him, his sons liked him better than they liked Pandora, who screamed at them from morning till night. *She's a screamer, both in and out of bed,* he once told Gibbs. His mom had learned long ago not to intervene or say anything when Pandora was in one of her stormy, our-sons-are-dirty-filthy-creatures moods, but his dad, whom he'd reminded time and again that it was best to let her blow herself out, was a different story. "Something's not right in the head with her," his dad liked to say, in front of her, which of course just made matters worse. Moses suspected that part of his dad's butting in had to do with how much pleasure he took in winding Pandora up even further, then sitting back to watch her spectacular implosion.

Moses thought of returning the phone, then decided to shove it in his pocket, for Pandora would be out for another couple of hours, which would buy him some time. Usually, she never slept in, up at the crack of dawn to see the boys off to school or sometimes to meet her dad for breakfast—that is, when he was in town and not gallivanting off to the Caribbean with his floozy du jour. It amazed him that she seemed to love her dad as much as she despised her mom. For years she'd had nothing at all to do with her, even though she lived just a few miles away. He envied Pandora's relationship with her dad even as he fought against scolding her for holding a grudge against the woman who had brought her into the world. It's not that he didn't understand the strain between mother and daughter or couldn't sympathize with her decision to cut the woman, good or bad, out of her grandkids' lives. But even horrible parents, Moses knew, could make remarkable grandparents, often trying to make up for their failure and neglect of their own kids by heaping loads of attention on the next generation. This made him think about how his dad may have intentionally broken his son's fingers, and he realized that not even this, the simplest of charitable, grandfatherly characterizations, could be applied to Julian. Moses sighed, following Dexter down the stairs and into the kitchen, where the boys were gathered on stools around the island, his dad at the stove wearing an apron, already spooning the pancake batter onto the griddle. "I want to flip them," Baxter said, standing beside his paw-paw, who handed him the spatula.

"Where're Mom and Aunt Thistle?" Moses asked, training one nervous eye on his dad, the other on Baxter.

"They're in there," his dad said, indicating the guest room.

"Keep an eye on your paw-paw," Moses said, leaning down and whispering into Bronson's ear. "I'll be right back."

He hurried out of the kitchen and through the den, passing the wall of glass, where he briefly caught his reflection and beyond that, the shadowed, sunless backyard, the dark green grass, the slate-colored flagstones, and the pool, everything seemingly in place, though not quite right, as if in the night they'd had an earthquake, which had shifted the world around and tilted it ever so slightly. Moses pressed on, though, for he had no time to dawdle, not then anyway, not with so much riding on what he might or might not find within the locked confines of Pandora's phone, which buzzed frantically in his pocket and played the theme to *The Twilight Zone*—Pandora's alarm. He silenced it, then headed for her office down the long, narrow, unlit hallway at the far back of the horseshoe-shaped house.

Here, he knocked cautiously, a silly involuntary reflex, as if he might find her inside—when she was in her office, he knew enough not to disturb her—then entered the Fortress of Disquietude, as he called it, this room into which she disappeared for hours and which was the central nervous system of her thriving online business—*Pandora's Box: The Mommy's Treasure Trove of Family-Friendly Fun in Los Angeles!*—an email newsletter that reached eighty thousand families, Jewish and Gentile alike, in the Valley and beyond.

He hadn't been in her office for months and here, too, everything looked exactly as it always did, though also slightly out of whack. Keeping one ear on his sons' voices, Moses brushed his eyes over the desk, skimming it for something, anything, that would help him get into her phone. His fingers quested through her papers, then the drawers, yet nothing leaped out at him, only that what he was doing was in direct violation of the rules they had set down ages ago—no one, including Moses, was ever to be in her office without her express permission. Not only was he breaking this rule, he was also trying to break into her phone, and that's when it struck him that if she ever found out about any of this, she really would divorce him. Her phone buzzed and pinged again, announcing another text, then another and another—*Someone is desperate to get in touch with her, someone who isn't me,* he thought, leaving her office and heading back into the kitchen, where his dad was serving the first round of pancakes.

The boys slathered them with Irish butter and real maple syrup—his dad was a stickler that his pancakes had to be served with the genuine (pronounced: gen-u-ayn) article, which he'd brought with him all the way from Texas, because, as he said, "It's clear you'd feed them that Aunt Jemima slop. I'd like them to grow up with a modicum of taste. Can you blame me for trying?"

The door behind him opened and out rolled his mom, pushed along by Edith, who was shaking her head and mouthing something he was having a hard time deciphering, though it looked like she was saying "I hate this," but she might have been saying "I hate him," meaning their dad. And that's when Moses had a moment of eureka, grinning a big dopey grin that stretched from ear to ear. "Good morning, Mo," his mom said. "Did you just have one of your father's pancakes, or did you just win the lottery? I love seeing you smile."

"Morning, Ma," he said, reaching for Dexter and drawing him out of the kitchen in midbite, the fork still grasped in his little fingers. "We'll be right back," and he led the boy to the wall of glass and stopped, retrieving Pandora's phone from his pocket. "Okay, I want you to try this: Try saying 'I hate Moses.'"

"Dad, you're being a big silly," he said.

"Just try it," he said, handing the phone to Dexter, who whispered the three words into it, handed it back to him with a sad, disappointed shrug, then raced into the kitchen to finish his pancakes with his brothers.

Moses looked down at the phone, which, finally unlocked, lit up in his palm. It did not surprise him that Pandora had changed only one word in the passphrase, for she was nothing if not predictable, even in her scorn. *First things first,* he thought, and searched the phone for the video, which he found without much trouble. He played it, and he saw what Edith had seen earlier—their dad, tampering with their mother's spare oxygen tank in the back of the minivan. It did look as though Julian had had no idea he was being recorded, just as Edith said. But Moses, unlike his sister, understood instantly that his dad had done something to their mother's spare oxygen tank. He played the video again, just to make sure, slowing it down frame by frame when he got to the end, but even then he couldn't exactly see what his father was doing, only that he was doing something. He glanced up from the phone in the direction of the kitchen, fuming, in shock. He tasted bile in the back of his throat, thought he might be sick, and rushed into the bathroom, stuffing Pandora's phone into his back pocket. He turned on the taps and held his face under the water, wondering why his own wife had kept the video from him, then quickly understanding that she had kept it from him precisely because she knew him and knew what the video would do to him. He reached for the toilet, not to vomit but to sit down, forgetting about Pandora's phone, which made a sharp, unforgettable crack the moment he sat down on the lid.

"Ruck me funning," he said, jumping up and removing the phone from his back pocket to find a single fissure in the glass, from top to bottom, a split that ran directly through the center of Pandora and him, who were angled toward each other and holding hands, separating them as if it knew. Moses forwarded the video to himself and Edith—he would have to explain that traceable offense to Pandora later—then left the bathroom. He snuck up the stairs and into the bedroom, knowing the right thing to do was to have the glass replaced, yet sometimes the right thing was negated by too many wrong things. Just as he was setting the phone on the floor, it buzzed and lit up again in his hand—another text. Before he knew what he was doing, he was opening it and reading.

It was from Gibbs, asking Pandora about this evening and if she thought it was such a good idea for him to come. It seemed odd to Moses that he was expressing concern to his wife rather than to Moses himself. After all, Pandora had wanted to keep the evening small and exclusive to the family, whereas Moses understood that having Gibbs around would up the ratings. His appearance at the Jacobson table would surely draw millions of viewers, including industry heads, who, Moses was hoping, might see them interacting and offer them a new show, at least the chance of one. He had hoped Pandora would support him on this, as it was to her benefit as well. She hadn't, and they'd fought. At the time, some weeks back, Moses had just assumed the fight had to do with Passover. This morning, however, while absently scrolling through a previous and surprisingly lengthy text exchange between Pandora and Gibbs from a couple of days ago, he realized something else—that while he'd been at an audition for a commercial for a new kind of hemorrhoid cream in downtown L.A., Pandora had taken the boys over to Gibbs's house to go swimming. Gibbs could still afford the exorbitant pool tax. This meant nothing in and of itself, except for one small detail—neither Gibbs nor Pandora nor even the boys had mentioned it to him.

Kneeling down, Moses set the locked phone on the floor, stood, backed up a few paces, walked toward the bed, then deliberately stepped on the phone. "Oh, crap," he said in what he hoped was one of his best performances. He bent down and picked the phone back up, then roused Pandora, who was already in the process of waking. "Hey, honey, morning," he said. She removed the mask and the earplugs and sat up, running a hand through her preternaturally coiffed platinum hair. She went to bed ravishing and woke up ravishing and it was all Moses could do not to climb into bed and fuck her between her delicious 34DDs. "Shoot, honey, I accidentally stepped on your phone. It must have fallen off the bed. You'll need to get the glass replaced," and he leaned in to kiss her as she reared back and away from him.

"You what? What did you just say?" she asked, grabbing for the phone. He handed it to her gently, for he was trying to maintain his composure, to come to her with openness and light, trying to salvage what was left of the rubble of their marriage. Even from where he was, he could see that stepping on the phone had caused the initial crack to fissure even further into a veritable spiderweb. "Dammit, Mo. I don't have time to deal with this today," she whined. "I'll just have to go buy another one after I take the kids to Krav Maga."

"Pandora, darling, that's eleven hundred dollars we don't have," he said, feeling as though he were losing his shit, both literally and figuratively, for the anger was rising in his face and his bowels were clanging and bucking like radiators whose valves were stuck on off. He felt himself about to blow and rushed into the bathroom.

"IBS acting up again?" she asked from the doorway, where she stood with what looked like a giant grin on her face, though he couldn't be sure in the bathroom's windowless gloom. "You know what they say—weak bowels, weak will."

"Is that what they say?" he said, flushing and rising.

Though he'd just relieved himself, Moses felt worse, the pulleys of gravity tugging him down even further. He moved as if through quicksand toward the door, while behind him Pandora murmured about the bowels and souls of men, the noxious, sulfurous stink trailing him out into the hall, where he paused to consider the enormity of the situation and his own part in it—his part, and what was slowly dawning on him as Gibbs's part, as well.

Moses found the boys seated on the sofa, his dad in the middle telling them the story of Passover. "And then the angel of death came sweeping over the land of Egypt, but she 'passed over' the Jewish homes because they were smart and marked the lintels of the doors with the blood of a slaughtered spring lamb," which, at the sound of blood, made them even more hyperactive than they already were and fall into one another, playing dead.

"A slotted spring lamp?" asked Baxter, the wiseass of the two.

"That doesn't even make sense," said Bran, rolling his eyes.

"Why is the angel of death a girl?" asked Dexter, who sat at the far end, next to Brendan, who was deeply involved with his iMuse.

"Because angels of death are always feminine," his dad said, "or gay."

"Boys, disregard everything Paw-Paw just said," Pandora said, appearing on the stairs. "Men are the true harbingers of death," and she held up her phone and glared at Moses, who glared right back. "Julian, both my brothers are gay and contrary to how you feel about your own son, I love them and will not have them bashed in front of me or my children. Is that clear?"

"Moses, tell your wife she needs to lighten up," his dad said.

"Tell her yourself," Moses said, turning to the boys. "Go and grab your backpacks and head to the car. I don't want you to be late to Krav Maga again. So . . . chop-chop."

"But I want to stay and hear Paw-Paw tell us about the plagues!" Baxter said, screaming and throwing what Moses knew was to be merely his first tantrum of the day.

"I'll tell you all about them when you get home later," his dad said, reaching out and hugging Baxter, to Moses's horror and chagrin, for he'd never seen his dad hug any of the kids before, nor could he recall a single memory of his dad ever hugging him.

Moses was about to call the network to ask what time the technician would be at the house when his phone rang—a prerecorded message from the Lost Hills Sheriff Station asking him to accept a collect call from Jacob Jacobson. "Um, yes," he said uncertainly, heading into the hall toward the bathroom, for he felt another clench and jangle in his intestines.

"Mo, you need to come here and bail us out," Jacob said, his voice barely recognizable for the shame and anguish in it.

"What the—what are you talking about?" he asked, confounded.

"Later. I'll explain it all later," Jacob said.

"Jesus H. Christ," Moses said, the clenching and jangling subsiding. "How much is the bail?" When Jacob told him it was going to be ten thousand dollars—five thousand apiece—Moses laughed, because the only other alternative was to cry. "What in the hell did you do?"

"It doesn't matter," Jacob said. "Can you do it? We'll pay you back."

"With what?" he asked. "Your good looks and his—"

But the line crackled and went dead. *Un-fucking-believable,* he thought. So now on top of all the other stuff he had to take care of that day, he also had to figure out where he was going to get ten thousand dollars, then drive to the Lost Hills Sheriff Station and bail his incompetent younger brother and his anti-Semite boyfriend out of jail, while also trying to come up with an appropriate time and place to ambush his dad, convince him to pull up stakes and disappear for good. The only thing Moses wanted was to go back to Gibbs's house, jump into his pool, sink to the bottom, and never come up again—not that he'd ever do anything like that to his sons or give Pandora the satisfaction.

Speaking of Pandora, he thought, rushing into the garage to find her scolding the boys. Moses tapped on the glass with his wedding band, thinking of the first time he met her fourteen years ago for a date at Jerry's Famous Deli, in Thousand Oaks. They'd found each other on www.modernyenta.com, a dating site for Jews founded by a meddling grandma cum media mogul. He recalled driving away from the date, which had lasted all of forty-five minutes, and calling his mom and dad in Dallas to tell them he'd just met his future ex-wife, laughing at his own joke, because he'd never imagined Pandora marrying him, much less ever seeing him again. Yet Pandora had surprised him the same night by texting him to invite him to Shabbat dinner at her dad's apartment in Beverly Hills. Two years later, they were married, she was pregnant with the triplets, and a billboard of them went up on Sunset Boulevard, proclaiming them another perfect union and Modern Yenta an undeniable success. Sadly, after a skinhead posing as a Jew raped and tortured a young woman in Tarzana, the site had to be shuttered and was no more, just as Moses feared he and Pandora were soon to be no more.

"What?" Pandora asked, rolling down her window. As Moses explained the situation to her, her eyes went wide and wild, first with shock, then with knowing. "We'll never recoup a single penny, you know that, right? But do what you've got to do, Mo. It's not like you care what I think anyway."

"Pandora, that's not fair," he said. "I'm asking you now: What do you think I should do?"

"If you have to ask me what to do about your brother, I think it says something pretty sad about you, doesn't it?" And with that, she rolled up the window and reversed out of the garage.

The game between them was simple, yet it was a game Moses kept finding himself losing because the rules kept changing. Marriage was like this, he understood, a dance that drove everyone crazy at times, yet this dance with Pandora was wearing him out, until what he thought he'd always wanted—a reconciliation, a new beginning—made about as much sense as finding Gibbs's texts on her phone. Or too much sense, for he was starting to realize that perhaps Pandora was cheating on him with his best friend. *Impossible,* thought Moses. Even Pandora had better scruples than that, at least the Pandora he used to know. Yet this was a new Pandora, less likely to laugh with him, less likely to stand up for him, less likely to sit with him, drink wine coolers, and watch the sunset from the roof of the house. He missed her. He missed the people they'd been, the people who'd promised each other they'd never turn into their parents—she a child of divorce, he a child of untold emotional abuse. He had kept his promise, while she had banged around the house like a poltergeist, threatening and shrieking and lodging complaints, as if he were the innkeeper and she an unhappy, dissatisfied guest. He wondered if Pandora knew how good she actually had it, if anyone ever did.

As he passed the wall of glass on his way to find Edith, Moses glanced at the backyard again, and again was unsettled by some detail about it. Yet he had no time to figure out what it was, for he was already in the kitchen, telling his sister about Jacob and the German.

"Keep the parental units busy and don't tell them," he said. "It'll kill Mom."

"Unless you-know-who beats me to it," she said. "That was a joke, Mo. Jeez, lighten up," and she grabbed hold of his arm and smooched him on the cheek. "Are you sure you don't want me to come with you?"

"Negative," he said. "Just keep your phone on you and text me when the tech guy arrives."

"Roger that," she said, holding up one of the soggy, wilted pancakes. "Did you have one of these? Like sawdust," she added as she ripped it in half. "And, Mo, don't you be mean to Dietrich. Jacob loves him. And, well, he's as good as family now, if you know what I mean."

Moses thought this over in the car, speeding down Mulholland Drive. He thought about this when he came to a flashing police cruiser blocking the entrance to the 101, the cop directing traffic onto the frontage road, which meant there'd been another major accident or another suicide bombing, both of which filled him with anger and pathos. He thought about this while he inched along like a little worm behind all the other little worms, then thought about this some more when he finally arrived at the sheriff's station some 7.2 miles and two hours later. He thought about this as he paid their bail and thought about this while he waited for them to walk through the security doors. He thought about this as he studied the list of the FBI's Most Wanted, tacked up on a corkboard near the door, trying his best to avert his eyes from one face in particular—a young woman who was wanted in connection with the maiming and subsequent death by arson of several residents at a Jewish assisted-living facility in Encino. He thought about this while he composed a text to Pandora in which he asked her if the man she'd been having an "emotional affair" with since their separation—he knew there was someone, though she'd refused to give Moses a name—was Gibbs and thought about this some more as he deleted the text, then composed a new one to Gibbs, asking him the same thing, which he then also deleted. He was distraught. He was floundering. He was unable to think about anything else but the idea of Gibbs and his wife together. But then that other thought crept back in, the thought his sister had planted in his brain, about the German being as good as family now—and Moses was still looking at his phone, at the frantic message he'd just received from Edith, who texted him that their mom had taken a tumble, when Jacob and Dietrich pushed through the security doors at last. He was replying to Edith—*Is she all right? WTF happened?*—when he glanced up at Jacob and Dietrich making their way toward him, but something about them wasn't right. What wasn't right was so wrong, so utterly, horribly, disgustingly wrong, that it was nearly indescribable, nearly but not quite, for there was Jacob in the schmatte with the yellow Star of David embroidered into the pocket and there was Dietrich in the SS uniform, shiny black leather boots and all. Just like that, Moses didn't want to know anything about any of it.

The drive back to the beach to get Jacob's rental car took a supremely long time. To drown out the suffocating silence, Moses put on the radio, while Jacob sat beside him, gazing out the window, just as he used to do when they were kids, and Dietrich tried his best to make conversation with Moses, who refused to engage him. "You're being rude," Jacob said at one point and Moses just grimaced, turning the volume up.

One bad song passed into another, then the disc jockeys broke in for a news and traffic update, alerting any and all drivers that many miles of the 101, which included several exits in Agoura Hills, were closed to traffic in both directions until further notice due to terrorist activity. This time, three cars had exploded simultaneously, two on the northbound side, one on the southbound, and while no one except the drivers had been killed, the shrapnel from the exploding cars was scattered for miles all across the Ventura Freeway. "No one has claimed responsibility for the incident yet, but Daesh released another video late last night denouncing the abhorrent portrayal of Muslims on TV and in the movies and accusing corrupt Jewish politicians and businessmen of colluding with 'the evil Jews of Hollywood who own all of Los Angeles,'" one of the disc jockeys reported.

"Welcome to L.A.," Moses said, shutting off the radio and glancing into the rearview mirror at Dietrich in his preposterous outfit.

"They gave Israel back, and still it's not enough for them?" Jacob asked. "What the fuck do they want?"

"They didn't give Israel back," Moses said. "It was stolen."

"I think what Jacob means is—"

"I know what Jacob means," Moses said. "And to answer your question—they want what they've always wanted: to drive us into the sea. Apparently any old sea will do, even the Pacific."

"I have read that those attacks happen there in America much more often than anywhere else currently," Dietrich said. "It is bad for the Jews everywhere, but there it is even worse, I think."

"Yes, Dietrich, but you mean *here* it is even worse," Moses said. "Thanks for overstating the obvious."

"Shut up, Mo," Jacob said. "He was only trying to make conversation."

"This is okay, *Schatz,*" Dietrich said. "But, Moses, I want to say directly to you now: You can hold a grudge against me for what my country did a long time ago and you are completely within your rights to despise me, but I will not sit there and let you come between Jacob and me. Do not make him choose you or me. It is unfair."

"That was a pretty little speech," Moses said, "but let me tell you what's unfair—what's unfair is that I just had to shell out ten thousand dollars to bail your stupid, sorry asses out of jail and now, to add insult to injury, I have to sit here with you dressed in a fucking Nazi uniform. Does that even remotely register at all with you? And as for you, Jacob, you ought to be ashamed of yourself. You better hope Ma's still at the doc-in-the-box when we get home because if she sees you in that, it will kill her. And I can only imagine what the old man's going to say. Maybe, just maybe, it'll kill *him* and all of our problems will be solved. We can only pray. Shall we pray?"

"What do you mean 'still at the doc-in-the-box'?" Jacob asked with alarm.

"She fell. It doesn't sound serious, but who knows because Thistle won't return my texts."

"Have you tried calling her?" Jacob asked.

"Have you seen me call her? You walked out in that getup right when I got the news."

Some thirty utterly silent minutes later, they arrived at the beach, where Jacob and Dietrich hopped out without a word and Moses watched them go, still so disgusted that he wasn't sure he'd ever be able to look his brother in the eye again. It was one thing for Jacob to practice his perverted sexual rituals in the privacy of his own home, yet it was another thing altogether to make someone else a witness to it. The idea that his brother found excitement in demeaning himself and that Dietrich found equal if not more excitement in demeaning him only helped further clarify something that had been on his mind for quite some time—that in some way, their dad was responsible, that in some way Jacob had discovered the perfect partner in Dietrich. Still, he had to admit he'd never seen his brother this happy.

Moses drove quickly and beat Jacob and Dietrich back to the house, arriving just as his watch let out twelve cuckoos, tolling noon. Somewhere between the police station and here, it had begun keeping time and tracking his heartbeat again, both of which reappeared on the small black screen, though the color of the digital heart had changed—instead of a fiery, incandescent red, it was fainter and softer, as if he'd left his heart out in the rain one too many times. Which would have worried him if he let it, but he had no time to worry about such things, for he had realized a monumental thing about himself—that after this was all over, after the TV special, after confronting his dad, after making sure his dad was never seen or heard from again, after he either reconciled with Pandora or they went their separate ways, he would have no reason to worry again, for all of his reasons for worrying were caught up in these relationships. He could start acting more like the man he used to be. For as long as he could remember, Moses had been the guiding force within the Jacobson family, the ever do-gooding brother and son. He'd tried and tried and tried to get his dad's attention and approval, yet the more he tried to secure it, the more elusive it was. He'd known that his dad had no respect for him or for his career, his objections showing up in subtle and not-so-subtle ways, movies Moses starred in that went unseen and unremarked upon. He'd spent many hours of his day thinking about how his dad saw him, because, although he might not have respected Moses's choices, Moses understood that out of all of his siblings, he was his dad's favorite, which was often made clear in how he bad-mouthed Jacob and Edith to him behind their backs—Jacob a ne'er-do-well, lazy queer, Edith a cobwebbed-womb spinster.

Yet somewhere along the way, Moses had stopped defending them to him, because he thought it was high time they defended themselves. What he hadn't realized, until a couple of months ago, was just how far-reaching his dad's disappointment in all of them was and how deeply vindictive he could be. Mo suspected that over the last few weeks his dad had been setting his own plan in motion and that this plan had a three-prong approach—first, to poison their mom against the three of them, second, to render her non compos mentis, and third, to get power of attorney, thereby kinging himself. For it still seemed far too coincidental to Moses that his mother, the wife of a research pulmonologist who specialized in rare forms of progressive and life-threatening lung diseases, should contract one herself, this one as particularly pernicious as it was idiopathic, meaning that no one, not the doctors who treated her or the specialists in the field, had any idea where it came from, although Moses thought he might: his dad. How easy it would have been for his dad to figure out the precipitating factors that could lead to the disease and then introduce them to her environment. A particular aerosol, perhaps, or a cleaning agent that she used on the floor, the fumes of which only she would breathe while he was safely away in his lab miles away. An airborne toxin, maybe, administered while she slept and that irritated and damaged her lungs, and her lungs only, for he'd be certain not to let himself come into contact with it. There were countless ways to kill someone and Moses wondered if his dad hadn't figured out the best way possible. From a young age, Moses had understood that a vein of greed ran directly through his dad, who had controlled every single aspect of the family's finances, including his wife's inheritance, with a ruthlessness that bordered on the fanatical. While his children fell into financial wrack and ruin, his dad sat by and watched it happen with furtive glee.

"I can't wait for the day when all of you are off my dime," his dad used to tell them. This coming from the man who'd retired practically the day Grandpa Ernie died and bought a brand-new Mercedes convertible while Edith drowned under a mountain of debt after her divorce. This from the man who'd showed up at the house with a used barbecue, for which Moses had thanked him, but then who'd thrown a tantrum because Moses hadn't thanked him quite enough.

As he got out of his car and wandered into the house, Moses wanted to tell his siblings that even if they managed to talk their dad into leaving, he wasn't about to go quietly and certainly not without what he thought he deserved—a chunk of change commensurate with the years he'd spent as a father and a husband, however incompetent he'd been at both. There was no way Moses saw them getting rid of him that easily, no way without involving their mom, whom they'd sworn to keep all of this from. In some odd way, he understood, this was her fault more than anyone else's, for if she'd only left him when she'd had the chance, they never would have had to discuss such grisly plans. *Yet here we are,* Moses thought, knocking on the guest room door and entering to find his mom resting on her bed, reading a magazine.

"You're alive," he said, delighted to see her free of a bandage or a cast.

"I tripped," she said, looking up, her face a blend of emotions, seriousness and sorrow among them. "I've never fallen in my life," and she patted the bed. "Come sit with me for a few minutes."

"Sure, Ma," he said, taking a seat beside her. "Do you want to tell me what happened?"

"Honestly, I'm still not sure," she said, rubbing the back of her head. "Dad and I were taking a walk around the cul-de-sac—the doctor said I need to get as much cardiovascular exercise as possible—and we were on our fourth or fifth loop, and I just went down. Well, down and backward. You should have seen your dad, Mo. Absolutely beside himself. He says I must have slipped on a patch of oil."

Moses studied his mom, the clear plastic tube of oxygen running from the tank to her nose. The sight made his insides run cold. He studied her to see what she wasn't telling him, or rather what she was telling him without telling him. Yet her face remained impassive and darkly gleaming with whatever secrets she was keeping. *Perhaps these secrets are the only things keeping her alive,* he thought. "Are you still on your first tank?" he asked.

"Oh, yes, they last me a few weeks," she said. "Why do you ask?"

"Just curious," he said, thinking of the video. Should he show it to her and let her come to her own conclusions, or should he wait for the three of them to confront their dad when the time was right? What if the time was never right and they missed their tiny window of opportunity? His parents were scheduled to leave tomorrow morning to drive back to Texas because she had an appointment with her pulmonologist on Wednesday. The hours were shrinking away from him, and Moses decided then and there that his mom could never comprehend the depths of his dad's depravity.

"Do me a favor, will you? Do something nice and take your dad fishing. Get him out of the house. He keeps hovering, and it's driving me nuts," she said.

"I will if I have time," he said.

"Good. Now I'm going to rest up before tonight's big event," she said. "Pandora told me the network's sending a gal over to do our hair and makeup!"

"Yes, they always do that," he said, rising and kissing her on the cheek.

"What was that for?" she asked.

"No reason," he said. "Because you're my mom, and I love you."

He hadn't seen her cry in ages, not since he'd left home for college, and when the tears started falling from her eyes, it was all he could do not to cry himself. He didn't blame her, not like Jacob, who he suspected only wanted to off their dad to get back at their mom. Jacob was nothing if not vengeful himself, although Moses knew exactly where his unforgiving spirit came from—those nights his mom visited him, but also from someplace else, a single moment in time when they were still boys and Moses palmed him in the nose and they'd had to stop at IHOP on the way to the airport. It was a memory Jacob had relayed to him only yesterday, one that Jacob said had returned to him years after the fact, when he was already living in Brooklyn and was writing his first play, *Possessive Plural*, about an incestuous affair between a mother and a son, who, after murdering the boy's father, sold the family house, bought a new car, and went on a road trip, stopping off in every IHOP along the way to fuck in the bathroom. The memory kept returning, long after he'd finished writing the play and found a theater to produce it. On Friday, while Edith was in Claremont and Dietrich was napping, Moses had taken Jacob for a drive, ending at Calabasas Lake. It was there, in the gazebo at the lake's edge, where Jacob recalled that morning thirty years ago—the day after Edith's bat mitzvah—when their mom had piled them into the car and headed for the airport.

"You never apologized for hitting me in the nose," Jacob began.

"You were being a twerp." He shrugged. "You had it coming."

"You were my big brother," Jacob said. "And, no, I didn't."

"You want me to tell you I'm sorry?" Moses asked.

"It'd be a start," he reasoned. "Considering."

"Considering?"

"What else happened to me that morning."

"What else happened to you?"

"You're not going to like what I'm about to tell you," Jacob said, pausing. "Mom kissed me."

"Mom kissed you? Mom kissed you how? What are you talking about?"

"She was wiping the blood off my chest and leaned in and kissed me on the lips," Jacob said. "That's the truth, Mo."

"No, it's not," he choked. "That did not happen."

"It happened. I can't prove it, but I did write an entire play about it. I have no reason to lie. Not anymore."

They stared silently at each other.

"She . . . our mother . . . kissed you?" Moses repeated, his voice full of disgust, though he wasn't sure if it was directed at Jacob or at the very idea of what he was saying or that he was saying it with such candor, as if it could have actually happened.

"She didn't just kiss me," he admitted. "She French-kissed me."

"She did not French-kiss you, Jacob. Stop making stuff up," Moses snapped. "You always made stuff up when we were kids. You're a consummate, pathological liar. Isn't that what Dad used to say? I never wanted to believe it, but today I just might. You're talking about a woman who's dying, Jacob. It's . . . so utterly preposterous I really should bash you in the nose again for old time's sake."

"I know all that, Mo, but she wasn't always dying. She packed us into the car and drove away from the house. She was leaving him, Mo, I'm certain of it. Then you punched me in the face and we had to stop because I was bleeding and she took me into that bathroom to clean me up and . . . she kissed me," Jacob said helplessly. "I'm not saying that what she did was right or wrong. I'm not ascribing judgment. Well, maybe a little. But it's something that happened, and I had to tell you. But I'm not going to sit here and take your crap, either. I'm not about to let you or anyone else tell me I can't trust my own memories, because that's what our asshole father has tried to do to us our entire lives."

"I don't know what to say," Moses said, beyond stunned. He wanted to ask Jacob if there was a word for that, but he hated his brother too much at that moment to ask him much of anything.

"Then we left the bathroom and joined you guys. We ate our pancakes and drove back to the house," Jacob said. "Dad never knew we left home. He never even knew she was going to leave with us."

"He knew," Moses corrected. "Because I told him. Later."

"That explains it then," Jacob said.

"What does it explain?" he asked.

"Why he was nice to us for about a minute," Jacob replied. "I always wondered about that. I just thought he'd changed. I was wrong."

"You were always right about him," Moses conceded. "I'm sorry."

"For my nose?"

"No, for not listening to you," Moses said. "And I guess for your nose."

This exchange rattled around in Moses's head as he left the guest room and shut the door, running into his dad, who he had assumed had driven Edith to Claremont, for the minivan had not been in the driveway upon his return. The front door opened again, and this time Jacob and Dietrich strolled in, no longer wearing those insulting, despicable getups, but back in jeans and T-shirts.

"The tech guy's here," Jacob said, ushering Dietrich up the stairs.

Sure enough, the front door swung open yet again and in walked a tall, skinny kid in a black T-shirt with THE JACOBSONS! in white block letters emblazoned across the front. On the back, the show's tagline: 5 X THE LOVE, 10 X THE VOLUME.

"Hey, Mr. Orenstein-Jacobson. I'd like to start on the room this shindig is happening in," Chandler said. "Take some measurements. Do the do. Cam it up."

Moses led him into the dining room, which sat off the kitchen at the far end of the horseshoe and directly opposite Pandora's office, though unlike Pandora's office, the dining room was made up of two glass walls—one that looked directly out onto the backyard, the other onto a grassy declivity separating the Jacobson property from their neighbors', the dreaded, cantankerous Frieda and Milton Rothman, an older, retired Jewish couple who were as prickly as their precious cacti, Pandora liked to say. When they'd first taken possession of the house from Pandora's own cuckoo of a dad—a gift to them and a tax write-off for him—Pandora had beseeched the couple to have the cacti removed, yet Frieda and Milton had remained adamantly opposed to her request. They had seen the new homeowners as interlopers on what had been a peaceful, quiet block, "until the arrival of your unruly boys and your hotheaded wife," according to Frieda, the ornerier of the two, who had mentioned this to Moses a few days after what became known as Cactusgate around Edelweiss Estates.

"They're old," Moses told Pandora. "And they've been here a lot longer than we have."

"They're evil," she said. "And it's just like you to take the side that isn't mine."

"I'm not taking anyone's side," he said.

"Exactly!" she said.

So Moses went over to try to convince the Rothmans and again the request was shot down, though this time Frieda asked him to stay for a cup of tea, which he did, because he thought it might help down the line. Though in trying to accommodate and placate both parties, he knew that sooner or later he'd merely just wind up alienating one or the other.

"Having grown up with a combative, litigious dad, the last thing I wanted was to become him, so instead, what did I do?" Moses asked Frieda as he sipped his tea. "I traded him in for Pandora," he said, joking somewhat. "No, but really, her bark is worse than her bite."

"Well, I just hope she doesn't snap at us again," Frieda said and

Moses detected an accent, "because then I will be forced to call the pound," and she smiled, the first time he'd seen it. "I am sure she's a nice, reasonable woman. She just wants to protect her children."

"Yes, that's true, she does," he said. "So it sounds like you're from Germany?"

"Austria. From Innsbruck," she said and he detected the tiniest of blushes rising in her face.

"My grandparents were Viennese. They took my brother to Innsbruck when he was a kid. He came back with one of those funny green felt hats. He wore it around the house for weeks until our dad made fun of him and told him he looked like a prancing gay leprechaun."

"Your father said that?" she asked, surprised.

"My dad said many hateful things to us," he said. "That was tame by comparison."

"No one should speak to a child like that," she pronounced firmly. "Milton and I have a son. He was born here, in California. We never see him." This came as a shock to Moses. "He married a Catholic girl against his father's wishes. It was terrible. Milton never got over it."

"Just for marrying a non-Jew? That seems . . . harsh," Moses offered tentatively.

"He married outside the faith," she said. "I was hurt, but not like Milton. What some of our own relatives lived through only to have our boy disavow his own Judaism? It was a betrayal. Unforgivable to some," and she poured herself another cup of tea. "I speak to him on occasion. Don't tell Milton." Moses said he wouldn't dream of it. "We have three grandchildren who Milton doesn't even know exist. If I bring Ezra up, Milton just changes the subject. They own a house a few miles from here, in Tarzana. Can you imagine living so close and yet so far?"

Yes, Moses could imagine it, because that's how he'd felt while growing up in his dad's house. "I'm sorry you have to go through that," he said.

"It's Milton who suffers for it, not me," she said. "Oh, he'd never admit it, but I know he does. I catch him looking at Ezra's baby pictures sometimes and know his heart's still breaking. But sometimes what we believe in is more important than whom we believe in."

Some two years later, nothing much had changed between the neighbors, except that Milton had taken ill and was housebound and Frieda left him alone for hours at a time to go visit Ezra and her grandchildren. Moses only knew that because he saw her at the Commons once, in the window of Slices of Heaven Bakery, seated at a table with a man, who looked like a younger version of Milton, and three teens, who could have only been her grandchildren. The cacti still remained an unresolved contention, with Moses still caught between Frieda, who would not budge, and Pandora, who regularly slipped notes into the Rothmans' mailbox with landscaping brochures and estimates.

But now that Edith had arrived, Moses was hoping to be able to put the issue to bed at last. Edith, with her mediation skills and her powers of persuasion, which she'd been honing for years, starting at home by brokering deals between Moses and Jacob when they were deadlocked on whose turn it was to take out the trash or mow the yard. It was Edith, Moses suspected, who'd insinuated herself between her parents after their Point Dume proclamation, and who must have talked their mother into giving their father another chance. He couldn't be sure of it, yet it seemed completely plausible, more so now that he was having his own marital troubles, and he wondered if he shouldn't encourage his sister to whisper in Pandora's ear. Not that Pandora would ever listen to her or take her advice, but this was an arena in which Edith did seem to excel. Yes, he and Pandora were in the middle of it and because of that they had lost their perspectives. Their marriage had become a house in which the power had gone out and everything was shadows and dark corners and sharp edges and broken glass. And he was tired of cutting his feet on Pandora's disappointment and running into new walls she kept erecting, just as Pandora was tired of talking to the specter of his former self and feeling as if he didn't care. He didn't want to lose his wife or his family. That said, he was pretty sure he didn't want to give his sister any incentive to meddle in his affairs, although that's what she would do whether asked her to or not. "I was only trying to help," she'd say—but he knew Pandora wouldn't take unsolicited advice, good or bad, from anyone, especially not from Edith. No, if Edith really wanted to help, she should keep her nose out of it. Which was not to say that Moses wouldn't enlist her to smooth out relations with the Rothmans, though this weekend was probably the worst of all possible times to go about it.

Moses left Chandler the tech guy on the stepladder, installing the first of the four webcams, then headed for the door to the garage and went out to see if the dirt bike he'd run over could be salvaged. He'd reminded the boys time and again not to leave their bikes in the driveway, but they kept doing it anyway. At the height of their marital trouble a couple of months ago, when Pandora finally said she'd had enough and accused him of not caring about their marriage anymore, he'd turned to her and accused her of sabotage. "You tell them to do it, don't you?" he asked. "You tell them to drop their bikes wherever they want."

"Oh, please," she said, "give me a little credit. If I wanted to antagonize you through them, I'd be a lot craftier than that. And besides, I'd never put our boys in that position. I'd never use them the way you do."

"I have never used our boys to get back at you," he said, thinking about his dad and how, when he and his mom were fighting, he often showed up at home with presents for each of them. Not that the presents ever reflected the slightest expenditure of thought or spirit on his part, for they were as generic and impersonal as if they'd come from a distant relative and not someone who lived among them, not someone who knew them—for Jacob another new chemistry set, though he never played with the old one; for Edith another new Nancy Drew mystery, though she'd already read the entire series, twice; for Moses another new model airplane kit, though he still had the one he'd gotten for Chanukah in his closet, untouched and unopened. Oh, Moses always thanked him and pretended he was happy, knowing that if he hesitated even slightly in ripping through the plastic, his dad would turn, not on Moses, but on his mom, screaming at her and blaming her for the way Moses had turned out. So they all feigned gratitude, although they hated what he gave them, and they all feigned love, because they knew better than to withhold it. And in this way Moses grew up learning three important facts—that his dad would always get it wrong, that his mom would spend her entire life trying to make it right, and that it didn't matter anyway, because kids loved whom they loved. Moses saw through his dad and swore that when he had kids of his own, he'd never play such a sad, pathetic game with them, and he hadn't, whatever Pandora might think.

Moses had never wanted to re-create his parents' marriage and had thought, when he'd met Pandora—this tattooed, free-spirited, buoyant, and affectionate woman—that he'd been spared this particular hardship. They were a combination that worked, until they stopped working, and if he didn't get out of his own way, Pandora would leave him and take his kids with her. Thinking about her still managed to excite him and raise his pulse—the digital heart was racing—and he tugged at his shorts to hide his erection, which vanished the moment he heard his dad on the other side of the garage doors. He went over and pressed an ear against one of them, but whatever his dad was saying was too muffled to make out. He laughed at himself, the curiosity and paranoia still alive and well inside him. How many times had he stood outside their bedroom door, listening to his parents whispering about him or Jacob or Edith—about his poor performance at school, about Edith's rigidity and moral self-righteousness, about Jacob's constant snooping through their drawers? "You gave birth to a bunch of liars, dimwits, and thieves," his dad used to say to his wife.

"I'm sure they'll all outgrow it," his mom replied.

"Schlemiels, the lot of them," his dad had said, and that was enough for Moses, who went to shoot hoops until it got dark and he was called in for dinner, during which he sat in stony silence, imagining what it would be like to remove his dad's larynx with his spoon, to carve out his eyes with his fork, to cut out his tongue with his butter knife.

Moses worked on the bike for about half an hour before he got too warm and had to put up the doors to let in some fresh air. As the doors went up, he saw his dad hosing down the minivan. He wandered out of the garage into the day, which was like every other, like the last three hundred, full of nothing but sunshine and heat, as if they were living in a kind of upside-down Noah's flood in which God was trying to desiccate rather than drown all that he'd created. He was baffled by his dad's utter frivolity with the water, especially because Moses had reminded him only yesterday about the exorbitant fines and taxes after he'd taken a ten-minute shower that was going to cost them well over fifty dollars. Water was not to be used for anything cosmetic, not for watering the lawn or washing a car. "Hey, ever hear of something called a drought?" Moses tried for levity, though fearing the angry tone in his voice had given him away.

"You ever hear of spousal privilege?" his dad sniped and kept hosing the minivan down.

"What's that supposed to mean?" he said.

"It means, genius, that your wife said it was okay."

"Pandora told you it was okay? Look, I don't mean to be an asshole, but I doubt very seriously that my wife said this was okay. Water costs a fortune, Dad."

"Then why's the pool full?"

"Those little monsters," Moses said, following the hose around the corner of the house. Across the gully and halfway between his backyard and the Rothmans', he found his green hose connected to an orange one and followed the trail of this hose across his neighbors' patchy, brown yard and there it was, the spigot out of which the water was flowing. Someone, most likely one of the trips, had married the Rothmans' orange hose with his green one and was siphoning water from the Rothmans, God only knew how many gallons' worth or the cost, though as he turned off the water and heard his dad yelling, he estimated that it was probably in the thousands of dollars and this didn't include the steep fines Moses was going to have to pay, should the Rothmans ever find out, or the jail time, if it came down to that.

Moses quickly detached his own hose, then hurried with it back across the gully and reconnected it to his spigot. Then he went into the backyard and there it was, that thing he couldn't quite place that morning: water, lapping daintily against the sides of the pool, sloshing over onto the stones, wetting and darkening them, the sun touching the water and making it gleam like liquid lapis lazuli. For a moment, he looked around for the peacock, then remembered that he'd stashed it. With everything else going on, the peacock was the last of his worries and could wait, he reasoned, until tomorrow, after whatever was going to happen happened. The wind came along and blew a few white feathers into the air, where they twirled briefly before dropping into the otherwise pristine water. Someone had also switched on the saline pump and the Polaris, which was patrolling the bottom. The pool hadn't been filled since before the show got canceled, before the city banned swimming pools outright and water became a luxury item, as expensive and as precious as oil. And before he knew what he was doing he jumped into the ice-cold water, sinking to the bottom, and while he was down there he had a chance to think: He thought about the last time he'd fucked his wife, some eight weeks ago, and the last time they sat out under the stars holding hands, and about the day they brought the trips home from the hospital and then later the twins, and how happy he had been because here was his family, and they were all going to live forever and no one was ever going to die and no one was ever going to grow old because this was California, where everyone aged in reverse, including his wife. She'd begun her injections shortly after the trips turned five, the collagen in her lips and the Botox in her forehead and around her mouth, and then the breast implants, after the twins turned two, until she was virtually unrecognizable as the woman he'd married. No less beautiful, just enhanced, more of who she was, not less, ravishing Pandora, who didn't want for anything—a dream house in Calabasas, a dream marriage to a well-known actor, a dream life of leisure in which all that was required of her was that she never age. He imagined, as he bobbed along the glimmering surface, that he'd created her, this Pandora, out of the parts of himself that he felt needed the most improving, a projection of his own worst fears about aging and dying, about his mom.

On his back, Moses floated from one end of the pool to the other, gazing up at the swarm of helicopters hovering in the clear blue sky. Perhaps they were on their way to the site of the wreckage on the 101, where several jihadists had given their lives. Yes, the world was a new, shiny, and terrifying place, made up of the same foes as always, but they were closer now, tucked in among the good people of Edelweiss Estates. He hadn't wanted to move into this house, not even when Pandora presented it as a golden opportunity to start afresh. They did need the extra room, yet he had learned from his dad not to be beholden to anyone, not even his eccentric father-in-law, whom he liked despite his womanizing ways.

The world spun around him as Moses plunged through the water, weightless, somersaulting and doing handstands and ten years old again. Then he swam laps, feeling his muscles stretch and tighten, the exertion a miracle, the water a baptismal font in which he was reborn—not as Moses Jacobson, son of Rosalyn and Julian Jacobson, but as Moses come to lead his people out of Egypt. *Go down, Moses*, he thought, imagining the world free of those people who kept getting in his way and holding him back, the parts he didn't land because he was "too old," "not old enough," "too muscular," "not muscular enough" (and certainly because he was "too Jewish" rather than "not Jewish enough"). Had it really come to this? Here, in America, where Jews had been living peaceably for almost two hundred and fifty years? It was terrifying to confront, and he pushed the thought away as he pushed himself up and out of the pool. He grabbed a towel from the cabana to dry himself off. Then he covered the pool with the solar-paneled tarp, which would heat the water nicely, although what he really wanted to do was to drain the pool just to teach the boys a lesson.

It was closing in on 2:30 P.M., but he thought he'd pay a visit to the Rothmans, to check on Milton and maybe mention the purloined water. He was halfway down the sidewalk when he recalled his mom's request for him to take his dad fishing. Though the last thing he needed was to spend time he didn't have entertaining a man he didn't like, a plan, still rudimentary, bloomed in the back of his mind, guaranteeing, he hoped, that if his dad wouldn't leave voluntarily, that these next few hours would be the old man's last on Earth. The idea both cheered and fortified him.

He approached his dad, who was wiping down the inside of the minivan with a skin-colored chamois. His dad took meticulous care of all of his cars, washing them and detailing them by hand, running the sponge over the paint with the loving, soothing attention of a masseur. "Hey, Pop, think you might want to do a little fishing later with me? I was thinking we'd go into Malibu and fish off the pier. There's a bait stand and all."

"Do I look like a low-rent Mexican to you, boy? Because that's who fishes off piers where I come from," he scoffed, exactly the response Moses had expected to lay the groundwork for the next phase of his plan. Introduce the idea of fishing. Check. Then later offer up an alternative that was more in keeping with his father's sense of self-importance. "By the way, you're lucky I'd already finished rinsing down my vehicle, or else you and I'd have a serious problem."

"You know about the water situation here," Moses reiterated. "Besides, I didn't come out here to argue with you."

"No one's arguing. I'm just saying," his dad said. "Now, let me get back to work. I'm not driving home tomorrow with all this dust hanging around. It aggravates your mom's condition."

"Then I guess you're also not interested in fishing with Gibbs later, either," he blurted out without thinking. He hadn't checked with Gibbs to see if this was even a possibility. But from the look on his dad's face, he'd found a way in, hitting the sweet spot he'd been hoping for. Now he just had to reel the old man in. "He invited us out on his boat this evening. He says the flounder are running. What do you think?"

"Well, why in hell didn't you lead with that? Now that's what I call a plan," his dad said, brightening. "Fishing with the Gibbs."

"And all of your children," Moses said. "He invited Edith and Jacob, too."

"Just so long as they keep their mouths shut and don't scare the fish, I'm game," he said. "I haven't been night fishing in years. Probably the last time was with you out on Canyon Lake. Remember that? The Evinrude conked out on us and we had to row to shore."

"Yeah, good times," Moses said, although it hadn't been a good time, because no time with his dad was a good time. "Well, I'll leave you to it," he said, turning to go. He'd only taken a couple of steps when his dad snapped him on the back of the neck with the moist chamois. Moses paused, his heart galloping. He shut his eyes and clenched his teeth. "Why did you do that?" he asked, an angry, red welt already forming.

"Do what?" his dad said innocently, the chamois dangling in his fingers. He was smirking that awful smirk of his, the lower half of his jaw thrust out, which Moses wanted to slam shut, and by slam shut he meant slam his dad's face into the dashboard.

"You got me," he said. "Very funny," and he turned once more, but before he could take another step, his dad snapped him again, stinging him on the back of his right arm.

This time Moses didn't stop or say a word. He just kept walking toward the garage, even as his dad called out, laughing, "Damn them mosquitoes! They sure sting. Just another reason not to live in California!"

In the garage, Moses grabbed the hammer, which was hanging on a hook on the wall above his worktable, and stood there, peering under hooded eyes at his dad, the welts on his neck and arm red and painful, though not nearly as red and painful as his dad's head was going to be after he bashed it in. He held the hammer in one hand and tapped the clawed end of it on the palm of the other. His dad never looked at him, never glanced up from the dashboard, but Moses knew that he must have seen him and the hammer. There were so many ways to hurt him without inflicting an ounce of physical pain—like putting a big dent in the minivan or smashing the headlights. But he knew his dad would call the police, he'd done it before—not to him but to Jacob, who'd once borrowed the car and stayed out past curfew, and when he came home the cops were waiting for him. His dad spun a tale about how Jacob had taken the car without permission—"He stole my vehicle!"—and how he wanted him arrested to teach him a lesson.

He remembered the night of Jacob's accident, when he flipped the car, and how hysterical his mom was when they got the call, although Jacob was okay. Moses went with his dad to the site of the accident, not because he wanted to, but because he was afraid of what his dad was going to do and say to Jacob, who had just turned sixteen and had only been driving for a week. That didn't matter to the old man, who, the second he saw the extent of the damage—the car was totaled; it was a miracle Jacob walked away unscathed—announced to all of the bystanders who had gathered, "Look at what that moron did to my vehicle!"

He screamed at Jacob, who was sitting on the curb, sobbing. No display of compassion, or love, or even gratitude that his younger son was still alive, just contempt piled on top of more contempt.

Moses tapped the hammer in his palm, thinking about all the hurt his dad had inflicted on them, and he yearned to smash the smirk off his face forever, until he was pulp, chum for the fish in the deep blue sea. But they had a plan and he was going to stick to it, *and the plan,* he thought, *is coalescing nicely.* That thing about fishing with Gibbs tonight was a stroke of genius, he had to admit, returning the hammer to the wall, then going inside to grab his car keys. He poked his head into the guest room and asked his mom if she wanted to come with him to pick up her grandsons from Krav Maga.

"No, thank you, dear," she said. "I'm still recovering, but I should be fine for tonight."

"You didn't see the boys tampering with the hose, did you? I think one of them, or all of them, filled the pool."

"I don't know anything about that," she said. "I thought you weren't allowed to use water for that."

"We're not," he confirmed, omitting where the water had come from. Then he told her about taking his dad floundering later, with Gibbs.

"Oh, he'll enjoy that so much," she exclaimed. "It'll be nice to see Gary again. It's a shame about his divorce. No one stays married anymore. Except your father and me." She glanced down at her wedding ring, then back up at Moses, who thought he imagined tears in her eyes. "You and your brother and sister still think I should have divorced him, don't you?"

"Why didn't you?" he asked hesitantly, for they'd never discussed it, and he worried she might suspect something, bringing it up now.

"I think I wanted to prove everyone wrong," she said, turning her oxygen up a notch, which meant her discomfort with this conversation was increasing her heart rate. "Of course, that's a lousy reason for staying married. I also wanted you kids to grow up with a father. Better a dad like yours than none at all. That was my reasoning, like it or lump it."

"I see," he said.

"Do you? Do you see that I only had all of my children's best interests at heart?" she asked, her eyes now definitely moist.

"I do, Ma, yes. I don't blame you," he said. *Not like Jacob does,* he thought. "I'm going to get the boys now. I'll see you later," and with that, he shut the door behind him, wondering if he shouldn't ask Jacob and the German if they wanted to come along, but he was still too incensed with his brother and worried that he'd only say something he'd regret.

After heading into the garage, Moses found his dad tinkering with the dirt bike. "The frame's bent," he observed, "and so is one of the rims."

"Yeah, I know. I'll have to buy him a new one," Moses said, as his dad reached into his pocket and pulled up a couple of crisp hundred-dollar bills.

"Here," he said, extending the money to Moses. "Go on. Take it." From time immemorial, this had always been his dad's way. First the lightning anger and fork-tongued insults, then the cooldown and the payoff. Moses took the money because he'd never not taken it, thus resetting the buttons and beginning the cycle anew. "Buy him a new one," his dad said, wandering back into the house, probably to brag to his wife about this latest mitzvah of his.

Moses climbed into his car and began reversing out of the driveway just as Edith pulled up to the house in her ridiculous cargo van. She climbed out, then hurried over to his car, opened the right-side door, and hurled herself into the passenger seat. "That was an absolute nightmare. But luckily the damage isn't as bad as I thought. I'll just say someone backed into me," she said.

"How did you get to Claremont?" he asked, confused, for none of them had driven her there.

"I took an Uber," she replied, though Moses didn't quite believe her. *Probably some guy she met on a hookup app and talked into driving her,* he thought, feeling smug and sorry for her as ever. "And where are you sneaking off to?" she asked, leaning into him. She smelled gamy, and her face was both puffy and drawn. Her breath stank of mint mouthwash.

"I have to run up to the kids' school and pick them up, Thistle," he said. It'd been the boys' idea to sign up for these Saturday self-defense classes, choosing Krav Maga over Muay Thai, for they liked the poses and the lightning-quick reflexes of their hands and feet— the roundhouse kick especially titillated them. Moses was all too happy to pay for the expensive lessons, for how could he possibly deny or object to his boys' wishes to protect themselves? Pandora was just as supportive, though it was the last time in recent memory, Moses thought, that they'd been able to come to an agreement on anything. "If you're coming, strap yourself in. If not, I'll be right back," he added, though it seemed to him that she hadn't heard a word he'd just said because she was looking at the house.

"Do you think he has any concept of what he did to us? I mean, an actual, concrete idea of what a prick he was?" She whipped her head back around. "Did I . . . Did I ever tell you—nah, I don't think I ever did because why would I have?—how he convinced me that Mom was a witch? I was terrified of her. Like, she scared the bejesus out of me, Mo. But that's what he wanted, and I fell for it. I spent the entirety of my childhood afraid of the wrong parent. Priceless, huh? Well, it just goes to show what a great judge of character I am. My mother's daughter after all, I guess."

"Edith, why don't you stay here and take care of yourself," he said, having neither the desire nor the time to discuss the moral ramifications of her having driven while intoxicated. He wasn't about to mention how dangerous it was, even more so if she'd gotten pulled over by the wrong cop—driving while under the influence and driving while Jewish, a double whammy that might have ended disastrously for his sad sister. He didn't want to scare her, so he didn't mention the rumor that Pandora had passed down to him last week about the mysterious disappearance of several Jewish women who'd said good-bye to their husbands and kids, headed to the grocery store, and were never seen or heard from again, their cars abandoned in parking lots or by the sides of the road. He nearly told her about the pool, wanting to suggest she go for a little swim to sober herself up, then thought better of it, for who knew if she just might not drown in the process.

"Do you think he ever went down on Ma?" she asked. "I ask because Elias never once went down on me. What kind of a person marries a guy who won't go down on her? Me, your sister, that's who," and she opened up her door, yet didn't make a move to go.

"You know something? I'm going to tell you a little secret before you go—I always wanted to date a guy named Moses so I could sing 'Go down on me, Moses, way down,'" and she broke out into one of her uncontrollable hyena laughs, her eyes springing with tears.

"Jesus, Edith," he said, "what the hell is wrong with you?"

"Oh, I don't know. I might have gotten the teensiest bit high," she said, laughing again. "Not drunk. Just magnificently high. With Zion. Out the window of his dorm room."

"You got high with Zion? Sheik Cohen's son?" he asked, her poor judgment confounding him despite her dismal track record. He knew this was not the first time she'd let herself fall prey to her own wayward impulses. "Are you out of your goddamn mind?"

"The Magic Eight Ball says . . . all signs point to yes," she gasped with laughter, launching into a monologue about how she hadn't planned to contact Zion, but then she'd seen him and he looked so much like Sheik that she just couldn't not get in touch with him, because she thought talking to the son might help her put to rest her past with his father. She'd emailed him under a false name and gave him false credentials—the address formula for Pomona students embarrassingly easy to deduce—explaining that she was visiting with her son who was keen on going to school there. "I told him my son was on a campus tour and asked if he wanted to meet," she finished. "I know, I know," she said when Moses scoffed. "Look, please don't be mean to me right now. I'm . . . I'm dealing the best I can, Mo, but a few months from now she's . . ." And her voice trailed away. Moses wanted to comfort her, but he was too fixated on how it was that they, he and she, had both come from the same parents.

"Anyway, we met for a coffee, then took a walk around campus. He's such a nice young man, the kind I wish I'd met when I was his age. Tell him who you are, I kept thinking. Tell him you're sorry for terrifying him when he was a boy, that it was a different version of you who used to stalk him and his father. It happened so long ago, but the way he spoke to me, it was almost as if he knew exactly who

I was and why I'd come. I didn't have to say anything because Zion, unlike his father, has an incredible amount of compassion. I told him that I'd seen him speak yesterday and that it had moved me. Then he said that he realized that I was the lady who had driven the van onto the quad and how fucking awesome it was."

She was rambling, which she did when she was high or drunk, and Moses sat there in silence, trying his best to withhold judgment. He couldn't possibly judge her as harshly as he suspected she was judging herself.

"Long story short, he invited me up to his dorm room and before I knew it we were smoking a joint and gazing out over the campus, and he kissed me or I kissed him. Please don't hate me, Mo. I . . ."

"You need to get out of my car right now," he said. "Before I start accelerating and push you out."

"Don't be so damn sanctimonious, unless of course you enjoy sounding like Daddy. So I kissed him. So what?"

"So what? Let me tell you about so what," and he launched into all the reasons it might not have been such a grand idea to get high with, then kiss, then do God only knows what else with Zion Abdul-lah Cohen, for he didn't believe she'd really stopped there. "Do you not remember what happened in D.C., because I sure do. You also kissed and fucked that boy's father and see where that got you. You tried to commit suicide, and you worried all of us to death. Look, it's not my place to criticize anyone's love life"—thinking about the state of his own marriage—"but you have some serious sexual hang-ups that you haven't dealt with. I'm not blaming you. I want to see you happy, and you aren't. You aren't, Thistle."

"I don't remember the last time I was happy," she said. "Oh, wait, yes, I do. It was about three hours ago, when I was sitting on Zion's bed. And for the record, you don't seem very happy to me, either. But the difference between us is that I'm doing—did—something about it. I told him exactly who I was before I left and do you know what he said to me? He said that his father treated him and his mother like absolute shit and that he had all sorts of women on the side. I've been idealizing that man for years and he was fucking everything that moved? All I ever wanted was to love Sheik Cohen. I thought I would have been perfectly happy had I been given that chance. But the moment I tried to get close to him, he shut down and turned me into a shrew. You know he told me that his marriage was over? That they were divorcing? Oldest trick in the book and I fell for it. I fell for the whole damn thing, because that's what people with hearts do. They fall. Headfirst. And they either swim or they don't. They either make it to the opposite shore or they drown."

His sister was one who swam, he thought, giving her credit for finally taking some responsibility for it all. "And besides," she went on, "Sheik got a fucking novel out of it, but what did I get? A restraining order barring me from coming within five hundred yards of them and an indelible scarlet letter on my record. I admit that I was obsessed and that I stalked him, but that's all I did. I didn't do the terrible things in the story. I thought you believed me at least."

"I do, Edith," he said, yet this news about Zion only managed to reshape how he assembled the past. "And that boy at Emory? With the sexual harassment suit?"

"Alleged," she corrected.

"Okay. Alleged harassment," he said. "That's all it is, though, right? Alleged?"

"What kind of professor and person do you think I am?" she said. "I don't fuck my students, Mo. It's completely unethical. I'd fuck any number of them if they weren't my students because they're beautiful and I like sex and some of them remind me of the way I was at that age—all awkward and gawky and yearning to be loved by someone. But I don't fuck them, Mo. I never have. And the one who's suing me isn't my type at all, if you want to get right down to it. He's skinny and hairless and bony and looks like a child. I like men. The crafty little asshole trumped up the charges because he didn't get the grade he thought he deserved. I have plenty of other students who don't get the grades they think they deserve, but they don't lie and distort scenarios that never happened. It'd be nice if my own brother took my word for it. If the roles were reversed, I'd defend you, Mo. But I guess that's another way we differ."

Yes, it is, he thought, recalling what Jacob had told him yesterday about the kiss. He wanted to tell Edith about it, but then checked his watch. "Look, Pandora's going to tear me a new one if I'm late getting the kids," he said. "Just go inside and make nice with everyone until I get back. We can talk more about this later."

"Or . . . we can just forget the whole thing," she said, stepping out and slamming the door. As she went, he thought he heard her singing, "I'm the good witch lollipop . . ."

All of the boys attended Ilan Ramon Day School, a private Jewish day school in Agoura Hills. With the 101 still closed in both directions, the trip took longer than usual, but he didn't mind because it gave him time to collect himself and go over how he was going to attack the question of the water. His boys liked to close ranks, protecting one another when accused of misdeeds, in this particular case, of grand larceny, for California had made stealing water a serious offense, punishable with jail time and steep fines. The law was the first of its kind, though other states, like Nevada, Arizona, New Mexico, and Texas were about to pass similar measures. There wasn't enough water for the state, the population of which had reached a staggering forty-one million people, according to the last census, huge numbers of them displaced Israelis, who found the climate and terrain familiar. Desalination plants were springing up all along the Pacific Coast corridor, but they weren't desalinating fast enough, not yet anyway.

To get onto the school's campus, Moses had to pass two security checkpoints—one at the bottom of the hill, another at the top, each time presenting a laminated badge, which the guard swiped through a card reader, raising the mechanical arm. The school itself was heavily fortified, full of a private security presence bought and paid for by the parents that he'd also come to take for granted and found as ordinary as the flags of Israel that the school refused to take down. He didn't like seeing the ubiquitous armed guards, who were stationed at every entrance and exit, yet they were living through some incredibly rough, menacing times, and he supposed this was just the way it had to be. If water was California's most precious commodity, then the boys were his and he was more than happy to show ID if it meant their protection and survival—jihadists and violent anti-Semites had already bombed a couple of yeshivas, one in Beverly Hills, the other in West Hollywood.

The boys were lined up and waiting for him, Bronson, whose turn it was to sit in front, hopping in beside Moses, while the rest scattered into the back and the way back. Moses figured that the one who sat farthest away was the trip with the most to hide—and so he directed his questioning at Brandon, who promptly denied having any part in Pool-water-gate. "Then which one of you did it?" he demanded, while Bronson sat beside him, humming "Dayenu," which they'd practiced again yesterday in assembly. "I'm not angry and neither is your mom. I just need you to be honest with me."

"It wasn't us, Dad," said Brendan, followed by Dexter, who was then followed by Baxter, a chorus of denials.

"Fine," Moses said. "If that's the way you want to play it, then you leave me no choice. When we get home, I want all of you to go to your rooms. No Wii, no PlayStation, no tablets, no computers. And absolutely no TV."

"But, Dad," whined four, but not Bronson, who remained utterly removed, which made Moses wonder if he should have been questioning his favorite little oddball, this boy of his who cared nothing for family drama or politics and preferred to sit all of it out, even as his mom screamed at him and tried to drag him into it. This boy who never had an unkind word to say about anyone and who drifted through his life as if everything were already laid out before him. Moses loved Bronson best and most, for he saw him as a superior being, the apotheosis of who Moses wished he could be and a paradigm for the rest of them to follow and emulate. *My own little messiah,* he thought, turning to him.

"So is there anything you'd like to tell me, Bronze?" he whispered. "Anything you'd like to add? Tell me who did it, okay?"

"No, Dad, I took a solemn oath not to tell," he said. "I made a promise."

"You made a promise to whom? Which one of your brothers did it?" Moses asked, growing irritated. He was bending under the weight of his own life and starting to think that when it all came crashing down, he'd welcome the fall. "I'm your dad. See how that trumps everything else?"

"I'm no snitch," he said, imitating a movie gangster.

"You disappoint me," Moses said. "I never thought I'd see the day, but here it is."

"You're breaking my heart," Bronson said. "And I'm only twelve. I never thought I'd see the day when my own dad would want me to break a promise. I'm just as disappointed in you as you are in me," and he turned his face to the window and said nothing more.

If it weren't for the other four, who would certainly bear witness to his fury and blab to their mom about it, he might have pulled over to give Bronson a good and thorough thrashing. Yet he'd learned patience and he'd learned reserve and he wasn't about to let his boys see him come apart. He focused on the road while he seethed, beads of perspiration popping out on his forehead and his heart thumping wildly in his chest, the digital heart galloping so fast that he was afraid it might simply leap off the screen or short-circuit the watch again.

Once they got home, all the boys leaped out, hooting and hollering and karate-chopping one another as they ran inside, probably to tattle on him and complain to their mom and grandparents about how Daddy was being mean and unfair. Only Bronson remained, still refusing to look at him. "One day none of this is going to matter," he said. "All of it's going to disappear."

"What are you talking about, Bronze?" he asked. "Did Paw-Paw say something to you? You shouldn't listen to him whatever it is."

"Nothing," the boy said, turning to face Moses at last, an expression of pure calm and resignation in his face. "C'mon, Dad. Look around you. Look at where we are," then he opened the door, climbed out, and headed into the house as well.

It was a sobering moment, and it lingered even after Moses climbed out of the car, put down the garage door, and went inside, where he found the boys in the kitchen. "Okay, grab your snacks and then up to your rooms," he said. "If I hear even a single beep, I'm taking away all your electronic privileges for a month. Got it?"

He heard his dad in the next room, where he was having an animated discussion with Chandler, the tech guy, about the necessity of an education. "In a few years, even a secondary degree might be worthless. Ask my sons—one got his MFA in something useless like playwriting, the other in something even more useless like acting," and he laughed derisively and far too loudly. "The humanities are going the way of the dinosaurs. What you need is a PhD in computer engineering coupled with a law degree in intellectual property, and you'll be golden. You'll be the future of this country."

"What I need is to marry a rich woman," Chandler said, laughing.

"Like I did," his dad said, or at least that's what Moses thought he heard, for the boys were clanking around in the fridge.

Pandora appeared in the doorway and asked Moses if she could speak to him. "In a second," he said, hoping to overhear his dad say another disparaging remark or ten.

"Now," Pandora insisted. "It's important."

"What? What is it, O light of my loins?" he asked once they were back in the garage and sitting in the Expedition, where they often went to speak and to fight and even to fuck sometimes so that the boys couldn't hear them.

"Jacob and Dietrich are packed up and ready to head to the airport," she informed him. "I don't know what you did or said to them, but you need to go in there and apologize."

"You want me to apologize to them?" he asked.

"Actually Roz does," she said. "But I do, too. He's your brother and quite frankly he's the only other one of you, besides your mom, whom I can stand. So if you can't do it for her, do it for me."

"You do realize why they were arrested, right? I mean, if anything, they're the ones who should be apologizing. It's despicable what they were doing in those outfits down there on the beach."

"Oh, don't be such a puritanical prick," Pandora said. "What happened, happened, Mo, and there's nothing any of us can do to change it, but harboring all of these hateful feelings isn't good for anyone. Jacob is all set to fly back to Berlin, and you'll never see him again if you don't get over yourself. And wouldn't your dad just love that," and she kissed him, the first kiss in eight weeks, and left him sitting in the front seat to contemplate what she'd just said. Pandora was right—his dad would get tremendous pleasure from Jacob's leaving, and more, knowing Moses was to blame.

Back in the house, Moses went upstairs to the guest room, where he knocked on the door and was told to enter. They were just zipping up their suitcases when he shut the door behind him and said, not to Jacob but to Dietrich, "What you have to understand about me is that I try superhard to be a good guy in every aspect of my life, but sometimes I'm a little dense. Jacob knows this. I don't mean to hurt anybody's feelings, I don't, but on occasion, like this morning, I'm caught off guard, and I do and say things I generally don't mean. So I hope you can forgive me for my behavior, because there's nothing I want more right now than for you to unpack that suitcase, find your swimming trunks, and come downstairs with me," and he turned to look at Jacob, who remained at the window, his back to them.

"I can appreciate that sentiment," Dietrich said, "but I think it is better if I go."

"You? I thought both of you were leaving," Moses said. "Please don't leave because of what I said."

"No, it is not about this," Dietrich said. "It is about that other thing. I've told Jacob my thoughts, but now I must tell you. I might come from a long line of warring barbarians, but that does not make me one of them. I wish I had been asleep when Jacob told me what you were planning to do, but since I know this I cannot stay here and pretend it doesn't bother me. Right now, I'm just someone who knows a secret. After, I'm an accomplice. And then there is this other matter of all of you being completely out of your minds. If you want to murder your father, I can't stop you, but I don't want to be there when, and if, you do."

"Well, luckily for you, I may have a better way out," Moses said.

"Better than blackmailing him?" Jacob asked. "Because Diet's pretty sure that isn't going to work anyway."

"Why not?" Moses asked Dietrich.

"It is not hard to see that your father is invested in his marriage," he explained. "Whether it is for love or for money or for another reason altogether, he will not let it go easily. Blackmailing him will only make him more adamant about staying. It will blow down in your faces. You will give him the reason he has been seeking to isolate you from your mother even further."

"Wow, I see someone's given this some thought," Moses said.

"He has," Jacob said, turning around at last. "I still think the only way out of this is a knife through his heart. But that's me."

"If you truly want to get rid of him, you're going to have to be subtler. You need to manipulate him into leaving without letting him know this is what you're doing," Dietrich said. "In other words—"

"It needs to be his idea," Moses said.

"Think of your father as an unwanted guest who has overstayed his welcome. How do you get rid of an unwanted guest? You make life as miserable as possible for him, so he has no other choice but to leave," he said.

Moses chilled. Leave it to the German to come up with such an inventive, diabolical plan. "That's great and all, but I still don't think you understand whom we're dealing with here," he observed. "Nothing, but nothing, is going to separate him from our mom.

That's why he has to die," and as Moses said this, he glanced at Jacob and understood that this was it, the one incontrovertible truth that none of them could deny any longer. All that talk of blackmail and bribery, all this talk of psychological warfare—it didn't matter, because the only way to get rid of their dad was not to make life in the house miserable for him, but to bring the entire rotten building down on top of him.

"This is where we differ, and this is why I cannot stay," Dietrich said, as Edith burst into the room.

"Pandora said you're leaving?" she exclaimed. "Well, I forbid it. I just forbid it," and she crawled over to Dietrich's suitcase and sat down on it. "You're family now. Tell him, Mo. Tell him he's family. You are. We love Jacob, Jacob loves you, and thus we love you, too."

"Don't mind her. She's high as a kite," Moses said.

"Do not do that," she barked. "Do not patronize me. I may be stoned, but I also lived through the nightmare of Julian Jacobson, and I demand your respect. I'm ready to torture the son of the bitch. He tried to kill me. He tried to kill all of us. Did you know that?" She directed this last bit at Dietrich, whose eyes went big, then narrowed into slits, which either meant he believed her wholeheartedly or not at all.

"You are pulling the river over my eyes with an oar," Dietrich said.

"You pull the wool over someone's eyes. You send someone down the river without a paddle," Jacob corrected.

"But this isn't possible," Dietrich argued, ignoring him. "He may be crass, but he isn't violent. No, you must be mistaken."

Then Moses told Dietrich about it all, all the ways in which their dad had set out to annihilate them. He told him about the baseball and about the figs and about making Jacob watch horror movies that kept him up for weeks, until he was sleep deprived and half out of his mind with fear. "You don't understand, because you didn't live through it," Moses concluded. "The only one who really knows is our mom and she has yet to admit he's ever done anything wrong to us, much less to her. She's lived with this fantasy of him, that he was the best dad he could be, when in reality his best is someone else's worst. I don't expect you to understand. Hell, I don't even understand it, but there it is. We just want to give our mom a few months of peace. That's all. We think she deserves it."

"And revenge," Jacob said. "I'd just like a little revenge, plain and simple."

Dietrich just stood there, unspeaking, looking dazed, staring at each of them. He took his time, lingering first on Moses, then on Edith, then finally on Jacob. "No, it is too much to process," he said at last. "It's not that I can't believe fathers like this exist, because of course they do, but where is the empirical data, the proof?"

"The proof is us, *Schatz,*" Jacob said. "We're the proof. We're still here, despite his intentions to the contrary."

"He wants proof, I'll give him proof," Moses said, irascible, sick of trying to justify to everyone, including himself, why his dad had to die. He went to the door, opened it, and shouted for Dexter, who entered cautiously after a moment. "Dexter, tell your aunt and uncle what Paw-Paw did to you. Go on." The boy gazed up at Moses, then around the room at the other grown-ups, and shook his head. Moses kneeled down in front of the boy. "Tell them, Dexter. Tell them for Daddy."

"It was an accident," he said slowly. "It was my fault."

"But you told me that Paw-Paw slammed it down on your fingers," Moses urged. "Why are you lying? You know what happens to boys who lie. They get baked in a cake and served for dessert."

"Moses!" Edith rebuked him, as the boy began to cry.

"I'm not lying," Dexter wailed, rubbing at his eyes, then tore out of the room.

"Well, whatever. He's lying. I have no idea why," Moses said, ashamed of himself for being unprecedentedly cruel to his boy. But he could feel it now, the cruelty, coursing through him, and for a moment he saw the world as his dad must have seen it—his power-hungry, craven dad, who lashed out at those who could not protect themselves against him. And standing there, he could almost understand it, how it all might have started and how impossible it was to control or to stop. Even as he left the room, left them all there to chastise and discuss him in his absence, Moses felt the years of suppressed rage and disappointment gaining strength within him, thinking that if he hadn't been saddled with five demanding kids and an equally demanding wife, he might have made something different of his life. Was this how his dad had seen them? Was this where his ferocious need to destroy them came from?

Moses went into the bedroom, shut the door, drew the blinds, and climbed into bed. He yanked the covers over his face and then he cried, quietly at first, then louder. He cried until he had no more tears left in him, then dried his eyes, blew his nose in the sheets, and fell asleep.

Moses awoke sometime later with a tongue licking his ear, at least that was the sensation, though there was no one there and nothing but the quiet stillness of the bedroom surrounding him. Peering down at his watch, he saw that the tiny screen was black again and sighed. Gibbs had given him the watch after becoming a spokesperson for Apple—he was plastered all over town on billboards and buses. *Leave it to Gibbs to give me his leftovers and a dud at that,* he thought, climbing out of bed and going to the window to pull up the blinds. The sun hung in the west, dripping yellow light on the backyard and his five boys, all of whom were stationed around the pool, the tarp rolled back, the shadow of something splashing, dark and shapeless, in the water. He opened the window and called down to them, "Is that Nieves? Don't just stand there. Help her out!"

"It's not Nieves," one of the trips said. "Aunt Thistle said a coyote got her."

"What is it then? Where's your mom?" he called back.

They all pointed to the house and that's when he heard Pandora, shouting her ferocious Jewish San Fernando Valley lungs out, shattering the quiet. Moses realized that he'd overslept and that it was approaching game time, for the sun was rapidly descending, which meant he only had about twenty minutes to shower, shave, and shit, though not necessarily in that order. But first—the pool. He was there, in a flash, looking down with his boys into the crystal water, not at Nieves, but at a mangy, bedraggled opossum, which had been terrorizing the dog and the backyard for weeks. The oversize rodent scratched at the smooth, tiled side, trying to gain traction and lift itself up, the momentum of which kept launching it backward. There were whispery fingers of blood leaking into the water from what must have been a gash in the animal's underside. One of its eyes was missing and one of its back legs was bent at a sickening angle, broken, which must have precipitated its fall into the water. It made no sound, no cry for help, which, for reasons beyond him, made Moses incredibly sad. He watched it, as the boys watched it, the twins who pointed, laughed, and screamed in delight as it sank beneath the surface only to appear again, and the trips who stood back and watched in silent wonder, for they were older and wiser and understood a little bit more about the world. "Did any of you . . . Please tell me that none of you had anything to do with this," Moses said, turning to face his brood. They shook their little heads.

If he pretended it wasn't happening, then he could go inside and come out hours later to find that it had tired itself out and drowned. And while a part of him wanted nothing more than to do just that, another part of him, the better part, knew what had to be done. "Boys, go inside and get ready," he instructed them. "Put on your dress clothes and dress shoes. Have Mommy or Maw-Maw brush your hair."

"But, Daddy," the twins said. "We want to swim, too!"

"Don't be dumb," the trips said, leading the twins away from the pool and into the house, Bronson glancing over his shoulder with an eerie, knowing look on his face.

After they were gone, Moses fetched the long mesh scoop from the pool house. It had grown dusty and cobwebby, for he had not needed to clean the pool for over a year. He returned to the pool, where the opossum was kicking with its three good legs, spinning in graceless circles, somersaulting in the ever-reddening water. It wouldn't live long once he got it out of the pool. He lowered the scoop under the rodent and it somehow managed to understand what Moses was doing, for it gripped the edge of the mesh with its claws as Moses swooped it out, dropping the animal onto the deck, where it looked up at him for one tiny second before limping off slowly into the grass, leaving a trail of blood in its wake. Moses set the scoop down, breathing heavily, and when he glanced at the house, he saw his entire family gathered at the wall of glass, watching him. He waved feebly, the sun sinking even further behind him, the backyard darkening by degrees as his family broke apart until only his siblings remained, waiting for him. He went into the house, where everything looked and smelled and sounded different to him, as if between here and the pool he'd taken a turn somewhere and had either found his footing or lost it completely. Pandora wasn't screaming and the boys weren't arguing and his dad wasn't nitpicking and the air didn't contain the scent of despair, as if the house were preparing itself to usher in the holiday, this spring feast of matzo. It was time, he realized, running upstairs to prepare himself as well.

He took a brisk shower, then a beautiful crap. Someone from the network had chosen his clothes for him—the marketing department declaring he skewed best in "casual-L.A.-formal," which apparently meant dark slacks, a powder-pink button-down, no jacket, nothing to obscure that hallmark body part of his, his hairy chest, which they wanted him to show off to his fan base, lonely housewives and their gay best friends. He was not to shave his face but to remain swarthy and to leave his curly black hair untouched, applying just a smidge of mousse to keep the frizz away, but that was it. He found these instructions taped to the bathroom mirror and followed them to the letter, down to the gold Star of David necklace, which he extracted from a small blue Tiffany box on the counter. They'd all been told to keep them on throughout the show, even the twins, who hated wearing anything around their necks.

Downstairs, the house was percolating with activity, a bubbling over with conversation and frenetic energy. The caterers from Canter's Deli set up each course in a separate corner of the kitchen and lit the Sterno to keep the soup and the brisket and the potatoes warm. The florist arrived with the centerpieces, two exquisitely arranged bouquets of heliotrope and anemones, which had been Israel's national flower. Vera Wang Wedgwood of Beverly Hills donated the table settings, Steuben of Thousand Oaks the stemware, which Moses somehow had to manage to plug during dinner, for product placement was paramount to the network. Their clothes, every last stitch, came from Barneys of L.A., whose representative called Moses now to make sure his mom's clothes had been satisfactorily altered, and if the black pearl earrings, which she would wear, had arrived.

Moses answered the call outside in the gloaming, taking in the purple-hued sky. "Yes, thank you," he said and was told that the moment the hour-long special was finished, they were to replace the clothes and the pearls back in the traveling bags and boxes and that a sales associate, who was standing by, would collect them. "Yes, fine," he said, the rep wishing him a good Yom Tov. "Same to you," he said, understanding suddenly that all of these sponsors, many of them Jewish owned and operated, were counting on him, which only further aggravated his already aggravated nerves.

Sunset that night was at 7:25 P.M., which coincided perfectly with the 7:30 airtime of *A Very JacobSONS Passover*. He hung up the phone, then went into the house, where Pandora was setting tapers in two silver candlesticks, for it was customary to light and say a blessing over the candles to usher in the holiday—his dad reminding everyone that because of Pesach they would have to add a special phrase to the blessing. It amazed him that his dad remembered any of this garbage, yet he was nothing if not a traditional Jew deep down, having grown up in a strictly kosher home to Orthodox parents. Once her husband was dead, however, Grammy Esther, his dad's plucky, redheaded mother, had thrown out the kosher dishes and stocked the fridge with treyf—ham, pork, lobster, you name it—which she'd been eating on the sly for their entire marriage.

Twenty minutes before sundown, Gibson Gould arrived to great fanfare, all the boys crowding around him, as if he were their long-lost best friend returned. Moses looked upon the scene and felt a growing disturbance in his bowels, imagining what it would be like to lose Pandora and his kids to Gibbs. He quickly pushed away the unsettling vision by shaking Gibbs's hand, a firm, steady handshake that contained the history of everything between them in it—all the love and jealousy and hope and regret of being two men from the same town who chose the same career, Gibbs's thriving, Moses's paling, each perhaps wanting what the other had—Moses, better roles, and Gibbs, Pandora.

"So it begins," Gibbs said, heading for the wall of glass and the backyard beyond. Moses followed, for it seemed his old friend had something to tell him, but before they could slip out the door, his dad was upon them.

"Gary Goldstein, how the heck have you been?" his dad asked, smiling from stem to stern.

"I'm doing well, Dr. Jacobson," Gibbs said.

"Dad, he hasn't gone by Gary in twenty years," Moses corrected him.

"Nah, it's fine, Mo," Gibbs said. "It's not every day I'm in the company of a brilliant mind like your dad. I mean, brilliance is hard to come by out here, if you know what I mean, sir."

"I do, I do," his dad purred, for Gibbs had always known exactly which part of his dad's ego to stroke. "How's that new house of yours? You liking Calabasas?"

"I like being closer to this guy right here," he said, wrapping an arm around Moses's shoulders. "Who would've guessed we'd end up here?"

"I was shocked to hear about your divorce," his dad said. "Just shocked. I was telling Roz the other day that out of all of Moses's friends, I was sure you'd stay married."

"Dad," he said. "I don't think Gary—Gibbs—wants to talk about his divorce."

"I will discuss anything Dr. Jacobson throws my way. I am, as they say, an open book, but only for certain people." Gibbs winked.

"I watched that *Spotted in Hollywood* program the other day, and they reported that you were 'romantically involved' with a mystery lady," he probed. "They even hinted that you'd moved to Calabasas to be closer to her. Roz and I were trying to guess who she was, but Roz is lousy with names. Is it that Israeli girl, the singer with one name?"

"Bathsheba," Moses said.

"Right," his dad said. "See, I'm not the only Jacobson who follows your life," and he turned to Moses. "Maybe Gary will introduce you to his manager if you ask him nicely."

"Jesus, Dad, enough," he said, too loudly, so that his dad took a step back. "I don't need Gibbs introducing me to anyone. I've done perfectly well on my own, thanks."

"Oh, is that what they're calling failure these days?" his dad sniped.

"Now, c'mon, Dr. Jacobson, I think you're being too hard on him." Gibbs stepped in. "He might be in a bit of a slump, but we all go through that in the business. If there's anyone who can pull himself back up, it's Moses. He's got the acting chops and the movie-star good looks, which, I must say, he got from you and your beautiful wife. I totally believe in him."

"Oh, I believe in him, too," his dad said, swelling up. Moses wished he had a pin to pop him. "I believe he should have gone to law school, like I told him to twenty years ago. Then he wouldn't be in the situation he's in now—all this sneaking off to your house every night and creeping back before we all wake up. It's shameful. You didn't think your mom and I knew about that, did you?"

But I've been so careful not to make a sound, Moses thought, wondering how his father had figured it out, if Pandora might have let it slip, though they'd both agreed to keep it a secret. No, the old man must have concluded it all on his own, for even when they were children he'd had an incredible knack for sniffing out and making the most of their fears and failures.

Leave it to his dad to bring up the two most troubling chinks in his armor—the waning of his career and the implosion of his marriage. "I plead the fifth," he said, because he couldn't think of anything else to say.

"The fifth?" his dad asked. "I think they teach it in law school, but you wouldn't know that, would you?"

"Mom's calling you," Moses said, sending him off to look for his wife.

"I see things are still status quo with the old man," Gibbs noted. "Maybe even worse?"

"Far worse," he agreed. "So, look, I was wondering if I could borrow your boat tonight," and he explained that he and his siblings wanted to take his dad out fishing later. "You know how much he loves to fish."

It was a simple plan, and would be so easy to carry out—utter darkness, a mishap on the boat, an accident. *He always did love fishing,* their mother would tell the police later. And the three bedraggled, shocked siblings would agree, these three eyewitnesses who—choking up, aggrieved—couldn't believe their father was gone.

"Yeah, sure, you know where the keys are. I've got a date later, so I probably won't be around. You have the run of chez Gould. There's a stash of kosher for Passover beer in the fridge. Anything for Dr. Jacobson," he consented. "And for you," and again he wrapped an arm around Moses's shoulders, the gesture of which felt both forced and spurious, as if Gibbs were drawing him close only to pick his pocket.

"I think Pandora's in the kitchen," Moses said. "Go say hello," then he left to take another call.

It was Ronnie, the producer of the show, calling to tell Moses that they'd be going live in ten minutes and to remind him about the list of items to plug. "This is live TV. No commercial breaks, no ad revenue, Mo," the producer said. "Be doubly aware of that. And remember: You're not trying to teach anyone about Judaism, so not too much explaining. We'll direct viewers to our own Wiki page, where they can find myriad information about Passover, et cetera. And when you mention the angel of death, please use the gender-neutral pronoun 'it.' The audience development team feels the use of 'he' or 'she' might alienate certain viewers. And also when you get to the plagues, we'd prefer that you say 'The unfortunate and unfair slaying of the firstborn son' rather than just 'The slaying of the firstborn son.'"

"But that changes the entire meaning," Moses protested. "Besides, it wasn't unfortunate or unfair. It's in the Torah, in black and white. It was used as a threat against Pharaoh. It was supposed to soften his heart."

"This is focus-group-tested, and we'd like it if you complied," the producer stressed.

After Moses hung up, he announced that it was "go time" and that they were live, giving everyone the thumbs-up and calling them to gather together to light the Sabbath candles. Thus, the entire Jacobson clan, as well as Dietrich, who had apparently decided not to leave after all, and Gibson Gould, hovered around Pandora, who'd covered her head with a shawl. Bronson struck a match and handed it to her, then she touched the flame to the candlewicks, reciting the blessing over them. Moses stood just behind his wife and beside his mom, who held on to his arm for support. He could feel her grip through his shirtsleeve, the solidness of it, yet also the frailty, the clinging. His dad spoke over Pandora, reciting the Passover add-on—*lihadlik ner shel Yom Tov*—then they all said "Amen," the boys scattering away as everyone else shuffled into the dining room to take his or her place at the table.

Moses was still miffed about his conversation with the producer, but what could he do? The only person who'd probably notice the change anyway was his dad and he just prayed he got it past him without enduring the usual high dudgeon and self-righteousness.

This was his hope as he took his chair at the head of the table, Pandora to his left—Pandora, who looked stunning in her short black crepe de chine dress and black patent-leather heels, the Jewish star necklace draped lusciously around her throat. His mom, too, looked beautiful in a black pantsuit and flats, the black pearl earrings accenting her eyes, her face rubicund in the soft light, looking far healthier than he'd seen it in ages. Edith was in a knee-length black herringbone skirt, a white blouse, and a heather-gray bolero, which showed off her hourglass figure. A choker and bracelet gave her the appearance of a 1950s starlet, for the makeup artist had even penciled a mole, à la Marilyn Monroe, right above her lip. She looked amazing and everyone except their dad had told her so.

Moses glanced lovingly around the Passover table, his eyes falling on the five empty seats that should have contained his sons, who, he imagined, were upstairs playing videogames. He was about to head upstairs to fetch them when they all burst through the door in the glass wall en masse, huffing and puffing and taking their seats at the far end of the table near Jacob and Dietrich and Gibbs, Jacob looking as if he hadn't showered in days and so over it all that Moses wondered if he'd even make it through the entire hour before getting up and leaving. Well, the main attraction wasn't his brother or his lover, but Gibson Gould, who sat exactly opposite Moses at the foot of the table. Moses glanced at his boys, who were looking everywhere else than at him, and noticed that their faces were splashed with what looked like red freckles. Their hair was messy and their ties askew. "So glad you could join us, boys," he said, smiling avidly at them. "Before I tell you the story of Passover, I just want to thank my parents, Roz and Julian, my brother, Jacob, his boyfriend, Dietrich, and my sister, Edith, for coming all this way to celebrate the holiday with us," Moses continued. "I also want to wish my best friend, Gibson Gould, a big welcome. So happy you're all here."

The trick with reality TV was to act as natural as possible, and Mo relaxed into his groove about ten minutes into the show—after he'd explained the significance of Passover and what it meant to the

Jews. Like the actor he was, he never once looked at the webcams, though he did enunciate his words slowly and carefully. "Boys, can you tell your maw-maw and paw-paw what the definition of Seder is?" he asked, adjusting his yarmulke in the hopes that his sons would take the hint and put theirs on. No such luck.

The boys gazed sheepishly across the table at him as he waited for one of them to make him a proud Jewish papa. It was messianic Bronson, with the most abundant of the red freckles splattered across his cheeks and nose and chin, who said, "Order. Seder means order."

"Good job, Bronson," he said. "Now, the first order of business is the Kiddush. I'm going to let my dad lead us in the blessings, while I prep you boys for the Four Questions," and he rose and motioned for his sons to follow him. "We'll be right back."

He marched them through the kitchen and into the bathroom, where they all crammed in together, then flipped on the light and shut the door. He wasn't sure if the bathroom was a hot spot. He glanced up and sure enough found a single webcam, its red light blinking, which meant it was recording, though Moses had no idea if they'd cut to follow him in here with his sons.

"Okay, spill it," he said. "What did you do?" He turned Baxter around and studied his face, which looked as if one of his brothers had taken a red felt-tipped marker to his cheeks. "Will one of you tell me what's on your faces, please?"

Again, it was Bronson, fearless and determined, who stepped out of the huddle and right up to Moses and spoke for them all, saying, "It's blood."

"Blood? As in . . . *blood*?" he asked, horrified. "Whose? Yours? Is one of you hurt?"

"No, it's from the . . . opossum," he explained. "We needed a sacrifice, and there weren't any lambs around to slaughter, so we settled."

"I want you to tell me exactly what you and your brothers did with the opossum."

"We didn't want anyone to die when the angel of death came down," Bronson mumbled. "So we painted the front doors with blood."

"You painted the front doors with blood," Moses repeated and pushed through his brood to slump down on the toilet, no longer caring if the webcam picked any of this up or not. "Let me get this straight: You killed the opossum, sliced it open, then used the blood to ward off the angel of death?"

"It was already dead," Bronson said. "We found it in the grass. Think it'll work? Think he'll pass over?" he asked.

"It," Moses corrected him. "From now on, let's use the gender-neutral pronoun 'it,' when discussing the angel of death," looking up at the webcam beseechingly.

"You and me and Paw-Paw . . . we're all firstborns," Bronson said, wrapping his arms around his brothers. It was true—Bronson had been born first.

"You said front doors, though," Moses realized. "What other doors are we talking about besides ours?" Suspecting the extent of what they'd done, he shut his eyes, leaning his head against the wall, his bowels bucking like a pissed-off bull. "How many doors?"

"We kind of ran out of blood after we did ours and the Rothmans'," Bron admitted.

The Rothmans, Moses thought. Perfect. Just perfect. "Where's the opossum right now? What did you do with it?" he asked.

"We pitched it over the fence."

"Our fence?" Moses asked as the room went swirling around him. The Orenstein-Jacobson fence backed up onto a slight declination that ended in a plateau on which sat a mobile-home park.

"Our fence."

"Okay, well, there's nothing we can do about it right now. Wash your faces and let's practice the Four Questions."

Traditionally, the twins, who were the youngest, were supposed to recite the Four Questions—*Why is this night different from all other nights? Why do we eat matzo? Why all the dipping of bitter herbs? Why do we recline?*—but Moses and Pandora had agreed that it would be better television if they all did it.

Once they'd gone through the Four Questions, *which didn't sound half bad,* thought Moses, they filed out of the bathroom and returned to the table, where his dad was incanting, "Salt water to remind us of the bitter tears we cried when we were slaves in Egypt." Moses and the boys resettled themselves, while the rest of the table dipped the bitter parsley in salt water, everyone making the same sour face as they chewed. Moses glanced down the table, surprised to see a new addition—Elias Plunkett, who sat beside Edith. He'd wondered about the two empty seats and the two empty place settings—growing up, they'd always reserved one chair for the prophet Elijah, who was welcomed in by an open door at the end of the meal. The boys, especially Bronson, loved this tradition. While it was true that there was absolutely nothing in the liturgy about saving a seat for Elijah, the tradition had passed itself down, as Jewish traditions did, and Moses had kept it, though he wondered why Elijah would ever want to join them for Passover considering how unlikable three-fourths of the table was.

Moses said hello to Elias, then reclaimed the reins of his table, noting that his dad had made remarkably good progress on the service—they only had an hour to cram in what usually took four or five hours, for Passover was full of bawdy songs and four glasses of wine, although there'd never been any singing when Moses had been a boy and the four glasses of wine only made everyone even meaner. They moved on to Yachatz, the breaking of the matzo, in which the middle matzo was broken in half, one piece to be eaten later, the other used as the Afikoman and hidden somewhere in the house for the children to hunt for and find. When they were children, whoever found the Afikoman was given a silver dollar. Correcting for inflation, that silver dollar had become a twenty-dollar bill. This was a highlight for the boys, who chomped at the bit every year, waiting for permission to get up and search. It usually ended in tears, for his dad inevitably hid it in the same place, which meant a beeline for the familiar spot, and that the fastest boy, usually Brendan, got to it first.

"Do me a favor and hide it somewhere else," Moses muttered to his dad, handing the broken matzo to him.

"Don't you worry about that," his dad said. "You just focus on steering the Seder ship to shore."

"Boys, are you ready?" Moses asked, for it was time to recite the Four Questions.

They stood up and gathered against the wall of glass, the trips in the middle, with the twins bookending them. Their singing was indescribably beautiful, the melody coming up and out of them as if they all had the lungs of opera singers and the talent to boot. Perhaps it was the shape of the room or the acoustics or the love that Moses was beaming out to them with his eyes and his smile, but the song moved Pandora to reach under the table and grab his hand, as if to say, *Look at what we made.* There was joy, a copious amount of it, and it dripped off everything and went ringing through every room in the house, trembling the air. The caterers poked their heads out of the kitchen to listen to Moses's cherubs with their angelic voices, drawing Moses out of himself and into the holiday. If he shut his eyes, he might not have been sitting at a table in Calabasas but in an ancient house with sand floors and fire pits and baked mud for walls. Then the singing ended, yet Moses wanted it to go on and on, for it had paused time for him—in those few minutes nothing evil had happened in the world, not here, not anywhere. But then it all came whooshing back and his phone was vibrating and Pandora let go of his hand to return to her texting, and he noticed that every time she texted, Gibbs glanced down at the phone sitting next to his plate. The joy fizzled.

"Stunning, guys. Just stunning. Thank you," Moses said, clapping.

"Encore, encore," Jacob called.

"I think you two might have the next big boy band on your

hands," Gibbs said. "In the tradition of the Jacksons and the Jonases, I give you the Jacobson Five."

Moses looked down at the text he'd received. It was from the producer, who wanted him to speed things along. "Okay, now it's time for the telling of the Passover tale, so please remove the iPad minis, which you'll find under your plates, open iBooks, click on the Haggadah icon, and flip to page twenty-seven. I want to thank the folks at Apple for being one of tonight's sponsors," he said. "And that goes for all of our sponsors," and he rattled off the list. "Okay, let's just go around the table and everyone can read for a bit," which was what they did. And when they came to the ten plagues, "which King Pharaoh brought upon himself by refusing to let the Israelites go," Moses said, the boys lit up and watched him with rapt attention.

Moses recited them in the order he found them:

"1) And God turned the Nile to blood,
 2) And sent frogs to rain from the sky,
 3) And he sent bugs up from the earth to torment the Egyptians,
 4) And wild beasts to ravage the lands,
 5) And a pestilence to destroy all of the Egyptian livestock,
 6) And boils to burst out upon man and beast,
 7) And hail to pulverize and crush all of those who did not believe,
 8) And swarms of locusts to blot out the sun and ruin what was left of the crops,
 9) And a teeming darkness to blind the Egyptians and fill them with terror,
 10) And the worst of them all, the unfortunate and unfair slaying of the firstborn son."

"What was that?" his dad asked after Moses had finished. "The last one. That's not the way it goes."

"Leave it alone, Dad," Moses whispered.

"I will not leave it alone," he said.

"You have to admit that it was pretty unfortunate and unfair," said Gibbs.

"Have all of you lost your minds?" his dad asked, pushing away from the table and huffing out of the room.

His mom got up to go after him, a slow and painful ascent that showed in her face. "Ma, no. Let him be," Edith said, helping her back into her seat.

It was then that the doorbell rang, and the boys jumped out of their seats. "Elijah! Elijah's here," they said, running out of the room, Moses apologizing to the table and getting up to see who was at the door.

When he got there, his dad had already opened the door and let Frieda Rothman into the house. "Angel of death! Angel of death!" the boys shouted as Frieda grimaced, shooed them away, then walked right up to Moses, slapping him in the face.

He stood there in a stupefied daze, rubbing his cheek against the sting. "She just hit Daddy," he heard the boys telling the guests at the table, who then got up to see the commotion for themselves.

"Your boys," Frieda said. "They're menaces. Now I have proof. I'm going to call my son. He's a lawyer, you know."

"Get out of my house," Pandora snarled, coming between Moses and their next-door neighbor.

"Pandora, let me handle this, please," he begged, knowing they were all being watched and that it was imperative he diffused the situation before it escalated. "Look, we're right in the middle of our Seder," he said. "Couldn't this wait until a little later?" He knew she was there about the blood on the door, but this was the last thing he wanted mentioned in front of the entire world. "I promise I'll come over after and we can talk."

"I like you, Moses, but your boys have gone too far," Frieda countered. "What they wrote—well, I won't repeat the words in polite company because I'm not that kind of person. Suffice it to say,

I'm shocked and horrified. Milton and I both are. To think we live next door to such a bunch of hateful, insensitive hooligans and Jews no less. It's disgraceful. Just disgraceful."

"Words? What words? What did they write?" Moses asked.

"Ask them," she said, pointing to his sons.

"Boys, what did you write?" he demanded of them.

"We didn't write anything," Bronson protested. "We just . . . painted."

"It's on your door as well. Come here. Look."

He followed Frieda outside, where Moses knew for certain that a camera had been installed, and where his dad was already standing, shaking his head in dismay. Moses glanced at the lintel, which was indeed streaked with blood, but there was more to it than that, for on top of the blood in big, black letters were the words DIRTY STINKING PIG JEWS. "Boys, what have you done? Why would you write this?" he cried, appalled.

"I'll tell you why," his dad broke in. "Because like father, like son. You never had any sense and neither do they. Look at the way you live, well beyond your means, and look at how they're growing up. You spoil them rotten, and then wonder why they are the way they are? You made a mockery of our family with that stupid show for three years, and you're making a mockery of it again tonight. I only agreed to this because your mother had her heart set on spending what is probably going to be her last Passover out here with her family. And you subject her—you subject me—to this bullshit. Congratulations, you've confirmed to the world what a bunch of idiots we raised."

Moses had no response, because what was there to say to that? What was there to say to such a man, such a father, such a grandfather?

"We didn't write it," Bronson remarked.

Yeah, sure you didn't, Moses thought, but then he noticed a van with the network's logo in the driveway. And he was startled by his own rash reaction and felt ashamed for doubting his sons, especially

Bronson, who stood there with his sad, stern face. For in his face he saw other faces, his own, his brother's, his sister's, and thought, *I am nothing like you, Dad, and my boys will be nothing like you. This night, I will be the kind of father you never were.*

He passed through the yard and rapped on the door of the van. Chandler slid it open, holding a sandwich in one hand, his phone in the other. Moses caught the glow of a computer screen on which Chandler was monitoring everything. "Did you see who defaced the door?" Moses asked.

"It looked like a couple of kids, but they had on hoodies and were carrying bats. They were here and then they were gone, man. I didn't see their faces," Chandler said.

"Well, were you going to tell us about it at some point?" Moses asked.

"I'm not supposed to interfere or get involved, man." He shrugged. "I just do my job."

"Nice job," Moses said, speculating that the thugs must have seen the live feed and wanted to be a part of it, part of this show that was devolving into *A Very JacobSONS Nightmare.*

"But it's cool, because I'm getting all of this," he continued. "I put a camera up there." He gestured at the lemon tree. "Excellent stuff, really personal and controversial. Beats the hell out of the Kardashian reunion I shot a few months ago."

"I'm glad you're enjoying yourself," Moses said. "Now kindly fuck off."

"Dude, you can't say that on live TV."

"Oops. Well, I just did, didn't I?" Moses said, turning to his family, but they'd all gone back into the house.

For a moment, all he wanted to do was to get into his car and drive away where no one could find him, least of all his producer, who was going to ream him out. It didn't matter. The whole night was a complete fiasco from start to finish and now he had this crime to contend with, these awful words to sand away come morning. Frieda was still in her yard, gazing out into the dark, her face stricken.

"Do you and Milton want to join us?" Moses called.

If she heard him or not, he couldn't tell, for she turned and hurried into her house, slamming the door. The porch light went out a moment later, though he knew she'd be keeping vigil all night, worrying that whoever had desecrated their door would come back to do worse. Things like this happened, had been happening for a few years.

Back in his own house, Moses found his family at the windows, peering out. "It's over," he said, though he had no idea to what he was referring—the vandalism, the Seder, the show, his marriage, his mother's life, his career. Everything caught in those two little words as he moved past them all and back into the dining room, picking up his fork and clinking it against the side of his wineglass. They shuffled in, reluctant to begin again, *but begin again we must,* he thought, trying not to look at his father, who sat with a self-satisfied smirk on his face, as if he were somehow happy about all of this. *I'm so much better than this,* said that pernicious smirk of his. *I'm so much better than you.*

They all settled back in their seats and the Seder went on, because it had to, although Moses would have liked to bash every single webcam, and his father, for good measure. But this was important, this special, and Moses, ever the professional, dredged up a camera-ready smile. The meal was served and conversation resumed, wine was poured and drunk, spirits lifted, smiling facades went up, and everything was forgiven and forgotten, at least while they were all on live television. His dad had done a terrific job hiding the Afikoman on his own person, so that none of the boys could find it, but this was cause for laughter that night. His dad deposited one gold coin apiece into his grandsons' open, expectant palms, then continued eating his brisket. Pandora kept checking her phone and Gibbs kept glancing down at his, but even this didn't matter to

Moses anymore. He was thinking about the man beside him, his dad, their own angel of death, their own walking ten plagues, who sat there, absorbed in the world of his dinner, licking his fingers when he thought no one was watching—except of course the entire world was watching. The world had seen him for what he was when he roared at Moses in the front yard, indicting him for his terrible parenting skills. The cameras saw and heard it. Now Moses thought back to all the death threats the trips had gotten, even after they'd changed their email addresses, and he realized that it had to have been his dad who sent them. It all made sense now, considering what he'd just said out on the lawn. Those threatening emails—"Hitler had the right idea," "There's no good Jew like a dead Jew," "Gas the women and children first"—it had been his dad all along, trying to get the show canceled. Oh, he understood why his dad might not want the world to see into their lives. But to threaten his grandsons simply out of embarrassment?

It's unforgivable, Moses thought, reaching for his fork and wanting to jam it into his dad's neck. *Now those would be some ratings,* he mused, stabbing a piece of tangy, juicy meat and sliding it into his mouth. They ate and they laughed, they told stories about their lives, Jacob and Dietrich about Berlin, Edith about Atlanta. It was a good time. And his dad sat there in silent judgment, feeding his face, and his mom sat beside him, fiddling with her oxygen, trying not to let anyone see her do it. But Moses saw, and he took a sip of wine and then another to wash the bitterness of it down.

Moses opened the doors to the backyard to let in some fresh air, the candles fluttering in the breeze. When he sat back down, he noticed a peculiar thing—his dad's face was bright red and he was clawing at his throat. His mom was turned to Edith and Elias, and Pandora was glued to her phone, texting Gibbs, no doubt. The boys were huddled around Jacob and Dietrich, who were telling them about the Brandenburg Gate, and no one but Moses himself seemed to take notice or care that Julian was choking. He stared at him in awe and wonder, for he couldn't quite believe his eyes or his luck—their luck. It wouldn't be long now, a couple more minutes. He could say and do nothing, and it would all be over. Yet Moses realized he couldn't let it happen like this, he couldn't allow himself to be implicated on live TV. Against his better judgment he leaped up and grabbed his dad and pummeled him from behind, expelling the piece of gristle that had lodged itself in his dad's esophagus—all of this before the rapt audience at the table and in living rooms and dens across America. His dad reached for a glass of water, his eyes on Moses the entire time, and Moses knew then that his dad knew that he'd hesitated a second too long.

"It went down the wrong way, Roz," he moaned petulantly. "I was choking. I couldn't breathe."

"You're okay now, Julian. Moses saved you," his mom soothed, stroking his hand and glancing up at Moses with the strangest look on her face.

Ten minutes later, the webcam lights went dark simultaneously; the broadcast was finished. Moses pushed away from the table, exhausted yet energized at once. He'd saved his dad's life—a life that in a few hours he was going to end—and he couldn't help laughing at the incredible irony of it all, at the twisted logic of the universe.

"Why the hell didn't you just let him choke?" Jacob asked later, cornering him in the pantry, where Moses had stashed a package of Oreos, verboten and against Passover law. Moses shook his head at Jacob's question. "Yeah, letting him die on national television would have won me lots of points with the network. And the police," he said.

"It would have solved our problem, that's all I'm saying," Jacob said. "Because we're running out of time for the plan to work." From the pantry, Moses could see that Edith and Elias were sitting in the backyard, having some kind of serious discussion that only they could have. Edith's face was drawn and Elias's strained and he wondered if she was telling him about her afternoon with Zion

Abdullah Cohen, justifying it all over again, though perhaps this time looking at it through the eyes of someone she had once been intimate with, as intimate, he understood, as Edith could be with anyone. He hoped, for her sake, that what she'd learned from Zion had broken whatever juvenile spell Sheik had had on her, that from now on she'd be able to proceed more cautiously with men who weren't wildly and wholly inappropriate for her and that she'd mended one fence, Elias, at the very least, a fence that would serve to corral her desire, say, the next time a male student showed up in her office, distraught over his grade and beside himself with personal sorrow. Edith, good, kindhearted Edith, had done what any person would, reaching out to comfort the boy. But she wasn't just any person— she was his professor. How exactly she was going to untangle herself from it all Moses still had to wonder, but he hoped she would.

While his dad roamed the backyard, shaking his head in disappointment while kicking at large clumps of the freshly mown, dried grass, which, Moses knew, his dad had expected Jacob or Moses himself to have raked up and bagged, and Elias and Edith chatted, Moses told Jacob about the backup plan, in case the video blackmail failed. "Fishing on Lake Calabasas." Jacob grinned. "It's kind of genius. I'm surprised I didn't think of it first. I think we should just bypass plan A and head straight to plan B," he said, lightly punching Moses on the arm. "Good work, *mein Bruder*."

"Keep the German to a minimum, okay?"

"So when is this happening?" Jacob asked, a little too excitedly, thought Moses, who was not excited at all. There was nothing about this that was right, not in the strictest sense of the word, and he had to keep reminding himself of what his dad had shouted on the lawn, as if this and not everything that came before it were the proof he and his conscience needed to carry the plan out.

"Soon," Moses said. "I just want to give him some time to recuperate."

"It's after nine already," Jacob complained.

"We'll get him out on the boat. We'll present the evidence we have, and he'll go for it or he won't," he said, pulling an Oreo apart and eating the middle. "Good for him if he does. Good for us if he doesn't. We win, regardless."

"You mean Ma wins," Jacob amended, depositing an Oreo whole in his mouth and chewing.

Moses remained in the pantry after Jacob left to go check on Dietrich. He liked it in the cool, silent dark, nibbling on his private stash of cookies and imagining waking up in the morning free of his dad either way. After eating another six cookies, Moses left the pantry and went to knock on the guest room door. His mom was already in bed in her nightgown, her makeup removed, the oxygen tank beside the bed, the clear tubes running from it to her nose. "That was a lovely Seder." She smiled. "Do you think your producer was happy with it?"

"I haven't heard from him, so probably not. It doesn't matter. Not really. I'm just glad you were able to be here."

"Me, too," she said as his dad stepped out of the bathroom. Moses was surprised to see him in his pajamas, and his heart sank. "Your dad wants to be on the road bright and early."

"Five in the morning." His dad nodded. "Beat this damn L.A. traffic."

"Tomorrow's Easter," Moses pointed out. "No traffic."

"Still," his dad said, "we have a long drive ahead of us."

"So I take it you don't feel like going out on the boat?" he asked.

"Another time," his dad said, eyeing him. "Tell Gary thanks anyway."

"Of course," he said. "But are you sure? When's the last time we all went fishing together?"

"I told your father he should go, at least for a little while, but he doesn't want to leave my side."

"My place is here, with your mom." His dad leered, smirking that horrible smirk again. *He knows,* Moses thought. *He's got to know.*

Well, it'd be easy enough to whip out his phone right then and there, to finally show his mom that this man, who didn't want to leave her side, had tampered with her spare oxygen tank. He pulled out his phone—it was now or never—his heart racing a mile a minute, his stomach doing cartwheels. He sent a text to Edith, telling her to get Jacob and meet him in the downstairs guest room. *Hurry*, he wrote.

"Ma, I—we—want to show you something," he started, as his dad climbed into bed beside her.

"What is it, Mo? Pictures of the boys?" she asked, sitting up. "They have such gorgeous voices. Don't they, Julian?"

"They sounded like castrati. You know castrati? The little boys they castrated so they would sing like girls," his dad said. "You know who had a truly remarkable voice, though, was my sister. She sang in the choir at the synagogue. We used to joke that she had a schwartze living inside her."

"Julian, you know I don't like that word," his mom said.

"Which word?" He snickered.

"You know what's always amazed me about you," Moses said to him. "Just how utterly oblivious you are to everyone around you. It takes a special kind of chutzpah to use a word that you know is offensive to everyone, especially when you're talking about my sons to me. You can't say something bigoted and horrible like that."

"Boy, you watch who you're talking to." His dad glowered.

"Or what? What can you possibly do to me that you haven't already done?" Moses asked. "Embarrass me on national TV? Done that. Make sure I know what a worthless piece of shit I am? Done that, too."

"You embarrassed yourself," his dad said, sneering. "And you are a worthless piece of shit most of the time."

"Julian! Moses! Both of you knock it off," his mom commanded as the door swung open and in walked Jacob and Edith.

"Sounds like we're missing all the fun, Thistle," Jacob said to Edith, who glanced at the rollaway, then knowingly back at him.

"I take it, Mo, that we're not going fishing as planned. Well, that's a pity. I was so looking forward to spending some real quality time out on the lake with you, Dad, so you could tell me again how bad my last play was and how I should have gone to law school. I've always wondered if you wanted to raise children or lawyers."

His dad just sat there. None of them had ever spoken to him quite like this before. *Perhaps if we had, we wouldn't be in this particular situation,* Moses thought. "I just wanted to raise children who'd actually make me and your mother proud, that's all," he said. "Instead, we got you—a faggot playwright, a barren, spinster sex offender, and a talentless cuckold. Your mother and I have so much to be thankful for in you."

"Do not speak for me, Julian," his mom exclaimed. "You have been at them their entire lives, and I want it to stop. They are your children. They are our children."

"They haven't been children of mine since they walked out of my house. Do you three want to know a little secret? If it hadn't been for your mother, I would have left years ago. You don't think I couldn't have found someone else? You don't think I couldn't have had loving kids who appreciated all that I did for them? Think again. You all have been nothing but constant disappointments since the day you took your first breaths. Each of you damaged in some spectacular way. No doubt you blame me for most of it. But as far as I remember it, you grew up with two loving, adoring parents. And here's another little secret—I blame you for not living up to the Jacobson name, and now I have to watch the same thing happen to those five boys. It's despicable."

Moses stood there, unmoving and numb. He'd always suspected that his dad felt this way about them. He could tell that Jacob and Edith were as stunned as he was. "No, Daddy, you're the despicable one," Edith whispered at last. "You never loved us because you can't. You rob everyone around you of sympathy, but you have nothing to give back. You expect love. You demand servitude. You always have to have your own way, or you throw a tantrum like one of your five-year-old grandsons. Daddy, you're an abuser, and if Ma weren't here right now, I'd kill you myself with my bare hands."

Their dad started to speak, but Jacob cut him off. "Show her the video, Mo," he ordered.

"Ah, the video," their dad jeered. "I was wondering when that was going to surface."

"I've already seen it," their mom said. They all took steps back, as if they'd been smacked in unison. "Your father showed it to me."

"It really just proves how depraved all of you are to think I'd tamper with your mom's oxygen tank," their dad said.

"But you did," Edith said, the first of them to recompose herself. "I picked it up, Ma, to put it back in the minivan. It was much lighter."

"Lighter than what? Air? What exactly do you have to go on?" their dad asked, smirking.

"I checked the tank myself, Thistle. It weighs exactly the same as this one when it was full," and their mom touched the tank sitting on the floor beside her.

"That's not possible." Jacob shook his head in disbelief. "He's clearly doing something to it in the video."

"I'm . . . moving it," their dad said. "That's all. Arrest me if that's a crime. Go on."

"We want you to leave." Mo found his voice. "We want you to go away and never come back. You slammed the lid of the barbecue down on my son's hand on purpose. And even if we can't prove it and Ma doesn't believe it, you tampered with that tank, and you've never once apologized or taken any responsibility for any wrongdoing—not when you hurled that baseball at me, not when you fed Edith figs, not when you made Jacob watch all of those horror movies with you, knowing that he was too young and that he'd have nightmares for years. You are not, nor have you ever been, a real father. We can take care of Ma, the three of us."

"Don't make me laugh," their dad taunted. "You can't even take care of yourselves, much less a dying woman who needs constant care."

At this, their mom swiveled out of the bed into her wheelchair. "Let me know how all of this ends," she said with dismissive finality, rolling to the door, which Moses opened for her.

"That's just great," their dad snapped. "Now you've upset her."

"Now? I think she's been upset for over forty years thanks to you," Jacob said. "And just who the hell are you to criticize any of us?"

"Do you know why none of this matters to me at all and why I'll sleep like a baby tonight?" their dad asked. "Because tomorrow I get to drive away from here and never think about any of you wretched, ungrateful losers again. I'm cutting you all off and that includes whatever inheritance you thought you were getting. Your mom and I are going on a three-month cruise. She wants to see the world, and I'm happy to give that to her. Now if you don't mind, I need to get some sleep," and he shut off the light, slid under the covers, and shut his eyes. "You can all leave anytime."

Edith marched over to the rollaway. Moses was sure she was going to reach for the syringe, though now was not the time for it, he wanted to tell her. They would have to wait until everyone was gone. Instead, she closed the rollaway, latched it, then pushed it out of the room, Jacob and Moses following. She left it by the wall of glass and went out to speak to Elias, who kept peering in at Jacob and Moses. It seemed Gibbs had left, for Moses had a text from him asking if they were fishing or not. He texted back that they weren't. Then he went to find Pandora, but she was not in their bedroom or anywhere in the house. She'd grabbed his hand at dinner, briefly giving him hope, but that was fading already. He found her in the garage with his mom, sitting in the front seat of the Expedition. They were chatting, and he didn't want to disturb them, so he just waved. They waved back, their faces gaunt and expressionless, which he took as a terrible sign.

Jacob said he was going upstairs to talk to Dietrich, to tell him

about what had just happened, and Moses told him that Dietrich
was welcome back there anytime. The confrontation with his dad
had burned away Moses's resentment toward Dietrich, toward anyone who wasn't his father. The last couple of days had brought him
closer to his siblings and to his mom and he wouldn't have traded
that for anything in the world—*well, maybe for our dad's death,* he
thought, stepping out into the front yard to appraise the damage to
the door again. It wouldn't have surprised him if his dad had vandalized it himself.

Edith and Elias came out of the front door and Moses shook his
hand and said good-bye. It'd been years since he'd seen him, but his
opinion of Elias hadn't changed—he and Edith were still just as un-
suited for each other as his mom and dad were. Edith walked him to
his car and said her own good-bye, and as she and Moses wandered
inside she asked him if he thought Pandora would mind if she set the
rollaway up in her office.

"You'd have to ask her," he said just as Pandora returned from
the garage with their mom, who looked as if she'd been crying.
Moses's heart broke when he saw her, so frail and so old, and he
wondered how it had happened, how he'd let her age behind his
back. He kissed his mom good night, told her to wake him up before they left, then followed Pandora upstairs. They had missed
their chance to get rid of their dad, and Moses regretted that he
hadn't let him choke to death at dinner. He went to check on the
boys, all of whom were fast asleep. But he roused Dexter, because
he just had to know.

"Did you tell Paw-Paw about the video you made of him by the
minivan?" he asked softly. "I won't be mad if you did." Moses hated
to take advantage of the boy in his sleepy, vulnerable state, yet he
didn't see any way around it. Still, he thought twice about what he
was doing, for he felt terrible about implicating his own child in
this horror show. But then Dexter was reaching under his pillow
and pulling out two crisp hundred-dollar bills. He handed them ea-

gerly to Moses, whose face went dark as he took them from his son. "Paw-Paw gave this to you?"

"He told me it was from the Truth Fairy," he chirped. "He told me to keep it a secret, even from you, and that if I told anyone, the Truth Fairy would get supermad and steal the money back and turn me into a—a forearm." He sniffled, darting his eyes back and forth with a keen vigilance, on the lookout, no doubt, for the Truth Fairy. A forearm? But surely the boy didn't mean that. *Firearm* wasn't right, either, but it popped into Moses's head. No, it must have been a more threatening word—this was Julian Jacobson after all—though for the life of him he had no idea what it might be. "Are you sure Paw-Paw said forearm?" he asked.

Dexter pushed his face into the pillow to dry his eyes, for he was crying now. "If I told, Paw-Paw said the Truth Fairy would make everybody dead. He said I'd never see you again, and I'd have to go live in Dallas. I don't want to live in Dallas! Their house stinks like farts!"

"Hey, language," Moses scolded, thinking of his dad and the threat to turn Dexter into an orphan, the word buzzing hideously through his head. "Look, Paw-Paw was just teasing. Nothing's going to happen to me or to Mommy or to your brothers," he said, wrapping the shivering, frightened boy in his arms. "But I need you to be very brave and tell me if you showed Paw-Paw the video on Mommy's phone. The video you made of him. I'm in pretty good with the Truth Fairy. I bet she'll buy you whatever toy you want when she hears how brave you're being. So what about it, champ? Did you show Paw-Paw the video?"

"You mean the one where he's sticking a shot into that green torpedo?" he asked.

"A shot? You mean you saw Paw-Paw injecting a shot into the tank?" he asked, his heart racing.

"Yeah," Dexter said. "I dropped the phone," which accounted for the sudden shot of the grass. "He was shooting it." He had seen what Moses had not, what wasn't shown in the video. He'd been there and had observed his paw-paw using the syringe.

"Thank you," Moses whispered, kissing him on the forehead. "Now have yourself some good dreams and sleep well."

"Good night, Daddy," he murmured, slipping back under the covers and shutting his eyes, though Moses had a feeling that he'd spend the entire night on high alert, watching the shadows for the Truth Fairy.

Moses left the room, hurried to the upstairs guest room, knocked quickly, then entered. "Jacob, I need to talk to you," he said.

In the hall, Moses told him what Dexter had just told him. "You have got to be shitting me," Jacob said.

"I don't know what's in that syringe Edith found, but I'm pretty sure he planted it," Moses said. "I'm pretty sure that one of these days, if Ma, God forbid, dies 'unexpectedly,' the police are going to come snooping around and pay the three of us a visit. They'll check all of her tanks and see they've been tampered with. You don't think that's been his plan all along, do you? I mean, to implicate us in her death?"

"That incredible son of a bitch."

"It must contain hydrochloric or sulfuric acid or a very potent chloroform," Moses conjectured, not really knowing much about chemicals but knowing his dad. "Something that would degrade the lining of the tank, something lethal when it was inhaled. If anyone would know about that kind of thing, he would."

"Okay," Jacob said. "Then what's the new plan?"

"We don't have a choice now." Moses scrubbed a hand over his face. "He'll kill her if we don't kill him. It's as simple as that. We could confront him again, but he'd only find another excuse."

"Then we have to do it between now and five o'clock," Jacob said. The brothers came up with a plan right then and there. "I'll tell Edith," and off he ran to find their sister.

Moses went into the bedroom and found Pandora already in bed, playing on her phone. He shut the door and kept waiting for her to tell him to leave, but she didn't. And when he undressed and slid into bed beside her, she did not protest as she usually did. She glanced up from her phone and said, "I take it you're staying. Well, it's about time," and leaned down and kissed him. "Look, I know you know about that dalliance of mine with Gibbs. I want to say that it didn't mean anything, but it did, Mo. As clichéd as this is going to sound, he listened to me in ways you haven't since we got married." *And texted you in ways I never have, either,* Moses thought bitterly. But she was right. "I texted him tonight that it was over, though. You don't think I appreciate what I have and what we've built together, but I do. Seeing the way your dad's been behaving on this trip put it into perspective for me. But let's get one thing straight. If I ever see or hear you treat our boys the way your father treated—still treats—you, I will take them away and divorce you. Is it a deal? Can you live with that?"

"I can live with that," he said, kissing her back, though he wondered if he could live with himself for lying to her, by omission, about what he was about to do. *What does "living with it" even mean?* Moses thought.

"Some night," she said. "Have you heard from our producer?"

"Not yet. I'm sure he's not thrilled with the way things went," he said.

"I'm thrilled with the way things went," she told him. "You're a hero, Moses Orenstein-Jacobson. You're my hero. I'm sorry for everything."

"Me, too. Sorrier than you'll ever know."

"Just promise me we'll never turn into your parents," she said. "Your poor mom. She should come and live with us after their cruise."

Moses started laughing. "Do you know something I don't?" he asked.

"Not a thing. I was just thinking it'd be nice if she didn't have him around. God, what an albatross."

"What were you guys talking about anyway?" he asked.

"Girl things," she said and left it at that. He knew then he'd never get it out of her. Pandora was like that—and he wouldn't have had her any other way.

"I'm going to lock up," he said, throwing on his robe and slippers and heading downstairs.

He went from room to room, switching off lights, then stood at the wall of glass, surveying the moonless backyard, wondering if Edith had been right about what she'd seen—Nieves being carried away. Well, it certainly wasn't like her to run off and not come back and he had a terrible, queasy feeling that she had been eaten. He tapped the tint button on the controller and the glass went opaque, the backyard a memory.

The rollaway was gone, and he heard the echo of Edith's voice— she was talking animatedly on her phone, probably to Elias, thought Moses, for it sounded as if she'd known the caller forever, using a kind of Jacobson shorthand with him that Moses recognized in his own speech patterns with his wife—coming from the long, dark hallway, where a sliver of light escaped from under the office door. He was about to go back upstairs when he caught a faint reddish glow in the kitchen and went to investigate, thinking that one of the boys had left the fridge door open again. It wasn't the fridge, but the candles, which were still burning, remarkable considering that it was some two and a half hours later. They threw a soft, warm aura upon the walls and the sleek, titanium appliances. Here was modernity entwined with the medieval, here was his life entwined with the lives of his forefathers, and he was transfixed by the candles and by his own luck, for he had never thought of himself as lucky until that second, standing in his kitchen and listening to the sounds of his house settling around him. *Things actually have a way of working out for the best, if you wait long enough, if you believe strongly enough,* he considered, thinking about Pandora, who was awaiting his return upstairs, and about Gibbs, who'd been doing his best to woo her away. *Some things also have a way of unraveling, even the closest of friendships,* and he left the candles to burn themselves out. Instead of going upstairs, however, he grabbed his keys and went into the garage, heading straight to the freezer chest. He peered down at the large black garbage bag, which he removed. It was heavy, but then dead bodies often were.

Moses loaded the bag into the back of the Expedition, climbed into the front seat, and headed in the direction of Calabasas Lake. The roads were empty, and he made incredible time, pulling up to the house twenty minutes later. He parked in the driveway, unsure whether Gibbs was at home or not, though when he peeked into the garage he saw that both cars—the Bentley and the Hummer—were there. The house was enormous, twice the size of Moses's, with an atrium and fountains and a giant greenhouse, where Gibbs raised rare hothouse flowers. He'd done well for himself and deserved every ounce of his success. Action films, dramas, period pieces, thrillers, and comedies—he was about the most versatile actor in Hollywood these days, with an emotional range that took Moses's breath away.

Moses grabbed the garbage bag from the back of the car, then lugged it over his shoulder and into the house, where he set it down before collecting his toiletries and the odd assortment of clothes he'd left in the guest room. He set all of it by the front door, then picked up the garbage bag and headed for the French doors that opened up onto a sprawling backyard full of real Grecian statuary, a white marble gazebo, several white Adirondack chairs, and a lap pool, which was painted a majestic empyreal blue, the bottom adorned with a giant stencil of Gibbs's winking face. *A remarkable likeness,* thought Moses, who pulled out his dick and urinated into the water directly into the actor's smiling, parted lips. When he was finished, he grabbed the bag and dumped its contents into the water—the frozen remains of the white peacock immediately sank to the bottom, covering up Gibbs's huge right eye and half of his nose—a pert little thing he'd had done when they were still kids, a gift from his parents on the occasion of his bar mitzvah. Then he removed the watch and chucked it into the pool as well, shouting, "Time to leave my wife alone."

A light inside went on and Moses flew back into the house, nearly stumbling in his slippers, scooped up his possessions, and raced out the door, tossing the house key onto the sidewalk. He had just gotten into the car when Gibbs stepped out, yawning and rubbing his eyes. They stared at each other for a moment, then Moses peeled out of the drive, gunning the gas.

Moses sped through the dark, quiet streets, making it home and into bed again in fifteen minutes flat. He lay on his back and laughed silently to himself, thinking of Gary Goldstein and the white peacock thawing out on the bottom of his pool. Before falling asleep, he set the alarm on his phone to wake him up at the usual time, 3:30, though not for the usual reason of getting to the gym. Rather, he set it so he could join his brother and sister in kidnapping their dad, incinerating his body, and returning home before anyone was the wiser—all this before their mom woke up to find that her husband had changed his mind about leaving early and had instead gone fishing.

ROSALYN JACOBSON;
OR, THE WORLD TO COME

Sunday, April 17, 2022

J ULIAN WAS HOVERING OVER HER. SHE SENSED HIM BY his breathing, which was steady and bellicose, and by his scent, which was recognizable and pungent, as if he'd bathed in cayenne pepper before getting into bed, and she kept her eyes shut. It had been happening this way every night for the last few months, ever since he started that regimen of sleeping drafts and aids, a concoction of dandelion root and melatonin, then an iSleep PM lozenge, Apple's first foray into the multitrillion-dollar pharmaceutical market. She waited for him to lean down and kiss her, as he usually did, then to shuffle out of the room, to attend to whatever adventure or misadventure his sleepwalking had in store for him.

Mostly, it took him into the yard, where he gardened, some light weeding and heavy deadheading of the roses. She wondered why he couldn't get through the day like that. He was so much more agreeable asleep than awake. She hadn't married him because he was easy, but because she'd found him infinitely interesting, yet interesting, like love, as she'd come to learn, faded over the years. She wished someone had warned her beforehand, but that was old news, old and yellow and tied up with string in the attic.

But how interesting he had once been. He could finish her sentences and she thought this the most magical thing in the world—a man who could read her mind! It was straight out of a fairy tale, if a fairy tale existed in which a Jewish postdoc from Dallas meets a Catholic typist from Little Neck and after a few dates invites her to a Seder, her first. At this Seder he asks her probingly about her family, he's interested in *her*. She tells him about her parents, her childhood, how wonderful it had been to grow up so close to the city, how she'd always dreamed of being a Rockette but had to settle for a secretarial job, "which I love, don't get me wrong, but only because I don't have legs for days and was born with two left feet."

"They'd be crazy to turn away those legs, at least that's what it looks like from where I'm sitting," he said, which made her blush and lean in closer to him, feeling as if she'd met HIM—Her Incredible Man, she told her friends later, after she got home from the Seder, after she'd had a chance to think about that other thing he asked her, which she kept wanting to bring up with her parents but was having trouble inserting it into their conversations. Why had Julian asked if she was Jewish? How could he have simply looked at her and surmised that she might be? It didn't make any sense to her. But in the end, he had been right and she wondered what other things such a man could tell her about herself, what he'd see in her that she could not.

But it wasn't Julian standing over her now, for when she finally cracked open an eye, she saw one of the triplets instead, though she had no idea which one. Oh, she knew that Brendan didn't like peanut butter, that Brandon only ate pistachio ice cream, and that Bronson had an allergy to chocolate, bless his little heart, but as far as keeping their names straight she was as bad at it as Julian was good. Her inability to recognize which triplet was which drove him insane. Julian, who was perfect in every way, never had a problem differentiating them and often let Roz know how much better he was at it, at everything. She'd married a know-it-all, yet she'd had no idea just how little he actually knew. *The worst kind of know-it-all,* she thought, rising on her elbow and removing the oxygen from her nose, *the one who knows nothing.*

"Did you have a bad dream, baby?" she asked, not wanting the child to realize she didn't know his name.

"It's okay. I'm Bronson," he said, whispering. "Daddy said they named me after the brontosaurus, but that dinosaur was slow and stupid and had a tiny head. I prefer to think it was after Charles Bronson."

"Or Bronson Pinchot," she said. When he screwed up his face, she added, "He was in one of your dad's favorite movies when he was your age—*Beverly Hills Cop*. He must have seen it a hundred times. He used to enlist your aunt and uncle to play *Beverly Hills Cop* with him. He was always the good guy and he always got his man." The boy was silent, a strung-out look of concern and consternation on his tired face. His big blue eyes sparkled in the light of the digital clock, which told her it was 2:39 in the morning. "What can I do you for, Bronson?" she asked.

"Paw-Paw's in my bed," he explained. "Well, he was in my bed, but now he's playing Wii."

"Shall we go have a talk with Paw-Paw?" she asked, switching on the light and standing up without much effort, a minor miracle.

She felt most like herself in the wee hours of the night, like the woman she used to be before the onset of this horrible illness. All of those abominable horse pills she had to swallow each day! All the fuss and pother people made over her! She hated it. But the pills—*the medication, Roz*—were keeping her alive and supposedly slowing the disease down, though they also gave her ferocious diarrhea and horrible muscle cramps and headaches the likes of which she'd never experienced before. Was it any way to live? Yes. And no. Yet this was her life, and she was sticking to it, for now at least.

She followed the boy upstairs, having to pause on each one to catch her breath, but ascending anyway, which she couldn't do in the afternoon or evening, when her lungs were in full revolution, inflamed and angry at her for having dared use them throughout the day. She held on to the banister, feeling woozy but refusing to give in to the feeling of helplessness that accompanied her so often these days. She'd been alive for seventy-two long, difficult, beautiful, rapturous, overwrought years, nearly two-thirds of them tied to Julian, and she wasn't about to let this condition get the best of her, not when she was going on an around-the-world cruise for three months, then docking in Los Angeles again to attend the triplets' bar mitzvahs in October. True, she'd never get better, only worse, but hell if she weren't going to make the most out of her final few months. She had not told Julian about her last doctor's appointment, when she'd gotten this terminal time line, wanting to keep it secret, though in a moment of absolute weakness, she had told Pandora.

Bronson took her hand and together they crossed the catwalk to the playroom and there he was, her seventy-year-old husband, playing Wii Tennis in his pajamas. And she recalled how vigorous he used to be, playing squash three times a week for years, trim and athletic, and oh, how fantastic their sex life had once been, when they were younger and thinner and still cared about the taste and texture of each other's skin, back when he was still Jules Jacobson, grad student at Rutgers University in Camden. They'd met by accident in a stairwell in Yorktown, on Eighty-first Street and First Avenue, in a crummy fifth-floor walkup, where Julian had gone to pick up a different woman, Roz's roommate, as it turned out. A week later, Julian was back, only this time to take Roz on a first date to a hamburger joint around the corner—New York City in the late '70s. Pure heaven. And that was that. A splendid, fairy-tale courtship of flowers and chocolate, and oh, what a gentleman he'd been, laying his jacket down in a puddle for her to step on. Who would believe this about him today? Not his poor children, who loathed him.

He really had been lovely at one time. She supposed he still loved her, though the reasons had grown grubby and tarnished with age, and she was pretty sure that if she asked him why he'd married her, he wouldn't be able to tell her the truth anymore—he'd just smile slyly and say, "For your money, of course, Roz. For your money." Which at this point wasn't far from the truth, was it? Yes, she knew. Of course she did. She knew things, felt things—she was the antidote to Julian in every way, but she hadn't always needed to be.

"Let's put you back to bed," she whispered to Bronson, leading him into his room, where his brothers were sleeping soundly. *The smell of boys,* she thought, and she suddenly missed her own, although they were only a few feet away. Her sons. Had she let them down the way Julian had? She hated to think so. She'd done her best, after all. Once Bronson was safely tucked up under the covers, she leaned over and kissed him good night, noticing so much of Moses in his face, so much of Julian there as well. How had it come to this? Well, it had, and that's what she had to focus on now or else she'd be lost. "You sleep well," she whispered into his ear, but he was already asleep. The magic and mystery of children, to renounce the world the moment they shut their eyes. She wished for Julian's sake that he still possessed some childlike magic, yet he didn't. Slowly but surely, he'd turned into his nasty, spiteful mother right before her eyes, her mother-in-law who once told her that she was an uppity Yankee whom no one in the family could stand. That was Roz's world for a time, until she had Moses, who had nearly killed her in childbirth and had nearly died himself.

When he was sleepwalking, Julian was pliable, suggestible, and she now whispered into his ear that it was time for him to stop playing tennis, he'd beaten Ivan Lendl again, and he had to go to the locker room to speak to the reporters. For a moment, she thought he hadn't heard her, or that he was ignoring her, as he did when he was awake much of the time, but then he was putting down the pretend racket and wiping his brow with the imaginary towel she handed him (oh, how she indulged him, even in sleep).

It was closing in on 3:00 A.M., which meant she didn't have much time. Moses would be getting up soon to go to the gym, as he always did, except of course he wasn't planning to go to the gym this morning. Roz had sensed it during that unexpected, unfortunate argument in the guest room, the three of them turning on Julian like that, and it frightened her, because the last thing she wanted was for them to pay the price for her mistake. A plot was afoot, though she had no idea what it contained or how it would happen, or even if it would. This was her disaster, hers alone, and it was high time she took responsibility for it, for hadn't she had a hand in creating the monster and setting it loose upon them?

She had Dietrich to thank for cluing her in—Dietrich who'd told her on Thursday when they'd only just met about what Jacob had inadvertently revealed in the car. She suspected his confession had less to do with Julian, whom Dietrich hadn't even met, and everything to do with Jacob, whom he loved ferociously. Roz recognized love when she saw it. If Dietrich hadn't woken up and heard what he had, she might never have known about the plan—why they had all gathered in L.A. in the first place. How absolutely lovely it was of them to want to kill him for her. And how stupid and naive of them to think they would ever get away with it. She loved her kids dearly, but they were all rash and impulsive, and there was no telling how they might screw the whole thing up. Three of them meant three times the noise, six hands meant six times the mishaps, and thirty fingers meant thirty times the accidental smudges and leftover DNA. *Unless they wear gloves,* she thought, *but do they really have that kind of foresight?* They weren't murderers, these kids of hers, they were absolutely unprepared for such felonious acts. It would destroy them, their hearts and consciences. Hadn't Julian put them through enough already? She would not have his blood on their hands.

He floated down the stairs much more quickly than she did, and she lost sight of him in the dark. After making it down the last step, she paused to catch her breath, just for a moment. When she saw that the guest room door was open, she worried that he'd gone back to bed. She checked. He wasn't in bed or anywhere in the room. She grabbed her tank of oxygen, for all of this upstairs and downstairs and chasing after Julian business was tiring her out much faster than she'd imagined it would, and she wheeled it behind her out of the room to go look for him. But then she heard movement coming from the garage, a familiar rattling, and she knew, because he was nothing if not predictable, that he was off to mow the grass again.

She opened the front door and sure enough there he was, pushing the lawn mower through the yard. She was afraid he'd wake the entire household, so she went after him, but he was too fast for her. She was breathing heavily now, puffing for dear life, the sweat running down her scalp and into her eyes. When he rounded the corner of the house, Roz turned and headed toward the wall of glass, the oxygen tank bumping along the floor, clanging as she pushed through the door to meet Julian, this obstinate, bastard husband of hers. *For my brood,* she thought, and she charged down the steps and out into the yard, the sky teeming with the faint buzz of helicopters, six or seven of them hovering above the canyon, one of them right above them, so close that if she angled her face toward it, she could feel the rotation of wind on her cheeks and in her hair, cooling the sweat and fanning the flames of her certainty that this was the right thing, the only thing to do. She took careful steps toward Julian just as the yard lit up with errant light, the helicopter's spotlight, striking the blue water of the pool and the dark green of the grass, her husband in his faded pajamas and her in her nightgown and slippers, and then it fell on two coyotes in the far corner of the yard. They were ripping apart an opossum, a possible relative of the one Mo had scooped out of the pool. Well, it certainly wasn't Nieves, she thought, as Julian, perhaps sensing danger, angled the lawn mower away from them and toward her, where she was standing in the middle of the yard, but then the lawn mower hit one of the uneven flagstones by the pool and would go no farther, and Julian let his arms drop to his sides, the lawn mower giving out and going silent. The coyotes glanced up from their midnight snack, lifting their bloody snouts into the air, and oh, how she hoped they would lunge at Julian and rip his throat out, for then everything would end. But instead they turned their ragged faces to her, keenly aware of and able to sniff out weakness of any kind, these vagabond scavengers of the animal kingdom. When one of the coyotes took a step toward her, she took a step toward the pool, where Julian was standing over the water. She thought, *How perfect,* and she thought, *Jump,* although the water might wake him up and then where would she be?

Her heart was pounding with everything it had, but she was nearly there, nearly beside him, and when the coyote finally lunged, she went perfectly still and held her breath for as long as she could, which wasn't that long, but this seemed to do the trick, for the coyote swerved and pounced at Julian, knocking him into the water, the force of his fall sending up sprays of water against which Roz shut her eyes. When she opened them again, Julian was awake, splashing around in the pool and calling her name, the coyotes and the helicopter gone, the backyard once again shrouded in darkness.

"Julian, are you okay?" she asked, shuffling to the edge of the pool and looking down at him bobbing there, his glasses askew and one of the lenses gone, his pajamas bunched up around him, and the sight of him caused her to laugh.

"That's right, just go ahead and laugh," he said, rubbing at his face, still dazed. When he pulled his hand away, Roz saw something dark running down his chin and throat.

"Oh, Julian, I think you cut yourself," she said.

Julian brought his hand to his chin. "I must have scraped it on the bottom," he said, making his way to the side, toward her. "Well, don't just stand there. Go and get me a towel before I bleed to death." She looked down at this husband of hers, at the years of their lives together etched into his face and how the pajamas clung to his saggy flesh, and she couldn't stand the sight of him any more than he could stand the sight of her. "Roz, come on, I'm bleeding here," he said, touching the spot on his chin and wincing.

"Yes," she said but didn't move. "You are bleeding, Julian. It's true. It's probably the truest thing you've ever said."

"What? What are you talking about?" he asked, grabbing onto the side of the pool but lacking the strength to hoist himself up. "Just get me a towel, for crying out loud," he ordered.

"Get it yourself," she said.

He looked up at her, the blood trickling from the gash and falling daintily down his neck to land in the water. One drop, two, ten, twenty. "Are you looking forward to our cruise?" he asked suddenly. "I hope you are, Roz, because when we're out in the middle of the ocean, I'm going to throw your sorry, burdensome ass overboard."

"Yes, Julian, I figured," she said patiently. "It would have been a good plan except for one small detail."

"Oh, yeah, and what's that?" he asked belligerently.

"You're not coming with me," she said, drawing the oxygen tank up and over her head. And with all of her heart and with all of the might still left in her, she brought it down on him, listening to the crack of his skull and his nose, which smashed against the side of the pool. She was about to raise it above her head again but paused. She'd been Mrs. Julian Jacobson for so long she was unsure of how to be anyone else, especially around her children, who'd scold her for referring to herself like this and not simply as Rosalyn Jacobson, or just plain Roz. She gazed upon him with her tender smile and all the love she could still muster, because that's who she was—Mrs. Julian Jacobson, for forty-four years.

She looked down searchingly, expecting Julian to lift his head and scream at her. She didn't think she'd be able to bear another single word from this man who'd kept her in relative comfort this past year, ever since her life-changing diagnosis, yet who'd also stopped her from living what little life she had left. He'd been waiting for her to take her last breath. In the beginning, Julian's brand of love had been his own—neither demonstrative nor tender—but she'd thought as time went on, as they grew closer and she gave him children, that this might change. It hadn't. In fact, she never could have imagined what it would eventually become, perverting even that first year, the best year they had, in her recollection, and all but erasing the sweet intimacy that had come before. *Well, now it was way too late,* she thought, raising the tank above her head at last and bringing it down on Julian again, until his fingers slackened and he finally let go, sinking beneath the surface, the water blooming with his blood.

As Roz collapsed now on one of the lounge chairs, she surprised herself by crying. Rather than the tears of relief she had expected, however, she felt sorrow and anguish for the life she'd just taken, a life that had been wedded to hers for more than four decades. A life she had cared for and nurtured and, yes, had even loved. Julian was spinning in slow arcs through the water, his arms outstretched as if reaching for Roz, but Roz, lying back and shutting her eyes, was feeling more alive than she had in ages. The hairs on her arms stood on end, her skin prickled with goose bumps, and the cool night breeze slipped over her, whispering, *Julian is dead. Live your life.*

When she was breathing normally again, Roz got up and looked down into the pool, where Julian floated faceup, his nose smashed and pulpy, the pajama top puffed up with air like a life jacket. *Dead jacket is more like it,* she thought. *Gallows humor,* she thought. She kneeled down to clean his hair and skin from the bottom of the dented tank, rinsing it in the water that she herself had stolen from the neighbors next door—the pool hadn't actually featured in her plan; she'd filled it merely to thank Dietrich, who loved to swim, for alerting her to her kids' scheme, and besides, the Rothmans could go fuck themselves. No one mistreated her grandsons and got away with it.

If Julian had been beside her, he would have cackled at the irony, ribbing her, for she finally understood that if she'd been a better mother, she would not have let him mistreat her children as horribly as he had. And though she'd made an uneasy and, for the most part, a resigned peace with this some ages ago, she'd never understood his monstrous unwillingness to attach to his children, especially to Jacob. Although Roz understood she wasn't supposed to have a favorite, it was all too clear that she had preferred her youngest, though this was probably because he was the most vulnerable and most prone to Julian's ridicule, given his boyhood tendencies to dress up in her nightgowns and stomp around the house in her high heels. Things that made her chuckle but that offended Julian to the core, Julian who took these moments personally—acts of transgression, he called them. They disgusted him—disgusted him so much that at one point, when Jacob was seven, he cornered his terrified son and shouted at him, "You were born a boy. Start acting like one, for God's sake."

She might have loved all of her children equally, but she found she had the most in common with Jacob—that he was a homosexual made no difference. In fact, she might have learned a thing or two about men from him, she thought, and a memory came to her, bubbling to the surface as Julian's last and final breath bubbled to the surface: her very first PFLAG meeting, which she'd attended alone because Julian wouldn't hear of coming with her.

She had sat among other mothers and fathers in quiet discomfort, thinking that it would have been nice if Julian had at least shown some interest in coming with her, for Jacob's sake. But Julian wouldn't dream of it. "It's not an issue for me, Roz," he'd said, though of course it was. She'd seen how Julian behaved when Jacob came out to them, how Jacob had felt so terrorized by Julian's reaction that he'd flown back to L.A. that very day. How cruel Julian had been. Though several years had passed since then, she'd seen how Jacob's sexuality had become something else Julian could use against him, spurring interactions between them that she was forced to defend.

Granted, it was an odd memory for her to have at that moment, as her husband sank to the bottom of the pool, but in some way her recollection of the utter aloneness she'd felt at that meeting was indicative of her entire marriage and helped further justify her own feelings about killing him, feelings that went beyond trying to save her brood.

Without another thought, remorseful or otherwise, Roz went back into the house, where she rinsed off, changed into a fresh nightgown, then climbed back into bed, waiting for Dietrich to set the next part of their plan into motion. Following the Seder, when everyone was busy returning clothes to hangers and jewelry to boxes, she'd taken him into the downstairs guest room and briefed him.

She lay in the dark, gazing at Julian's side of the bed, the digital clock on the nightstand reading 3:23. A couple of minutes later, she heard the floor creak as Dietrich made his way downstairs "to go for a swim because he couldn't sleep." Dietrich tapped on the door and entered, whispering, "Mrs. Jacobson, it is I."

He was wearing a pair of swimming trunks, his long, lean body angular and defined, with a ridged stomach and a tiny trail of blond hair that led down into the elastic of his suit. Seeing him in his bathing suit recalled all the family trips they had taken down to the Gulf of Mexico when the kids were small and she wanted to ask him about his own family, if they'd ever taken trips and where, but it would have to wait for another time, for she needed to rise and feign surprise. "Yes," she said. "Now it's time to wake the house. Well, only my children."

"I will get up Jacob. He will do the rest," he said, and she thought he smiled.

"Thank you, Dietrich," she said.

She waited, hearing footsteps rushing past her door and whispers, loud and fretful, from Edith. She heard an enormous thud, as if something large and weighty had been dropped, and shushing and more heated whispers, a door being opened and shut. She got up and dressed, waiting for the alarm to go off, which it finally did—4:00 A.M. She shut it off and left the room, dragging her oxygen tank behind her into the den, where she met Jacob, Edith, and Moses, who'd just come in from outside. "You're all so thoughtful to get up to see us off," she said. "Is Dad loading the minivan?"

She hated to deceive her kids like this, but deceive them she must, for their own sake and for the sake of her grandsons. "Ma, it looks like . . . Daddy's had an accident," Edith started, glancing at her brothers and looking away. "He's dead, Ma. Daddy's dead."

"Dead? But, Thistle, that can't be. He was . . . we were asleep," she said.

"Come see for yourself," said Jacob, his voice strangely devoid of sorrow or cheer, simply uninflected and matter-of-fact, as if he were reporting the weather.

She followed her children into the garage and there he was, propped up in the backseat of Mo's Expedition, looking like he was waiting to be chauffeured around. "Why is he in there?" she asked, slightly unnerved. This was not part of the plan, which had involved capitalizing on the rampant rise of anti-Semitic attacks and a faceless (fabricated) assailant, whom Dietrich was supposed to have seen fleeing the scene, a bat in his hand. She could not have been any clearer with him that this was how it had to go, that it was the perfect explanation to a perfect crime. Nowhere in this foolproof plan of hers had she accounted for the possibility—the certainty, she now saw—that her children would bungle it all so spectacularly by moving the body. To her utter dismay, Dietrich had not been able to convince them that he'd seen someone about, they weren't buying his death-by-unknown-anti-Semite explanation, and now she had to deal with the fallout of his failure. "What have you three done?" How inept were her children that they couldn't even spin a narrative about a dead body served up to them on a silver platter? Had they all just simply panicked and taken leave of their imaginations? She couldn't blame Edith or Moses for such a response, but Jacob? Her youngest had imagination in spades. Perhaps this had just been too much for him and he had simply short-circuited. Whatever the case, she was horrified by what they'd done and how they'd managed to screw up her inspired work.

"We just wanted to give you some peace," Moses explained, clearly believing that one of his siblings had killed his father. *Well, if this is how it's going to play itself out, then so be it,* she thought. *Better that than having them turn on one another.* "We can take care of you. You can move out here now. We'll build you a cottage, and you can be closer to your grandsons. You'd like that, wouldn't you, Ma?"

"I'd like to know which one of you killed him," she said, deciding the only way to secure their silence was to make them all believe one of them had done it without the others' approval. They all began to bicker, hurling accusations, until Roz stepped in. "Well, I suppose it doesn't really matter now, does it? What's done is done," hoping this would be the end of it.

"We should have just left him where he was," Edith said plaintively. "We should have just listened to Dietrich; he saw someone running away. But no, 'Don't listen to the German,' you said, Mo. We shouldn't have listened to you! What Dietrich said would have worked. It would have made sense to the police. Now we have this, which doesn't make any sense at all."

Edith was clearly coming apart, and Roz turned to her and grabbed her hand. "Thistle, enough. You can't put him back. The only way is forward."

"Forward?" She sniffled.

Roz knew this day had been coming, though she'd had no idea how or when. She'd hoped for Julian to keel over from one of his heart attacks, like his dad and grandfather. No such luck, for the man was destined—had been destined—to outlive them all. It was just a happy coincidence that Dietrich had told her anything at all about what her children were up to.

"We're going on a road trip," she announced, turning to the freezer and opening it. She pulled out a bottle of vodka and handed it to Edith. "Fortify yourself, dear." Edith took a swig, then passed it to her brothers. "Now, listen to me. I'm still your mother and I still love you no matter what you've done, so Edith, you're going to take another few sips of vodka while you, Jacob and Moses, are going to move your father into the minivan. And you," she said to Dietrich, who'd just stepped into the garage, "are going to drive us because we are all going to drink until we get to where we're going. Pass the vodka back to your sister, Moses."

"And where's that, Ma? Where are we going?" Edith asked, taking the bottle and sipping from it as instructed. "Because Jacob has a crematorium on call."

"Edith," Jacob shouted.

"Oh, please, like it matters anymore if she knows," Edith replied. "So I guess you should call Clarence and tell him we're on our way," all of her features contorting and turning her face into one giant grimace. "Asses to asses, Daddy . . ." An old joke Julian used to make at the expense of one dead relative or another.

Jacob moved toward the door, but Roz interjected: "Darling, don't make that call just yet," as she had other plans for disposing of the body. "I'm pretty sure there are legal channels to go through before a cremation can happen."

"But, Clarence . . . ," Jacob stuttered.

"I think it would look quite suspicious if Clarence lit up the cemetery, let alone an oven, at this time of night, don't you? Does he still hate you, Jacob? Are you willing to find out? He might have alerted the cops already, and they might be waiting to pounce the moment you drive up with a body. You did kill his peacock, after all. Why would you think you could trust him?" It amazed her again how it was she'd raised such smart children only to have them not think any of this through or even understand that everything would have to be explained in what was becoming a very complicated lie.

Better to do it my way, she thought, sending her sons off on their appointed task, while she lingered in the garage with Edith, who leaned against the wall, eyes shut, and took an occasional sip from the bottle. Roz herself gazed at the tools—the hoe, the shears, the trowel—suspended on the wall, each of them corresponding to the ones Julian had back in Dallas, the very same arrangement. She smiled when she pictured the garage sale she was going to have. Or she might just keep it all, not for any sentimental reason but out of respect for Julian and his memory, for Julian loved his garden. Maybe she would keep pulling the weeds up for him; it was the least she could do.

After the boys got their father into the back of the minivan, Dietrich came around and helped her into the passenger seat. And then they were ready, Dietrich behind the wheel—he was worried about not having a license and having only just learned to drive, but Roz reassured him that it would be okay, saying that she trusted him to drive more than her own children in their shocked states. The three others got into the backseat. She turned the dial on her oxygen tank up one notch, from two to three, as they climbed into the hills of Malibu Canyon, the sky dark, the moon overhead dangling like a bare bulb, which she wanted to reach up and shatter.

Roz glanced in the rearview mirror every so often to catch sight of her three dumbfounded children. Edith sat between her brothers, her unfocused eyes opening and closing. Mo had his arms crossed on his chest, his long, shaggy black hair peppered with gray, although his beard, to her constant wonder and surprise, remained as black as the day he'd appeared with it onscreen two decades ago. Jacob told her it came out of a bottle. She'd laughed at his willingness to tattle on his brother even then and at Mo's ongoing vanity, which he had yet to outgrow. Jacob, too, was turning gray at the temples, and this made him look even more handsome, as distinguished as Julian had been at his age. All of them bore a profound resemblance to their father, who was strapped into the seat in the far back of the minivan, looking as if he were sound asleep, his head lolling forward every so often, then rolling back on his spongy neck. She half expected him to open his eyes and holler at her, but then the dead had but one directive—to stay dead.

Dietrich followed the directions of the state-of-the-art navigation system and drove with German precision, his hands gripping the wheel at twenty-two and fourteen, as Jacob had prescribed. He used the turn signal religiously and obeyed the rules of the road as if he'd been driving his entire life. It didn't surprise her that he'd been willing to carry out this task for them. *For Jacob,* she thought, correcting herself, and turned to Dietrich, who, she hoped, might still one day become her son-in-law.

"Thank you for . . . cooperating," she whispered.

"That's my pleasure," he said.

She imagined Jacob, intractable grammar Nazi that he was, scolding him for the mismanagement of the English language. *He definitely has some of his father in him,* she thought, an untamed, untrammeled part that he still needed to watch. It made her sad to think that Jacob—that any of her kids—had it in them to speak as roughly to their loved ones as Julian had spoken to them.

"My husband said some egregious things to you," she said. "I'm not sure he meant half of them."

"It's okay," Dietrich said, holding his eyes firmly on the tortuous, narrow road. "I am German. I think probably I am somewhat to blame. Jacob tells me I should be less of a *Besserwisser*—a know-it-all. I think probably I should not have come to Los Angeles but stayed behind in Berlin. It would have been easier on all of you if I were not present."

"Jacob's father is—was—a wisenheimer, too," she said. "My kids gravitate toward people with that quality as well. Better that than the alternative, someone like me. I'm not exactly the smartest person in the world. You heard my husband. If I'd seen a doctor sooner—"

"Mrs. Jacobson, please," he interrupted, "now is not the time to beat up yourself. It's possible your condition will improve, that it will go away on its own. Many medical distresses come and then go without fuss. They caught it, and you are dealing with it."

No, she thought, *you're wrong. Now is the perfect time to beat myself up because I know it's not improving. I know it's only getting worse.* "Please drop the formalities and call me Roz. Before I became Roz Jacobson, director of membership at the JCC and a damn good housewife to boot," she told him, "I was Rosalyn Overland, originally Oberlander, daughter of Ernie and Trudy, of Little

Neck, Long Island. My parents were immigrants. Viennese. In 1938. The Anschluss. I don't know if Jacob ever mentioned that."

"Yes, he did. As I'm sure he told you, we traveled by train to Wien for his birthday last year. It was an eye-soaping experience."

She laughed, coughing and grappling for breath, and reached down to increase the flow of oxygen. "Eye-opening," she corrected at last, because she simply could not help herself. Jacob might have inherited his temper and impatience from Julian, but he'd inherited a love of language and books from her. He was the best and worst of them.

"Yes, this is what I meant," Dietrich said, taking his eyes off the road to smile at her. "You are a warm, kind woman, very unlike my own mother. It is impossible for us Germans to disavow our mothers, although sometimes they should be disavowed."

"Dietrich, do you think you and Jacob will make it?" she asked, blurting out the words before she could stop herself. In the bathroom mirror at Mo's and Pandora's, she'd rehearsed the question, and now that she had asked it, she wished she could call it back. Contrary to what her husband claimed, she didn't like to pry.

Before he could respond, however, the navigation system announced, too loudly, "Exit 32 onto Las Virgenes Road," which Dietrich took. Edith poked her head into the front seat.

"Are we there yet?" she asked, transporting Roz to a different time, when the five of them—the kids not yet teenagers, she and Julian in their thirties—had made this same journey. They'd followed the Pacific Coast Highway, pausing along the way in Big Sur, San Luis Obispo, Solvang, Santa Barbara, then in Malibu. Julian refused to let Roz drive, which was fine by her, she remembered, gazing out the window at the still-shadowed Malibu Canyon. It felt odd to remember that trip now. She and Julian had stood at the edge of one of the cliffs at Point Dume, the sea spreading out like a pool of liquid silver under the smelting heat of the sun. The kids were down the road, using the bathroom and most likely squabbling over the array of snacks in the vending machine, while she was up there with this husband she loved, discussing if they shouldn't separate permanently.

Edith asked again and Roz said, "Not yet, Thistle," remembering the origin of her nickname and how looking upon her blossoming daughter had once unnerved Roz. She'd had a hard time not superimposing onto Edith her ideas of what Julian had been like as an unassuming, bespectacled boy. She didn't want to see this boy reflected in her daughter's face, reminding her of her own girlhood and all those thousands of delicate and indelicate steps that had led her to become Dr. Julian Jacobson's wife. Against nearly everyone's wishes—her mother, her friends, everyone except her father, who liked Julian as much as Roz did—she'd renounced her baptism, converted to Judaism (well, technically, back to Judaism), and married him.

Everyone but her father had been right, of course, but she wouldn't give them the satisfaction of knowing it. It was impossible to keep it from her kids, however, because they'd witnessed his brutal ferocity up close. Because Mo arrived first, he bore the worst of it, along with Roz herself. Her little Moses, who tried to act as her protector, her pint-sized, pigeon-toed son with his stutter and lazy eye, all thankfully corrected in time, though not before Julian had committed these weaknesses to memory and used them against him. How had she allowed it all to happen? History made fools out of them all, though mostly out of Roz, who had only recently begun to take stock of her circumstances. Better late than never, she supposed. A few months, the doctors told her, but that was a few months ago, so what did they know?

They'd been driving for about twenty minutes and had another twenty to go before they got to the bluff at Point Dume. "I only ask because I need to use the little girls' room, Ma," Edith said, though Roz suspected that she simply wanted out of the minivan and away from them. She was still and forever Daddy's little girl, after all, and had been the most outspoken of the three the last time they were all at Point Dume, after they had all climbed back into the station wagon and Julian explained that once they got back to Dallas, he was moving out.

"Your mother thinks it's best," he'd said, pulling out of the scenic overlook.

Even then, he refused to take any responsibility for himself, Roz thought. At the time, though, she'd thought she'd finally taken her shot at sparing her children and herself even more grief, though she hadn't been brave enough to go through with it in the end. Several years later she would try once more, with an equal lack of success. Her inability to leave the man kept surprising her, as if her attachment to him was a separate entity with separate wants and desires and not a part of her—*how different our lives might have been if I had been able to control it,* she murmured.

"What? What was that, Ma?" Edith asked, and for the first time that morning, Roz registered fear in her daughter's voice.

"You think I'm stupid, dear?" she asked, eyeing Dietrich, who she imagined gave her a conspiratorial grin out of the side of his mouth. "You must think I'm a monster. Well, maybe I am. But I can't possibly let you out of the car just yet."

"You can justify this any way you want to, Ma, but this thing we're doing is just plain uncivilized. I know what kind of man he is—was," her daughter said. "Only weren't you always telling us to blame his behavior on the way he was raised? Blame the environment, not the individual, you said. Besides, he was my father and now his skin's all blue and he's sloshing around in wet pajamas, freezing to death. It's indecent. You could at least turn on the heat back here, Ma. Dietrich, make her turn on the heat."

Roz couldn't help herself and laughed quietly, wheezing for breath. She could feel her heartbeat, a terrible sign, a thick, boisterous thwack against her rib cage. "I'll humor you," she said, removing the oxygen from her nose to turn around in her seat and address her dead husband directly. "Julian, your daughter thinks that you're freezing to death. I'd like to point out the black humor in her use of the phrase, and ask you if it's true: Are you freezing to death? You can tell me, but you'll have to speak up," then she laughed again, which rousted the others from sleep, though not Julian, who remained *quite dead to the world,* she thought, mirthful. *Oh, what pun I'm having.*

"Oh, Ma, for shame," Edith scolded.

"What? What's going on?" Mo asked with a start. "I dreamed I found where the old man stashed the Afikoman, and every last one of those Krugerrands was mine."

"Those coins belonged to my parents," Roz said. How utterly like Julian to turn a happy, innocent game into a blood sport, pitting his kids and grandkids one against the other. This year he'd even outdone himself by hiding it on his own person, which was, even for Julian, beyond the pale. "He had no right to them. No right at all," she said indignantly. "When we get home, I'll divide the coins up."

"Isn't it a little late now to find your inner feminist, Ma?" Edith asked. "I mean, no offense, but it seems pretty silly to cry over spilled doubloons since you spent your entire life letting him hold your money hostage."

"Edith, how about showing some compassion, huh?" Jacob said.

"Oh, you mean like she's showing Daddy? Like she's showing any of us?" she asked. "I cannot believe I'm a party to this. I teach ethics, for fuck's sake! They're going to chuck me out of the academy. But we can make it right if we just turn the van around, go back to Mo's, and call the authorities. What do you say, y'all?" Edith's adopted Georgian brogue deepened whenever she was nervous.

"Now, Jacob, your sister has a good point," Roz said. "I don't want any of you to think I'd ever stop loving you or hold a grudge if you didn't want to help." She had expected their loyalty and cooperation but realized that making them accessories after the fact only intensified her sense of wrongdoing.

For a second, the air in the car went stiff and silent, as they descended the steep, winding hills of the canyon, Roz's ears popping from the change in altitude. Jacob leaned forward and set his hands on Dietrich's shoulders, kneading them gently. The sight of her son being so open with his sexuality had an odd, calming effect on her, and she shut her eyes, imagining Julian's fingers on her own shoulders. She could not recall a single moment in her marriage when Julian had reached out spontaneously to stroke her cheek or grab her hand or tousle her hair. Physical affection hadn't been in his DNA, and she'd come to terms with that, because she'd had her kids, most of all Jacob, to love her.

After that moment on the cliff, when they'd made their decision and then unmade it, Roz stopped examining the life she might have led without Julian and instead began to live the life she had chosen with him. The decision had really been made years ago at her mikveh, her Jewish cleansing ritual, when she'd been reborn as Rifka, a testament to her revived covenant to Adonai and His reclamation of her, as the rabbi who supervised her conversion explained.

As Julian liked to remind her, she was already a Jew because her mother had been born one, so it was an utter waste of time to go through the hoopla of converting back. But it wasn't for herself that she'd embraced the conversion, attending Torah study three nights a week and brushing up on the trials, intifadas, inquisitions, and tribulations of the Jewish people—all these rituals and rites of passage she should have already been familiar with but wasn't because she'd been brought up a staunch Catholic, the religion forced upon her by her fearful immigrant parents. No, Roz converted back for Julian, because she wanted to be a good Jewish wife to him and a good Jewish mother to his children, which was why she'd gone to such lengths to renounce Christ. And in the beginning, she attended services at the synagogue with a fervent dedication and really got into Shabbat, the rituals surrounding that most holy of days. Yet like everything else, Julian let her know where she faltered and when, how she kept bungling the blessings over the candles, how her Hebrew was rudimentary, until she felt as if she'd converted for nothing—she felt fraudulent, not Jewish enough for Julian or for her in-laws, who looked down on her, and certainly an absolute failure in her mother's eyes—"What rational, thinking person," Trudy Overland had asked her on her wedding day, "chooses Judaism willingly? Not even for love would I have done what you did, Rosalyn. And you'll find that Julian Jacobson will make the worst kind of husband because he is the worst kind of Jew."

Flabbergasted, Roz decided never to speak to her again. She told Julian that her mother was nothing more than a self-hating Jewess masquerading as a disillusioned, bitter hausfrau. She omitted what her mother had said about him because why give her the satisfaction? That Trudy disliked him because he was a Jew made about as much sense as her fervent belief that her German neighbors were Nazis. All of it preying on Gertrude Oberlander's imagination until she ended up drowning herself in the duck pond at the end of the block.

Roz heard heated murmurs in the backseat, Edith's beseeching recriminations and her brothers' replies, all of it inaudible to Roz, who detected mutiny and decided to deal with it justly and swiftly, or else lose the fight or, even worse, her children. She was about to give the rebellious trio a much-needed pep talk about loyalty when the front seat filled with humming. Soft and gentle, then increasingly loud, and she understood then what Dietrich was trying to do.

At first, Roz was outraged that he would hum what sounded like the German national anthem. Though far less vituperative than Julian on the subject of the Holocaust, Roz still took offense with Dietrich's tasteless choice in tunes until she realized what it was and looked upon this blond-haired, blue-eyed young man differently. Julian had loathed Dietrich's Aryan looks, going so far as to ask him during a lull in the Seder if he'd packed his Hugo Boss, a crass reference to the supplier of the uniforms of the SS and the Hitler Youth, a query that seemed to cause great consternation among her three children and resulted in a breathtaking sequence of dirty looks and silent exchanges between them, though she couldn't figure out why they'd taken such exception to this particular offense of Julian's.

Roz didn't laugh along with Julian, yet she also did nothing to rebuke him. She had learned long ago that it was better to let Julian have his bit of fun than to interfere.

Looking at Dietrich sitting there with his back straight and his fingers still gripped around the wheel precisely, she cringed at the uncomfortable memory. For years, she'd been complicit, had said and done nothing to protest against Julian—*alas,* she thought, *Edith was right*—and for the first time since she'd hovered at the edge of the pool and looked down at the body of her husband spinning in slow motion through the bloody water, she understood that she herself might have been the agent of her own demise, her own angel of death. How much longer could her body have borne the swallowing down of regret, disgrace, shame, rage, and hostility? Of course it had broken down under the weight of her silence.

She glanced out the window at the rushing blur of inky-black hills, while Jacob jumped in at the beginning of the second verse and then Mo came around and joined them in the third. It took Edith until the sixth, yet there she was, singing along with her brothers and Dietrich, who led them in this rendition of "Dayenu," which was exactly what she'd had—enough—when she'd begun to hatch her plan after Dietrich's confession on Thursday.

"'Day-Day-yenu, Day-Day-yenu, Day-Day-yenu, Dayenu Day-enu,'" they sang, their voices filling every crevice of the minivan and crowding out the unnatural darkness that had seeped out of the far backseat. She had tried her best to be a good, caring wife and a good mother to his children. She had left her childhood home, family, and friends behind in New York and had followed him down to Dallas, because she knew without having to be told that that's what you did for the man you loved—*like Jacob had done for Dietrich,* she thought, listening to them harmonizing, Jacob a tenor, Dietrich a baritone. So what if they sang off key; at least they were singing.

She and Julian never sang. They had sex twice a month, then not at all these last dozen or so years. They took walks around their planned and gated community. They met friends for dinner and went to the movies. Mostly he chose, just as he chose where they went on vacation, how long they would stay, and how they would get there. The idea that she would live out the rest of her days alone in that gigantic house on Christopher Columbus Court suddenly overcame her. If her children had been listening, they might have misconstrued her nervous giggles for sobbing. She kept her face turned to the glass, humming to herself, *Ding, dong, the kvetch is dead.*

While the kids went on singing and the eastern sky gradually undid the dark, Roz increased the dial on her portable tank another notch, drinking in the rush of oxygen, which made her giddy, as if she'd swallowed a magnum of champagne. She was drunk, twirling around with Julian at Edith's bat-mitzvah reception, the last time they ever danced together, and then she was sneaking off to meet Doug Butterfield behind the bema, where, among the black choir robes, they held hands and kissed like the star-crossed high-school sweethearts they had once been. No one suspected a thing. A second chance, a way to redeem her failure after Point Dume, to untangle from Julian, to resettle in her beloved New York City, to renounce Judaism. She could divorce Julian and remove her children from his house, from the arid wasteland that was Dallas, and return herself and them to civilization, the sumptuous offerings of Manhattan: the Metropolitan Museum of Art, the Frick, the New York Public Library, Lincoln Center, the Metropolitan Opera, Walter Reade Theater, and even the streets themselves, which teemed with life. She would make it up to them for having had to endure the unbridled tyranny of Julian Jacobson and detoxify them by exposing them to New York—now wouldn't that be something.

The next day, the Sunday of Edith's bat-mitzvah weekend, Julian and Roz were to hold a brunch at their house for the out-of-town guests and relatives. Well before dawn, Roz woke the kids, told them to get dressed, then hurried them to the car, Edith sniffling, whining, and asking where they were going without Daddy. "On a trip," Roz said. "You'd like that, wouldn't you?"

"No," the girl snapped, then fell quickly back to sleep. Mo sat in the passenger seat, sullen and contemptuous of Roz for having interrupted his sleep—he was like his father that way, not a morning person at all—while Jacob, in back of Mo, wet his finger and drew on the window. She glanced in the rearview mirror to see what he was writing and froze, because it looked as if he'd spelled out D-O-U-G, though when she blinked, she saw he'd formed a word even more eerie and surprising: D-E-A-T-H.

"Jacob, are you all right, honey?" she asked soothingly.

"Oh, yeah, I'm swell. I was just thinking that what you're doing will kill him."

She understood what he meant—that this would ruin Julian, that it would take him a long time to get over it, if he ever did. But hadn't she heard the faintest whisper of hope in his voice when he'd said it? "Jacob, honey, you don't actually want your father to die, do you?" she asked tentatively.

"What you're doing is good, Mom. It's a good plan," he said. "It's not like he doesn't deserve it. The only problem is, well, I guess it might not kill him. A few months from now, he'll just find another woman to marry, then she'll give him a new family to torture. So it's a good plan, but it's also a faulty one. If you want to kill him, I think there are better ways to go about it." Leave it to Jacob, her death-obsessed, precocious boy, to say what was on his mind and, if she were honest, what was on her mind as well, as chilling and disturbing as it might have been. "I mean, there are ways to go about torturing him the way he—"

"Jacob, stop," Mo said.

"—tortures us. You could, for example, leave him for another man. I mean, that's what I would do," and he pressed himself against the front seat, his hot, sour breath in her ear. "That's what you're doing, isn't it? So who is he, Mom? Is it that guy at Edith's reception, the big one who looked like a fat Ken doll?"

The light changed to green, but Roz couldn't make the car go. She sat there, staring with hard, glassy eyes at the light, which turned amber, then red again. She never could put anything over on Jacob, who knew her better than anyone, including her own husband. There it was again, that tremendous bond of theirs, which even Roz occasionally found unnatural. Jacob knew she was being crushed under the profound, indelicate weight of her marriage, as a woman, a wife, a mother. She had to get out from under it or it was going to pulverize her. Jacob had been begging her for a while to leave Julian's house and never look back.

"Who? Huh? What are you babbling about, Jacob? Mom's not leaving Dad for a guy named Ken. Are you, Mom?" Mo asked, absolutely unable to believe that she, Roz, would ever do such a thing. Moses, her eldest, her dumb jock of a son, did not possess an ounce of Jacob's self-awareness. Another reason she had to leave. It pained her to think he might become more like his father with age and that under Julian's tutelage she could turn around one day to find Moses an equally unseeing, narcissistic, and supercilious man. She feared he was becoming a bully. And just to prove her right, he reached back and smacked Jacob in the face with the open palm of his hand.

Jacob howled, waking Edith, who screamed, "Mom, Jacob's nose is gushing," while Roz pressed down on the gas, and they shot through the light.

By the time Roz pulled the car into the IHOP parking lot down the road, Jacob's chin was dripping with blood, soaking the neck of his T-shirt. Now they had to flee for sure or else face Julian's wrath once he laid eyes on his youngest. *There is no way I can manage it, any of it,* she thought, settling Mo and Edith into a booth—"She'll have a sugar-free hot chocolate with sugar-free marshmallows, if there is such a thing," she said to the waiter, who looked upon her with pity. She gave him an awkward half-grin, then led Jacob into the women's toilet to take care of what she feared was a broken nose.

After inspecting it, she determined the nose was merely bruised— she knew broken when she saw it thanks to football- and basketball-playing Mo, whose nose had already been reset twice in his fourteen years. The bridge was swollen, the skin throbbing, yet Jacob was far calmer than she was, even as he demanded that she make Mo apologize for his brutality and then turned the scrutiny on himself.

"I'm sorry, Mom, I was being disrespectful to you," he said. She found his restraint unnerving. In the mirror, she caught sight of herself, her wide, sleepless eyes, the unmade-up face with its new lines that she was sure had not been there yesterday, and shockingly, streaks of her son's blood in her long flaxen hair.

She rinsed out her hair—she had no memory of running her fingers through it, but then it wasn't every day she wound up with blood on her hands. She looked at the dizzying profusion of blood that had run down his chin and neck, sopping his T-shirt. The sight of him conjured in her a fierce resentment toward her eldest, but she tamped it down and told herself to let it go because this wasn't her battle, it was Jacob's. Still, she wondered if it'd go down in that little notebook of his: *May 26, 1994, Mo bashed me in the nose with the palm of his hand. I'm sure he'll never apologize.*

Roz cleaned him up as best she could, using the last of the paper towels in the dispenser, dabbing gently at his nose, the blood caking his nostrils. She was surprised he didn't balk when she moved down his long, lean torso, wiping away the dark speckles. He remained his usual pliant self, bending and bowing to her every command without pother or back talk. It was the sort of moment between them that imbued her with the hope of a renewed intimacy between mother and son, a return of the casual comfort that they hadn't had since he'd become more aware of his body. If it'd been either of the other two, she would have had a rebellion on her hands, but not with Jacob, whose concern was the only thing that stood between her and the oblivion of her marriage. She'd been so lonely for so long and here, finally, was an ally, a vital piece of herself that had gone missing ages ago and that had been made flesh again in Jacob.

Roz stood facing him. She felt oddly stung, not by Jacob but by time itself, that her younger son was growing so quickly. "You'll tower over all of us soon enough," she said, her voice warbling. She swept the curls of golden-brown hair off his forehead. She turned and caught his reflection in the mirror and in that moment he looked exactly like his father, though a softer, gentler, and far kinder version of him, a version she'd kept hoping would reappear one day, if she could somehow do everything right. Here, standing before her, was Julian and not Julian, a spitting image of the man she married when that man was a boy and also a complete unlikeness, so different from his father in every way that she wondered where he'd come from—far too sensitive, far too perceptive and thoughtful for his age. And he loved her with an all-encompassing love that never once failed to eclipse a bad day or another fight with Julian, because she always had Jacob just down the hall, ready to hold her and she him, to comfort him against the bullies at school and the bully at home. She knew how deep his grievances against Julian ran, thanks to that small black notebook of his, which she'd come across by accident while changing his sheets and pillowcases one morning and had been unable to resist peeking into. She'd flipped through the pages without reading any of what he'd written, then replaced the notebook and left the room, though she hadn't stopped thinking about her discovery all day.

Still, her curiosity to see what he'd written, if any of it pertained to her, became intolerable, a thirst she had to slake. Just a tiny peek, that's all she was going to take, so she stole back into his room the next day, slid out the notebook, this record he kept of the wrongs committed against him, and peeked, finding it full of rotten, hard-to-swallow fragments and sentences filled with sour complaints and dusted with a bitter, powdery perception. She wanted to go to Jacob, to talk about it with him, but if she did, she knew he'd never forgive her and that she'd forfeit his trust. And she'd never be able to live with that.

Roz sat with it for a couple of days, vacillating between confiding in one of her friends, another mother with a son Jacob's age, who, she thought, might explain to her why he was keeping such a horrible, detailed record, and forgetting she'd ever read it, much less stumbled upon it in the first place. She felt a driving sense of duty to understand Jacob better and what exactly this notebook was. What made him come home every day from school, disappear into his room, and jot down things, in her opinion, that were nothing more than everyday eventualities best ignored, as much a part of life's rich pageant as the joy of winning the lottery or the misery of going bankrupt? Life was one long glorious miscalculation, she might have told him, a series of teachable moments that often resulted in a desire to do it all differently, though ending up in the same place, clutching the same soggy bag of drowned kittens—ultimately, life was random, nonsensical, and chiefly unfair. Roz knew what a total waste of energy it was to hold on to the unpleasant, to plaster the rooms of one's life with the ugly, contemptible faces of those who wished and did us harm, and worst of all, to tally every slight, both major and minor, we suffered along the way.

" 'My Manifest of Meanness.' That's what he called it," Roz said into the silence that fell after the last verse of the song, turning and speaking directly to Dietrich. "Did Jacob ever tell you about it, the catalog of every mean thing anyone ever did or said to him? Most of the entries—is that what you call them, dear?—he devoted to his dad, naturally, because his dad was a very mean man. But can you believe? Page after page of hurt and injustice going back years, some of it spectacular reading, I must say."

"You . . . read my journal," Jacob said, his voice a squeak from the backseat. She immediately regretted having said anything, for she now understood the severity of what she'd done. "And now you're discussing it before a live studio audience? Great. Just fucking great. Like I want to revisit it—"

"But don't you see, Jacob, that you are letting the world know anyway," interjected Dietrich, whom she couldn't have adored more than at that moment.

"Your plays, dear," she said. "I'm sorry I read it, but I'm even sorrier for the way you felt. I wish you could have just come to me," although in saying it, she wondered how she might have reacted if he had. "And before you ask—no, I never told your father about any of it. It would have only hurt him," she said, taking a tiny breath before continuing. "As you kids know, I spent my entire life doing my best to shield you from him and him from you. And it's killed me. So much hatred among you and there I was, trapped in the middle of it. So yes, something was bound to give, but don't think for a second this is how I wanted to spend Passover with my five grandsons or that I'm the least bit proud of any of this." *There he was,* she thought angrily, *lying in the pool, like a drowned gift horse, and instead of listening to Dietrich, you just had to look into its mouth. And here we are. I gave you the perfect setup and you blew it. You blew it!* She took shallow sucks of air; for the first time since they had strapped Julian into the far backseat and headed for Point Dume, she wondered if Edith might not be right. They could still turn around and go back to Mo and Pandora's. There was still time to undo this and make things over—and if not over, at least more palatable. She could let her kids scatter as they had the moment they reached adulthood, leaving her behind. She'd resented them for it, if she were being honest, because they continued to be the best and worst parts of her, the best and worst parts of Julian.

Dietrich eventually left the road and angled the minivan into a deserted rest area off the main thoroughfare with an extraordinary view of the Pacific Ocean. The navigation system announced, "You have arrived at your destination," and kept announcing it until Edith barked at Dietrich to shut it off.

The moment Dietrich came to a stop, Edith leaped out, grumbling curse words under her breath and clutching herself as she walked. She hurried for the bathrooms, a thatched, faux-wood-sided hut replete with a chimney, which resembled a quaint English cottage, a vast improvement on the old structure. The boys leaped out as well, clearing the van and running in circles, regressing momentarily to adolescence, drunk and loopy from the morning's events. Dietrich shut off the engine, then climbed out, walking around to the passenger side to help Roz out.

"You're a good boy. Jacob had better appreciate you. If he doesn't, you let me know, and I'll disinherit him," she joked.

"Vould you like me to grab ze vheelchair, Mrs. Yacobson?" Dietrich asked. *What was that? Did I just hear him correctly?* she wondered. Had his German accent become more noticeable and far more pronounced outside? She supposed he might be delirious with fatigue, his eyes confusing the rolling hills of Malibu for his native Bavaria and sending misguided signals to the speech center in his brain. But no, he was smiling, a big, toothy smile that showed off all of his small, stained teeth. It was only a joke, but my heavens, the accent was enough to scare the breath out of her, recalling her parents and how stringently they'd adhered to removing any trace of German in their voices, forbidding German in the house, especially in front of Roz, whom they were only protecting, they'd said later when she asked. And she damn well asked later, after she'd called off the wedding to Doug Butterfield because she'd met this man, Julian Bernard Jacobson, a PhD candidate in respiratory physiology—"The definition's not that hard to remember, people: the study and function of the lungs," Julian used to holler at anyone who was curious. And he finished her sentences and he didn't hide or sugarcoat things, and he'd asked her if she was Jewish, had a hunch she might be—he was the reason she was there in Little Neck, confronting her parents about their past and pleading with them to leave nothing out.

"Are we Jewish?" she'd asked them.

"What does it matter?" Trudy responded.

"It matters," she said, "because I've fallen in love with a Jewish man."

"*Mein Gott,*" said Trudy, the only time she'd ever spoken German and invoked God in front of Roz.

"We're born Jewish, but if anything, we're agnostics," Ernie said.

"We are? But you raised me a Catholic?" Roz asked. "I drank the blood and ate the body of Christ every single Sunday."

"It was a different time," Ernie said.

"We're born-again atheists," Trudy had said, correcting her husband. "Tell your Jewish boyfriend that the next time he asks."

Now she heard Dietrich ask again about the wheelchair. "It won't be necessary," she told him, taking a step, then another, testing the ground, testing her own stamina. She took what felt like belated breaths, as if her lungs were out of sync with the rest of her body, yet found if she gulped the air as deeply as she could, she just might be able to make it without having to resort to the chair or the tank. She'd been preparing for this—okay, not for this precisely, not the removal of Julian's body from the minivan, but for something just as momentous: the triplets' upcoming bar mitzvahs. She wanted to walk up the steps of the pulpit and stand together with her entire family. For months now, she'd been attending physical therapy— well, when Julian would let her, for it exhausted and winded her and he didn't want her to tire herself out. She'd fought him, and it was proving to have been worth it, as she arrived at the back of the minivan. She peered inside the back window, the overhead throwing off a diffuse spray of light just enough for her to make out her dead husband, whose head had fallen forward on his neck. Seated in this position, the back of Julian's head was on full display, and Roz had an unobstructed view into his brain cavity; a large chunk of skull was missing.

"If only I had my melon baller," she said as her kids reappeared, knitting themselves around her.

"Ma! Don't be ghoulish!" Edith said, though she was pretty sure that at least Mo had laughed. Undone by the sight of her daddy in the backseat, Edith scolded her: "Daddy might be beneath your contempt, but he was still a person. He gave the three of us life, after all."

"And you all plotted and schemed to take it away," she said, turning to face them. "Eventually, I would like to know which one of you suggested it, though I already have my suspicions, Jacob, or am I barking up the wrong tree?"

"What makes you think it was Jacob?" Mo asked from inside his hoodie, which softened his voice into a muffled echo. "Maybe one of your other children loves you as much as Jacob? Is it out of the realm of possibility that Edith or I wanted to do something nice for you? No, I suppose it had to be Jacob, your favorite. I mean, am I wrong?"

"Fuck you, Mo," Jacob hissed. "Take it back."

"Yeah, right. Dream on, little dreamer," Mo said, like a parrot of Julian with the same scoff and dismissal in his voice.

"Stop it. You just stop it right now," Edith interjected, banging a fist on the minivan and sending the car alarm squawking, the lights flashing on and off. Here, out in the wide open, the sound traveled everywhere, expanding and intensifying, rippling in still louder and shriller arcs with each passing second.

Mo tried the driver-side door, but it was locked, as all the doors were locked. "Where's the German?" he asked. "Find your damn German, Jacob." And Jacob departed, searching for Dietrich, who seemed to have vanished. "Did he tell you about the guy's grandparents? They were fucking Nazis in charge of confiscating works by Jewish artists. Degenerate art, they called it. Fucking Germans."

"Yes, Mo, I'm well aware of that," Roz said, although she wasn't. A fast and furious chill descended upon her and raised the hair on her arms, though it originated not from the chilly air but from the icy breath of the past, which contained within it a slide show of her parents fleeing Vienna on a night train bound for Istanbul and carrying only what they could take with them—a few articles of clothing, a photograph or two, and her mother's prized and priceless possession, an original self-portrait by the Austrian master Egon Schiele, the only painting that fit inside Gertrude's suitcase.

Jacob returned with the keys and shut off the minivan's alarm, saying, "He's taking a nap on a picnic table."

It was at that moment that Roz knew exactly how all of this had to go. She also knew that, judging by the sky, they didn't have much time left, so it had to be now or never. "Jacob, you're going to pull the van around the cottage and back it up to the picnic table," she said. "Then, Mo, you and your brother are going to lift your father out and lay him down, while your sister—where is Thistle?"

Jacob pointed at the vending machines, and sure enough there she was, a dim aura cast on her consternated face. She was just standing there, swaying a bit in place, as if she were six years old again and wondering why her bag of chips hadn't fallen. Roz shuffled toward her daughter, her breathing shallow but steady, shooing her boys off to their tasks. Once she got to Edith, Roz reached into her pocket and pulled out a ten-dollar bill. "Go crazy, Thistle," she said, sliding the bill into her daughter's hand.

Edith dropped the bill to the ground, while Roz ran a hand through her tangled red curls, smoothing the tangles out as best she could. She was tired, Roz knew, and aggrieved and in shock, but now was not the time to turn her fiercely ethical mind against her family. Edith backed away from her and kneeled down, running her hands along the dirt. When she stood up again, she had a stone in her hand, a flat stone the size of a baby's fist, and she took a couple of steps toward the vending machine, wound up her arm, and sent the stone through the glass, shattering it. "I've been dreaming of that for decades," Edith said, triumphant, reaching past the shards of glass and pulling out bag after bag of chips and pretzels and those awful neon-orange cheese crackers.

Roz took her by the elbow and led her around the side of the cottage, where the boys had laid Julian out on the picnic table, just as she'd asked them to do. "While you've been dreaming of that, Thistle, I have been dreaming of this," Roz said, standing over her husband. She dialed up the oxygen on the tank while Dietrich walked around the minivan and climbed in. For a moment, Roz was worried that he would take off and strand them. "Jacob, go see what he's up to," she directed, but before Jacob could take his first step, the air around them shifted, filling with what sounded like a string quartet.

Ah, how lovely, Roz thought, studying Julian's left hand, on which he wore his gold wedding band. She lifted the hand up, his arm already stiffening, his fingers swelling, and knew she'd never get the ring off. Her children stood near her, just out of the circumference of their dead father, as if they feared he might awaken and pick up where he'd left off, screaming at and insulting them. They had lived in Julian's shadow their entire lives, and it would take some time before any of them got used to living in the light. She feared that without Julian to hate, her children might turn their hatred on one another, or inward, or toward her. She wondered if in killing Julian she'd opened herself up to this, for she had not been innocent, she had done her part in fueling the anger that burned brightly in all of them. If she'd only left him when she'd had the chance—well, as Julian liked to say, *If if were a skiff, we'd go boating.*

"I think I might need some help," Roz said, struggling with Julian's ring. But then out of the shadows came Dietrich and he reached out and bent the finger back and broke it, the sound reverberating wildly in Roz's ears. He spit on the finger, then slid the ring off and handed it to her. How she'd longed for this over the years, to be free of him. Julian had never deserved the love she'd given him, she saw that now as she undressed him, his skin as white as the porcelain toilet over which Roz had spent every one of her pregnancies—the most horrid morning sickness of anyone she knew. And Julian had made fun of her for that, saying she wasn't woman enough to carry his children. He'd said vicious things and still she'd stayed. He said things, then showed up with flowers. He said things, then took her to a fancy dinner and later bought her a new house and a new car and everything she'd ever wanted, all of this to make up for the fact that he did not have it within him to say that he was sorry. She'd only once, ever, heard him say it. *And even that had been under serious duress.* Yet that, too, no longer mattered, for she had her children and her grandchildren, and what was left of her health. She would not tarry in mourning Julian Jacobson. She finally saw just how irredeemable he truly was, a black hole into which he sucked all light and luck and love, manipulating them into giving it to him when he had no love to give in return. A vacancy. An absence. That's all he'd ever been.

"Well, here we are," she said, turning to her kids, who were standing around the picnic table gazing down at the body of their dad. In his hand, Moses held the chamois, which was dripping with water and which traveled with Julian everywhere they went, and Moses began to run it over his dad, washing him, a ritual that went back thousands of years—the cleansing of a Jewish corpse. Each of her kids took a turn, even Jacob, who washed his dad's feet, so lovingly and so gently that Roz felt prouder of him then than she ever had.

"Would anyone like to say anything?" she asked, staring down at this husband of hers, at the blood-soaked pajamas she held in her hands. No one had any words to say. *A pity,* she thought, *yet what could they say about him that hadn't been said already?* Then they were all hoisting him off the table, even Edith, who said quietly, "I'm sorry, Daddy." Roz knew that her daughter would have the hardest time of it, that it would take her years to get over her grief, but that one day she would. One day she'd wake up and see that this was necessary, exactly how it had to happen, and that she was better off without him.

They came to the edge of the bluff, the sea pounding at the rocks below, and Roz counted to three—and then they released him, tossing him unceremoniously over the side. They did not watch him fall, nor did they hear a splash. After it was over, her kids wandered away, toward the bathrooms to clean themselves up, saying nothing. Only Roz remained. She took one quick look over the edge, just to make sure, for she was worried that with Julian's luck he'd awakened and was clinging to a vine or a tree root and at any moment would be yelling at her to pull him up. But Julian was gone, and there was nothing but the sea and the rocks and the fish, which she hoped were already feasting on him. *You had to be good for something,* she thought, joining her brood in the bathroom, where she rinsed herself off, then they all headed back to the minivan, where Roz instructed Jacob to grab his father's fishing gear—his prized rod and reel, his tackle box—from out of the back, then toss it all over the side of the cliff, which he did, returning to the minivan with an eerie, gleeful smile on his face, the same smile she remembered him wearing when she and Julian announced all those years ago, and in the very same spot, that they were divorcing.

I T ALL WENT ACCORDING TO PLAN, WELL, TO THE AMENDED plan, the one upon which they all agreed on the drive back to Von Trapp Lane. Mo put on an Oscar-worthy performance for the police officer they called, distraught as he recounted his predawn fishing trip with his dad, in which the two waded out into the surf and fished for a couple of placid hours before they were ambushed by a group of bat-wielding, neo-Nazi skinheads who rushed into the surf and surrounded Julian, taunting and terrorizing him. His dad, he said, had begged him to flee to the safety of the shore. He'd accidentally dropped his phone in the process, which was why he hadn't been able to call for help immediately. He'd stood there, watching helplessly as Julian was hit in the head with a bat. He'd be hearing that sound forever, Mo said, the echoing crunch of his dad's skull caving in. Then his dad disappeared under the waves, good as dead, he imagined, and the group then turned in unison and headed for him. He'd raced to the car, climbed in, and sped away.

Roz pointed out the graffiti on the door of the house, leading the officer to draw his own connection between last night's crime and that morning's, which claimed the life of her children's dear, beloved father and her own dear, beloved husband. Edith, wretched with shame, took to her bed and remained there, taking personal leave from Emory, and Jacob and Dietrich changed their tickets, not once but twice, Jacob more than ready to go but Dietrich reassuring him that he'd regret it if they did. For two weeks, Roz, the dowager, came to grips with her widowhood and began to plan a new future, one that did not in any way resemble the one she'd been facing when Julian was still alive and they were heading off on a cruise, during which, she was fairly certain, he'd been planning to kill her. And so it happened that on the fifteenth day after Julian's death, Roz awoke and decided it was time, well, to decide.

She could stay indefinitely, or she could leave and go home. She could get on a plane and fly to Paris or sit in the sun in the backyard for hours on end. Her days were her own again and for the first time in forty-four years, she had absolutely no idea how she was going to fill them up. This did not frighten her. What frightened her was how little she missed Julian, yet how much his death meant to her. She sat in the backyard, fiddling with Julian's ring, as her children came and went, leaving her with Dietrich, who sat in the lounge chair beside her. "Go and get my handbag, dear," she whispered to him at one point. Once he returned, she pulled out the spare checkbook that Julian made her carry around on the utterly slim-to-none chance that he ever misplaced his or got it stolen. That day, however, she wrote her first check in years and presented it to Dietrich. "That ought to be enough for you and Jacob to buy an apartment. I'll let you know when Julian's will clears probate and it's safe to deposit," she said. It was more than enough for two apartments in Berlin, and he thanked her profusely, then went to show Jacob, who was lingering at the wall of glass, having taken up his father's role as protector of the dying queen. She would do these things for her children, because she loved them and because it felt good to give them what was going to be rightfully theirs someday soon anyway. And then Jacob was beside her and she told him, "Please be happy. Please make a life with him," meaning with Dietrich, only Dietrich, for she had come to love him like a third son, and so what if they never had children.

"We will make a beautiful life together, Mrs. Jacobson—Roz," he said, hovering over Jacob. "I do not . . . for the first time, I am lost words."

"At a loss for words," Jacob said gently, taking his hand and squeezing it. Then he turned to her. "Mommy," he whispered, which was all he needed to say. It was everything and it was nothing, all of it wrapped up inside that one word.

"We didn't need your friend Clarence, after all," she said. He looked at her askance, and she saw his eyes darken with the revelation that she'd known about their plan to kill Julian all along, that Dietrich must have told her about it the Thursday they'd arrived. "But make sure to wish him well for me. Will you do that, Jacob? And about his ostrich, well, I'm sure he won't hate you forever. Accidents do happen."

"They certainly do," he said, kissing her on the cheek. "But you can thank him and wish him well in person. I thought I'd take Diet to see where Bugsy Siegel is buried. Dad used to . . ." But he stopped himself, unexpectedly choked up. *How people do surprise us,* she thought.

"When Jacob was a boy, his father liked to tell him Bugsy Siegel would kill him in his sleep," Roz explained to Dietrich, "because that's what Bugsy Siegel did to all bad boys."

"You are right, Jacob. Your father was a psychopath." Dietrich nodded. "I do not have another explanation for his behavior."

"Julian was many things," Roz agreed. *If I can say anything about him,* she thought, *I can say this—he was terribly good at hiding his worst parts from the world and saving them all up for us. In some ways, he was a better actor than Mo.*

"Anyway, what do you say, Mom? Want to come with us?" Jacob asked. "It'll be fun."

"I think I'd like to go home," she said.

"Shouldn't one of us drive with you?" Edith asked a little later, as Mo and Jacob shoved her suitcases into the minivan.

"Yeah, I don't think it's such a good idea if you go alone," Jacob said.

"I second that, Ma," Moses said. "What if . . . ," But he didn't finish his sentence, although she knew they were all thinking the same thing, all of them including her.

But she needed them to understand that this was something she had to do on her own and told them so, told them that if she started to feel dizzy or unwell, she would pull off the highway and find the nearest hospital, that she would check in with them every hour, if it made them feel better.

"Every hour on the hour, Ma," Edith said.

"And if you have any trouble at all, one of us will be there in a flash," Jacob said.

Then Roz was saying good-bye to them and to Pandora, who appeared from out of the house and to whom she felt closer after sharing her plan in the garage the night of the Seder. It had been important to Roz that she know, just in case. Next came five teary hugs with her grandsons, all of whom wanted to go with her, all of them except for Bronson, who held himself back, held himself aloof, as if he weren't buying any of it, as if he knew what had happened to his paw-paw. She thought about her dead husband and how he'd never taken the chance to know any of them, not perhaps because he didn't want to but because he simply didn't know how. And this more than anything else saddened Roz, who hugged and kissed them all one more time, then climbed into the minivan and pulled away, waving to her children and to Dietrich, who called out, "*Auf Wiedersehen!*"

She drove for about half an hour before the fuel light came on, and she took the next exit. She pumped her own gas, which she hadn't done in forever, and when she was finished, she went around to the back of the minivan and grabbed the spare oxygen tank, the one she suspected Julian of tampering with, and dragged it behind her on the way to the Dumpster. Her breath was short and labored, and when she climbed back into the minivan, it took all of her strength to reach under the passenger seat, where she retrieved the slimmer, lighter, more portable spare tank, which she'd kept hidden for months, just in case—only a five-day supply of oxygen, but enough to get her home.

Roz headed east on I-10, bound for Texas. She was driving straight into the sun and flipped down the visor, dislodging an old

Polaroid—it couldn't be, but there it was, a picture of the five of them, she and Julian so young, so thin, and the kids and that cruddy brown Oldsmobile station wagon. The picture had been taken at Point Dume moments before the kids ran off and she and Julian had stood at the edge of the bluff and talked about separating. It hadn't been a good day, or even a good trip, Julian irascible as ever and the kids punchy in the backseat, wanting out, and she in the passenger seat, wanting out as well, wanting out from all of it. But here, in this photo, the facts of the day, of the trip, of their life, were absent. Here, they were smiling. Here they were, smiling.

And suddenly Roz was getting off the interstate and turning the minivan around, back toward L.A., for this had been her destination all along, there with her family. She was relieved to finally be heading in the right direction, and though she knew this disease would kill her eventually, she couldn't help imagining that she was already breathing better, for her chest felt lighter, and she rolled down the window and let the wind into the car to take the last of Julian's scent away.

It had been Roz's impulse to get back into the minivan and drive it home, yet she realized as she pulled onto Von Trapp Lane some forty-five minutes later that she hadn't thought this part of the plan through enough, or at all. She liked her house, but it was just a house, and she liked her things, but they were just things, easily packed up and moved. She'd find a nice, quiet place on the beach, in Malibu, close enough to Mo and Pandora but not too close. She had no desire to be a burden. And when her friends asked, she'd just tell them the truth—that she'd never liked Dallas, that her doctors had prescribed a drier climate, and that she wanted to be near her family. Besides, Texas was no safer than California. It had become a hotbed of intolerance, too, and hadn't she already lost her husband to the scourge that was virulent anti-Semitism?

Roz parked the minivan in the drive, then made her way slowly into the house, where she was met by her grandsons, who were delighted to see her again so soon, especially the twins, who asked her about Paw-Paw, as though in the last hour they'd already forgotten what Mo and Pandora had explained to them—that Paw-Paw wasn't coming back. Roz glanced past them through the wall of glass to the shimmering pool. She'd given Mo a check before she left with instructions to keep it permanently full. And she thought about that moment when she'd struck Julian and how extraordinary it had felt, and how she wasn't going to apologize for any of it, not for that, and not for telling the twins that Paw-Paw was looking down at them from heaven and that he'd loved them very much.

Roz decided to stay with Mo and Pandora while she settled up her life in Texas. Even after she'd set herself up in the guest room again, she kept expecting the police to arrive on Von Trapp Lane with new evidence disputing their account. But they never did. No particular effort seemed to be going to catching the assailants. Another unsolved attack for the backlogged LAPD. Sometimes she was surprised by her guilt, for never in her life would she have ever imagined that in removing Julian from the world, she'd had to, in some way, become him. Jacob reminded her that her actions had been good and just, which did a little to allay her guilt, though it never completely went away. And how could it, when she'd spent her entire life with Julian, loving and caring for him, this man who had been slowly poisoning her by tampering with her oxygen? It was hard to forgive him, yet Roz understood that forgiveness was the only way through. And the more she forgave him, the better she felt, and the better she felt, the easier it was to breathe, at least this was the way she imagined it, even if it weren't exactly true. Without Julian, Roz breathed easier—was it really as simple as that?

As the weeks became months, the boys stopped asking about Paw-Paw altogether, all of them except for Bronson, who refused to let it go, who kept at his parents, especially Moses. Which was why on a dry, warm day a couple of days after his bar mitzvah—yes, it was a miracle that here it was October and Roz was still alive—she sat him down and told him the story from start to finish, the story of their lives together, the story of Julian's reign of terror, and when she was done, Bronson got up and hugged her, just like that, and he whispered in her ear, "He was a bad man and bad men have to be punished," almost as if he'd known all along. He never mentioned it again after that, yet she could tell that it continued to affect him, as it continued to affect all of her children in surprising ways. The next few months were full of small miracles—Moses landed a big part in a movie and Jacob wrote a new play, *Edelweiss, Edelweiss,* which was picked up by a small production company in New York City and performed across the country.

Edith, dear Edith, went back to Emory to find that in light of "new evidence," the board had no other choice than to recommend her immediate and swift resignation, as she told her family at the trips' bar mitzvah. She could finish out the year but then had to go. She was not about to accept this and filed an action against the college, demanding her case be reexamined. She drummed up support from colleagues and students alike in the form of affidavits and letters, filing this and that document, careful not to make a single mistake, although she was tired beyond tired and couldn't wait for winter break, which was quickly approaching. All of her documentation had to be in before end of term, so two days before winter vacation she was leaving her office late once again. She was throwing her briefcase into the backseat of her car and was about to climb in when a car slowed down and stopped, blocking her in. The driver, who was wearing a balaclava and aiming a gun right at her, told her not to move. He said her name—Edith Jacobson Plunkett— and called her a filthy kike bitch, telling her that he knew where she lived, reciting her address, laughing. "Gonna gut you, you stupid Jew cunt," he said, cocking the gun.

Edith shut her eyes, the fear overtaking her as her bladder let go, the piss streaming down her thighs, and he laughed again, and in that laugh she heard her father, heard the sound of her death. But he did not kill her. He fired a bullet through the windshield, the sound of which exploded through the cavernous parking garage, the glass shattering and spraying her so that she was still picking tiny fragments of glass from her hair days later. She screamed as he tore away, her voice resounding in her ears, which continued to ring from the blast, her eyes squeezed shut until she was sure that he had gone. She got out her phone, called the campus police, who arrived to take her statement and escort her home, where she locked and chained the door and kept all the lights off, cowering in darkness that night. In the morning, unable to bring herself to set foot on campus, she called Roz and told her what had happened. "I hate to say this," Roz said. "But I have to agree with what your father always said—fuck Emory. Come here, my darling."

Edith bought a ticket to L.A., booked a rental car—no vans!—and headed to the airport just a couple of hours later.

After selling the house in Dallas through a real estate agent who specialized in remote sales, Roz bought a three-bedroom house with a skylight in every room. It sat right on the beach in Malibu, and it was there that Edith came. Roz welcomed her only daughter and put her in the room beside hers, just steps from the Pacific, not far from Julian's last resting place. Roz took care of Edith and Edith took care of Roz, who had made a recovery of sorts, no longer needing the wheelchair as often to get around, her health taking a turn for the better—everyone attributed it to the drier climate, but Roz knew differently, attributing it to happiness, to her proximity to her children and grandchildren, to living without Julian and those poisoned tanks. She grew stronger and took fairly long walks on the beach with Edith, who only rarely spoke about her dad these days.

"Do you ever miss him?" she asked Roz once. It was a warm, sunny day in June, the ocean gleaming and glassy, the tide high and wetting their feet as they strolled.

"Maybe like a pain one gets used to," she mused. "When the pain finally goes away, another one takes its place."

"Are you in pain, Ma?" Edith asked.

"Not that kind of pain." She smiled, reaching for her daughter's hand. "I won't see the boys graduate from high school, or Jacob and Dietrich's apartment, or Moses win an Academy Award, or you get married again, if you meet a man and decide that's what you want to do."

"You'll see other things, I promise," Edith reassured her.

"Oh, I'm not complaining, Thistle," she said. "But you asked."

"I miss him a lot," she offered

"You need to find a boyfriend, dear," Roz suggested. "Sex is the ultimate distraction."

"Ma!"

"Your dad and I used to have so much sex when we were younger." She laughed, stopping herself from elaborating, and added, "Before you kids came along and frightened him to death."

It was something of a golden age for the Jacobson family, for even the boys prospered. Not long after that disastrous Passover special, they received calls from record companies, the producers of which wanted to harness the talent they'd seen and heard. And thus the Jacobson 5 was born—to their parents' wary, overprotective chagrin. The boys fast-tracked a single, "This Night Is Different," that slowly penetrated the airways of L.A., then was picked up nationally, gaining momentum and popularity, eventually climbing as high as number 32 on the Billboard charts. Then the boys were asked to sing at a gala to raise money for the new JCC in downtown L.A. During their set, which was heavily attended, several members of the audience stood up and began to shout anti-Semitic slurs, lobbing bags of fecal matter at the boys, which exploded upon impact, dousing them and forcing them to flee the stage. And that was that—Mo and Pandora put an end to the Jacobson 5, without much argument from their sons, save for Bronson, who thought it was an overreaction and sulked for days until Roz took him aside and explained that he needed to cut his parents and brothers some slack, that they were only looking out for him.

"Yeah, I get that, Maw-Maw, but that's not the point, is it?" he said, that precociousness of his roaring out of him.

"Well, then, what is the point?" Roz asked, growing ever more concerned that her grandsons, Bronson in particular, understood far too well what was happening all around them.

"If we disappear, it means they win," he announced. "And I am not about to disappear."

"You can't lose unless you believe you've lost," she said sagely, trying not to think about what might be coming, the world that Bronson was about to inherit.

"Everything not saved will be lost," he said cryptically. When Roz repeated what he'd said to Moses later that night, he just laughed and said that Bronson was quoting the warning message from his Wii, the one that flashed across the screen whenever it crashed.

"You can't take him too seriously, Ma," Moses said.

While Bronson continued to bemoan the state of the world, Moses's comeback continued. He landed a starring role in the latest J. J. Abrams film, a remake of *Splash* in which all the roles were reversed—Moses reprising Daryl Hannah's role playing the mermaid, merman, technically—and Ronnie, one of the executive producers on *The JacobSONS*, was so impressed with the way Moses had handled himself on the night of the Seder that he offered him his own late-night talk show, eponymously called *Moses!*

"The country is in love with you," Ronnie decreed at their initial meeting. "Well, most of the country. Anyone who tuned in that night to watch you save your father. That, my friend, was spectacular. It continues to be one of the most viewed and talked-about episodes in the network's history."

When Moses told Roz about the offer that night over dinner on her deck—it was just the two of them because Edith was at the movies with Elias, whom she'd been seeing a lot more of lately, and Pandora was at home with the kids—Roz set her fork down and stared at her elder son.

"We both know how it could have gone," she proffered, taking long, slow breaths. The water twinkled with the reflection of the stars above, the houses up and down the beach glowing. "No, let me rephrase that: We both know how you wished it could have gone. You've never been scrutinized for it, but don't think for a second I didn't see you, because I did. You hesitated, Moses, and you can't possibly think I'm the only one who noticed. Dietrich saw you as well. He told me so later that night." She hated to lie to him, but she needed him to know that there was just no way Moses could do the show, not with so much at stake. "All it takes is one crack-pot or one guest who has it in for you, one question followed by one misplaced answer, and the whole thing comes crashing down on top of you—on top of us. You're a very good actor, but no one's that good." Moses sighed and in that sigh Roz heard his acknowl-edgment and resignation. "Let's keep this between us," she said, determined to maintain peace among her children. "You will have other opportunities, Moses." Shutting her eyes, she reached for the nosepiece on the portable oxygen tank and inserted it—*inverted it,* she thought, smiling to herself, remembering when Jacob had told her about Dietrich's malapropism—her breath instantly returning.

"Are you okay, Ma?" Moses asked.

"Just . . . I'm just a little worn out," she said, hearing movement inside the house, then Edith was calling out for her.

"Out here," Moses cried.

"Ma, there you are." Edith kissed Roz on the cheek. "You had me worried there for a sec. I didn't know where you were."

"Where's Eliass?" asked Moses, who'd taken to adding another *s* to Elias's name, something, Roz thought, Julian would have ap-proved of, though she herself did not.

"He has an early meeting with a client tomorrow," Edith said, shooting her brother the middle finger, while Roz looked on, think-ing about her dead husband and the real reason she'd called off the divorce that first time. It was true that Julian had been nastier than usual in the days leading up to that road trip to California, which had culminated with the two of them standing on the bluff at Point Dume, where Roz, emboldened by the sight of the silvery, endless sea, had finally told him that she was done and wanted a divorce. She'd felt lighter than light itself after she said it, as if she'd given herself over to the sun and had become one with it. The drive back to Texas was unusually pleasant with a cowed Julian on his best behavior. She would have assumed anything but this from him when he'd been told in no uncertain terms that he was to pack his bags and leave the moment they got home. And that's exactly what he did. He stacked his bags by the door, then went to say good-bye to the kids, while Roz waited in the bedroom, terrified that she'd change her mind.

Julian stepped into the bedroom and shut the door behind him. He kneeled down on the carpet and wrapped his arms around her, muttering that he was sorry—and that one word, *sorry*, froze Roz in place, for she'd never heard it come out of his mouth before. "I'm sorry I was mean to you," he said, and the word bloomed like a flower and it was as if Julian had filled the entire room with fresh-cut red roses. She raked a delicate path through his thick head of hair, sighing a sigh that held in it the acceptance of a woman resigned to her fate. And that was that—she let Julian back, because it was the first time and sadly, she now thought, the only time he ever took responsibility for himself, that he ever said that he was sorry. She must have told her children that he'd apologized, yet this explanation must have gotten lost among all the others—that she still loved him, that she wanted them to grow up with a father, that keeping her family intact was more important to her than being right. "And happiness?" Jacob had asked. "What about that?" Everything was implied in that one word—*happiness*—though Roz had only been thinking about her own, because if she were happy she'd be able to share her happiness with all of them, her children, and that happiness would certainly protect them, wouldn't it?

Well, no, Roz thought that night, as Edith escorted her back into the house and into her bedroom, *because the problem with happiness is that there's never enough to go around.* Roz changed into her nightgown, then lay down on the bed, calling for Moses, who came in to say good night. "Be nicer to your sister," she said, kissing his face. *Say you're sorry,* she thought.

She turned the dial up on her oxygen, while she and her daughter watched the news, which, as she liked to confirm nightly, didn't contain any new leads in the Julian Jacobson investigation, though it did mention the Great Drought: The Sequel.

The last time it had rained in L.A. was that morning in April 2022 when Jacob and Dietrich had arrived for Passover, in fact. And now here it was more than a year later, and they hadn't had a single drop. President Cox issued another state of emergency in California, as crops fell into ruin and farmers had to abandon their land. According to the news, unless something was done or it rained soon, food prices would continue to soar across the country, from Seattle to New York City, where many grocery stores had more demand than they did supply.

"How was the movie?" Roz asked.

"It was fine," Edith replied, though something in her daughter's voice alerted Roz to the fact that it hadn't been fine at all.

"What happened?" Roz asked.

"Well, you know how some theaters show those three-minute movies about the terrible poverty ravaging the Israeli refugees and then they have a rep go around collecting donations? Well, when the rep went around, he was booed out of the theater. Elias wanted to leave, but I talked him out of it. The movie was fun, though. A stupid rom-com starring Apple Paltrow."

Yes, it is bad, Roz thought, *and only getting worse*—for the Israeli refugees and, by default, the American Jews, if she were to believe what she heard on "Jews in the News," the nightly news segment that highlighted the day's instances of anti-Semitism in the United States and around the world. Most of the time, Roz switched the news off before this segment. She couldn't bear to hear about another attack on a synagogue or another suicide bombing of a school bus full of Jewish children. It was all just too much and though she wanted to remain informed, she hated to feed her fears like this. On some level she understood that while reporting these atrocities was necessary, it was also playing directly into the hands of those who wished to do the Jews harm—it focused as much attention on the neo-Nazi skinheads and the white supremacists and ISIS and whoever else had it in for the Jews as it did on the bereaved families and innocent bystanders who'd lost their own lives in the process. The ADL had made this argument, she'd read, to try to get networks to remove the segment, but there it was, still on the air, still alarming every Jewish person that he or she could be targeted next. Roz switched off the TV, as there was only so much bad news they could take. But oddly, there seemed one bright spot in the world amid all of this mishegas.

Whenever Jacob called, he told them all how good it was in Berlin, how Jews from all over Europe, especially France, were flocking to Deutschland, where they were protected under the law. Roz wanted to believe that he was living in a new Germany, but she couldn't quite keep the worry out of her voice, thinking that even if it were terrible here in America, she couldn't imagine being a Jew in that country. Diet called out from somewhere in the flat that they should come visit and Jacob echoed him before asking Roz how she was doing.

"Not great, but not terrible." She shrugged, finding it more difficult to breathe that day for whatever reason. It didn't take much to irritate her lungs anymore.

"Do you want me to come?" Jacob asked. "You only have to say it and I'm there, Mom."

She wanted nothing more than to have all of her children nearby, but she was happy that at least one of them didn't have to face the hatred that swirled like dust in the air. *If you think you're safer in Berlin, then that's where you should be,* she thought, still unsure that Jacob wasn't exaggerating, but there was Dietrich, who would not lie to her, and so when he finally showed his face, she asked him about it all, for she wanted to hear it from the mouth of a bona fide German.

"It is not ideal, no, but it is better than it is in America," he confirmed. He told her about an article in *Der Spiegel* claiming that 73 percent of American Jews polled said they had experienced a direct threat in the last six months and that 61 percent of non-Jewish Americans blamed the Jews for the country's economic and ecological woes. "This is not the case in Germany, Roz," he said. "I am not telling you what to do, but it seems fairly clear that things there are only going to get worse. You are always welcome here," he added, smiling. "It will be our pleasure to have you, all of you. We have the space, thanks to you."

The idea of moving again, however, gave Roz real pause because she worried she'd never survive the trip. She was feeling run-down. She'd outlasted her prognosis by well over a year—but one day soon she figured her luck was going to run out. And so it did, for on an afternoon a few days before Yom Kippur, while Edith was substitute teaching at the Malibu Jewish Center and Synagogue and Moses was on set at Paramount Studios, Roz lay down for a nap and never woke up.

JACOB JACOBSON;
OR, THE BEST UNVEILING EVER

October 7, 2024

T HEY STOOD TOGETHER ON THE BLUFF ON THAT SUNNY, fall morning, Moses and Thistle flanking Jacob, who clutched the urn to his chest, a beautiful round canister of Delft-blue enamel, which they'd picked out together last year at Eternal Hollywood, Clarence offering them the chapel to say a few parting words before they escorted their mother's body to the crematorium. They stood alone on the bluff, which was exactly how Jacob wanted it, just the three of them. He'd been trying to persuade them to move to Berlin, but that conversation had faded to silence when they'd climbed out of the car and walked to the edge of Point Dume.

The sea spread out before Jacob and for a moment, as he unscrewed the lid on the urn, he recalled that morning when they'd disposed of their father's body. *It seems only natural and befitting,* he thought, *to dispose of our mother's cremains here as well, where everything changed.* It had been far too late to reverse the damage Julian Jacobson had done to any of them, especially to his poor mother, who had deserved so much better than him, that ex-husband of hers, which was how Jacob had taken to thinking about him—that lousy, no-good ex-husband of hers. He hoped the last year of her life without him had been able to make up for the forty-four with him. Edith had told him it had, when she called to let him know their mom had passed away in her sleep, sobbing as she told him about finding her in bed and how utterly at peace she'd looked. Just an easy quiet and the exhalation of her last breath, though Edith did have a moment of hysterics, scream-crying that if she'd only gotten home sooner, if she'd only not taken that stupid subbing job, if only, if only, if only . . . To which Jacob replied: "Enough. You did more than enough. She knows that. We all do."

Jacob handed the lid to Mo, who slipped it into one pocket, then from the other removed three yarmulkes from the trips' bar mitzvahs—small, blue leather kippahs with black stitching, inscribed with the trips' names and the date of the blessed event.

"Mom," Jacob began, but the rest of what he wanted to say got bunched up in his throat. "Mom," he tried again, but there was nothing, just his dry tongue trying to form the appropriate words to say good-bye. "Mom." One last time, before Edith wrapped an arm around him and she said, "Ma," softly, leaning her head against her brother's shoulder. Mo stood beside them in silent contemplation, and Jacob thought, *My sweet, dumb older brother,* but then he wrapped an arm around Jacob and whispered, "Mommy," that word and only that word.

Suddenly, Jacob was a boy again, in the backyard of their house in Dallas, crouching behind a shrub and sobbing his eyes out because he'd just come to the realization that one day his mom was going to die—six years old and kneeling in the rocky dirt, not being able to wrap his mind around such an enormous concept. If he could just stop picturing it, maybe it wouldn't happen. But now here he was and he no longer had to picture it, for he was holding the result of his childhood in his hands. He was thirty-four years older than the boy he'd been, but he felt again his knees packed into the rough earth and the branches of the shrubbery scraping his face as his mom found him cowering behind the house, and she lifted him into her arms and asked him what was wrong and he told her that he didn't ever want her to die. For a time after that, he tried to never let his mom out of his sight.

"When I was six," he began, "I had this horrible thought that Mom was going to die. I didn't know how or when, but I also didn't have any idea someone else in that house actually wanted her to die. I lived my entire life pretending she wouldn't. He lived his entire life hoping she would."

"Jacob," Edith interjected gently, "is this really the time?"

"Let him speak," Mo said.

"Mom spent the better part of our lives fighting him off," Jacob continued. "And it weakened everything about her. She was never able to say what she needed to say and that, for me, is the greatest tragedy of all. So, Mom, I'm saying it for you now." He turned his face up to the sun and said, "I'm sorry I wasn't strong enough to stand up to him for you. I'm sorry about what I said in the car that time because if I hadn't, Mo wouldn't have hit me in the face and my nose wouldn't have bled, and we would have gotten to the airport on time and flown away. I'm sorry I didn't visit you more, later, but I just couldn't stand to be around him or watch how he treated you. I'm sorry you never understood how much better you were than him, but you have to know that I—that we—knew it. I hate you for not understanding that you were going to die one day and that you could have made your life as beautiful as possible—without him."

"Oh, Jacob." Edith sighed. "Jacob, Jacob, Jacob," and she grabbed hold of his hand and squeezed it tightly. "Try to see it differently. Try to see that Ma made a choice. She loved him, Jacob, but that doesn't mean she didn't love us. You can love a monster and still know what he is."

But Jacob was inconsolable. He let go of his sister's hand, recognizing the pointlessness of doing battle with time, and he resigned himself to the idea that none of it could have gone any other way than the way it had. It had all been meant to play out exactly this way—with the three of them standing on this bluff on this morning to say good-bye to their mom for the last time. This gave him a momentary peace, enough to join his siblings in the Mourner's Kaddish. They did not have a minyan, but so the fuck what—they were ten adults if they were anything, for they had lived countless lives already, reinventing themselves in different images, each as unalike their father as possible.

They recited the prayer in unison, and Jacob knew that Edith was secretly reciting it for their father, too, whom no one had said a single word for after they'd tossed his body into the sea—an unheard kersplash and then it was gone

Now Jacob tipped the urn, ceremoniously scattering little bits of his mother into the sea at a time. *Fish food,* he thought, watching the ashes go and peering over the edge, which he hadn't done that morning two years ago. It was a long way down onto the jagged rocks and the sea below and for one brief moment he imagined his mom's ashes reconfiguring themselves just below the surface, imagined a fin, her fin, and then she was a shark searching the depths for her prey, their father, smiling as she did, for here was Jacob's idea of an afterlife—his mother leaping at their father to devour him over and over again.

Jacob handed the urn to Edith, who lowered her head and whispered, "Good-bye, Ma. I love you," into the mouth of the urn, then took a step forward and poured out some of the ash, most of which ended up on her shoes, as Moses pointed out later, after he had taken his turn with the ashes and they stood there in silence for a full sixty seconds. It seemed to Jacob the longest minute of his life, longer than the plane ride over from Berlin, longer than the drive from the airport to Calabasas, even longer than the seventeen years he'd spent in his father's house. Sixty seconds. Blink and it was gone. Blink and they were back in the car and Mo was saying to Edith that she had some of Ma on her, and Edith was giving him the finger, even as she wiped their mother off her shoes, and Jacob was smiling, the first smile in days. He had not thought he was up to coming to L.A. and only agreed to go because Diet told him that he'd regret it if he didn't. Diet who was waiting for them at Canter's Deli, along with Pandora, his nephews, and Elias, none of whom even asked to come along to scatter the ashes, for they knew: The Jacobson children needed to do this alone.

Jacob drove to Canter's while Mo sat beside him and Edith in the backseat, crying softly, Jacob noticed, when he glanced at her in the rearview mirror. "Thistle," he said.

"I was just thinking about all the times I went into Ma's closet, hunting for any sign that she was a witch," she sobbed. "God, I was a stupid kid."

"You were definitely a stupid kid, but you're not a stupid adult. You gave Ma a lot of joy," Mo said.

"You know what," she said, blowing her nose. "I don't miss a single thing about Atlanta. Leaving gave me . . . it gave us . . . This is going to sound strange, but I think I would have left even if . . . Those last few months with Ma were some of the happiest—and the hardest—of my life, but I wouldn't take any of it back. Not even if Emory had gotten on its hands and knees and begged me to return. Funny, isn't it? Daddy was right about the place. Still, it makes me wonder about . . . Well, you don't think he—"

"Please don't make this about him," Jacob interrupted, knowing exactly where she was heading.

"Then how did the advisory committee know about Zion?" she asked. " 'In light of this startling new evidence, Dr. Jacobson, we have no other choice but to dismiss you.' I know you didn't tell them, Mo, and Jacob didn't because, oh, I guess I never told you about Zion, unless you did, Mo"—Mo shook his head that he hadn't—"and Elias wouldn't ever do such a thing, which only leaves—"

"Who the hell is Zion?" Jacob asked.

"Later, Jacob," Mo said.

"Daddy," Edith finished. "But you don't think he . . ."

"He was a saboteur," Jacob said incredulously. He knew nothing about Zion but everything about how their father operated. "Of course he told them. So please stop defending him, because I just . . . I just . . ."

"Jacob, calm down," Mo said, then turned to Edith and conceded that their father must have overheard her talking with Elias the night of the Seder or on the phone with Elias in Pandora's office that night. "It's the simplest explanation," he said. "The only one."

"But he died that night," Edith said, "which means . . . well, I don't know what it means."

"Um, how long do you think it takes to send a two-sentence email? Thirty seconds at the most, if you know what you're saying and to whom it's going," Mo said.

While Mo and Thistle continued to rehash the mystery of the anonymous evidence and why Julian would have done it, Jacob tuned out, thinking about their dearly departed despot. *You keep trying to come up with reasons to explain why he was the way he was,* Jacob thought, *which means you still contend that he could have been different. But he was born a black hole. He hid out in the dark, where no one knew where to look for him. But I did.*

Jacob pulled the rental car into the lot and parked, recalling the last time he'd been at Canter's, where he'd met his siblings right after taking his final exams at UCLA. Twenty-one years old and hankering for a life in New York City, for the chance to blossom into a playwright. *Though I had no earthly idea how to make it happen, other than knowing I had to get as far away from L.A. as possible,* he thought. His brother and sister climbed out into the day, which was already gaining heat and momentum, but he hung back, walking in circles around the car, thinking back to two and a half years ago when he and Diet arrived at LAX. He recalled the accident on the 405 and the Jaws of Life—*the Jews of Life,* he thought—which cut through the steel and glass like a can opener, dislodging that young man's lifeless body. It could have been any of them, he realized, and still could be, the longer his family remained here.

Jacob shook the thought off and entered the deli to join his family at a booth by the window, where he took his place beside Diet.

"Baby, you are back," he said. "Mazel tov," smiling that big German smile of his. Who would have believed that four years after that dreadful Christmas Eve in Berlin they'd still be together, that they'd still love each other enough?

He had a harder time imagining how he was going to convince his family that it was time for them to go, which was the other crucial reason he'd come back to L.A.—to persuade them, gently at first and then with force if necessary—force being Diet, who would explain to them that the Bundesrepublik had declared every Jew who stepped onto German soil an instant citizen, granting them the same privileges as if they'd been born there. That the government had come out with *Die Liste der genehmigten geschützten Arten—The Approved List of Protected Species*—which made it a capital offense to harm in any way or kill a person of Jewish descent. That the new Jews of Germany were integrating slowly but surely into the fabric of German life and he would tell them so, again and again, until they got it, until Mo and Edith said good-bye to their lives here and emigrated. *Whether or not they are in imminent danger is beside the point,* Jacob thought, and all they had to do was take one look at the news to see that he was right. But his siblings had grown complacent and believed, like countless Jews before them, that it could never happen here. *And it probably won't, but why take the chance?* Diet had pointed out how easily it could turn, how easily night could overtake the day, understanding better than any of them. *But Germany? Seriously? What about the horrible, snowy winters and the terrible food and, well, what about living in a place like that, with such a gruesome history?* he thought, having no trouble at all imagining what they'd say.

Yes, okay, but think about the boys, Jacob would say. *Think about all the opportunities they won't have here in America, not the way things are going.*

But now was not the time to mention how things were going. They were there, in Canter's, to celebrate their mother's life, and they ordered all kinds of food in her honor—matzo ball soup and chicken soup and lox and bagels and blintzes and potato knishes, pancakes and waffles and Denver omelets, chocolate pudding and chocolate doughnuts—foods that had sustained them as children and that their mother had made when they were sick or sad, comfort food that stuck to their ribs and put smiles on their flu-stricken faces. And at one point Mo held up his mimosa as Pandora shushed the boys and the table went quiet.

"I'd like to make a toast." Mo raised his glass high into the air. "To my mother, who taught me revenge is a foul substitute for forgiveness," winking at Jacob, to whom he'd confessed his dumping of the peacock in Gibbs's pool only this morning.

"That was . . . interesting, Mo," Edith said, rising. "I'd also like to make a toast. To Ma, who never ceased to cast her spells of love over all of us, even when some of us didn't believe in them or deserve them."

Then it was Jacob who stood to meet his family, the sunlight spilling through the plate-glass window, shining across all of their faces, all except Bronson's. He was lost in his own world as usual, just as Jacob might have been at that age. "To my mom, who never once made it into the pages of my Manifest of Meanness," he said, as everyone clinked glasses, including the twins, who wanted to say toasters of their own.

"Toasts, with an *s*," Mo corrected them. The food kept coming until there was next to no room left on the table yet still the family noshed and noshed some more, diets and acid reflux and IBS be damned.

"For Ma," Edith cheered, slathering a potato latke in applesauce and drenching it in sour cream before offering it to Elias, who gobbled it down. It was nice to see her with Elias, and even nicer to see

Mo and Pandora laughing again and surreptitiously holding hands under the table. He and Diet discussed extending their visit and then perhaps coming again for Passover and Edith said that was a lovely idea and that they were welcome to stay with her at the beach house in Malibu.

"At least until we grow bored from that perfect weather of yours." Diet laughed and in his laugh Jacob was abruptly struck by the realization that his mother was gone and wasn't coming back. The idea hit him between the shoulder blades, so utterly incomprehensible and unpalatable that it was all he could do not to throw up. Instead, he got up and went outside, Diet following after him and asking if he was okay, but Jacob was not okay.

"It's just . . . it's been a year and it hasn't gotten any easier," he choked.

"Oh, *mein Schatz*, didn't anyone ever tell you?" Diet asked. "This is the pain that will inform all other pains from now on. You have lost your mother. That is the primal pain, what we call it in German. There will never be another pain like this pain. You cannot ready yourself for it because it is unimaginable. But I am here and you are here and your brother and your sister and Roz, she is here, too. She is everywhere. You are meant to be sad and you will be sad for a long, long time, and I cannot say this will ever stop being sad, but when it gets bad, I mean really bad, all you have to do is remember the last few months of her life and how extraordinary you and your siblings made them. You gave her an afterlife before she went away, Jacob. Be happy for this, *mein Schatz*. Let this be soothing to you. I promised your mother we would live a beautiful life and we are, we will."

Jacob didn't know what to say. He stared at this man and he could feel himself filling up with love, and it went brimming over inside of him and spilled out of his eyes, more bereft than he'd ever been and yet more in love with the world than ever—all thanks to his mother and to this man, this German, whom he hugged close, squeezing and holding on to him as if for the first and last time. The world was changing, he sensed it even then, as the two separated and Diet went back into the deli and Jacob climbed into the rental car, just sitting there, watching his family through the glass, seeing it all differently and imagining the play he might write one day—a play set in the near future in which his nephews grew up into self-assured, handsome men who married and had children of their own and lived within twenty minutes of one another and within a few blocks of him and Diet in Berlin. In the play, Germany experienced a second enlightenment and the German people continued to prosper, even with the influx of millions of displaced persons, Israelis and American Jews, and the entire Jacobson family was there to-gether to see it, Mo and Edith and Pandora, a second Weimar Re-public, a time of peace and prosperity in a place that had at one time been the center of such gross and indecent incivility. In Jacob's play, those who were most in need, of course, were the American Jews, who were systematically being run out of their country through a series of governmental shifts and insidious propaganda campaigns, the likes of which the modern world had not seen since Adolf Hitler rose to power. In this play, the Jews of Germany would flourish and repopulate the land, giving rise to more and more Jewish schools and kosher grocery stores and butcher shops, in Berlin and all over the country as new synagogues were consecrated and no Jew ever had to fear persecution for being who he was, for they were all safe under the law.

Jacob let his imagination run further, declaring Germany the new Jewish homeland, the German people sworn protectors of Jew-ish life, all life, in fact. It was one of the most beautiful achievements in the history of man and softened the world's heart to the Germans, this magnanimous, misunderstood people, who had never forgiven themselves for the part their ancestors had played in the virtual an-nihilation of the Jews of Europe. The countries surrounding Ger-many, however, would not be nearly as welcoming or as kind, for once a Jewish person stepped into France or Belgium, Poland or Austria—at least in this version of the future Jacob was dreaming

400

up that day behind the wheel of his rental car—he would feel the hostility and the medieval darkness and hurry back across the border into Deutschland, a rare and endangered person. (It would add to the dramatic tension of the piece, he felt certain.)

Edith and Mo joined him in the car with a smuggled pitcher of mimosas and told him to drive. "Anyone want to join me in a trip down the Ganja River?" Mo asked, pulling out a joint, a gift from Pandora, apparently. "We'll meet them all later back at the house, but first I want to show you something." He instructed Jacob where to go.

Jacob felt a momentary guilt for leaving Diet behind, but he knew Diet would understand and so he followed Mo's directions, a right here and a left there, then straight ahead for a couple of miles until they were on Sunset and Mo said, "Look." Jacob slowed the car down and the three of them looked up and there was Mo, larger than life, on one of those giant billboards, an advertisement for his upcoming film, *Splash.*

"Oh my God." Edith giggled as she took a sip from the pitcher, then handed it to Jacob, who took a gulp before passing it to Mo, who declined and lit the joint, taking a long, slow drag.

"You must be so excited," Edith exclaimed. "We're so proud of you, Mo."

"It's basically soft-core porn," he said glumly. "I'm naked—half-naked—through most of it, but I am in every scene except for one, so I guess that's saying something."

"That's saying a lot," Jacob said robustly, glancing up at the facsimile of his older brother, then back at the flesh-and-blood version beside him. "Mom would have loved it."

"Mom would have shit her pants," Mo said.

"Mom would have bought the first ticket and been the first in line to see it," Edith warbled, her voice faltering, and Jacob thought she was about to cry. Instead, she leaned forward and laughed. "This is the best unveiling ever," she gasped, and just a couple of tears plunged down her face.

As they sat there, gazing up at this giant poster on which Mo, half-clad, with a fishtail, was perched on a rock in the middle of New York Harbor, Jacob saw how the ending of his play might go. He couldn't wait to start writing, for if anything would see him through the loss of his mother it would be this new work of his, which he would dedicate to her.

After taking a hit off the joint and passing it to Edith, who took a hit as well, he thought about how his fictional Jacobsons, after having lived for dozens of years in peace and harmony in Germany, would all wake up one morning—older and grayer and virtually unrecognizable, with wrinkles and cataracts and hearing aids, the life of a Jacobson in old age—and leave their homes to meet for breakfast, just as they had been doing for years. Except that on that day, one that none of them would ever forget and that would prove the indomitable supremacy of history yet again, they would all pass newsstands, each a different one, for they all lived in different corners of Berlin, and they would pause to read the headlines, which were the same on every paper and said the same thing, in German and in English—that the Bundesrat had ratified and updated *The Approved List of Protected Species* and had, by a count of 56 to 13, struck the word *Jew* from it completely.

ACKNOWLEDGMENTS

I CANNOT LIE—I NEARLY DIDN'T WRITE *Tell Me How This Ends Well* because I agonized over the day I'd also have to write the acknowledgments page. Well, here I am, and I did write the book, which you've just finished reading, and here you are at the dreaded page, which I fear will not live up to expectations. You, dear reader and possible friend, may not find your name and for that I am truly sorry, especially if I know you and especially if you thought, well, that you might find your name included here. But given the constraint of space, I can only thank a few people in the end. Thus—an enormous thanks to Sheila Fiona Black, Cliff Hudder, Kimberly Elkins, Steven Volynets, and Robbie Goolrick for all of the talks; Jeff Goldberg and Erika Halstead for being there; Emily Wirt and Adam Ross for the company; Joseph Skibell for the Shabbat lunches; Janice Convoy-Hellmann and her family for their Southern hospitality; Hannah Conway, location scout extraordinaire; the creative writing department at Emory University; all of my students; and finally to the great city of Atlanta, where I wrote the novel. Major, major, major thanks also to the fantastic team at Hogarth; my amazingly patient, funny, and brilliant editor, Hilary Rubin Teeman; and my equally brilliant, patient, and supportive agent, Richard Abate, without whom I wouldn't have had to agonize over this page of thank-yous at all. But I'm not kvetching, Richard. Believe me, I am not kvetching a single bit . . .

THIS BOOK IS FOR MY MOTHER AND FOR ANYONE WHO'S ever been terrorized and bullied—you are not alone.

ABOUT THE AUTHOR

DAVID SAMUEL LEVINSON is the author of the novel *Antonia Lively Breaks the Silence* and the story collection *Most of Us Are Here Against Our Will*. He has been nominated for the Pushcart Prize and has received fellowships from Yaddo, the Jentel Foundation, Ledig House, the Santa Fe Arts Institute, the Sewanee Writers' Conference, and the Marguerite and Lamar Smith Fellowship for Writers. He won an award for his fiction in *The Atlantic*, and his stories have been published in *RE:AL, storySouth, The James White Review, The New Penguin Book of Gay Short Stories, The Brooklyn Review, Prairie Schooner, The Toronto Quarterly, West Branch,* and *Post Road,* among others. He has served as the Emerging Writer Lecturer at Gettysburg College and as the Fellow in Fiction at Emory University.